Advance Praise for the *The Patriarch*

"This multitalented spinner-of-stories paints on the canvas of the arcane, turbulent world of governmental shenanigans gone awry in the ethics-be-damned universe of world oil markets ... Political anarchy? It's always just a page away ... in this smashingly entertaining novel by a writer of prodigious skill."

—**Robert E. Fuisz**, Emmy and Peabody Award-Winning Writer and Producer

"A good story. In search of his own sense of self, a complicated young journalist probes the origins of power that built a revered New England dynasty. Buffington makes your head spin with what's really at stake 'from whale oil to crude oil,' as he poses the question: Is the party in power the reincarnation of the Crusades, and is it out to 'kill the messenger?'"

—**Alfred R. Kelman**, Emmy Award-Winning Producer and Director

THE
PATRIARCH

THE
PATRIARCH

A Novel of Corruption and Terrorism, Love and Loss

G. N. Buffington

iUniverse, Inc.

New York Lincoln Shanghai

The Patriarch
A Novel of Corruption and Terrorism, Love and Loss

iUniverse books may be ordered through booksellers or by contacting:

iUniverse
2021 Pine Lake Road, Suite 100
Lincoln, NE 68512
www.iuniverse.com
1-800-Authors (1-800-288-4677)

Because of the dynamic nature of the Internet, any Web addresses or links contained in this book may have changed since publication and may no longer be valid.

This is a work of fiction. All of the characters, names, incidents, organizations, and dialogue in this novel are either the products of the author's imagination or are used fictitiously.

ISBN: 978-0-595-44881-4 (pbk)
ISBN: 978-0-595-69072-5 (cloth)
ISBN: 978-0-595-89206-8 (ebk)

Printed in the United States of America

In Appreciation

Much credit goes to my wife Pamela,
a constructive critic and
always an encouraging supporter
of my writing, past and present.

"Whether 'tis nobler in the mind to suffer
The slings and arrows of outrageous fortune,
Or to take up arms against a sea of troubles,
And by opposing end them?"

—William Shakespeare

Prologue

His name was Jacob. He was a descendant of Germans who settled in the Midwest to farm land in the New World. They came from the old country full of hope and Martin Luther's doctrine. Some were Mennonites, insisting on preserving the old ways. They fought Indians, cleared land, and built log houses and fences out of pine and hardwood. They were patriarchal, deeply religious, and hardworking. Jacob's forebears, venturing west to the edge of the Great Plains, were archetypical pioneers. Their farms were not large, maybe half a section. They planted corn, wheat, oats, and hay for the stock. Unlike their Amish cousins, they eventually gave up teams of horse power for tractors and mechanized reapers. They sent their children to the decentralized rural school system, often consisting of one-room schoolhouses with first to eighth grades. It was a good but demanding life. Belief in God and hard work were the cornerstones of existence. Extreme weather provided the principal hardship in the winter, with tornadoes in the summer.

Jacob Sellars was born in modern times. But some farming families were slow to modernize. Growing up did not come easily. In his early teens, he began to feel the restless energies of puberty. It was a powerful force. The open displays of sex in the magazine racks at the supermarket had already caught his eye, but he shunned them as being far beyond the risks he was willing to take. He preferred books anyway. When browsing in the public library, as he did frequently on the slate-gray days of winter, he stumbled onto books of romance and love. A few included lovemaking scenes, some merely suggestive and others graphic and raw, like the books of Henry Miller, at which he managed furtive peeks. The images were both unsettling and exciting. But he was much too embarrassed to check out the volumes at a desk presided over by the stern, spectacled librarian. It wasn't until he discovered *Anthony Adverse,* the Victorian coming-of-age story of a young English boy, that he decided to take a chance and face the woman behind the desk. The book seemed harmless enough to pass muster—a venerable work, yet erotically revealing. He took it home where he could read it in privacy, in the attic, in the barn, and, on warmer days, in a secluded glen in the pasture. He read and reread the well-thumbed passage about the seduction of the youth by his nurse. It was, for Jacob, a powerful vignette of arousal. Although plagued by guilt and anxiety afterward, he learned to pleasure himself and relieve the yearning.

These experiences were immense and defining—at least until he was caught in the act. One cold winter afternoon in his room when Jacob was feeling reckless, his father walked in on him in the heat of his self-absorption. As he struggled to cover himself, he watched his father rip the pages from the book. The commotion brought his mother to witness the awful crime. Invoking the Bible like a preacher, his father, trembling at the lip with righteousness, told him that he was going against God and the teachings of Christ and that he was unclean and unworthy of manhood. Storming out of the room, he tossed his last bomb—the suggestion of homosexuality. It was a defining moment. The implication was not overt, and Jacob later was never able to remember just how his father had put it. He couldn't help but wonder why there was none of the forgiveness he kept hearing from his devout Amish friends. His mother had stood beside him during the scene, transfixed and unable to speak. In the awkward silence that followed, she laid her hand on his shoulder and squeezed—was it at least her forgiveness? That's how Jacob wanted to read it. The guilt lingered long after, especially when Jacob continued to give in to his passions. It wasn't until much later that he learned from friends that his father's violent reaction was excessive and out of date. After his first run-in with *Anthony Adverse,* however, all his activities of self-discovery were conducted with meticulous privacy.

Jacob agonized about these early experiences and came to resent his father's cruel words. In fact, there were times when he wondered whether his father might even hate him. There certainly was little warmth in their relationship. Jacob began to doubt himself—was he somehow unworthy and unlike other boys? The lack of any warmth in the relationship between his parents puzzled him. Late at night, there was often the rumble of angry words invoking God and Jesus—mostly in his father's deep growl. He was tempted to sneak to the door and listen, but he feared being caught treading the creaky floor.

Like most children his age, Jacob had a fertile imagination. He made up stories about his father, contriving all kinds of doubt-driven fantasies. He spent a lot of time studying his own image in the mirror. His thick brown hair, rather shaggy falling over one side of his brow, and the band of pale freckles across his nose were unlike the features of the old man's long, lugubrious face, with deep-set eyes staring out of a florid, Germanic countenance. Jacob was small boned, his father, a giant. His overactive imagination, enriched by reading, conjured up all kinds of mysterious scenarios. Mr. Baum, a quiet bachelor farmer who lived next door, was a frequent visitor. To escape the loneliness of his big house down the road, he often dropped by to talk, sometimes when Jacob's father was out in the fields. Mr. Baum seemed always happy to see Jacob and, in a way, even loving—arm around his shoulders and supportive of the boy's reading interests. Jacob wished his own father was like this. The visitor was obviously fond of his mother, too—touching her arm, her hand as they talked. One night when his father was called out of town to attend a funeral, Mr. Baum dropped by late in the evening, and Jacob watched from his window on a moonlit night. His heart beat and his stomach churned as he watched them embrace. He forced himself back to bed and lay awake for a long time trying to make sense out of what he had witnessed.

Life on the farm was never easy, even on the good days. There was something about the work which required more discipline and perseverance than intellect— mending fences, feeding stock, tending the kitchen garden, cleaning horse stalls, stacking bales of hay and straw. The chores seemed endless. The sheer weight of the work did not leave much time for daydreaming. Spring, summer, and fall went by quickly. By contrast, the harsh winters passed slowly. That was when Jacob did his reading. On his sixteenth birthday, Mr. Baum gave him a copy of *Men of Iron,* a romantic coming-of-age story from the Middle Ages about an evil black knight. Loving it, Jacob swept through the book and delved into other tales of medieval history. He was drawn to the darkness of evil. He spent many winter afternoons in the Appleton library combing through the shelves, randomly picking out books, discarding those which bored him and devouring those he liked. Gradually, he developed his own tastes. Biographies of the famous and infamous fascinated him. He spent hours wading through Sandburg's *Lincoln,* who, in his moody isolation, was an appealing, sympathetic character for Jacob. This interest led him to other more intimate studies of the moody side of Lincoln. In fact, it was this dark side of humankind that preoccupied Jacob as he progressed, largely on his own, through a wide swath of introspective literature, including Dostoyevsky's *Crime and Punishment,* Shakespeare's *King Lear,* and Albert Camus' *The Fall.* It was during this period that he discovered what he perceived to be his own dark side. It happened on one of those bleak winter afternoons in fading light. Jacob could never understand his inexplicable attraction to Christy in the shadows of the barn—a memory that would remain to haunt him.

Jacob's early intellectual development was largely self-taught. His parents wanted him to be more gregarious and worried that his heavy outside reading was interfering with his schoolwork. His marks never got much above the C level, although his IQ tested high. He ignored the advice to get rid of the books and concentrate on his studies and neglected social life. To assuage his father's worries, he acquired a girlfriend—because it was expected of him. That was Sylvia. But after he went on to college to pursue journalism, he gradually lost interest in her.

Away from the farm and his father, Jacob's darker side was suffused beneath multiple layers of consciousness. While he struggled to bury it, the darkness kept returning in his dreams and visions. It seemed to control his life.

CHAPTER 1

It was bound to happen, and it would happen. Iraq was an open invitation to the terrorist as well as his training ground. There was always a way.

Ahmed and his men and one woman were carefully chosen by the Imam because they were of mixed blood—light skinned—and U.S. citizens. But their loyalties were to Islam. They had not been brainwashed by any madrassa. They had watched the crusade against Islam evolve from the inside—the racial profiling, detention at the border, strip searches, prejudice of employers, and, above all, the ugly occupation of Iraq. The Americans had stayed to kill Iraqis and control the oil. The patriotism of Ahmed and his friends had been unquestioned as they joined up. The need for military manpower had simply obscured suspicions of any kind.

Ahmed, who was known in his Stryker Brigade as Sergeant Jack Sala, drove slowly, leading his convoy of Humvees out of Kadhimiya and along the Tigris River into the center of the city. At several checkpoints along the way, he got the friendly wave-off he expected. Ahmed had arranged clearance for a detail of soldiers assigned as a special security force. There had been reliable threats that al Qaeda would attack the Green Zone that night. As Arabic speakers, Ahmed's people had been handpicked to monitor checkpoints and question any suspicious visitors. Members of Parliament had numerous aides who could take advantage of special passes, too easily given. Ahmed had made a point of impressing his superiors with knowledge of possible offenders in this category. He smiled as he considered the delicious irony—defending against his own attack. In fact, Ahmed had himself planted the al Qaeda threat.

His heart was beating fast, pounding against his chest. But he maintained a steely control over his emotions. His focus was total. There were no other thoughts in his mind—not even his beloved Tanya. He had said his farewells, and with them her image had disappeared from memory. He was confident that his group was equally disciplined.

The convoy crossed the Tigris slowly on the wobbly temporary bridge installed after the permanent structure had been blown up. As they approached the main checkpoint at the entrance of the Green Zone, guards stepped out with their weapons pointed at the first Humvee, and Ahmed leaned through the open window and waved.

"Hey, Jack," the officer had recognized him, "yer late!"

"Your clock might be a little fast, Lieutenant."

"Whatever. How many of your guys do I get?"

"I'm giving you the fourth truckload—there are six of them. The corporal knows the drill. If you do have visitors you don't like, he'll do the interviews. He knows a lot of faces. Made a career out of it."

"Okay." He approached and shook hands as Ahmed offered his. "Geez, I hope there's no trouble, Jack. We got some Congressional mucky-mucks visiting. Your boys all prepped on this, you know, like where they sleep and stuff?"

"You bet we are!" Ahmed tried to keep the irony from his tone. "We'll catch the bad guys if they have the guts to come. It'd be a pretty brazen move, though. I don't expect any trouble."

The Lieutenant waved his arm admitting the convoy and disappeared behind a wall of sandbags and concrete barriers.

The time had come. Ahmed knew where he wanted to go, and he led the convoy along the route still at a moderate pace, but only until it was about two city blocks from the entrance. In a planned maneuver, the convoy picked up speed—there was just enough room to reach fifty miles per hour—and crashed through a pedestrian gate, tearing at the metal sides of the Humvees as they penetrated the barriers. Continuing to accelerate as small arms fire began to pelt the vehicles, one after the other crashed into the building at the front portal and blew up in a deafening series of roars. Just before the explosions, Ahmed's cry could be heard to echo off the walls—"Allah Akbar, Allah Akbar!"

Jacob left in the dark to catch an early morning train to Boston. The three-hour trip would get him to Back Bay well before the funeral. Penn Station was already crowded when he arrived to pick up his reserved ticket, but the lines were short at the counter. The train scheduled for that time originated in Miami, so the accommodations were a cut above the usual commuter fare. Jacob did not like the wild rock and roll of the Acela. He picked out a window seat on what would be the sunny side. The chill of the dark predawn had gotten to him.

He settled in and was dozing when the train lurched to a start and began tunneling out of Manhattan. As his car emerged from underground, Hell Gate and the lights on the East River bridges popped into view. There was just the beginning of a winter dawn in the eastern sky, and planes were already dipping into La Guardia, navigation lights blinking reassuringly. It was almost nine years after the first terrorist attacks—but still not enough time to cure his bad taste for flying. This was made doubly so by the continued episodes of al Qaeda terror in the Middle East, Europe, and Asia. In fact, there had even been several unsuccessful attacks at the Port of New York with explosives, but the administration would not say what kind—because of security. There was talk of a dirty bomb, but it was never proven. The events were minor incidents compared to September 11, 2001. Homeland Security periodically reactivated its silly color codes—now showing bright orange, one level below the maximum red. It was difficult to understand what was useful about such alerts, other than to make one even more leery about travel of any kind. The political motives were clear enough—Congressional elections were only months off. The fear talk from Washington was unabated. The Republicans had won the White House for a third time and wanted to keep control of Congress.

The current president had been one of George W. Bush's loyal apologists. In fact, he was among those most vocal in support of the invasion of Iraq. His close relationship with the neoconservative community gave him a unique credibility for some as leader in the war on terror, a phrase still very prominent in the political lexicon. Not surprisingly, he had little trouble keeping the dread of terrorism at a fever pitch, largely fostered by a barrage of suspected al Qaeda plots and threats announced from time to time by officials of Homeland Security. As his first initiative, the new president, like his predecessor, had insisted on increasing forces in Iraq to make America safer. It was unclear how more troops accomplished this. But it had kept the violence under a modicum of control while the insurgency in Iraq continued to simmer, pinning down two hundred thousand U.S. troops for an indefinite future. The message was still the same threadbare assertion that "we must fight al Qaeda in Iraq, so we don't have to fight them at home." The president's second proposal was a new military program, calling on eighteen- to twenty-five-year-olds to do two years of national service—only vaguely defined. It was just a euphemism for an old-fashioned draft. It didn't fool anyone.

Conditions elsewhere in the Middle East had required another expansion in overall troop strength. The volunteer army wasn't working. Outside of Iraq, hostilities in the conflicts between Israel and the Palestinians and the Hezbollah in

Lebanon were always threatening to flare into full-blown war. There had been efforts to curb the power of Israel and limit its own nuclear weaponry, but the intense influence of the Israeli lobby in Washington proved to be too overwhelming. Oil refineries in Kuwait and Dubai had been bombed by terrorists, causing gasoline prices in the United States to spike at $6 a gallon. Pipelines in the Middle East were under constant attack. The rise in worldwide energy costs was beginning to depress the global economy.

The Muslim Brotherhood had taken over parts of Egypt. The army had imposed emergency powers in Pakistan to quell the growing political instability. In Afghanistan, the Taliban had occupied several Eastern provinces, and pitched battles with the government, or firefights as they were called, periodically flared up. Islam in Indonesia and Thailand was becoming more restive and threatening to bring down the military authority. To keep citizen concerns about the carnage in Iraq in check, casualties among U.S. forces in the area were downplayed and sometimes covered up. Total American dead was now over eight thousand. But there were new devious ways of tallying combat casualties. Of course, many Iraqis were lost, too. Private sources had estimated more than one million had died. Reporting from the Middle East remained under strict control by the military. The trend to embed journalists had returned. Only a few independent reporters were left.

It had become clear that an Iraqi army or police force was an impossible dream. Iraq was a country of disparate regions, the people of which had little in common with neighbors. The Shiites, Sunnis, and Kurds each had their own armed forces, with only sectarian loyalties. There was de facto partition of the country. After an abortive Israeli effort to bomb a suspected nuclear facility near Teheran, an outraged Iran allied itself with Shiites around Basra, and together they were trying to take over the southern oil fields. Sunnis and Kurds had become only occasional U.S. allies. The foreigners with al Qaeda were still using Baghdad as a training ground, killing Americans and murdering Iraqis working for the local government. U.S. forces in Iraq seemed to be paralyzed by the indecision of their generals.

It was a stunning irony that under Bush, the invasion of Iraq had begun as Operation Iraqi Freedom. The word "freedom" hung awkwardly in the smoky air of Baghdad these days. The swagger had dissipated. The first try at names, Operation Iraqi Liberation, had been quickly abandoned after a sharp-eyed bureaucrat saw that the acronym would spell "oil." The Freudian slip revealed all. The mission was never adequately defined—except as "bringing democracy to the Middle East," now just an embarrassing memory. "Democracy" really only meant allegiance to the United States. The weapons of mass destruction, initially suspected but not found, were now a reality. Sadly, the fiasco in Iraq had turned most of Islam and the rest of the world against the United States.

Bush left office under a cloud, after narrowly defeating an impeachment effort, declaring victory and leaving the cleanup to his successor. But even now there were no new ideas, no exit strategy, and no solution to the sectarian strife. The so-called cleanup legacy of the Bush administration seemed insurmountable in human and fiscal terms. The stiff-necked diplomacy with Iran and foundering negotiations with North Korea had done little to slow the nuclear ambitions of either country. The new president had better reason than his predecessor to accuse Iran of interference in both Iraq and Lebanon. The damaged credibility of the United States and Israel was fast diminishing hope of cooperation from Europe. A last-minute legacy effort by Bush toward détente with Iran had only a fleeting moment on the world stage before it fizzled. The United Nations floundered under stagnation by veto power, and U.S. diplomacy, still mired in attitude, refused to negotiate with either Syria or Iran on continued Israeli incursions into Lebanon.

The Republicans had won the 2008 election narrowly in a campaign filled with the usual acrimony, mudslinging, and chauvinism. The Democratic campaign had done little to build an effective opposition. The drumbeat of fear tactics, patriotism, and chest thumping continued unabated. Critics were labeled as weak and disloyal. The new propaganda machine ground up the opposition as it did under Bush. With the constantly increasing levels of snooping by the National Security Agency and the CIA, little privacy remained for U.S. citizens. Executive powers of the president had been expanded by a skewed Supreme Court to the point where the Republican Congress was nothing more than a cheering section. The United States had lost its direction and was scorned by most of the world.

Jacob had been immersed in the mundane level of political reporting, riding around the country in crowded, uncomfortable press buses and covering events with his own byline and responsibility to come up with the big story. Conflicted about the developing policy disaster, his Midwest roots whispered patriotism, but experience made him wary of the future. He wasn't much different from most American people. There didn't seem to be answers. Jacob gazed out the window at the endless stream of suburbs and wondered when the lives of Americans would be touched again by violence. It was only a matter of time.

He studied his reflection critically in the train window and decided he still looked like a thirty-six-year-old hayseed—a fresh, corn-fed face framed by long-ish brown hair. The image was of a slightly faded all-American boy. What saved him from an appearance of callowness were his prominent brows and deep-set eyes, which gave him a slightly haunted, but knowing expression. With a wiry build and good coordination, Jacob had achieved athletic prowess early and was always in demand for team sports. While it wasn't something he sought out, he followed the line of least resistance and participated in response to pressure from coaches and classmates. He got three varsity letters and a lot of attention but never lost his humility. He had resented these commitments as interfering with his reading pursuits.

The last ten years in the Big Apple had eroded any vestiges of his rural values, which were replaced by big-city wariness and toughness that weren't there before. Appleton seemed so distant. How long since he'd seen the farm? The southern Illinois countryside seemed lost in his past. His few visits back home had been surreal—bucolic Appleton still had only three thousand souls and two traffic lights. Life in Appleton had been centered in a small world consisting of family, church, Friday night basketball, and Saturday night sessions at the movies or at the Railroad Cafe. The depot had been converted after rail traffic died. In this sequestered atmosphere, the influences of the sexual revolution and its still-evolving presence had only lightly touched his contemporaries. He and Sylvia had dated for four years—under the watchful and approving eye of parents—with the understanding that they would end up as husband and wife after college. Of course, it hadn't worked out that way. Sylvia had married a classmate. Jacob's years at the university had been an eye-opener after life on the farm. The experience had changed him. His academic encounters with views different from those dominating small-town Middle America had pulled him into a different world. He decided early to major in journalism but was energetic in exploring other areas such as literature, philosophy, and even creative writing—the latter was always a tempting field for him. In his spare time, he had become an editor of the *Illini*, the school paper. He had worked hard on his studies, leaving little room for a social life. The comfortable routine of college life was over; he was facing graduation but was not quite ready for it.

His college thesis had been picked up by a small liberal magazine and had attracted some attention around the country. The publication had expanded his title to the more inflammatory "Failure of a Free Press—The Iran-Contra Affair." Jacob's modest fame traveled fast. His first journalistic effort had reached Apple-ton a few days after it was published. The town was a loyal bastion of the GOP.

He smiled, recalling his angry prose. He would never have described himself as a partisan. Not surprisingly, his father had written him an admonishing letter accusing him of being unpatriotic and followed up with a telephone call, his mother kibitzing on the line. It was about that same time that his breakup with Sylvia occurred.

On that memorable holiday trip home from college, the subject of the article created the first spark of friction in the family. He had done the unforgivable— question the honor of President Reagan. By the second night, he tired of reasoning with his parents, who continued attacking his politics. Instead, he called a friend, and they met at the local bar, where his fame had also preceded him. With beer flowing freely, the hostility followed him there. He escaped alone and walked the streets. The icy wind sharpened the taste of the unpleasant encounter. Swaying Christmas lights suspended over Main Street depressed him. He picked his way along the row of storefronts, avoiding icy patches from an earlier snowfall. Only a few people were out to brave the plunging temperatures. Rounding a corner, he ran into Sylvia. They hugged tentatively, and he invited her to have a cup of coffee. Taking her arm, he guided her to a nearby cafe. He was surprised to see lattes and espressos had found an eager audience in Appleton. The warmth of the steamy atmosphere was a welcome change. They found a booth and shed their coats. Holiday Musak was playing in the background.

"You just appear like ... like a ghost in the street, Jacob?" There was heavy sarcasm in her voice and not a little anger. They ordered two coffees. "Why haven't you called me?" she asked testily.

"Well, I, uh, just got home, uh, yesterday."

"I heard." She studied him. "So?" She pressed her point. "No calls from college, either."

He didn't have answers. After an uncomfortable silence, he said, "I was gonna call tomorrow." He couldn't meet her probing eyes.

"You haven't written for weeks."

He toyed with just telling her the truth—that he was no longer interested, that he had grown beyond their relationship, that he was, well, different. It wasn't as if he had met someone else. He had given no time to that sort of thing. The fact was that he just didn't love her anymore, and he hadn't for months. The realization had come over him gradually, in small doubts at first, then with more certainty. But he had never shared this with her. He was too embarrassed. He knew he was being unfair but couldn't bring himself to tell her how he felt. After previous visits, there was some guilt, but only until he became immersed again in academic life.

He glanced at her in the dim light of the cafe. While she had put on a little weight, she was still pretty, the shiny, curly hair falling across her shoulders like a shampoo ad. Her full lips began to tremble as the silence lengthened. Her eyes were locked on him, increasing the painful awkwardness of the moment.

"What's going on with us, Jacob?" she asked finally, her voice breaking with emotion. "Is there another girl?"

"No, it's nothing like that," he said quickly.

"Yeah, so what is it?"

"Look," he began, wanting her to understand, to approve of his change of heart. "College has changed a lot of things."

"Meaning you, I suppose."

"Yes, it has." He paused, searching for the right words. "I think we should, ah, slow down, live our lives a little before …"

"Slow down?" she spat back at him. "And live our lives a little before what?"

"Before we make any plans."

"Plans, meaning marriage?" Her anger was mounting.

"Yes."

There was another silence. Then she collected herself and asked evenly, "Why don't you level with me, Jacob? Tell me what you really mean. I can take it. For once, I want the truth out of you. You've been avoiding us for months now." She folded her hands on the table. "That's what you owe me; that's all you owe me. And I want to hear it from your own lips—now. I'm not going to say it for you."

He confessed, blundering into the admission so long denied. He told her that it was over, that it was his fault, that he was the one who had changed, and how he had resolved to find a life away from Appleton. He wouldn't soon forget the look on her face as tears streamed down her cheeks as she heard what she had already suspected. They hadn't promised each other anything, but after six long years, he was breaking a virtual engagement. She hung onto her composure, though, enough to gather her things, peck him on the forehead, and wish him luck. As he watched her march off into the frigid darkness, he felt as if he'd committed a heinous crime. They didn't meet again until after she had married Scott Travis, who worked for the local bank and eventually became a vice president.

The sun softened these unpleasant memories, breaking out from the horizon as the train rocked along. A lot had happened since that ordeal. After graduation Jacob had taken a job with the *Chicago News* on the city desk. He had not made a single trip back to Appleton since the breakup. Avoiding Sylvia was one motive, but there was also the more subtle fear of being drawn back into the fold. At first, the big city was a difficult adjustment. At times he was homesick for a simpler life and called his mother occasionally just to check in. She was having an easier time of it with his father having moved out. They were separated, but not divorced.

The big blustery city held new lessons for him. In the gritty streets of urban life, it was difficult to cling to the innocence of Appleton. Each morning he would greet the people in his adopted metropolis—the worn-out, probably abused waitress at the coffee shop, fellow reporters and hardened cops on the crime beat, cursing news vendors, courthouse bailiffs, and prison guards. The city desk was his home base off the streets. There were the inevitable murders, rapes, robberies, trials, and the court proceedings which followed. That was his beat, often late at night. There were the drunks, so many drunks, addicts, and the addled in the streets, always referred to by the establishment inaccurately as "the homeless." Maybe the idea of no housing was more bearable than the uglier and more complicated truth about these lost souls. Jacob was oddly drawn to this unforgiving world. It seemed to grow on him like a mold creeping into his psyche. By his third year of life on the city desk, he became restless and began to look beyond Chicago to the East, to the Big Apple. One day he got the call he'd been waiting for. The university placement service had tracked him down. *The New York News* had gotten his name in a list of honors graduates from the School of Journalism at Illinois and offered him a job with a nice salary increase and a promise of promotions. He didn't have to think about it much—he knew enough to realize that this was a good opportunity. It was the big time. His father had called the city Gomorrah, and that was precisely what made it appealing to Jacob.

He collected his few belongings and moved to the Big Apple. After a few years of grunt work at the *News* learning his way around the courthouse and City Hall, he had gotten his own byline on the local political scene. This was his trial period. His work began to show a rare astuteness about forecasting the political winds, and gradually he was admitted to the select group of journalists reporting on the national scene. It took him almost three years to be fully accepted by that tight little fraternity. Then, for reasons he couldn't fathom, he was chosen to write an in-depth piece on the Crane family. He would have much preferred sticking with politics or the war in Iraq, but there it was—a special assignment—with intimations of promotion possibilities and coverage of the national scene.

Joshua Coffin Crane, the New England oil billionaire, had just died, marking the close of a lurid chapter in the colorful history of a venerable Massachusetts family which had started in whale oil and eventually flourished in crude oil. Jacob opened his briefcase and sorted through his file until he found the *Boston Globe* obituary. This would be his fifth reading of it, along with other bits and pieces of background collected by the news staff. Each time, the force of the personalities revealed pulled on him, drawing him deeper into the family. For some reason he could not define, the story was beginning to take possession of him. The questions and implications left hanging were intriguing. He found himself creating images to go with the names. Smoothing out rumpled sheets of newsprint on his lap, he began to reread.

Joshua Coffin Crane Dies at 91
Marking the End of a Colorful
and Controversial Career

Boston, February 20, 2010. Joshua Coffin Crane, 91, died last night at his home in Manchester, after a brief illness. The cause was not disclosed. A service, for members of the immediate family only, will be held at nine on Saturday morning at the St. Martin's Episcopal Church in Gloucester. Friends are asked not to send flowers, but instead, make donations to the Fisherman's Fund. A memorial service will be held in Boston at four in the afternoon at Trinity Church. Later, there will be a family gathering at the Crane home on Nantucket.

Crane, chairman of The Crane Corporation and known to his friends and colleagues as "J. C.," is expected to leave an estate of almost one billion dollars. While most of this wealth is tied up in a family holding company controlling the Corporation, some shares are held directly by a few family members and others by financial institutions which had been corporate creditors in the past. Crane's early energy business has been predominantly in Latin America—one of the few U.S. companies accepted there. During the rapid growth of Crane's oil business, its aggressive exploration activities had a troubled and turbulent history. The Crane name had been linked to illegal arms trade, money laundering, and other activities thought to be at the center of its shadowy relationships in Latin American countries. But nothing was proven. More recently, Crane operations have spread into the Middle East and the Caucasus. It is a mystery how Crane has avoided any inquiry about its huge successes abroad, particularly in Latin countries, generally hostile to U.S. oil companies.

Little is known about what changes in ownership, if any, will occur as a result of Crane's death. His son, Joshua, Jr., who is now president and chief operating executive, will undoubtedly become CEO.

The Crane dynasty has a colorful past. In the nineteenth century, the family was heavily invested in whaling ventures and owned a fleet of ships. J. C. Crane's great-grandfather, Ezra Coffin, was a whaling ship's captain. Known to be a feisty character, Ezra, when a young mate, was aboard the Essex when it was sunk by a whale and its survivors were abandoned at sea for months. Ezra took charge and managed to save all the men who shared a lifeboat with him. The family ships were owned through Beacon Trading Company, which continued under the direction of subsequent generations of Cranes investing in other businesses after whaling died out. Beacon changed its name to The Crane Oil Trust a few years after it began oil exploration.

J. C. Crane had a colorful record in World War II as an early member of the Flying Tigers with General Chenault, and later as an Army Air Corps pilot in the Far East Theater, flying "the Hump," a supply route into Burma. After the war, he went to work in the family business and became president in 1952. About this time, the company began making investments in oil exploration in West Texas. During this period, young Crane met a local wildcatter named Alejandro Guzman, a Mexican national living in El Paso. They joined forces and developed a number of oil properties in the Southwest and in Mexico. When Crane and Guzman pooled their interests, The Crane Oil Trust was reorganized as The Crane-Guzman Oil Trust. Guzman was well-connected in Mexico, and with his help, the company was able to acquire ownership of newly discovered offshore oil fields. A little-noticed law was passed permitting Crane to own real estate and oil interests in Mexico. When Mexico began to limit foreign investment, Crane's interests were always grandfathered. Under the authority of this same exception, Crane affiliates were also granted offshore drilling rights in locations where large reserves were located. Guzman continued as a director and vice chairman of Crane until he died in 1996. Under the administration of President Zedillo, the special concessions to Crane were stopped, and the company began to look elsewhere for investment. At that time, the company changed its name to The Crane Corporation.

During the recent period of spiraling oil prices and short supplies, Crane has become active as a worldwide trader of oil and gas in the Middle East and the Caucasus. However, little information as to this activity is available. David Levine, an analyst with Day & Levine, energy industry specialists, advises, "Many key operations of the company have been concealed in foreign subsidiaries, and disclosure has been limited. The fall of Enron focused new attention on Crane, but in the current atmosphere of rising demand for and tighter supplies of oil, the company has been successful in holding off investigation." Success of the company's special pleading was in part due to its long-standing ties to the CIA, dating back to operations in Mexico. The relationship apparently began during the Cuban Missile Crisis when company contacts in Mexico provided back-channel access to the Russians in Havana.

Crane's son, Joshua, Jr., met briefly with the financial press in the company's New York office to state that his father had left Crane in good shape and that an orderly transition to new leadership was already underway. He refused to comment on the status of any investigation of the company.

Joshua Crane's only other child, daughter Emily, lives in Boston. She has been active in various charities and currently chairs Project Hope, an AIDS research fund. She is also antiwar and an outspoken critic of the Iraq invasion.

Outside the Boston area, Crane had homes in Manhattan, Paris, and Mexico. His second wife, Natasha Zilenko, a Russian national, is said to be living in Paris. Twenty years younger than Crane, she has been rumored to be separated from him. They married after Crane's first wife died of cancer. Company sources say that Zilenko has been instrumental in developing relationships in Russia and the Caucasus. Crane leaves two grandchildren, Ezra, an attorney in Boston, and Yvonne, who, like her aunt, is an antiwar activist and a graduate student at Harvard University.

Jacob put aside the paper. The piece raised many questions that cried out for answers. Stories about Joshua Crane, which he had combed through, were mostly the superficial stuff of gossip and trivia. He had not yet found the time to delve very deeply into financial reporting. Neither Crane's 10K reports nor the financial news Jacob had seen shed much light on what was going on inside the corporation. He had discussed the available data with the *News* business editor and learned that what bothered most analysts was the buildup of cash and, of course, the perennial mystery of Mexico, Crane's baffling successes in that country. The excessive cash could be attributable to the fact that The Crane Corporation does not pay dividends—a significant omission for an oil company and one not overlooked by angry family members. Only gossip and suspicion were offered as explanation for the company's outstanding successes in Mexico.

As he contemplated the job ahead, he smiled, remembering how his friend Rachel had gently pushed him to take this assignment. He still had his doubts.

He and Rachel had shared a good deal together. She was a colleague with more experience than he. Indeed, she had already published a book—based on an assignment in Afghanistan. He'd read the book and was captivated by her prose and the critical insights about the war on terrorism. He also admired her guts. It had been a dangerous assignment where several reporters were killed by hostile Taliban forces. She had actually witnessed the early stages of what became a very controversial massacre of Taliban by a warlord, acting as surrogate for the United States. Her article on this had been viciously attacked by the administration.

Rachel had the idea that the only way to break out of the pack during a war that everyone was reporting on was to do a story on a major misstep of the government. If the event was controversial, so much the better. She had often used that phrase, "break out of the pack," with Jacob. He hadn't realized he was in a pack of any kind. Jacob was only mildly ambitious and not at all pushy. Promotions came to him, he didn't seek them out. The comfortable familiarity of the job and his associates usually outweighed ambition. By contrast, Rachel was extremely competitive about her own career and now about his as well. In fact, she had taken an interest in his with a proprietary fervor that made Jacob uneasy. She liked his insights and pushed him to be more aggressive. She was very excited about the Crane project. They had spent the previous evening together discussing how he could turn it into a real opportunity—maybe even a future book. They often talked into the night about the insurgencies going on in Iraq, Afghanistan, and Lebanon and the politics and ideologies that seemed to be driving the administration. Rachel's disgust with the notion of preventive war was intense, although he reminded her that there was nothing new about this in U.S. history. Jacob could not match her fervor, and this frustrated her. She would go on to rant against control of foreign policy by the Defense Department and cynically suggested that we should return to the old title of War Department as more appropriate to its new role. Rachel had a strong sense of fairness, following wherever it took her. Her writings had attracted the wrath of the spin doctors at the White House. They tried to label her—a nice Jewish girl any mother would love to have for a daughter-in-law—as being anti-Semitic because of her harsh criticism of AIPAC, the hyperactive Israeli lobby in Washington. She was deeply offended by the shame of Guantanamo and the Attorney General's brazen attempt to legitimize torture. Jacob agreed with much of what Rachel had to say but was just not partisan enough to get himself worked up about it.

She admonished him for having talent, but no passion. Jacob would question her appraisal, but she always answered by saying, "You'll find it someday." These conversations occasionally ended in their having sex. They had been off-and-on lovers for more than a few years. Well, reconsidering the characterization, she was not really a lover. In contrast to her passion for politics, in bed there was a detachment about her, a reserve he couldn't understand. Come to think of it, the encounters were less than passionate for him. The term "love" was never used by either of them. Then there were those nights when she was not available. She denied adamantly that it was another guy. Jacob just chalked it off to her wanting to be alone. She was, indeed, a loner with few friends and a freelance job. She was Jacob's first prolonged adult relationship—one more intellectual than sensual. It had taken them awhile to get comfortable with intimacy. He decided that they were both repressed in this department.

As he gazed absently out at the passing scenery of towns and frozen country-side, he could feel himself reacting to the image of their lovemaking. The vivid picture of her slender, wiry body projected off his reflection in the window—her short dark hair tousled and face flushed—the quick culmination, almost hurried, he felt at times. These were odd experiences for Jacob. Before Rachel, his love life had been limited. He and Sylvia had stolen moments in the back seat of his car and on the couch at her house when her parents were out. These sessions, always partly clothed, were awkward and a little desperate for them both. There had been other heated trysts in college and during his working years, but they were never satisfactory—nothing more than the physical outlet, if it got that far. Of course, long before Sylvia, there was Christy. He instantly suppressed the thought and turned away from the window as if to block the unsettling memory.

The sex with Rachel had left him drained and empty, and he never had the feeling that they developed any relationship deeper than intellectual. Her interest was mostly in pushing him toward excellence and ambition for a larger career. There were days when he found the pressure from her over the top, sometimes to the point of his own resentment. In an odd way, though, he recognized that the pressure was good for him. He always looked forward to seeing her. Little by lit-tle, he had become convinced that their sexual relationship was probably unhealthy, but as a mentor, she was helping his career. In time, he came to regard these intimate encounters as a form of compensation for her support.

The glint of the plastic cover of his press pass in a pocket of his briefcase caught his eye and brought him back to the matter at hand. Digging around in the mess of papers, he found the dramatis personae he had prepared hastily of the Crane family and important friends. Joshua, Jr., had an impressive resume—a stint in the Marine Corps, MBA from Harvard Business School, a few years in the oil fields of Texas, working on offshore platform rigs off the coast of Mexico, and a brief assignment in the wild city of Baku in the Caucasus, always working for companies unrelated to Crane. The job in Azerbaijan was his last job outside the family corporation. Since then, Joshua had made his way through Crane's operations, moving inexorably to the top in a carefully planned progression designed by his father. Joshua had married very young. The match could have been part of a plan. Laura was the daughter of then Senator Lopez-Diaz, leader of the Mexican Senate and later minister of resource development in the administra-tion of President Salazar. He was very well connected. The photo of them on their wedding day revealed a lovely dark-haired Mexican beauty out of central casting. More recent pictures of Laura from the society pages were matronly without being dowdy. She was still a beauty. Time had been kind to her. The couple lived in Manhattan, where the head office of Crane was located.

There were no press photos of the children, Ezra and Yvonne. Ezra, from what reports there were, lived the circumspect life of a fledgling Boston lawyer and was regarded around town as an eligible bachelor. Sketchy reports of Yvonne presented a different picture—a headstrong young lady often given to public outbursts of exuberance that were hard to suppress from the public domain. One notable flare-up had taken place in the Hamptons a few years past when Yvonne drove a Ford Explorer into the swimming pool at a golf club on Long Island. While *The New York News* was able to get a good shot of the SUV partially submerged, there was none of Yvonne. At first, the boyfriend gallantly insisted that he was at the wheel for the dunking. But later, she relented, taking full responsibility and asserting that she did it as a protest against the golf club's discriminatory practices against blacks.

Of Crane's daughter, Emily, there was a strange dearth of any kind of background. She led a very private life and refused to meet with the press. The *Boston Herald* had recently carried a story about her companion at rare outings. According to the Boston tabloids, the woman, one Liza O'Leary, an active feminist of some fame, was involved in a longtime relationship with Emily. Both Emily and Yvonne had been identified in press stories with left-wing causes and, particularly in recent months, the antiwar movement. Both were vocal critics of the administration's policy in the Middle East.

Jacob couldn't find much about Natasha Zilenko, Crane's second wife, other than that she was probably Georgian, born in the city of Tiflis. There were rumors of her estrangement from Crane shortly before his death. One shadowy picture of her was in the file, however, showing a middle-aged woman of extraordinary beauty. The mystery that cloaked her life attracted all kinds of gossip and rumors, the most intriguing of which was that she played a role in getting a favorable reception in Russia for Crane's ambitions in the oil fields of the Caucasus. It was not known whether she would attend the funeral events. Other notables listed were various professional types—lawyers, bankers, accountants, lobbyists— with ties to The Crane Corporation or to Crane personally. Jacob glanced over the list and then folded his notes into his briefcase.

He hoped to attend two of the memorial events scheduled: the first, a public affair in Boston at the Old Trinity Church, and a second and more intimate one a day later at the family compound on Nantucket. He had already made arrangements to attend the memorial service in Boston but as yet had only a vague plan to wangle his way into the latter; he doubted that his press pass would help with Nantucket.

As the train swayed at high speed into the snow-patched New England countryside, he daydreamed about Rachel and then dozed off.

CHAPTER 2

Jacob was sipping coffee anxiously at a cafe in the Copley Square Hotel in Boston when his old friend from the *Globe* joined him—later than they had planned. Henry Mitchel came in through the street entrance in a gust of cold, dank air. He spotted Jacob immediately. In the patch of sky visible through buildings on the narrow street, Jacob had noticed that the cloud cover was thickening with a promise of snow. According to a noisy television tucked into a corner of the restaurant, a northeast storm expected to stay offshore had instead drifted west to threaten the coast.

"Geez, it's penetrating out there," Mitchel commented. "East wind with a taste of salt—bad sign." He shrugged out of his coat and doffed a scruffy black watch cap, which Sellars recognized as Mitchel's regular winter totem reserved for the coldest days. The effect was to sharpen the New England features protruding from his round face, a countenance reminiscent of the Addams family.

They greeted and hugged briefly. The hug part had become a ritual among men of their generation, and it always made Jacob a little uncomfortable. It didn't help much either that Mitchel was openly gay. The two-armed, one-over and one-under-the-shoulders embrace was, for Sellars, something to escape as quickly as possible. He wondered whether, like some European men, there would eventually be a kiss. He shuddered at the prospect and shook off the thought. They ordered coffee and caught up on each other's lives.

"You look good, Jacoby." It was Mitchel's exclusive sobriquet.

"Thanks. It's been awhile."

"Yes, altogether too long, old chap. This is kind of a new beat for you, isn't it?"

"Yeah, it is." The "old chap" was also slightly off-putting for Jacob. It was *so* Ivy League. "I've had enough of elections. They say the same stuff over and over.

I'm relieved to be doing something different." Jacob glanced at his good friend, surprised to note that the usual cherubic mien had become more lined since they had last met. Almost two years had passed. Mitchel had always been a little too boyish—and very vain about his appearance. To hide a bit of the inevitable aging process, there was a hint of light makeup around his eyes to distract from the puffiness of added weight and a receding hairline. "Hey, I hear that you have been creating quite a name for yourself with your latest *Bushwit II*," Jacob said.

"Yeah, some of the stuff that got overlooked when he was in office. It's my little gem, with or without the *w*. I had so much fun with it. And now, my sequel—a whole new set of idiocies. He just never stops, even as a civilian. Hah!"

"People are eating it up." Jacob had to laugh even thinking about some of the mixed-up syntax. "It's in every bookstore."

"Yeah, I guess it is. It was so easy."

"God! How blasé," Jacob teased, peering at his friend more closely. "Hey, let me look at you. You're getting to look a bit like another Bush critic I know."

"Who?"

"Michael Moore."

"God forbid!" Mitchel glanced over at a mirror display around a pillar nearby as if confirming that Jacob was not serious. "I shave," he said rather primly and then added in a hurt tone, "So, did you have a nice flight?"

"Mitch, I'm kidding, of course. He's a unique slob. I took the train. Survival of the Big Dig tunnels is too dicey."

"Come on, only one or two have actually died. We've fixed it," Mitchel said, as he removed a pair of slick leather gloves finger by finger. "Still fixing it." He grinned ghoulishly.

"Yeah, so I've read."

"Well, are you all set for our little adventure?" Mitchel asked, rubbing the cold from his hands.

"Yeah, but I'm wondering what will happen with the Nantucket party if this turns into a snowstorm." Jacob was prodding his friend a bit on promised arrangements.

"They'll go on with it anyway." Mitchel snorted, glancing at the increasing darkness of the street outside. "This is a whaling family, remember—like mine? And it's not a party, Jacob. Let's call it a grief get-together." He laughed too loudly at his corny pun.

Mitchel was part of another venerable New England family whose history was also rooted in whaling—and the slave trade, too—as were many whalers. In fact, he was remotely related to the Cranes. A distant Mitchel lady had, it seems, married a Crane. After bearing her first child, she was widowed when her young husband was lost in a storm somewhere in the Pacific. Henry was a descendant of this unfortunate union. Sellars was counting on his friend to wangle a visit to the Nantucket gathering. It would be his best opportunity to get a closer look at the family.

"Speaking of that, Mitch," Jacob began, "this Nantucket thing, how do reporters … how do we …?"

"We?" Mitchel teased. "On press passes? Hah!"

Jacob recognized this as a tease after his Michael Moore remark. "Come on, get serious. This is important."

"Let's get some lunch, and then I'll fill you in on our little plot for the intimate island séance—that's even a better term for it."

"Okay." Jacob signaled the waitress, and they ordered sandwiches and more coffee. He was worried that Mitchel wasn't taking his visit seriously enough. "Mitch, this is a chance for me to, ah, break out, you know …" He was trying without much success to avoid the whole quote from Rachel. "Do something significant, get some attention. *The New York News* is a tough paper with a lot of talent, all of them working their asses off to get a byline or a shot at TV." He said this with a touch of irony, trying not to sound pushy. Pushy just wasn't in his genes. The coffees came, and he surveyed his steamy cup while Mitchel busily doctored his with cream and a mystery sweet.

"I know, I know, it's dog-eat-dog out there. And the print guys are panicking about losing out to MSNBC and Fox. Advertising is off, and nobody reads anymore. You know, Jacoby, we should be in television. That's where the big opportunities are." Mitchel was a coffee stirrer—one of those who stirred and stirred until almost wearing a hole in the bottom of the cup. Jacob found the nonstop tinkle of the spoon irritating. Mitchel glanced again at the mirror, moving his head side to side. "Jacoby, don't you think I'd look great on HDTV?" It was always necessary to get through these little charades with Mitch. Then he became easier to take. Their friendship had been tested by time. They had started their careers together in Chicago, even rooming together until Mitch uncloseted himself and found a more suitable roommate.

"You're such a ham, Mitch. Yes, you're great on TV." Mitchel had already made a few appearances.

"You think, Jacoby?"

Their sandwiches arrived. "Okay, what's the plan?" Jacob pressed, ignoring the repeated "Jacobys," which had become a regular term of endearment rather than a put-down by his friend. He was always a little uneasy with Henry Coffin

Mitchel's New England roots. Jacob's regional inferiority complexes seemed to intensify as he contemplated this product of Eastern establishment, Harvard, and all the parochial trappings that went along.

Mitchel had to napkin a messy mouthful of egg salad. "You worry too much, old pal. I got it all set up for us. Hell, I'll even help write the piece with you, if you want." He laughed through an eggy residue. Mitchel had been an honors graduate at Harvard without even trying. But Mitchel—who disliked "Henry" and detested "Hank"—came with a lot of baggage, not the least of which was his out-of-the-closet brassiness. While he had always belittled his Ivy background, he was nonetheless cocky and confident—quite the opposite of Jacob. Despite his sophomoric chatter, he was no lightweight. Far from it. Jacob was always impressed with how well-read Mitchel was. With the appetites of a dilettante, it seemed as if he had dipped into every field of learning, old and new, and he knew the stuff cold and didn't mind showing off. Every time they got together, Jacob felt he was playing catch-up.

"You gotta brush up on the whaling industry, you know. I bet you didn't know that those survivors from the *Essex* may have been cannibalistic." Mitchel didn't miss Jacob's blank expression. "Ha! You didn't know that, did you?"

"I, uh, didn't. You mean the survivors, one of the Cranes, might have used the dead ones for their, uh … to …?"

"To eat, to survive," he chortled. "Yeah, that's right. You got it." He leaned back with satisfaction, licking his lips, and finally using a napkin to finish off the last flecks of egg. Jacob wondered whether one of Mitchel's forebears might also have been one of the lucky survivors.

The story dulled Jacob's appetite for the rest of his roast beef sandwich. "I'll have to read up on that." Jacob pushed back his unfinished plate. "Now, let's get back to the news business."

"Okay." Mitchel looked smug, enjoying his control over their situation. "First, the memorial service here in Boston is just a town sweeper—anybody can come, you know, even bums off the street." He smiled impishly. Jacob thought to himself, still the snob. "You won't even need a press pass. But I'll get us good seats—right behind the family."

"Yeah, but what about a reception after?"

"There's not going to be one. The family doesn't want the exposure here in town. You know, all the questions from the press. And, hell, they don't really trust that wild and woolly girl, Yvy. She can be a scene-maker anytime. She might bring out her protesters."

"That's the kid—Yvonne—the daughter who put the Ford Explorer in the pool?"

"The same one. But she's no kid anymore. Wait 'til you see her. She'll knock your socks off."

"How so?"

"Well, she's really gorgeous and dresses with a lot of … actually not a lot." He sniggered. "That's the trouble. Sometimes racy—retro sixties, but not very, uh, in today. Old for her age. Sometimes she looks—and acts—like a hooker—at least that's what her father told her once. He went public with that expression at a dance, and no one's forgotten it." Mitchel was enjoying his insider status. "The press call her 'Iffy.' Cute, eh? It's a corruption of Yvy."

"Very cute," Jacob agreed. "Sounds like a handful," he added, trying to visualize the scene at the dance. "Her parents must be pretty frustrated." He considered the problem a moment and then asked, "How old is she?"

"She's twenty-four and much more grown up now. I think she's still in some phase of graduate school and teaching or tutoring, too." He paused thoughtfully. "But the kid's no flake, Jacob. Yvy is one smart piece of work and a real rebel. She hates the company and all it stands for, as she sees it. She works with shareholder groups and raises all kinds of issues. Imagine, in defiance of her inheritance! Drives her old man nuts. And the crowning blow is that she may go to law school. It certainly would be a good fit—she was a government major at Harvard. Her parents wanted her to do fine arts, but she got bored. Now she wants to go to Yale for law school. It's more public policy oriented." Mitchel seemed to glow with admiration as he related this. "And she's real active in antiwar, anti-administration stuff." His pleased expression revealed where he, himself, stood. "And she's very clever about it, too."

"Sounds like you're close to the family?" Jacob was surprised that Mitchel knew so much about the personal lives of the Cranes.

He snorted in disagreement. "Used to be. Their hospitality has cooled a bit since I got known as a dangerous antiwar critic. I stay in touch with Emily, though. She keeps me filled in." He paused reflectively, smiling. "They didn't invite me to the little family thing in Gloucester."

"What was that all about?" Jacob had wondered himself.

"Oh, a tiny memorial for the historical Cranes, whaling and finagling."

"And they didn't ask you? I'm surprised."

"So am I," he said ruefully. "But I had my spies in church. Nothing happened. Yvonne, the only reason to go, didn't show. She stiffed them. That must have caused a real family fight," he added with satisfaction.

"So how do we do Nantucket?" Jacob wondered whether the cooling of the family might reflect more of a problem with Mitchel's lifestyle.

"Well, don't worry, babe, I got a nice invitation for that one—and I can bring a friend."

"A friend?" Jacob asked, suspecting an unlikely scenario. "Your date?" he asked, amused at the thought.

"No, just a friend." Mitchel was teasing again. "You okay with that?" He grinned broadly. "They won't know the difference."

"That's what I'm worried about."

"So I bring a straight friend. You can be my straight friend; you are my straight friend." Mitchel was having more fun with this than Jacob. "You know, we don't have to kiss or anything for them. Ha ha!"

Jacob played along with the joke. "Well, I guess I can't be too choosy."

"That's the deal then. We're in." He signaled the waitress for more coffee. "I got ferry tickets for us over to the Island."

"Ferry tickets?"

"Yeah, ferry. You know, the things that go on water to an island."

"Very funny." Jacob glanced nervously at the street outside, which was now in the shadow of a thick cloud cover. "It doesn't look like such good weather for a boat trip."

"It'll be fine, Jacoby. Just fine. Certainly better than flying in this weather—even if I could get us seats on those dreadful puddle hoppers that go over there."

Sellars wasn't reassured. But he had no choice. It was Mitchel's show.

The memorial service for the public was held at Trinity Church where the Boston Brahmins mend their souls and mourn their dead, a beautiful old 1877 Romanesque example of the architecture of Henry Hobson Richardson in the downtown and just a short walk from the Copley Square Hotel where Jacob was staying. Dwarfing the old church next door was the posh new tower of the Fairmont Copley Hotel, rooms starting at $550 a night. It was a typical mixed neighborhood of old and new Boston. The church was under extensive renovation and was laced with scaffolding.

As they arrived, a fine snow began to fall, swirling in a gusty breeze. A line of chilled mourners was waiting anxiously to file through security at the door. After a short wait, Mitchel got the attention of one of the ushers and whispered something conspiratorially into his ear. The wheels were well greased because they were led around the crowd through a side door to seats close to the front of the nave. As they slipped into one of the reserved pews, their guide winked at Mitchel and gave Jacob a casual once-over. The organ was playing background Bach as the church slowly filled up, the murmur of greetings and condolences blending with the music. Jacob glanced around with curiosity, sizing up the crowd and trying to find a familiar face. Snow-dusted Chesterfields and furs were being shrugged off to reveal dark suits and plain dresses mostly of an Ivy League caliber—far from being a town sweeper. There was every variation of demeanor, from grim to bright smiles. He turned his attention to the roped-off section in front just beginning to fill. While Mitchel greeted friends, Jacob stood briefly to get out of his coat and take a better look. Family members had not yet arrived. Registers in the aisles were pumping hot air, and it was getting oppressively warm. A few minutes later as the crowd quieted, Mitchel nudged him, nodding toward a side door to the right of the sanctuary.

"There they come," he whispered, as those around them began to crane for a glimpse.

Mitchel cued the arrival of the family, identifying each one sotto voce. In the subdued lighting of the cavernous old church, the family was passing directly in front of them only a few rows away—first, Joshua and his Mexican wife, Laura. She was every bit as beautiful as her pictures—fine-drawn, dark features, big eyes—posture erect and expression appropriately somber. Her hair, cut fashionably short, was curled demurely to the shape of her face. As she got closer, Jacob became aware of the beginning lines of middle age at her eyes and around her mouth, but these didn't detract at all from her natural beauty. Joshua walked beside her, his arm laced into hers. His steel-gray hair was cut short, emphasizing a rather angular face and sharp features. But his skin was smooth and line-free—like a priest. There was nothing effete about him. Indeed, you could see how in later life age would reveal the same craggy, seagoing look his father had. But it would never show the same character. As he drew nearer, his rather intense wide-set eyes seemed to survey the crowd and miss nothing. For just a moment, his eyes met Jacob's, leaving him with an oddly uncomfortable feeling. Following closely was a tall, angular woman, whom Mitchel identified as Emily. She walked head high and confident, keeping her distance from the couple, her eyes fixed ahead to avoid contact with the congregation. If her brother would someday favor their father, Emily was already a carbon copy. Not unattractive, she reminded Jacob of an old portrait from colonial days. Her thick hair was done up in a tight bun at the nape, and makeup was spare. Following the family, other middle-aged couples walked arm in arm. Mitchel identified these as cousins and close friends of the family. The group took seats at one end of the pew reserved for them, as the organist went through the final flourishes of music. Then there was silence.

"So where are the kids?" Jacob asked in a hushed whisper.

"You got me. Maybe they won't show."

Jacob peered around the heads in front of him looking for any signs of Yvonne and Ezra. Then he caught sight of two darting figures slipping into the far end of the front pew. From the back, the girl had long silky dark hair which she flung across her shoulder with a toss of her head.

"That's them, Yvy and Ezra!" Mitchel shouted in his ear over the blast of the organ as the first hymn began. "Pretty clever. No one even noticed." They both stretched to get a better look. "I bet Yvy insisted on dressing dramatically. Love to see what she has on underneath that coat." His curiosity piqued, Jacob was wondering the same thing.

A number of hymns were sung, including a nautical one about sailors at sea. A canon delivered the eulogy, a rather long, tedious one filled with references to family history. He even had a quaint anecdote from the whaling traditions of the family. The eulogy ended with—Jacob thought it was in poor taste—an unctuous appreciation for Joshua's "generosity" to the church in "both treasure and wisdom over the years." A few others, not immediate family, spoke more eloquently. The whole service seemed carefully scripted. Jacob discreetly made a few notes.

Afterward, a short receiving line collected at the back of the church, but only Joshua and his wife seemed to be doing the greeting. Others hung around to people watch and chat. Yvonne and her brother had disappeared. Jacob caught a glimpse of a few political types he recognized, while Mitchel insistently guided him to a side door.

"Come on, let's avoid the crowds," Mitchel said over his shoulder. "Unless, of course, you want to meet the royal couple." He laughed at his rhetorical suggestion. Tugging at Jacob's sleeve, he said, "I've got a better idea. Hurry."

A gust of icy wind and blowing snow greeted them at the door. The storm had picked up. Mitchel cast an eye skyward. "Glad we're not flying to Nantucket. I'm a real chicken about planes in this kind of weather."

"Will they cancel the ferry?" Jacob asked.

"Not a chance. A measly nor'easter won't stop them. We're salty folk here in New England," he added with an uncharacteristic flourish of macho.

As they hurried past the Public Gardens, the wet snow began to stick, covering the ground and dusting the statues with a powdery white glaze. It was a beautiful winter scene. Jacob had to lengthen his stride to keep up.

"Where we going?"

"To the Carlton for a pit stop. Don't you have to pee after all that coffee?" Mitchel was trying not very hard to suppress a secret smile. "And to introduce you to the gracious lady Emily, if we're in luck." He clapped Jacob on the back. "How'd you like that?"

Jacob slowed to catch his breath. "You're kidding. How did you arrange it?"

"I didn't. I saw her leave. She didn't wait for the family stuff, and I'm just counting on her habits. The second-floor tearoom is her favorite hangout. It's been there for years, and they didn't touch it in the big rehab." He grabbed Jacob's arm and leaned close. "It's become a rendezvous for upscale gays." He added something else, but Jacob lost it in the wind, which was blowing itself into a gale.

Desperately, Jacob began rehearsing how he should handle the improvised opportunity for his first family interview and what he should be asking. He had no clue and, despite the cold, began to sweat at the armpits. Mitchel led the way through the polished bronze revolving door, a relic from the past which, Jacob guessed, had also survived the rehab. No modern electric glass doors for the venerable Carlton. He followed Mitchel down a set of narrow marble stairs to the men's room.

"She should be here by now. Probably had a car bring her. Go easy on the questions. I'll break the ice first. You know, go at her indirectly, unthreatening. We don't want to get her mad. She's not too fond of the press." He hiked his coat open and stood up to the gray marble urinal. Jacob did the same. "She's basically a nice person, but very private," he continued, addressing the wall. "The press was a little nasty about her live-in friend. And you know how I feel about that." He shook it and backed away, tucking it into his pants. Mitchel wasn't modest. "She likes me," he added smugly. "She'll say what's on her mind. But let her choose the ground." He paused to let this sink in. "Okay with you?"

"Absolutely, you lead the way." Jacob was relieved, not feeling so much on the spot.

Various visions of Mitchel's relationship with Emily ran through Jacob's mind. None of them worked.

They climbed the stairs to the lobby and took the elevator to the second floor. As they approached the tearoom, Mitchel hissed, "There she is!"

Emily was seated alone in an upholstered wingback chair from another century, studying a steaming pot of tea. There was a plate of untouched sweets on the table. She seemed to be the only customer. Mitchel walked over to her table confidently and plucked one of the sweets from the plate and put it in his mouth, pulling up a chair at the same time.

"We just have a moment, Emily dear. The storm, you know, has just screwed up our schedule. You'll probably make the trip to the Island in greater style. What will it be? Yacht or company jet?" Mitchel didn't even wait for an answer. "But I'm so glad we ran into you. It's been far too long. Oh, yes, this is an old friend, Jacob Sellars. Jacob, this is Emily." He added minimum hand gestures to complete the introduction. "He's a journalist of some renown himself. *The New York News*—the Big Apple. And we both need a cup of tea," he added with a shrug of mock desperation. In his nonstop greeting, Mitchel had adopted the familiar gay style, which he seemed easily to shift in and out of depending on the company. Amused by the pose, Jacob couldn't smother a big grin at the performance. Not giving her a chance to speak, Mitchel was off again. "God, wasn't that a service at the church! Why did Canon George have to mention the whaling? Killing mammals and all, and then the money. Yucko. Disgusting business!"

By now Emily was giggling. "For God's sake, Henry, shut up. Let your friend speak." She offered her hand to Jacob. "I'd like to greet him properly. I can't even remember his name after all the guff."

"It's Jacob Sellars," he said, accepting her hand, warm to the touch. "It's nice to meet you." Jacob thought her crinkly smile revealed a well-developed sense of humor.

"Tell me, Mr. Sellars, do we really have a chance encounter here? Is that why I had to listen to all that bullshit?" Not waiting for a reply, she glanced sharply at Mitchel. It was obvious that they were close. "Grab a chair like pushy Henry did and sit down," she said with a wave of her hand, pleased with the intrusion in spite of herself.

"No. It was planned—at least on my part," Jacob improvised, surprised by his own invention. "Mitch didn't want to come. He didn't want me to spring this on you." Jacob studied her, wondering how far he should go with an idea that was popping into his mind at that moment. "Actually, I'm doing a story on the family." He took a deep breath and went on with his invention. "But not for my newspaper. As a freelance." Jacob hoped that explanation would make her less hostile.

"You're creative, anyway. And I don't believe a word—about Mitch, that is." She sipped her tea. "So you're freelancing, and you are a reporter for *The New York News*? How does that work?"

"Actually, I'd like to do a book about your family—which I think is, uh, very traditional and very American." What was he saying? He could sense Mitchel's surprised expression without looking. "And I'd like to do it with the family's help—and good wishes, of course." He added the last with some trepidation.

"My God." She gazed at him for a moment and then asked, "How old are you, young man?"

"Well, I'm, uh, thirty-six," he stammered, caught off guard by the question. He resisted the temptation to make it older.

"You don't look that old."

"Well, I've been in this game for awhile." He instantly regretted the swagger.

"Game? Is that what you call it?"

"Profession is a much better term," he conceded quickly. He realized he had to be nimble with this sharp lady.

"I suppose it is," she said doubtfully. "You're proposing to write a book on the Cranes?"

"Yes, or it could be an article, but only with the permission of the family. Nothing's written yet. It's just a concept."

She smiled and faked a huge sigh. "That's a relief."

Worried that she was making fun of the idea, he said, "I'm serious about this."

"I suspect you are, and I am kind of intrigued by the idea myself." A sly smile crept across her thin lips. "Do you have any idea, though, how impossible it will be to get any of the family to cooperate? We are a very secretive clan and in the middle of what could become a very untidy financial situation. And we have our differences—serious differences," she added cryptically. "But I rather like the cut of your jib, as we say in New England. There's a nice honesty and candor about you—at least on first impression. And you are a friend of Mitch's." She paused to study him a moment. "I should warn you that whatever good qualities you may have, you will probably lose some of them if you get too close to this family." She peered across the table, eyes still measuring him. Then she sat back and smiled. "Let me think about the idea. What would be your theme?"

"I rather like the concept 'from whale oil to crude oil.' It's an interesting history." Jacob wished that he had given more thought to his assignment before meeting her.

"Umm, that's a clever take, but I'm afraid it's not original. What about here and now, what's happening, I mean currently, with the company and in the family?"

"That's the main story, yes. But it's not complete without the history."

"Sounds like a tall order, Mr. Sellars." She paused, as though weighing the idea, and added, "There may be others who want to do the same thing. Maybe we could be first. I'll have to give it some thought. But we should start with something more modest like a magazine article. As you may have heard, I'm not fond of newspapers." She sipped at her tea and finished a tiny triangle of sandwich. "As I said, though, I like the cut of your jib."

She diverted conversation away from the subject and into talk of politics, taking measure of Jacob as she probed his thoughts. She was well-informed and had strong opinions. Mitchel didn't have much to say, allowing the dialogue to take its course. Jacob was impressed with her intellect and grasp of the issues.

Before they left, Mitchel bent over and gave Emily a hug, mumbling how sorry he was for their intrusion. Jacob shook hands formally and offered his appreciation of her hospitality. He knew he had been tested and hoped that he had passed muster.

"What the hell was all that stuff about a book, for God's sake?" Mitchel asked once they were outside in the weather, now showing signs of a real blizzard. "You surprised the hell out of me. I thought you were writing a personality column for your paper."

Jacob laughed. "I changed my mind. It just came over me. That's the truth, I swear," he added, seeing Mitchel's doubtful expression. "I just need to do something, uh, well, different—get out of the rut I've dug for myself. This could be the opportunity."

Mitchel rolled his eyes in disbelief as they hurried on, unable to converse in the blustery weather. "Geez, I'd settle for an article," he cried above the wind.

They returned to Jacob's hotel, picked up his bags, and left. Mitchel's car was covered with snow, and Jacob did the scraping while his friend started it up and got the defroster working. When the windows were mostly clear, Jacob climbed in. The heater was roaring, slowly bringing heat to the inside and melting the snow off their coats. The new Toyota Camry came to life reassuringly.

"I thought you might have an SUV by now, Mitch," Jacob said, taunting him.

"Ha, this baby is better—good mileage, easier on the old pocketbook, and the all-wheel drive and hybrid, just as good in snow as any SUV—you know, 'Saudi Utility Vehicles.' Those damn cars are an abomination, in the malls and on the road. I hate 'em."

"My, my, we've become the consummate radical."

Mitchel ignored the comment and guided the Toyota out of the parking spot and headed slowly for the highway. The traffic was light on the streets, but there was a line of cars waiting at the ramp to Route 3, the road to Cape Cod. The storm had not yet reached the whiteout stage, but was close to it. By the time they got on the highway, the snow was sticking and, predictably, cars began to skid off the road. They passed a bulbous black SUV turned over in the ditch.

"See that! It's Lincoln's answer to the Humvee," Mitchel cried triumphantly. "Those guys thought they were invincible in that damned monster. I'll tell you, when the going gets slick, the smart ones keep going." Distracted by the accident, Mitchel didn't notice the bright red taillights ahead.

"Watch out, Mitch!" Jacob yelled. Mitchel had the presence of mind to apply the brakes just enough to stop before skidding into the car in front of them. "Sorry," Jacob muttered, regretting his sudden outcry.

"It's okay, I needed that," Mitchel said, laughing nervously.

From then on, they rode in silence, Mitchel concentrating on the highway. Left to his thoughts, Jacob considered his reckless proposition to Emily. The idea of a book was silly. He could do a freelance article, but a book? He blamed the idea on Rachel. If Crane really had serious problems, the subject might be timely, particularly after all the price manipulation by the oil producers had been revealed. But financial matters were hardly his métier. He considered his own limitations. He had little experience with balance sheets, profit and loss statements, corporate finance, or international intrigue. Rachel could help a little or find help. She had done a brief stint on the financial page and had a few friends who knew a lot of that stuff. He had done some investigative work in the crime field. He let himself fantasize a moment. Scenes of his appearance on *The Today Show* and *Larry King* reeled through his fertile imagination. The theme of whale oil to crude oil, though not original, was appealing. Proving anything from financial statements would be tricky—like the rumors about cooking the books and money laundering, but from what? Would anyone in the family talk to him if crimes were involved? Was she suggesting that she could help him, without approval of others in the family? That would be a risky collaboration for both of them. He was pretty sure that Joshua would reject any intrusion. Emily had said as much. But the cooperation of at least one family member was an exciting prospect.

As they approached the bridge at Sandwich, the snow gave way to rain, and Mitchel, relaxing, picked up speed. "Okay, so talk to me. What's going on here—the book, I mean."

"Nothing. I told you I was just improvising."

"Yeah, well you could have fooled me."

"Do you think Emily will go along with the idea?"

"I really don't know, but I'm guessing that there is a germ of a proposition there. She's not close to Joshua, and as she said, they have their disagreements. And Ezra's hostility doesn't help matters."

"That's the young lawyer—the son?"

"Oh so. And precious, too. There's a guy who really thinks he farts through silk. Spaulding & Cabot has gone to his head. He got a job in that prissy white-shoe firm just because of Daddy and Grandpa, not because of any kind of distinction in law school. And he's so embarrassed that he has a gay aunt, not to mention his gay cousin, that he won't even send her a Christmas card. He's a real shit."

"I gather you don't like him," Jacob suggested, laughing as Mitchel rolled his eyes. "How would he interfere?"

"By being a little spy for his father, trying to ingratiate himself so he gets more company work for his firm."

"I see." Jacob made a mental note to follow up on this. "So, what do you think of my idea?" Then more to himself, he added, "I wonder if I could I do it."

Mitchel didn't answer right away. But Jacob waited. He valued his friend's judgment. When you set aside the gay stuff and the exaggerated personal opinions, he was very astute about the newspaper business. Recently, Mitchel had been asked by CBS to be a fill-in on a regular Sunday television critique of the media, and he had done a series on wartime journalism and the embedded press for PBS. The latter had gotten good reviews. Jacob regarded his friend as a real success story.

"Jacob, let me tell you something. I don't have any qualms about your abilities. You must know that. I just worry about your, uh, well frankly your … well, lack of experience with these kinds of people."

"Yeah, that bothers me, too." Jacob became thoughtful. "I've been around bad people, Mitch. It isn't that I lived a, uh, a sheltered life."

"I know, I know. Your father, the religion stuff, and the abuse were terrible. But this is different. These people are not nice. They play rough—at least the old man does, or did. Old Joshua dealt with some pretty shady characters in Mexico and more recently overseas. And it goes back in the family, to the ones that came before." His thought process seemed to be so intense that he instinctively slowed the car. "You probably don't know that an Ezra of a prior generation, in the whaling days, was a slaver on the side. After the whale oil was unloaded in England, some of his ships would head for Africa and buy slaves with the oil money and sell them in Brazil and the Bahamas. And that's after the Emancipation Proclamation. The current generation seems to be equally challenged, morally. Old J. C.—I've always gotten a kick out of those initials—got himself a sweetheart deal in Mexico buying influence." He rubbed the finger and thumb of one hand together. "And more recently, he was doing the same in Russia. Marrying Natasha, the Georgian beauty, didn't hurt that. She's an incredible lady." He paused and smiled slyly, adding, "I think the old devil had to—I mean marry. It wasn't a plan or anything like that. It came as a complete surprise to the family."

"You mean she was pregnant?"

He glanced at Jacob. "Yeah, that's the gossip. But no one really knows for sure."

"Wow! Did she have the baby?"

"Who knows? She stayed in Paris most of the time. That was almost twenty-five years ago. It's old gossip."

"That's a story I never heard."

Mitchel beamed with satisfaction. "Stick with me baby. There're a lot of skeletons in the Crane closets."

"So what else?"

"Natasha was plugged into the oil oligarchy, so the old man was able to corner a deal as an exclusive broker for Rusky oil and could be part of this—you know, to hide it. And Putin let it go on—never touched them." He paused to think. "There were other oil deals that may have gotten the Kremlin's blessing."

"Like?" Jacob asked.

"Maybe in the Caucasus. And some think the deals got an assist from the CIA."

"What would that have to do with the CIA?"

"See, that's why I worry about you taking on this story." He paused, shaking his head. "The old man never had a relationship that wasn't useful to him. The Crane family's connections with the intelligence apparatus are just as close as the Bushes'. And connections are the key, whether in Mexico, Russia, or right here in the U.S. Josh, Jr., is no different. It's why he married Laura, who incidentally is a very sweet person." Mitchel looked troubled, as if he wanted to say more about the Cranes. "You just have to suspect the worst. And as for Emily, she has to be real careful. She and Joshua, Jr., have never gotten along. It started even before her sexual orientation surfaced. That's why the old man made Joshua, Jr., sole trustee of the estate. If I'm right, then he's in control of most of the dough. It's in his hands to dish out." He paused, mulling this over. "I'm going to guess that if somehow Emily could get some leverage over him …" Mitchel didn't finish his speculation.

"Are you suggesting that she would use me to do that?"

"Yeah, I am. And this is all between you and me."

"Of course," Jacob agreed quickly, shaken by Mitchel's stories and wondering whether he was indeed out of his depth.

Glancing at his watch, Mitchel picked up speed. "We've got to move along if we're going to catch the ferry." But he hadn't finished with the Crane family. "Joshua is a chip off the block. The men in that family, I mean genetically, are all the same. They're rogues. Josh, Jr., is just a little slicker than his father—but maybe a little softer." A secret smile lurked around his mouth. "He looks remarkably like Jeff Skilling, don't you think? You know, the guy who ran Enron for awhile. I think the Business School clones their graduates—somehow."

By the time they reached Hyannis and had parked the car to board the ferry to Nantucket, the weather had deteriorated. The rain turned back to snow, and the wind blew harder. The storm seemed to be following them. The wind had kicked up a nasty chop in the harbor and more so out in the Sound, which was stirred by a wicked current. Icy gusts whipped at their coats. The conditions contrasted with the only other time Jacob had visited Hyannis, when the waters were smoother and sparkled in the summer sunlight. Mitchel led the way to the ticket booth on the dock, and after identifying themselves with drivers' licenses—a terror reminder, no doubt—they boarded the steamer and headed for the dank warmth of the cabin. Jacob could feel the gentle roll of the boat, even at the dock, and began to worry about the trip, hoping he would not get seasick. He wasn't the best sailor. They found a seat on the enclosed upper deck. The windows were steamed up, blocking any view, but, in fact, there was no view. A wipe-down of the glass revealed a virtual whiteout.

"Want some coffee or a beer?" Mitchel asked, after they were seated. "The only acceptable intake the ferry offers is the potables. The food is inedible."

"A beer?" Jacob shuddered at the thought. "How rough will it be?"

"This tub may roll a bit, but you'll barely notice it."

"I'm not much of a sailor, Mitch."

"I'll tell you what. Why don't we both get some tea? That's easier on the gut—just in case you get, you know, feeling, uh, unsettled." He got up, looking forward and aft searching for a sign for the food service. "I think on this boat it is aft. I'll see what I can rustle up." He disappeared through a door at one end of the cabin.

Just mentioning the seasick issue made Jacob feel queasy. Then he was startled by a blast of the boat's foghorn, which he guessed was a signal of their departure. Sure enough, the steel deck began to shudder with the engine vibration. He took another swipe at the window. Through the whirl of snow, he could make out the retreating pilings of the ferry slip. Now it was too late to get back to terra firma.

Mitchel returned with two teas in Styrofoam cups. "We're off. Headed for the open sea." Reacting to Jacob's sour expression, he quickly added, "Just kidding. Actually, it's just a little trip across the Sound. Relax."

They both settled in and sipped their teas. "I've been thinking about your plan—the book, or something more modest. You know, your timing couldn't be better. With all the hand-wringing about partition of Iraq and terror plots, there won't be much interest in the Cranes, at least for awhile. Joshua's death isn't even big news nationally. This gives you time to create something that will be right there in the bull's-eye for the Congressional races. And you could connect it to the gluttony for oil." He paused to sip his tea thoughtfully. "That is very timely. The media will be primed for the Crane family as a symptom of misrule and corruption."

"Yeah, maybe." Jacob saw how the Crane story could prove to be such fertile ground.

"Jacob, I can't give you chapter and verse, but let me tell you, there is plenty of big-time wrongdoing behind Crane's riches. Just look at political contributions, at the hangover of the Cheney oil policy, at wicked government contracts—oh, the potential is unlimited! It could be very relevant," he added with a flourish. "I'm not saying it will be easy to smoke out, but it can be done. And with Emily's cooperation, you could have yourself a real story." He rubbed his hands together. "I love it." Then he became more serious. "But this is also a dangerous idea. It could lead you into areas you don't want to go—like oil security. You could be risking your career. The crowd in Washington plays rough, too. Even now, they are trying to label any criticism as disloyalty and unpatriotic. You shouldn't do this as a lark. It has to be different, not just kiss-and-tell. It has to be tough and revealing. But most of all, it must be honest and not overstated."

The possibilities seemed staggering to Jacob. It made his improvised plan seem shallow and frivolous. It would be no simple task. But he was convinced that the story had a future.

For the rest of the trip, Mitchel dropped the subject and briefed Jacob on his plan for Nantucket and the reception at the Crane compound. Meanwhile the storm raged as the steamer rolled through the tide-ripped chop of Vineyard Sound. With the distraction of Mitchel's monologue about the cast of characters who might be at the Island affair, Jacob weathered the trip without getting sick. But he was very grateful when the boat rounded the breakwater and pulled into the protected waters of Nantucket Harbor. The snow had stopped. In the falling darkness of afternoon, the beam of the Brant Point Lighthouse swept the harbor reassuringly. They had made it safely to port.

CHAPTER 3

Two gray vans with engines running were parked near the dock waiting for the ferry to tie up. It seemed that most of the passengers arriving had endured the uncomfortable crossing to attend the Crane reception. Greeters in foul-weather gear held flapping placards identifying names, assuring a warm ride to hotels or to the Crane compound—for the lucky ones. Mitch and Jacob pushed through a line of local gawkers who were hoping to see a celebrity or politico and headed into town along Centre Street. The lights of shops and boutiques cast a beckoning glow onto the icy street. Gusts of wind lashed at their coats, and the blowing snow stung their eyes. Mitch had his ratty old watch cap pulled down to its limit and resembled one of those ridiculous bobbleheads, as he toiled along against the wind. Finally, he waved an arm weakly at a hotel sign which read "The Crawford Inn" and led the way up cobblestone steps into the warmth of the lobby where they registered, taking two rooms for the weekend. An aged bellman led them to a tiny elevator. Mitch said he wanted to make some calls.

Jacob's room was spare and very New England—a four-poster double bed, upholstered chairs, lace curtains and pull-down shades. Enhancing the nineteenth-century feel was a frame of frost around the paned windows. Radiators rattled with rising heat. Outside, the wind moaned, and the structure of the old inn creaked. For a moment he felt transported to much earlier times. He stood in the faded light looking out the window at the ghosts of swaying trees and, for just a moment, was overcome with an odd foreboding. Shivering in the drafty room, he thought of Ishmael, also on a stormy night, at the chapel in New Bedford. It was one verse of Father Mapple's sermon hymn that came back to him in a rush of memory—

> I saw the opening maw of hell,
> With endless pains and sorrows there;

Which none but they that feel can tell—
Oh, I was plunging to despair.

The words were indelibly imprinted in his mind. They were symbolic of his father, who had once, in the heat of his passion, quoted them to Jacob. In fact, it was his father who had first introduced him to *Moby Dick*. The words of the hymn had haunted Jacob for years. Here he was in Nantucket, a significant whaling port of the past, where memories were evoked by the buffeting storm. A sense of angst took possession of him.

His father's face appeared in the frosted window, eyes piercing the glaze. He shook himself, mentally, to get rid of the vision and sat on the bed, pressing his forehead between his fists. It was a vision he often endured at times like this, when he doubted himself. Later, in the bathroom, he dashed his face with cold water. Feeling better, he decided on a sudden whim to call Rachel. After several rings she picked up.

"You're home." The moment he said it, he regretted his slightly desperate tone.

"You okay? What's the matter?"

"I'm fine. I just needed to bounce an idea off you. Is this a good time?" All he really needed was her reassuring voice.

"You mean, am I in bed with someone?" Rachel always enjoyed taunting him about her slightly mysterious other life.

"Are you?" He fell in with her mood.

"Of course not. I've just been sitting here alone imagining your … big, ah, arms around me." She giggled at her suggestive foolishness.

"I've got a new tack on the article on the Cranes."

"Yeah, what is it?"

"A freelance article on my own. I write a revealing in-depth story on the Cranes, with the help of a family member." He didn't mention a book.

"Like a kiss-and-tell? Who's the family member dumb enough to let you do that?"

"I think I might have the old man's older daughter. Of course, I'm not sure yet. But it would be much more than a kiss-and-tell."

"Much more, huh," she said, not taking the idea seriously. "Is this the gal that has a female relationship?"

"She is gay, yes. That's the one—Emily."

There was a long pause. "Hmm. Are you serious about this? I mean, how long has the idea been germinating in that webby head of yours?"

"Well, uh," he stammered, embarrassed by the admission of impulsiveness. "Awhile."

"Awhile? Did I hear freelance?"

"Yep."

"My God, you've gone daft. Have you thought about the ramifications with your job, for starters? If you become a lone ranger, you're gonna be fired—quick." He could even hear the snap of her fingers. "Like that. And you'll be a pariah to the corporate media."

"I've thought about it, yes." Actually, he had given some thought to how this could affect his career.

"And?"

"I guess I don't care. You and I have talked about my getting out of a rut. I think this might be a good opportunity. This story may fit into what's going on—politics, oil policy, corruption, that kind of thing. Maybe you could help. You've freelanced, you know the ropes."

"Wow, that's sexy. You may be growing up, Jacob, finally. But do you think it's smart to kick over your job now? You don't have enough longevity at the *News* to get away with this. I thought you were on sort of a career path—you know, on your way to join the kowtowing old *Times*." She waited, further processing his news. "Jacob, are you doing this for the right reasons?"

"I hope so. I think I've been too satisfied, too careful. The risk-reward ratio of freelancing is much more interesting than a career path."

"Hey, you're preaching to the choir, honey. What have I been saying to you? Look, do the job you went up there for, write the assignment story for the paper, and then let's see where you are. Just don't lose your job—at least not yet."

"I think I might be able to get Mitch to help, too," he suggested, hoping to get a better reaction.

"Uh-uh. Bad idea. Anything you do, you should do alone—if you're bound and determined. You don't coauthor, ever. Do something yourself, that really tests your ability. He's not the right, uh, voice for you."

Jacob was not sure what she meant but decided not to ask. "We can talk about it. Anyway, I hope I'll be back by Monday or Tuesday. How about dinner?"

"A date with my new freelancer? Anytime. Just don't carry that freelancing stuff too far." She laughed. "Do you realize how funny it is that you suddenly discovered your independence in Boston? Must be in the water up there. Before you make any decisions, just write your piece for the *News*. Don't burn bridges. Okay? Bye." He could hear just the beginning of a comment to herself as she hung up.

As soon as he put the receiver down, the phone rang. It was a message from Mitch to say that he would meet him for breakfast. Relieved to be on his own for the evening, Jacob hooked up his laptop, checked e-mail, and then made a few notes on the events of the day. Restless, he went down to the bar and had a beer and munched chips. There was an Irish-style guitarist crooning from a makeshift stage partly obscured in the shadows of the candlelit room. Jacob was surprised that a small inn on Nantucket would be so generous as to offer live music in the off-season. The young crowd—somewhere between Y and X generations, accustomed to multitasking—was intent on the muted television's hockey game between the Bruins and Rangers. A hockey fan himself, Jacob was gradually drawn into the action as he picked at the junk food of chips and nuts.

"Ahoy there, mate, can I pull alongside?" A young woman had emerged from the darkness to take the next stool.

"Sure, why not." He had to laugh at the silly nautical pose.

"You a Rangers fan?" She nodded toward the screen. "Yeah, I watched you when they scored," she added smugly. "From the Big Apple, huh?" Her voice was big and gung ho, even for the noisy bar.

The neon signs for beers cast a pink light on her cheeks. She was young—in her early twenties—with short blond hair and a pretty face revealing lots of personality.

He swiveled his seat to face her. "Yes and yes to your two questions."

"That sounds like a lawyer."

Jacob laughed. "No, far from it. I'm a reporter. Journalist is a fancier name." He was reminded immediately of his newly self-appointed status. "Or a writer, if you like. Pick one," he suggested.

"Writer, I like that one. It's more impressive." As she peered myopically at him, he realized she was a little sloshed. "You, uh, like on vacation or somethin'?"

"No, I'm working."

She giggled. "Sitting on a barstool?"

He wondered whether it was worth having a conversation with her, but the reporter's instinct took over. Nantucket was a small island of many connections. "I'm working on a story about the late Joshua Crane. Know him?"

"Oh, my God!" she cried. She looked away for a moment. "Yeah, it figures. That reception out at the compound."

"Shh," he warned. "That's just between you and me," he added, feeling a little foolish.

"Oh, yeah, sorry. Of course. Sure. He's kind of an uncle, not really, but related on my mother's side. I've always called him Uncle Joshua. I sail with him—like used to, anyway." She took a deep breath trying to collect her impaired wits. "I go out with his grandson, too." She grinned, shaking her head. "You know, the grandson, his name is Ezra—get that. What a pompous ass. My dad didn't approve—Ezra's a cousin. And he's a crashing bore. He was like good for a dinner, but you better not be alone with him very long, otherwise you'd be sitting staring at your plate, like talking to yourself. Or defending your virtue." She laughed. "The only fun I had dating him was like when we went to his house for dinner—his parents are fun, sort of, especially his sister. She's a real pisser. God, she like entertains the whole table. Lots of laughs and she teases Ezra mercilessly." She waved at the bartender whom she seemed to know. "Hey, Frank—get me a cup of coffee." Then she whispered into Jacob's ear, "I need to sober up before I drive."

"It's probably a good idea. Young people shouldn't make that mistake." The remark sounded hopelessly stuffy.

"Young people? Like how old are you, for Chrissake?"

"Old enough to be your, ah, big brother." The bartender put a steaming china pot of coffee in front of her. "Want me to pour it for you?"

"Nah, I'm not that stoned." She grinned at him. "Don't have a big brother. Sure, go ahead, pour me some." She watched him, smiling. It was really a cute little smirk. "Thanks."

Jacob needed to get her back on track. "Now, tell me about your family. How are they related?"

"What do you want to know?" She was pensive a moment. "I'll tell you what. The food's crappy here. Let's get something to eat, and I'll tell you stuff. And you can tell me what you're writing." She took a big slurp of coffee and fumbled with her purse. Dropping a twenty dollar bill on the bar and slipping off the stool, she said, "Let's go." Waving an arm without looking back, she called, "Bye, Frank."

"You haven't finished the coffee." Feeling this might be a mistake, Jacob was stalling. "I'd have to get a coat. It's pretty bad out there."

"Come on. I can give you plenty for your story, if that's what you're doing. Like I'm related, remember?" She tugged at his arm. "My car has a super heater. You won't need your damn coat."

His indecision faded nearly as fast as it surfaced. What the hell, go along with it. Maybe she'd have something. She was also entertaining, he had to admit.

She held onto his arm and pulled him along. "My car's right in front." Jacob still looked doubtful. "And I'll drive you back, I promise." Jacob followed as she walked, with a boyish swagger, across the sanded sidewalk.

At the curb, she produced a key and clicked open a black Saab parked illegally a few steps from the hotel entrance. It was snowing again, but not as heavily. He scraped off the windows and then climbed in beside her.

Glancing at him out of the corner of one eye, she drove slowly down the snowpacked street, bumpy with its cobblestone surface. "I don't even know your name," she said, twisting the heater control knob.

"It's Jacob, Jacob Sellars."

She turned and gave him a quick once-over. "You pro-Israel—you know, that awful stuff going on in Lebanon?"

He laughed at her directness. "I'm not Jewish, if that's what you mean." He did not expect her to be following world affairs. "So, what's yours?"

"My race?"

"No, your name, for God's sake."

"Oh, probably English—my ancestors, I mean," she said, either not hearing him or ignoring his clarification. "Like my family has lived in Boston for a thousand years. Well, not quite, I guess."

"So your name?" he asked again.

"Oh, yeah—Coffin."

"Is there a first one?"

"Marilyn," she said. "I hate it. Like it's *so* common."

"Coffins seem to be everywhere?"

"Yeah, like I said, we're related."

Jacob was thinking that he had lucked into a better opportunity than he had hoped for.

"Here we are," she announced, pulling up in front of a brightly lit entrance that identified itself as "Blue Whale Plate."

Reacting to the sign, Jacob observed, "That's an odd combination. Is whale meat all they serve?"

"You're a riot, Sellars." He couldn't tell from her tone whether this was said in disgust or delight. Over her shoulder she explained, "No, dummy, they've just got like pictures of whales on all the plates." She got out of the car and without waiting bounded into the little cafe. Stepping carefully on the icy sidewalk, he followed her in. Of course, she seemed to know everyone in the place, and he began to worry that he might not be able to question her alone. But she ignored the shouted invitations from the bar and instead chose a secluded booth in the back, plunking herself down on the U-shaped banquette. Jacob slid in across from her. She ordered coffee, and he followed suit.

"Well, Coffin," he began, fitting in with her collegiate preference for last names, "let's talk about your relatives."

"Boy, you got like a one-track mind." She seemed to have sobered up a little. She eyed him critically. "Hey, you're a lot cuter than I thought—in that dark bar at the inn."

"Yeah?" he said, surprised at her come-on style. Jacob decided that she couldn't be older than twenty at most. "You're pretty well-preserved yourself."

She laughed and reached for his hand resting on the table between them. He met her gaze and held it. The sudden intimacy made him uncomfortable. He couldn't tell whether she was teasing or taunting him. Watch out, Sellars, his subconscious warned, as the old anxieties surfaced. He gently withdrew his hand.

"Okay," she finally said. "What would you like to know? Like I'm not very close to them anymore, and our families haven't ever gotten along well. The old man, Joshua, apparently stole the shipping business from my great grandfather, or at least that's the story I've been told. Then turned it into oil. He's awfully cagey and smart. Or was. Kind of hard to think he's gone." She studied her hands for a moment. "He stopped my dad from selling his stock in the company, which was good, of course, 'cause now we're rich, not like some of the others, but like comfortable, you know. They're scared to death that if too many strangers get Crane stock, bad stuff will get out.

"My dad was pretty high up in the company once. But he was forced out when I was little—some kind of disagreement with Uncle Joshua. The breakup was tough on my parents." All this bubbled out in a sudden surge. She stared into her cup for a moment, and Jacob could see tears welling up in her blue eyes. "They've separated." She wiped her eyes with the back of her hand and tried a smile. "On the brighter side, I've just been told that I'm getting something from the old man's will. It's complicated, like the lawyer said it's called a generation-skipping thingy, you know, to get out of taxes. He told me it was a trust fund of ten million bucks, in my name." She paused to be sure that she was in control of her feelings. "So you see, I'm rich. That's why I'm celebrating tonight." Her eyes fixed on his again, and her look was so intense that Jacob could feel his scalp crawl with panic. "That's why I'm so happy," she added, blinking away tears. Sensing what was coming, he looked around furtively, hoping no one was watching them.

"I want to go to bed with you." She reached for his hand. "Tonight." He tried but could not shake off her eyes.

"How old are you, Marilyn?" he asked, groping for a good way to handle himself. She was obviously still "stoned," as she would say.

"I thought we already covered that. I'm twenty-three." She flashed an embarrassing grin. "Old enough to know better. How old are you?"

"As I said, I'm certainly old enough to be your big brother, if not your father."

"Well, I don't have any brothers or sisters. I'm a one and only."

"I'm going to guess that you are, uh," he paused, taking a calculated risk, "more like nineteen, Miss Coffin."

"Wrong! Older. And you couldn't possibly be my father. That's bullshit," she snapped angrily. "Here, I'll show you my driver's license."

"I said 'big brother.' And I don't need to see your license."

"You don't like me." She put on a petulant pout. For a moment, he thought she might walk out.

"Yes, I do." He wanted to hold on to her long enough for more questions about her startling revelations. "But it wouldn't be right for me to, to do anything with you." He smiled, trying not to be condescending. "We just met."

"Yeah," she admitted sheepishly. "I guess that's right."

"But more important, if I did that sort of thing with anyone ... as a reporter, I wouldn't be keeping a job or my credibility very long. You're very pretty and fun, and I do like you, but that's got to be it." Jacob paused, feeling sorry about the hole she had dug for herself. He cast about for something more convincing. "Anyway, I have a girlfriend in New York. We love each other." It was an exaggeration, but it would do. "We're going to get married," he lied.

"Well, damn, isn't that my luck." She grinned impishly. "You could have a, uh, last fling, you know, like a bachelor's party." She lowered her voice, "I'm not a virgin, if that's what worries you."

He took a good look at her. She still had that childlike Lolita appeal. Her streaky-blond hair was casually tousled. She had shed her coat, revealing a slim, well-formed body in faded jeans.

"And you would have nothing but regrets and I, well, guilt about not treating you with, uh, respect—taking advantage of you." He paused. "And your, uh, condition isn't what worries me."

She softened a little. "Awesome. I knew you were special, actually." She studied him for a moment. "I hope you're happy with whoever she is. I envy her. I don't want to know her name, but if things don't work out, give me a call." She flashed a quick smile. "Come on, I promised to drive you back."

She led the way out, and they climbed into her car. Her generation just didn't like walking, he mused. "I thought you wanted something to eat."

"Nah, I changed my mind."

"But I have more questions."

She laughed as she started the car. "Boy, you must be an ace reporter. You just don't quit." Making a skidding U-turn, she drove—a little too fast for the road condition—back to the inn. She probably was still a little miffed about the rejection. Looking straight ahead with a poker face, she announced, "You can come to my room. The bar will be closed at the inn, like the rest of this hick town. We can talk there."

The suggestion took him off guard, and he didn't respond to her ploy immediately. He wondered whether he could handle the situation. He decided that he could, if that was what he had to do to get more of her story. She parked the car near the inn, this time legally. The snow had stopped, and the wind had softened, but the air was icy cold. A crescent moon peeked through the bare trees. The lobby was warm, and the bar crowd was gone, just as she had predicted. They passed the front desk, and Jacob could feel the eyes of the sleepy clerk following them—or did he just imagine it? He glanced at their images in a mirror at the elevator and was surprised to find that they looked rather well matched. At least he didn't look like some child molester—she didn't look like a child either.

In the room, she dumped her coat on the bed and flopped onto a couch, an amenity his room did not offer. Jacob nervously noticed that the bed had been turned down. Great, a perfect scene for seduction. But Marilyn seemed anxious to talk.

"Oh, come sit down here—I'm not going to rape you, for Chrissake." She patted the seat beside her. But Jacob remained standing. "Okay, suit yourself." She stretched out her long legs, as Jacob pulled up a small chair instead. "I know some of the story—at least from my point of view. You know, like the family stuff. Is that what you're interested in?"

"Sure, go ahead."

She stared at him. "I feel sorta like I'm in a shrink's office." She giggled nervously. "Just don't say, 'I see.'"

"I promise." Jacob was impressed with her cool.

She lay back without taking her eyes from Jacob's. She didn't look down and talk like most who relate hard-to-tell personal history. "I think my father and Uncle Joshua had a fight back then. Dad went to work for the company right after he got out of college. He did really well—he's older than Joshua, Jr.—and a lot smarter. Anyway, there was a breakup. It happened quite awhile ago." She paused. "You know, Dad is seventy-two years old now, a couple of years older than Mom. He was always closer in age to J. C. than Joshua. Maybe that was the problem." Oddly, the ages of her parents seemed to trouble her. "Mom was forty-eight when she had me. It wasn't easy for her at that age. There were complications and ..." She didn't finish the thought. "My parents don't like talk about this in front of me. Anyway, I think Joshua, Jr., got pissed off at J. C. for giving Dad, an outsider, all the authority." She seemed to have quite an adult grasp of the situation. "So, J. C. let Dad go—when he was, uh, fifty-eight or something like that. It's hard to jump into another job when you're that old." She blinked back tears. "So ..." she seemed reluctant to continue, "he wasn't happy." Her voice trailed off. "Even before ... some of the problems with J. C. were because he ..." she hesitated, unable to finish in what must have become an emotional moment for her.

"Because he what?" Jacob gently prodded, thinking of his own dysfunctional upbringing.

"Dad, uh, drank, too much after awhile." She took a deep breath and continued her story. A wistful expression full of memories crossed her face. "It was tough on all of us." The memory took possession of her for a moment. She gulped a breath of air as if she were drowning. "He finally quit, in AA. He like still goes to meetings. You won't believe this, but he's going to sail around the world—alone. Not in a race or anything like that, just on his own. I've begged him to take me, but he wants to do it alone." Her tone betrayed her admiration of her father. "He's got a lot of guts." She paused and frowned. "My mom thinks he's like trying to prove something—you know like his manhood. When she's mad, she says things like old J. C. emasculated him. That means cut his balls off," she explained angrily. "But he's got balls. He's a real strong person."

"You've had a difficult life," Jacob said, after she seemed to run out of steam. "Why are your parents separated, after all these years?"

"I don't know," she replied with resignation. "There's nobody else—for either of them. They don't like fool around." The smile that crept across her face was troublemaking. "They're different from me."

Jacob ignored the inference. Her story had made him feel very uncomfortable, as if he had just eavesdropped on a private conversation about one's most personal thoughts. But he felt a kinship. His own childhood hadn't been so average either. Now he saw this young woman, who could not have lived more than twenty years, as having the worldly experience and woes of middle age.

"I'm sorry you've had to deal with so much so soon." No wonder she was a little screwed up. "Talking about all this can't be easy. Why don't we call it a night?" He glanced at his watch to find the excuse. "It's after one. And I have an early meeting." He got up, a little stiffly from the undersized chair.

She uncurled herself from the couch more like a cat than a human being and yawned. Then she walked over and put her arms around his neck and kissed him on the mouth, hard. "There, that's for being such a patient listener." She kissed him again, this time letting her mouth open slightly. "And that's because I like you—a lot." Jacob pushed her away gently.

"Okay, that's enough." He couldn't hold back a smile, unable to conceal his captivation. "You know, I'm not that good at resisting your, ah, wiles."

"Oh, I hope not." She tried to kiss him again, but he turned away. She dropped onto the couch and beckoned him to follow.

"I have to go," he said. "Before I do, though, can you stand one more question?"

Feigning shock, she asked, "You didn't like my kisses?"

"I thought we had an understanding."

She bounced off the couch and laced her arms around his neck and roughed up his hair. "You are *so* difficult," she crooned. "Okay, yeah, what's the question?"

"I'm curious. The breakup between your father and J. C.—the way it happened, putting him out on the street at fifty-eight—that's really tough. I mean, just because his son is jealous. With all his faults, it doesn't seem that J. C. was the kind of guy who would fall for crybaby stuff."

She didn't answer right away. She just gazed at him. Then she smiled and said, "You know, that's what I'm hearing from a lot of people, but not until recently. Did you read the obituary in the paper?"

"Sure."

"There were other things. Uncle Joshua and Dad had disagreements. I mean like shady oil deals all over the world and other crap—money, what do you call it, cleaning."

"You mean laundering?"

"Yeah, that's it." She unwound her arms from his neck and stood back as if she needed to distance herself from these stories. "My father didn't like that stuff, and he wanted no part of it. It's just things I've overheard. I don't really understand what went on. All I do know is Dad said the company could have gotten along just fine without doing those things." She toyed absently with a small, but beautiful, ruby ring on her right hand. "But I guess Uncle Joshua didn't agree."

"Anyway, Dad's going sailing. And that's why Mom says he's emasculated. She wants him to stay home and fight—fight to get back into the company, or get even, something like that." She spread her arms out like wings. "I'm so sick of all this. I don't understand any of it. And I hate it all." She choked up again, dropping her arms in despair. "Mom even blames me for getting the money from Grandpa. My life is real shit." Looking at the floor, she murmured, her voice husky with emotion, "Jacob, please stay with me tonight." It was a plea, not a suggestion.

Jacob gazed at her but didn't see her. Instead, the old memory began to spin in fast-forward—a girl, blond curls, skinny legs, and a fuzz of hair on scrawny arms. She was the most beautiful little creature Jacob had ever seen. Christy was walking home with him. She lived on the road to his house and often tagged along for company. They had long talks on the two-mile trek, and he would describe books he was reading. She would cling to his every word and sometimes pepper him with questions. She would often take his hand, her warm smooth fingers squeezing his. Suddenly that winter day came alive for him. She had continued all the way home with him. Under the spell of some instinctive influence, he had led her to the barn in the fading light of dusk to finish the tale. In the seclusion of the hayloft, Jacob had touched her, and she had touched him. She was barely twelve, and he, seventeen, but the thrills and urges were intense for both. Shivering in the barn's chill, they had held each other close in their half-nakedness. Jacob would never forget her. It was a memory of a first love and dark guilt. In the years that followed, Jacob's relationships with the opposite sex had always been tainted with images of this day. It was panicking him now that years later, he was tempted again. The circumstances were too close for comfort. The familiar surge of remorse washed over him. He resisted the temptation to glance over his shoulder for the hovering image of his father, but he felt the presence.

"Marilyn, this isn't fair to you or to me." He could not resist taking her in his arms, if only to comfort them both. She clung to him, trembling. Her shoulders and arms were surprisingly hard and muscled. Still holding her, he took her chin in his hand. "Let's not spoil our friendship at a time when you are confusing an attraction with a need to work things out. Sex in desperation isn't the answer." She looked up at him. "Do you understand that?" She nodded through glistening tears. "Then let's say goodnight." He let go of her, and she fell back onto the couch.

"Goodnight, goodnight, sweet prince. That's Shakespeare, but I can't remember the damn play. Can you?"

"Hamlet."

As he closed the door, he took a last look at her, sitting on the couch gazing after him with an odd but knowing smile. At that moment, she seemed to be a woman, not a girl. He stood for a moment in the hall, trying to put the image out of his mind. It wasn't easy.

CHAPTER 4

Mitch was thirty minutes late for their breakfast date. But he had the decency to send a message to the dining room. When he finally walked in, he looked as if he had just been roused from sleep. In an attempt to distract from the circles under his eyes, he had added some eye shadow—a sure sign in his case that a "relationship," as he called it, had kept him up too late. Apparently, Mitch had not moderated his tomcatting. He seemed to have friends everywhere, friends Jacob hoped were HIV-free. But Jacob was never comfortable enough with the subject to caution his friend. Often, after a heavy encounter, Mitch would dress up and, with a little makeup, put on a personality more openly gay. This morning was no exception.

"Oh, God," he said, greeting Jacob with a squeeze and a Cheshire-cat smile. "You're so dear not to be too, too mad." He sat and ordered coffee. "I have to tell you," he lowered is voice, "I saw you with that Coffin girl last night." A waitress appeared and poured coffee. After taking a noisy, desperate slurp, he continued, "Now I'm not the one to play the morality police, but Jacoby, she is pretty young. Oh, I know—going on thirty. But really, you've got to be more discreet." He took another quick gulp and continued, "Everybody knows her here. It was just lucky for you that 'everybody' wasn't in the lobby when you two took the elevator—after midnight." The last phrase was punctuated by a shivery shrug of something like guilty voyeurism.

"Your implications are all wrong, Mitch. Nothing happened"—a characterization Jacob thought was literally the truth. "She's a very nice but mixed-up kid, and it was probably, as you suggest, risky using her as a source." He couldn't hide his satisfaction. "She did have some interesting things to say."

"Innocence preserved. That's a relief," Mitch said, apparently not as bothered as he'd seemed. "So, what did you get?"

"Things about her father, Amos Coffin, and old Joshua—like he worked for the company, had a fight with J. C. and got fired, family jealousy. Maybe, but that isn't the whole story. She's going to inherit a lot of money under the will. That surprised me. I would have thought that the row with her father would have soured J. C. on the whole family. There had to be other reasons for the breakup."

"Well, as to the money, Marilyn grew up to be quite a sailor, won races, and crewed in an ocean race or two with an all-girl crew. She caught J. C.'s attention. He was a shrewd businessman, but his seagoing genes were the strongest. As you probably already know, he, too, was an avid sailor. Had a down east fifty-foot schooner. In his later years, he developed physical problems so he needed help sailing. The crusty old devil couldn't get along with paid hands, and no other family member could stand his company on the boat for more than a day sail. The Coffin kid is tough and loved sailing, particularly in 'blue water,' as we call it. So he took her on, every summer and when she could wangle time off from school. She was as strong as a boy and twice as good on deck, and they got along well. He grew to love her like a daughter, and I guess she admired him. He did a nice thing for once in his life and left her some dough." He frowned into his coffee cup.

That would explain the hard little body, Jacob thought.

"On the other question … I don't know what happened between Amos and the old guy. But it had to be more than a petty family quarrel. Coffin was a straight arrow and did things by the book. There was talk of shenanigans in the company that bothered him. Maybe he wanted to change things. Maybe he threatened to go public. That's just a guess. I'm not sure that anyone else could explain it—except, of course, Coffin. And, speaking of the high seas, it's in his blood, too. He won't be around for long—maybe literally. He's taking off on a solo voyage around the world, I hear."

"Yeah, that's what Marilyn said. Assuming he'd talk to me, where could I find the guy?"

"In Marblehead. That's where he's outfitting his boat." Mitch giggled. "You know, we just might make a sailor out of you yet." He took a bite of coffee cake, tucking it into an ample cheek and adding, "He'll be a challenge, of course."

"I'm game."

"Sounds like a plan."

They both busied themselves with coffee and sweets for awhile. "About your night," Jacob was first to break the silence, "did you do anything, ah, fun?" It was time for his own quiz. "Where were you and your friend hiding in the lobby?"

"That's a loaded question, dear boy. You can't expect me to fall for that. I was sitting in the bar alone, so there!"

"Yeah, waiting for who?"

"That's *whom*, Mr. Smarty-man. And it's none of your business." His banter was nothing but good-natured. In fact, he seemed to be enjoying the attention. "I had two dates last night. One, with Ezra—how do you like that? I just happened to run into him late in the evening."

"Ezra Crane, the pompous boy lawyer?" Jacob, surprised by the revelation, considered this a moment and then asked, "A date? Is he gay?"

"I doubt it, and I really don't care. I just thought I'd try to find out some things for you."

"Like what?"

"Like what was going on in the company and were any of the darker suggestions in the obit true." Mitch allowed himself a smug smile. "See, I'm already looking out for your interests."

"I'm sure he was eager to share it all," Jacob said dryly.

"Well, he did seem eager to talk. He's very protective of his father, whom he admires and who, I suspect, he hopes will become a more important client of his firm. J. C. didn't like the kid and didn't steer much business his way." Mitch's attention span was interrupted as he spied the waitress emerging from the kitchen. "Let's get something else to eat. I'm starved."

After they ordered omelets and bagels, Jacob returned to Ezra. "So, what did Ezra tell you?"

"Well, it's kind of funny. I'm a manipulative son-of-a-bitch, as you know, and diabolically clever. First, I let him tell me how important he is at the firm, how he's on the verge of making partner, and the important cases he's working on. I get the impression that he's actually been shunted from the corporate side into criminal stuff. So, with all the crooked people saved by his smart defenses, I suggested to him that, golly gosh, his talents might come in handy at The Crane Corporation." It was obvious that Mitch was very pleased with himself as he relived his evening. "And he fell for it." Their breakfast arrived, and Mitch dove into it ravenously.

"Yeah, how did that play out?"

Between bites, he went on with his story. "He agreed with me. His dad did need help. J. C. left a mess of questionable deals behind, and in some cases, there were serious legal problems. I asked him whether any involved crimes, softening it a little with 'white-collar' crimes. Then he began to bubble over with tales of accounting irregularities and info about terrorist plots that helped the company buy favorable relationships with the CIA! How do you like that? It confirms what I always suspected. Most of this chicanery is going on in the Caucasus, I think. But more recently, there's been activity in the Mideast, Iraq especially. He described some of the deals but seemed to be parroting superficial stuff he'd over-heard—maybe from partners in the firm who knew what they were talking about—because when I questioned him more closely, he quickly ran out of facts. But he seemed confused by the CIA connection, asking rhetorically why the gov-ernment would prosecute if Crane was helping. He's so gullible. The partners probably keep the important business to themselves."

"That's all very ambiguous. Did he think a prosecution was likely?"

"He doesn't know. What saves the day for Crane is the obsession of Home-land Security in the hunt for terrorists. That's what this is about. The FBI has much more power to snoop now and is getting help from the CIA in the process. They've got some kind of slick way of tracking money. Somehow Crane is help-ing out. They must hear a lot of stuff. The CIA has all its undercover people who speak the language tied up in Iraq, but Crane has links to Arabs who actually know what is going on. So it doesn't take much imagination to dream up an odd synergy between Crane and the government."

Jacob was beginning to wonder whether he was out of his depth, but he was now hooked by the story and was determined to follow whatever leads were avail-able. Two avenues seemed promising—Emily Crane and Amos Coffin—but he would have to hurry to get Coffin before he sailed away.

"You're still thinking about freelancing this?" Mitch asked. "Don't get cold feet on me now."

"I'm not." Jacob flashed a reassuring smile.

Mitch shivered with premature excitement, rubbing his hands together in what Jacob took as real enthusiasm. "But you've got to promise to keep me up to date on every salacious bit you collect. Of course, it would all be in strictest confi-dence."

"Salacious?" Jacob was pleased with the support, but doubted the assurances. "I doubt there is much of that."

Mitch produced the gold pocket watch he sometimes sported on important occasions and popped the cover. "God, it's late. We have to run. We're lucky, though, because my dear friend Richard loaned us a car—kind of a heap, but it sure saves taxi fare." Like many threadbare Bostonians, Mitch was always able to scrounge up a favor from a well-heeled friend or relative. "I treated Ezra last night, so ..." He pushed the check in Jacob's direction and added with a wink, "We better get going. The house is out in Siasconset—the high-rent district."

Their drive in Richard's clunky BMW was a short one, as are all trips on the island. The roads had been plowed and sanded. The Crane compound was not impressive on first inspection. But it turned out that the entire cluster of Cape-Cod-style houses on the long point of land—some five or six—were part of the Crane estate. They drove into a sweeping driveway—freshly plowed—and were met by young valet-service employees who politely opened doors and offered a check for the keys, addressing them each as "sir." At the front door, they were greeted by a woman in a black uniform with a white apron who took their coats. If there had been a receiving line for the family, it had been disbanded by the time they arrived. But it didn't take Mitch long to find a Crane.

"Joshua!" Mitch wasn't the least bit shy about a frontal approach. Jacob recognized the young scion of the Crane clan as Mitch seized his outstretched hand. Joshua greeted his gay cousin coolly, and there was something about his smile that betrayed displeasure. Neither the eyes nor the face was in sync with the curve of the mouth.

"So nice you see you, Mitch." Joshua kept pumping his hand and smiling as if he were trying to think of something more to say, while his eyes darted around the room. "Please have a drink and make yourself at home. There are refreshments in the den." He turned to make his escape.

"Thanks, Joshua. But I came to offer my condolences." There was an obvious edge to Mitch's tone. "The death of your father is, of course, a sad day for all of us. He was, after all, the patriarch of a very, ah, renowned family." Mitch turned to Jacob. "I'd like you to meet Jacob Sellars, a colleague of mine."

Ignoring the introduction, Joshua said, "Indeed he was—a patriarch. Well put, Mitch." He placed his hand tentatively on Mitch's shoulder. Leaning in close, he added, "Now, I must greet my guests. Thanks for the sentiment. Enjoy yourselves. We'll talk later." Then, after giving Jacob a quick once-over, he was gone, evaporating into the knots of people spilling into other rooms.

"The guy's a little edgy, huh?" Jacob suggested, amused by Mitch's performance.

"'We'll talk later.' Did you get that?" he scoffed. "And the son-of-a-bitch didn't have the courtesy to even acknowledge you." He made a face.

"Well, he's on center stage today. It can't be easy."

"You're far too nice, Jacoby." He took his friend's arm. "Come on, let's prowl around and see who else is here and get a drink." He led the way through the crowd. He had a good nose. In another large adjoining room lined with books, probably the den, furniture had been moved aside to make room for small tables and two bars. At one bar, Jacob spotted Emily chatting with a tall woman, whose back was turned, revealing a sweep of long black hair which was remarkably thick and lustrous. As they approached, Emily recognized him and waved. Her companion turned to see who it was. Jacob was struck by what he saw—an exquisite beauty quite beyond description, big flashing eyes set wide apart, a slightly crooked smile—wider on one side—that was already making fun of him, and a lock of jet hair across her forehead just above one of those intense eyes.

"Nice to see you again, Mr. Sellars," Emily said warmly, adding "and Mitch." Jacob realized her companion had to be Yvonne. "Yvonne, this is Mitch's friend, Mr. Sellars, from New York. He's a newspaperman—a journalist, if I remember rightly." Jacob was trying hard to keep his eyes trained on Emily as she spoke, but he could feel the intensity of Yvonne's gaze.

"Oh, yeah," she said. "Are you here snooping on us?" The carefully plucked eyebrows arched with curiosity. As he studied her close up, she was even more beautiful—a finely sculpted face dominated by aquiline nose and high cheekbones. There was little, if any, makeup. She didn't need it. Her arrogance was softened by a sensuous mouth which relaxed now and then into the crooked smile. Contrary to Mitch's promise, her clothes were simple—jeans and a loose-fitting red sweater, not exactly right for a funeral.

"No," he stammered. "I, ah, just want to … well, yes, I guess you could say that about any, uh, reporter. But it's really not snooping. We're just following a story, and your family is a story." Her expression was hard to read. "I mean, it's very well known."

"I'm surprised you got in," she said, but her tone was friendly. "You a pal of Mitch's?" She glanced back and forth between them.

"Oh, Jacob and I go back quite a ways," Mitch said, unhelpfully.

"Jacob it is, huh?" Her laugh was disingenuous. "That's cute. Mitch, are you finally settling down? In a relationship, I mean. This guy is a distinct improvement over some of the others." She turned back to Sellars. "Jacob, what's your other name again?"

"Sellars, Jacob Sellars." He was searching desperately for a way to explain how he was not what she thought he was.

"Ah, you are Jewish?"

"No, German hardworking farmers." He tried lamely to match her snide humor, controlling his pique at her racial profiling. He hated bigotry in any form.

"God, this is priceless. A farm-raised significant other for dear Mitch! I can't believe your luck, Mitch." She studied Jacob with a critical eye. "And he's good-looking."

Finally Mitch, enjoying the situation, chimed in—a little late, Jacob thought. "No, you've misunderstood, Yvy. Jacob is among my few straight friends. He's not gay."

"Yeah, well, I might have guessed you would try to hide behind that story if things were really serious. It's okay, Mitch. I like him, and you don't need to hide him in the closet."

"That's ridiculous, he's not hiding anything," Jacob said, with an edge.

"You're still in the closet, Jacob?"

"No, I'm not," he replied, unable to conceal a smile at the absurdity of the situation. "You've simply made the wrong assumption. I am not gay. I have a girlfriend." The moment he admitted this he was sorry.

She studied him. "Oh, what's her name?"

"Rachel." Jacob tried to hold a grin that was fading. "Why are we talking about this—and who is the snoop now?"

"I guess I am." The crooked smile widened. "But I don't believe either of you." She took his arm forcefully. "Come on, Sellars. We'll find out about you. And if you're telling the truth, I'll tell you a family story that will make your hair curl. Your story will win a, what do you call that prize?"

"That's Pulitzer," Jacob offered.

"Whatever." She turned and walked away, assuming Jacob would follow.

Mitch watched them make their way through the room and disappear.

"That's not going to be a good match," Emily warned.

"He can take care of himself."

"Maybe." She sipped at her drink. "It was silly of her to persist with the gay thing."

"I bet it was just her way of flirting. He seems to attract women like flypaper. Isn't even aware of it. Last night he had to fight off the Coffin girl. I saw them going up in the elevator at the inn late last night, but he denied any hanky-panky—and I believe him."

"Interviewing her?"

"Yes, and getting an interesting story."

"I'm sure. He seems like a nice kid. I'm sure you're right that he doesn't even know he's attractive."

"Emily, he's not a kid. I think he's thirty-six or -seven."

"That's a kid to me. Anyway, he seems young for his age."

"He's been around," Mitch said.

They watched the crowd for awhile, both wrapped in their own thoughts about the new liaison. "You should warn him about Yvonne, Mitch. It's only fair."

"Jacob will go where the story is."

"Well, he won't get it from Marilyn Coffin."

"I suppose you're right, old thing. You usually are." He gave her a little hug.

Yvonne got them beers from a fridge in a large studio tacked onto the rambling house probably as an afterthought. At one end of the room there was a huge curved glass enclosure, like a solarium with a view of the harbor entrance. An easel was set up holding a half-finished landscape painting. A collection of pastel tubes and brushes were arranged on a nearby table. Two big windows looking east dominated the adjacent side of the room. The view was spectacular. With a sweep of her hand, Yvonne pointed out the landmarks. In the foreground was the secluded Polpis Harbor. To the east, the Great Point Lighthouse stood out stark white in the midday sun. From the southern beaches, the vast Atlantic stretched over the infinite horizon toward Spain, as the saying goes.

"Very beautiful and a little overwhelming. I can almost see the whalers starting out on their voyages."

"Yeah, this was the capital of whaling. My forebears were whalers."

"I know."

She glanced at him critically. "I wonder if you do." She walked over to the easel and fingered the partly filled canvas.

"Yours?" he asked.

"Are you kidding?" She laughed. "My mom's. I couldn't draw my hand."

He could feel Yvonne's presence. If a person had an aura, hers was intense. "She's good," he said, joining her for a view.

"Come sit." She flopped down on a deep couch facing the windows, her long legs stretched out in front of her. "Mom is a literal painter. She copies what she sees and is very good at that. Not much comes from the imagination."

Jacob took this as a negative appraisal of her mother's efforts. He joined her on the couch but kept his distance.

"Did you know the Cranes were also slavers?"

"Yes, I did." Jacob was pleased to be a step ahead of her.

"Ah, that's impressive. You've done your homework." She paused, gazing at him. "I could tell you things you don't know."

"I wish you would."

She continued to study him. "Okay, now level with me. You're not gay?"

"No, I already told you." Jacob laughed at her persistent interest in his sexual orientation.

"You came with Mitch. He doesn't show up often with a boyfriend he's not banging." She kicked off her shoes.

"Well, he did this time."

"So, you have a girlfriend?"

"Yes."

"A serious one?"

He studied her as she gazed up at the sky. "That's none of your business." He had to balance his increasing irritation with the need not to insult her.

"How old are you?"

He got up from the low couch with some difficulty, not as smoothly as he intended. "What's going on here? These are, well, they're just bizarre questions coming from someone like you."

"Like me?"

"Yes, like you—a young kid, who's just met a guy old enough …"

"Old enough for what, Jacob? God, I can't get over that name. It's *so*, uh, biblical." She laughed in her infectious way. "Old enough to be my father or just a big bossy brother?"

"I think I've heard this line before." He paused, oddly thinking of Marilyn Coffin. But he knew a show of anger would fend her off. "If I were your father, I might be tempted to send you to your room," he said, with as much severity as he could muster.

"That's a laugh." She reached for his hand. "Sit down and lighten up, Sellars."

"This is ridiculous." He started for the door.

"Hey, wait a minute," she cried, jumping up. "We're not through here."

Exasperated, he turned to face her. "You know what? I think you're a spoiled brat and a bore, in need of a good spanking." He wondered whether he was over-reacting, but he could not stop himself. He knew that these words might cut the deepest. But he also knew there was something bordering on sexual in his response.

She froze. Even with the bright light in his eyes, he could tell she was flushed with color. Then she slapped him. It was a pretty hefty blow that stung his cheek.

"And that was childish," he said, as he closed the door quietly behind him, feeling pleased with himself. He had touched a nerve of this all-too-confident young woman—but probably nothing else. He hoped that he hadn't lost her, but, oddly, he wasn't too worried.

He found Mitch and Emily together, sitting in a secluded nook. "What happened to your cheek?" Mitch asked, peering at him up close.

"Don't ask."

"She slapped him, obviously," Emily said. "That's what she does. You must have gotten to her. Congratulations. She only does things like that when she thinks she's losing."

"Or maybe you made a pass at her," Mitch suggested snidely. "After last night, a fair comment—eh, Jacob?"

"No. Passes she can handle easily. It's criticism she can't take," Emily said, ignoring Mitch's comment. "And your 'after last night' is off base."

Jacob suspected Mitch had already gossiped with Emily about what he had seen the previous night. "I think Emily has it about right. My only mistake was in going a bit overboard on reacting." He was beginning to have second thoughts about his hasty words. He realized that he wanted to see Yvonne again.

"I'll just say one other thing about her, Jacob. The fact that you got to her tells me that you made an impression. She wanted you to like her." Emily paused. "Next time, get her to talk politics. That's where she shines. You may not agree with her, but you'll find the conversation enlightening. She's a real powerhouse of ideas."

"If there is a next time," Jacob said.

"Oh, there will be. You can count on it. You got her attention." She took his arm. "But be careful with her. She can become, uh, well, she's complicated."

Mitch was restless and wandered off in search of friends, leaving Emily and Jacob alone. He pressed her for more information on the Coffin family, but she could not or would not add much to what Mitch had told him. She confirmed that the episode of Amos's leaving Crane was very murky and admitted that she had lost touch with him. She agreed that it would be a good idea to interview Coffin before he went off to sea. She told him Amos could be found by contacting the Preston Boatyard in Marblehead. But she warned that he was not a talkative man and probably wouldn't be very forthcoming. She wished him luck and asked that he touch base with her after the meeting so they could put their heads together and fill in some of the blanks. Her promising offer of continuing help was encouraging.

That night, Jacob couldn't stop thinking about Yvonne. She certainly was an extraordinary beauty—and a bitch. But what intrigued him most was her comment about the stories she could tell. This worldly young woman probably knew a good deal more than she should. He tried to recall his impression of her. There was something different—not just the beauty. She seemed older than her age, smarter. Her eyes were too wise, like those of a child of divorce. There was a foreign look about her—exotic. He was looking forward to seeing her again and hoped that he had not lost his chance. His interest had gone beyond a reporter's need of information.

On the ferry ride back to the mainland, Jacob was able to stand on deck and view the choppy waters of Nantucket Shoals and the land edging the horizon. There was a light breeze out of the northwest. To the south, Mitch pointed out the prominent lighthouse at the end of Cape Pogue, the first landfall of Martha's Vineyard from the east. The ferry churned along in the clear crisp air. East Chop light eventually appeared on the port bow, and in the distance the bluffs of West Chop were just poking over the horizon. The waters calmed as the ferry skirted shoal water marked by buoys tipped to the current. As the boat made its arcing turn to the east and Hyannis, the flashing strobe at the harbor entrance pierced the clear air. When they drew nearer, Jacob could make out a few stalwart fishermen trying their luck from the breakwater. They steamed into the harbor, and the ferry slowed to a crawl, turning into the dock. The deck rumbled with the reverse thrust of the engines. Jacob was pleased to find himself a pretty good "sailor" after all.

It had been difficult talking Mitch into making the trip to Marblehead. It was a long drive, and it was a Sunday. But he had relented after a hearty breakfast at the inn on Nantucket. His generous mood evaporated, however, when he found that his car had frozen up in the parking lot after the cold night. They had to get a mechanic to use jumper cables. Mitch had a bitchy temper fit over the ordeal. Jacob paid the guy with a nice tip. Mitch was silent and moody on the drive to Boston. But later, with an almost-empty interstate link to the North Shore, his mood improved.

"God, what a day!" He was smiling.

"Sorry I got you into this, Mitch."

"You're not really. Don't be a phony, Jacob."

"Have it your way."

After a short silence, Mitch said, "Let's make up. I can't do this whole trip without speaking."

"We don't have anything to make up, Mitch."

"I've been a prick all day."

"No, you haven't. I'm asking a lot of you."

"Well, your story is going to be a dilly. And I don't mind being a small part of it." He sniffed. "When you finish, you might want to mention me as, uh, a facilitator, you know, some little byline at the beginning."

"I feel like we're a long way from bylines." Jacob sighed, anticipating all that lay ahead. "I don't even have a good handle on a story yet."

"Your first story could be about the last couple of days—you know, the funeral, the personality stuff, maybe even the slap." He laughed. "That should satisfy your editor. Then you save the other stuff for the freelance work."

The sly little bastard, thought Jacob. It was good advice. It would give him a chance to keep his editor happy and buy some time to see whether his ambitious plan had merit.

"That's a good idea, Mitch, but not the slap," he said. "Anyway, if you do help me with the research, you'll get a mention." Too late, he remembered Rachel's advice against coauthorship.

"Then it's a deal."

Jacob knew Rachel would kick him for making the promise.

By the time they reached the exit for Marblehead, the day had warmed a little. Jacob thought at least he could see the place in good weather.

CHAPTER 5

Mitch seemed familiar with the streets of Marblehead as he drove to a small restaurant on the harbor. They chose a table with the best view of the sparkling water and a few boats swinging on their moorings to a gentle breeze. It was a late lunch, and Sellars was hungry. He could tell something was on Mitch's mind because he wasn't very interested in the fish chowder he had ordered.

"I'm going to make a call," he announced abruptly, extracting his cell phone and heading for a side door. Yet another friend? God, a guy in every port.

Jacob ate his fish slowly and enjoyed the scene. It was a perfect New England setting—the gray-shingled, white-trimmed houses with docks reaching out like fingers and the covey of cradled hulls at the boatyard dominating one end of the harbor. A few boats in the water sat in circles of floating "bubbler" devices. He had read somewhere that these were rigged to prevent any ice damage to the hull. There were still patches of snow on some of their decks. It was a strange sight in the middle of winter. A launch left one of the many docks and chugged into the harbor. A lone figure was dropped off at one of the boats. He slid open a hatch and disappeared below. In awhile he climbed back on deck with a large white bag of sails. Wrestling the canvas out on deck, the intrepid sailor began to slide one end of the big sail onto the boom. Jacob watched the man in fascination and with some envy. He had done a little sailing on Long Island Sound as a guest and wished he could do more. But neither time nor money proved to be adequate. Mitch reappeared, breaking Jacob's train of thought.

"Look, the guy is going out—in the middle of winter?" Jacob said, unable to tear himself away from the scene.

"There are still a few old salts who crank up in the cold. I don't know what the attraction is. I'm not even too fond of it in the summer, especially if I'm going to get wet." Mitch peered critically at the old sloop as it glided away from her mooring under the power of its mainsail. He shivered. "As a kid, I had to crew in boat races. I hated it."

"And you had me convinced that you were an old salt from a whaling family."

"Yeah, well, I wised up."

Studying the harbor, Mitch raised an arm slowly, pointing to the opposite shore where the clutter of mostly white hulls gleamed in the afternoon sun. "That's it, the big gray roof painted with 'Preston,' the yard where Coffin has his boat." The cradled fleet looked somehow awkward and naked out of their element. Jacob wondered how they got there. "Let's go." Still fretting over his earlier snit, Mitch picked up the check, leaving exact change.

"No more lunch?" Jacob asked.

"Not now." Mitch had apparently made other plans.

"Well, thanks for mine. It was great."

Driving slowly through the narrow streets, Mitch stopped in the boatyard entrance blocked by a forbidding cyclone fence. A watchman lounged at the gate with a big red stop sign with the intimidating warning "Owners Only."

"How do we get in?"

"This is as far as I go," Mitch said. "If old Amos catches sight of me, you'll learn nothing." Mitch smiled sympathetically. "You may get nothing anyway." Then changing his tone, he added, "But I bet you do. Your Midwestern sincerity will show right through the nosy reporter image." Mitch patted Jacob's knee reassuringly.

Jacob eyed the watchman doubtfully.

"Go ahead. Ask if Amos is around." He nudged Jacob. "I'll meet you back at the restaurant. Take all the time you need. Tell Coffin that's where you parked. He'll probably run you over in the launch."

Jacob took a deep breath. Somehow the scene—the boats, the "Owners Only," and the unknown quantity of Amos Coffin—made him uneasy. Despite the sunny day, there was a penetrating dankness in the air. He took a deep breath. "Okay, I'll give it a whirl." He knew he was good at softening up reluctant interviews. That was his best talent. The watchman admitted him when he mentioned Coffin and pointed to a collection of hulls at the edge of the harbor. "He's oveh theah. Big black boat. Cahn't miss huh." Jacob smiled at the Down East inflections. He waved to Mitch, indicating he had scored.

After getting additional directions from a loitering worker, Jacob picked his way through the maze of towering hulls. He marveled at the soft smooth lines—almost feminine in their suggestiveness. No wonder a boat was always a "she" to sailors. Circling the giant, empty cradle the worker had pointed out, he came to a large black hull glistening with fresh paint. A figure was standing at a makeshift desk of planks and sawhorses, studying a plan. Jacob watched for a moment as the man placed circular metal weights on a piece of plywood to flatten the blueprint. The boat was fully rigged and sat in a cradle on rails leading down to the edge of the harbor beside a long dock. There was a cluster of pilings that followed the track into deeper water.

Diverted by the nautical scene, he had not noticed that he had been discovered. "Can I help you?" The raspy voice took him by surprise.

Jacob took a couple of steps closer and put out his hand. "Hi. My name is Jacob Sellars. You are Amos Coffin?"

"Yeah. But I don't think I know you." Coffin was dressed in jeans and a black CPO shirt. He didn't offer his hand. The resemblance to pictures of the late Joshua Crane was remarkable—the piercing blue eyes, the sharp features, even to the lines arching around his prominent nose. Coffin slid off a black watch cap, leaving a full head of graying hair in a mess. His beard was a scruffy few days old.

"I'm a reporter with *The New York News.*" He hesitated, expecting a testy reply. Not getting one, he continued. "The paper has asked me to do a story on Joshua Crane. I believe he is your cousin." Coffin's face darkened, but Jacob went on, choosing to change the subject. He looked up at the black hull. "Gosh, that's a beautiful boat. I understand you're going to sail her around the world."

Coffin studied Jacob for a full minute more, and finally shook his head slowly and smiled. "Well, I'll be damned. A newshound. What part of the Crane family sent you up here to see me?"

"Well, sir, it was Emily. She thought I should meet you, particularly since you're about to embark on such a remarkable voyage. That is story enough for a visit."

"Is it now?"

"Yes, sir." Jacob could feel the intensity of Coffin's eyes as they searched for the other reasons.

"You don't have a cameraman with you?" Coffin looked around in a mock surveillance. "You should have because I'm about to put this craft on the water. You ever see a boat launched?"

"No, I haven't. But I'd love to see it." Jacob welcomed the distraction. "Can I help?"

Coffin stretched his cap back on at a jaunty angle. "Nope, just watch. Then we can talk." He started off toward the dock. "Come on."

There were shouts followed by warning beeps much like that used by a backing truck. A diesel engine rumbled from somewhere in the distance. From his vantage point on the dock, Jacob watched the cradle begin to move. He realized that the cradle was being slowly towed down the track by a set of steel cables. It was an impressive sight. As the sailboat settled into its waterline, it seemed smaller than it appeared to be on dry land. There were two masts and the teak deck was flush except for a small wheelhouse near the stern. A tangle of slack rigging swung as men moved quickly to secure the boat to pilings on the dock. Coffin had moved in to take charge of sorting out the rigging, quietly giving orders as he himself made adjustments and inspected the fittings. It took only a half hour to complete the job.

"What do you think of her?" Coffin asked after the men had left.

"She's beautiful," Jacob replied, in awe of the whole spectacle. "Does the boat have a name?"

"Are you a boat person?"

"I like them—sailboats, I mean. And I've done some sailing around Long Island—on other people's boats. But I really don't know a lot."

Coffin looked pleased. "Well, it's a start. If you do much more of it you'll get hooked, if it's in your blood."

"I'm afraid I don't have much of that. I was brought up on a farm in Illinois."

"Yeah, well, it could still get you." He paused and admired his craft. "*Saga*, that's her name. One meaning of that term is adventure, and the other is chronicle." He scratched his head and adjusted his cap, uncomfortable with the expression of his own romance. "But you're a writer, you already knew that."

He waited for a reaction.

"She's aptly named then."

"Yeah, I think so. I'm gonna paint it on her side when I get time. Big gold letters." He picked up a plank and laid it across the space between the dock and *Saga*'s deck at a gap in the lifelines. "Come aboard. Can't think of a better place to float your questions." He led the way. "Watch your step," he warned, as *Saga* rolled gently in the passing wake of a motorboat.

A stairway—Jacob later learned it was called a companionway—led below deck. Coffin disappeared down the steps into the shadows of the cabin. "Use the handholds," Coffin suggested, pointing to the wooden grips mounted on the ceiling and the walls of the companionway. "They're for rough weather."

Descending below, he was transported by the cozy, compact scene. The walls—Coffin called them bulkheads—were polished mahogany and teak. The galley stove was to port, the roomy navigation table to starboard, where charts and implements like dividers and compasses were stowed. There were two spacious couches, doubling as berths on either side, separated by a varnished table anchored to the floor. Kerosene lanterns sat in brackets fastened to the walls. Small windows, or portholes, admitted shafts of sunlight to warm the inside. At the end of the cabin, a door led forward to other accommodations in a separate cabin where bags of sails and other gear were stacked. It took several minutes for Jacob to take it all in. Based on the few boats he had seen, this one was definitely from another era. It even smelled different.

"Sit," Coffin said, indicating one of the bunks. He settled in across from Jacob. "This is where I will live and work for a couple of years." He spread his arms as if to embrace his surroundings. "I don't have to hurry. I got plenty of time." The suspicion of a satisfied smile cracked his weathered features.

It was obvious that this was a special boat—very traditional. Jacob was overcome with the exotic idea of being at sea alone in this environment—the motion, the roar of the wind, the shrill whistle in the rigging. He could only pretend to imagine. The vision was overpowering—alone on that endless ocean expanse, relying on your inner resources.

"She's an old boat. Rebuilt, of course, to toughen her up." He patted the cushion. "But still the same old ketch that was launched in 1950—all cedar planked and oak framed. I've kept her old-fashioned—even the oil lamps. There's not a drop of plastic in her. A guy named Joel Johnson up in Maine built *Saga,* but I suppose that wouldn't mean much to you. Good sea boat. Built for the likes of the Horn." There was something very reassuring about Coffin, an aura of confidence that made the prospect of a sea voyage seem safe. He slapped the table. "She's not like those modern racing machines."

"I can see that." Jacob took a deep breath to bring himself back to reality. "I have always liked stories about the sea. *Moby Dick* was a favorite of mine. The book got me to reading about sea voyages like the ones Captain Slocum took. He was a very brave fellow."

"So, you do have an interest in the sea. When I was very young, I had the good fortune to meet a few old salts like that Slocum fella. Learned a lot from them." He stroked his chin, studying Jacob closely. "A big-city reporter with nautical interests—that's a rarity, I'd say."

Jacob watched as Coffin busied himself tidying up the cabin, almost afraid to break the spell. He was beginning to like the guy.

"Want a cup of tea?" Coffin asked, but did not wait for an answer to pull down a kettle and rummage around his larder for tea containers. "Sorry, no booze on board." He held up a box of crackers. "I got some biscuits for munchies."

"Sounds good."

"Okay. That's what we'll have." Coffin moved quickly in his galley, lighting the propane stove and brewing cups of tea—real tea with a strainer. "She's been out of the water for only a few days. That's why I'm sorta provisioned. I'll be living on her while we get her ready for blue water. I plan to make a little shakedown cruise for a week or so. Gotta check out some of the electronic stuff—you know, self-steering, GPS, and such." He brought the mugs of tea and set them on the table and sat on the couch across from Jacob again. "I hate all that high-tech stuff. The only thing worth its weight is the radar, for fog." He waited for Jacob to take his first taste of tea, as if there were a formality at work.

"Mmm, good. Hits the spot."

"Okay, fire away."

Caught off guard, Jacob stumbled around for a place to start. "I, uh, am doing a story on Joshua ..."

"Yeah, you said that. But what the hell do I have to do with it?"

Jacob collected his thoughts. "You're part of the family."

"No, just a relative, a Coffin, not a Crane," he said firmly.

"Yes, that is a better way to put it. But you once worked for the company— The Crane Corporation."

Coffin became wary. "Yes, I did. Quite awhile ago. But tell me, what are you up to—looking for scandal or dirt on the Cranes? If it is, I'm not your man. You say you like *Moby Dick*—well, I can tell you about whaling. My family and the Crane family were neck deep in it, with a touch of slave trade on the side. That's a real story. This other stuff is just, oh, I don't know, stuff you'd rather leave under the rug for future generations to obsess over. It's raw now, too many people alive. Too many to get hurt. Sure, I know some things, things I'd rather forget." He studied his rough, callused hands and then looked at Jacob directly. "Do you know what I'm saying?"

"Of course. And I don't want to be out of line here. I respect your privacy. But the stuff—are we talking about the, uh, comments in the obituary, suggestions of accounting problems, company wheeling and dealing, or are you talking about things like, uh, the mysterious government connections? That's news, and I'm a journalist. I understand the company may also be under investigation on securities matters. Is this why you're reluctant to comment? If so, I want to respect that."

He chuckled. "That's a mouthful, I'd say. You been doing some homework. First, whatever's wrong here isn't the same ball of wax. That's past history. It should be left alone. On current matters, I'm not in the know at all. And I'm certainly not aware of any investigation. That doesn't mean there isn't one, but I just don't know. I try to stay away from the newspapers. I don't own a TV. I left the company years ago—I don't even remember how many."

Jacob took a chance. "But you remember why you left?"

A smile spread slowly across Coffin's face. "You're a cheeky son-of-a-bitch. You expect me to answer that?"

"You don't have to answer. But let me suggest a reason. You had a quarrel with Joshua, a disagreement over something major, like the direction of the company or its business practices. You had a problem with something you discovered, something you didn't like. It brought you to a crossroads with Joshua, and you had to leave or were asked to leave. Is that roughly correct?" Jacob anticipated an angry, defensive response and steeled himself for it.

Coffin picked up the teakettle and poured the hot water into the sink. Jacob wondered whether this was a prelude to his ending the interview.

"Who you been talking to? Is it Emily? Or someone else in the family? Emily, she's tight-lipped. Someone else?" He turned abruptly for the galley, hiding the hint of a smile. "Yvonne? Damn it. Yvonne's been shooting her mouth off!"

"I met Yvonne, but only briefly, not enough time for much of a conversation."

"None of her politics either?"

"No politics."

Coffin softened a little. "Then you missed an experience. She's a real wild one on that score." His comment seemed more one of approval than critical.

"So I gather from the stories."

"No, not that way. That's just gossip. Her political views on things are a bit, uh, outré." He laughed. "If Homeland Security finds out about her, she may end up down in Guantanamo Bay." He chuckled at the thought. "But she's right on some things others don't have the guts to say." He seemed to be filibustering.

Jacob tried again. "So, was my surmise close enough?"

"You already seem to know from someone else. No point in denying it. Sure, I came to a parting of the ways with Joshua. It was a family thing. He wanted Joshua, Jr., to take over. I think it was partly family loyalty. But the kid was too inexperienced, and the world far too devious for a youngster. But it was also because he could more easily get his way with Junior. And yes, I thought they were headed the wrong way. Joshua was letting the government get too, uh, close to the company. There were things of that nature I found offensive, but more important, it wasn't good business. It wasn't good for shareholders. So we parted ways." He paused, thinking over his next comment. "Now, the issues might be similar, but the venue has changed."

The government too close? What did that mean? But Jacob decided against pressing the point. "You mean to the Middle East?"

"Yeah, I guess so. And elsewhere."

"And the government? Was that the CIA?"

Amos just stared at him.

Jacob decided not to press the point. He had his answer. "Do you, ah, have bad feelings about Joshua, about the breakup?" Jacob was trying hard to conceal his own excitement. He sensed that he had the makings of a story.

"How can I have good feelings?" He paused, sitting again as if resigned to the invasion of his privacy. "It was a bad time to lose a job—at that age. It took a few years to get by," he said and then added, "but I've let all that go now."

"Do you want to talk about the practices that brought you and Joshua to an impasse? Like the government getting too close—and maybe even closer now?"

"No, that gets into what I said in the beginning. The whole nightmare comes back—I mean with the death of Joshua and the news coverage and maybe an investigation, like you say. Maybe trouble in the offing." It was obvious that Coffin had been following the company more closely than he was willing to admit. "I had my trip planned before all this recent stuff surfaced. Joshua was still alive and kicking with that young Russian wife of his, taking care of things like he wanted to. I'll tell you this. The old guy had all his testosterone to the very end." He leaned back and laced his hands behind his head. "We got along better toward the end. We're both seafaring men at heart. And that was good enough for me. The other stuff ..." He didn't finish. "Now, my only relationship is with *Saga* here. Don't need booze or Viagra for that. I've had her for a long time. We respect each other, take care of each other, live or die together."

Here was a man who knew who he was. Jacob realized that was why he liked him—and envied him.

A silence descended on the cabin. Jacob knew that he wasn't going to get any more from Coffin. The light had faded in the late afternoon sun, leaving pink shadows on the dark wood of the interior. Coffin sat forward and laid his hands on the table. "You know, I didn't mean to be critical of Yvy. She's a good kid and very smart. I don't know your politics, but you should hear her out. And in the process, you might also get more of what you're after. She knows more than anyone what's going on now. She's very down on the family. It's sad because they're all she's got." He took a breath with some emotion. "God, talk about dysfunctional. That family takes the cake." He chuckled. "Mine isn't a bed of roses either. Maybe it's in the genes." Jacob was beginning to admire this crusty, romantic old salt. His tragedy had made him larger in life, and the dangerous voyage ahead seemed to fit well with the way he had lived—honest with others as well as with himself. As he watched Amos clean up, he was struck by the likeness he bore to his daughter Marilyn. But he thought better of mentioning that encounter. The determined jaw and the kindness in the eyes, the vulnerability, were all there.

Before parting, Coffin offered Jacob a sail on *Saga* before he left on his voyage, but only if he could assure him that there would be no more reporter's questions. As predicted by Mitch, Coffin arranged to have a launch take him across the harbor.

"You were right about Coffin," Jacob told Mitch when they hooked up again. "He admitted that he had a falling-out with Joshua over more than just family, but wouldn't offer any details. And he did confirm that the old man wanted Joshua, Jr., to take over." Jacob did not mention Coffin's surprising admission to government ties. He wanted this for himself—at least for now.

"Was it worth it?" Mitch asked.

"Oh, yeah. Just to meet the guy—and see his boat. I liked him. He was onto Crane. He recognized that the old man wanted Junior because he was malleable—unlike Amos. And he as much as admitted that Joshua fired him. It was a dead end to press him on details." For the first time, Jacob was beginning to feel proprietary about his story. "It's harder for Amos now that Joshua is dead and authorities are looking at the company—and maybe dirty linen being aired." Jacob paused, reminded of his invitation. "And guess what? He agreed to take me sailing."

"You'd want to do that?"

"Sure—why not? I like boats. I'd like to have my own—someday."

"You must have made a hit with him."

"I hope so. He urged me to talk to Yvonne."

"To pump her?"

"No, just because she's interesting—politically."

"That's true." He glanced at Jacob. "But somehow I don't have a vision of that happening soon. I just remember the red mark on your face, old boy. And it wasn't lipstick," he said and giggled.

"We'll just have to see." Jacob didn't want to elaborate on Coffin's suggestion that Yvonne might be useful beyond politics. After the uncomfortable quiz that Coffin had put him through on his contacts, he thought it better to avoid involving Mitch, who seemed to elicit little warmth from Joshua, Jr.

On the drive back to the city, Mitch was in an expansive mood. He had spent the afternoon with friends at the Yacht Club, and he prattled on at length about his Harvard classmates and their racing boats. It was entertaining for Jacob, but it also made him feel like an outsider, as talk of the Eastern establishment usually did.

Back in his hotel room, Jacob checked voice mail and found one from Rachel. "I miss you. Just wanted to talk. Give me a call when you can." After making notes of his day with Amos, he got ready for bed, wondering whether 1:00 AM was too late to try her. Rachel was a night owl, but it was now late even for her. Once he had eased into bed, he gave in to the temptation anyway.

Four rings, five, six, and then, "Hello," an obviously out-of-a-dead-sleep voice croaked. Jacob thought that was a bad sign.

"Hi, it's Jacob. Sorry I …"

"I know who it is, for Chrissake. Do you know what time it is?"

"I thought you might be up."

"Well I'm not, wasn't, and am now." Her voice warmed a little.

"Not busy, are you?"

"Now what the hell does that mean?"

"Just kidding."

"Don't you know when you're away I just sit in my room and pine away for you?" For a moment neither of them knew where to go. "In a weak moment, I missed you. I think I left a message to that effect. Did you get it?"

"Yes. That's why I'm calling."

"So, you've been out gallivanting."

"I was up in Marblehead interviewing a relative of Joshua Crane. He's a sailor. He's going to sail around the world alone."

"One of those nuts. Did you get anything interesting?"

"Not really. But the guy did invite me to go out on his boat."

"That's great. A return to your *Moby Dick* days, huh?"

"Maybe. Want to go along?"

There was a long silence. She was either considering it or getting herself more comfortable. It turned out to be the latter.

"The last time I got that near the water was on a ferry to Fire Island—four years ago. I hate boating. I hate the beach. And I particularly hate sand in my mouth at picnics."

"Gosh, I didn't know you felt so strongly."

"Well, I do. How's the article coming? Are you going to trade it in for a trip around the world with some maniac trying to find his white whale?"

"That's an interesting idea, but no, I'm still on the story. I'm excited about it, too." He considered her jocular comment about the white whale to be oddly insightful.

"What else have you done?"

"Mitch got me into the reception on Nantucket. I met most of the family. The daughter of Joshua, Jr., may be a good source. She's alienated from the family and may be willing to talk to me." Jacob's confidence in this was tempered by the memory of the sting of Yvonne's slap.

"Is that the kid who put the Ford Explorer in the pool?"

"The same."

"She can't be credible."

"I think she is. She's apparently a smart cookie and not so crazy. Pretty radical and an outspoken critic of the administration."

"A twenty-something crazy is going to be a factor?"

"Maybe. Might be of help to me. Coffin, her uncle—the sailor—thought so."

"Coffin? That's his name? My God, how perfect."

"That's right. A lot of ship captains were Coffins."

There was another silence. "You're not, uh, interested in her, are you?"

"In whom?"

"The girl."

"Of course not," Jacob said quickly. "She's just a kid."

"Yeah, but so are you, and from what I've read, she's a pretty sleek chick, and wild, too." He didn't respond. "Do I need to worry about you?"

"You must be kidding."

"Okay, let's have telephone sex."

"How do you do that?"

"Well, we both could masturbate as we talk. Say sweet passionate things to each other." Her words about sex were always slightly off-key for Jacob. It was as if it were more a pretense than a reality.

"Uh-huh."

"Okay. Just a thought. Maybe we should just go to sleep and dream about it. When are you coming back?"

"In a few days. I have more interviews, with Emily, Joshua's sister. I've already got a raft of notes. But I will need to talk to some people in New York about the financial and legal stuff."

"I can help on that. I've got good sources on the Wall Street aspects—names and numbers."

"Great. I guess we should say goodnight. I miss you, too." But he had to force it out.

"Well, in a couple of days, then." She said, "Night-night," and was gone with a click.

Jacob put the phone down slowly. It was strange how they didn't ever use any words of endearment. It was just about sex. The thought bothered him. He doused the light but could not sleep right away. He tried to recapture the image of Yvonne until he drifted into a deep sleep.

CHAPTER 6

Jacob wakened as a narrow slant of sunlight through a gap in the curtains moved across his face. He took a moment to reconstruct the previous day. The *Saga* had floated in and out of his dreams all night. The image of Amos in the cabin returned, and gradually the details of their conversation. He needed to review his notes and begin to piece together the article. But as he lay in the comfortable warmth of his bedding, he couldn't help fantasizing an ocean voyage of his own.

As the shaft of sunlight moved away, Jacob drifted off in that half daydream state of early morning, his unconscious dredging up old images. He was holding Christy in his arms again. This time it was as his current self and she, still a child. They were naked. Her firm, undeveloped body was smooth and glowed in the moonlight. Then he woke up. His heart was pounding against his ribs. He rolled out of bed quickly to put the image out of his mind. Why had this nightmare come back, he asked himself for the hundredth time? Christy had been gone from his dreams for several years now. But this was a new twist, appearing with him as an adult and her as she was then, only twelve.

It was a dreadful picture. He wondered whether the dream was somehow seeded by Amos and his Ahab-like sea voyage. Had this beautiful Crane girl brought back the old guilt? Then there was the Coffin girl. He sat for a long time with his head in his hands, waiting for his angst to dissolve. It was an odd combination—the two young girls and then the old sailor. Was it an omen for him? Rising suddenly, he flung open the curtains and cried aloud, "Hah!" For heaven's sake, he was onto a good story. These people came from another planet, with all their money and family traditions. He surveyed the landscape of buildings stretching east to the harbor and the vast Atlantic Ocean beyond. He imagined Coffin's *Saga* slipping over the horizon and was a little envious of this possibility for escape. But escape from what? The odd feeling lingered. He remembered

Emily's warning about the family—something about losing one's innocence by getting too close to the family.

He sighed and stretched out on the bed again, noticing for the first time the alert light on the phone blinking. He must have slept through the call. Something told him it was his office reminding him of the deadline for the Crane story. He wasn't sure he was up to a conversation with Shanahan—an abrasive personality even on a good day. Struggling to pull himself together, he ordered breakfast from room service and checked his voice mail. The message was from Emily, received at 6:30 AM. She wanted to alert him to a call he might be getting from Luis Garon, a representative of The Crane Corporation. Garon would be asking about the newspaper article he was doing. Garon did not seem to know about any larger effort in the offing, and she did not bother to disabuse him. Her final comment seemed to be a warning.

"I'm going to be out for most of the day. But you should know that Luis is not likely to be, uh, very receptive to any kind of story on the business or the family. Be careful with him. He is dangerous." There was another voice shouting in the background, probably to hurry her. "Sorry I have to leave a message. But I did need to tell you about this fellow. We'll talk later. Bye."

Dangerous? Who in the company ordered him to call? Was it a reaction to Jacob's appearance at the Nantucket affair and concern about his assignment to do a story on the family? Jacob suspected that either Joshua, Jr., or his man Garon had already called the *News* and maybe talked to Shanahan, his editor. This thought was enough to persuade him to get started immediately on a story of the funeral in Boston and his trip to Nantucket, as Mitch had suggested. There was enough material for a good piece on that alone. He glanced at the clock on his bedside radio—9:45 AM. He would have to hurry to beat Shanahan.

Not bothering to dress, he set up his laptop and began a first draft. It went quickly. He paused only when he came to his encounter with Yvonne in the studio. He decided against including the slap or much of their brief conversation, except to comment on her being an unusual young woman, knowledgeable beyond her years. Of course, he decided to include only his impressions of Emily and Marilyn Coffin. Mostly, it was a story of local color—the church service, the snowy trip on the ferry, the memorial gathering in Nantucket, and a comment on Amos and his voyage without revealing the interview.

Pleased with his effort as he reread it, edited for the third time, he went online and forwarded it to the paper. Just as he pressed the send button, the phone rang with Shanahan.

"Hey, Jacob. We're gonna need a story on that Crane event in Boston ASAP. We're getting a hell of a lot of queries about that fat obit with all the innuendos—that sort of thing. Even had some curious bastard from Crane calling about the article you're doing. I know it's short notice, but I've got a timetable on this. Whatever you can put together." All this came in staccato speed with no pauses, almost as if it were recorded. Instructions from Shanahan were always off-the-cuff and nonstop on almost any topic—and usually came without any "how are you" amenities.

"The check's in the mail, Tom." Jacob was pretty sure that the bastard from Crane was Luis Garon.

"E-mail. God, that's great, Jake. Yeah, here it is." He was obviously monitoring his computer.

"I have to warn you, there's nothing about the more colorful stuff in this piece. That one's going to take awhile—until I can get more facts. But I'm working on it."

"Yeah, I'm reading. It ain't much, but it'll keep the wolves away for awhile. Actually, we've been able to confirm that an investigation of Crane is under way at the SEC. And the FBI wants to talk to Crane, Junior, although they deny that he or anyone there is a target." There was a gap in conversation while he finished reading. "Did you meet Coffin, this Amos Coffin?"

"Yeah."

"Well, what did he have to say? I understand he used to work for the company."

"He was pretty clammed up. We talked about sailing."

"Oh, that's real helpful. Anyway, it'll have to do."

"I'm meeting with a rep of the company today," Jacob volunteered, hoping Emily's alert would pan out.

"Stay with it, take as much time as you need. We'll be working our end. We can put our stuff together. We need to fill in the financial side." Then he had an afterthought. "Got a name?"

"You mean the guy I'm meeting?"

"Yeah."

"Garon. Luis Garon."

"That's the guy, from the New York office of Crane—very slick, very insistent—the same one I talked to."

"I'm getting the feeling that the company might be circling the wagons."

"Yeah, how so?"

"Just a gut feeling, Tom."

"If that proves to be the case, that's good news for a big story. They always do that when they're guilty—just like the government. Only their guys can't claim national security."

"Maybe they can."

"I take your point. You mean Crane's government contracts?"

"Something like that."

Finally, Shanahan was at a loss for words. He started to laugh. "Jake, you got a nose for trouble. How'd you get that out on the farm?"

"I've been in your big, mean cities for too long, I guess."

"Nope. Kids who grow up on farms seem to have more familiarity with bad stuff. You know, those long winters bring out the worst."

He hated it when Shanahan called him Jake. But, of course, he was right on farm kids, particularly this farm kid. He just didn't know how right. "If you say so."

He did his loud pleased-with-himself guffaw and hung up.

The warmth of the sun coming through the window felt good. He could relax now. Shanahan would keep for another few days. He wondered, however, whether he would be returning to New York as soon as he had planned. It was clear that the freelance project would have to wait until he had put together another more substantive story on Crane for his paper. As he gazed out on the cityscape below, he realized he would have to begin his story in Boston, from gossip, from family members who were willing to speak for the record, and some local research. There was a risk of being caught between kiss-and-tell stuff and the arcane intrigue of the multinational energy companies. The task seemed daunting, and now there was Garon.

A discreet tap on the door signaled his breakfast. Jacob was suddenly very hungry. As he sipped coffee after his meal, he made a list of contacts he might use in Boston. It was pretty skimpy. First, he would need to see Emily again. Amos Coffin had been more helpful than he realized. Jacob's first step would be to chase down the CIA connection. It could be a key to all the rumors.

His thoughts returned to Marilyn Coffin. Was she now a dead end? Certainly for him she was. There was Yvonne, beautiful Yvonne—he could still feel the sting of the slap and began to regret his sharp reaction at the time. Reconnecting with her would be awkward, to say the least. Now, more than ever, he needed her as a source. She was, after all, in the bosom of the family. Amos had said she knew a lot. Dealing with her would be tricky in a number of ways. He smiled as he considered again the singular coincidence of his two encounters—first the Coffin girl, and now Yvonne. The progeny of these adventurous seafarers were an odd lot. One wanted to go to bed with him, another slapped him, and Amos—already in his seventies—is going to sail around the world alone! Then there was the openly gay aunt. The patriarch of the family dies amidst rumors of international finagling and ominous CIA connections. The drive to live on the edge seemed to be embedded in the family's genes. They were all free spirits.

It was time to check in with Mitch. He knew he could not comfortably get close to any member of the Crane family without Mitch. Clearly, Mitch was probably not totally accepted by all the family, but he seemed to know how to hit the right buttons.

To touch base, Jacob first tried to reach Mitch at home. Of course, he was out and about—maybe even at the newspaper, although that seemed to play a minor role in his life these days. In any event, Jacob tried the office and left a message. Stymied for the moment for a next move, he decided to get a start on his larger story by making notes on all his interviews and impressions to date. It would make his life easier later.

Shortly after he'd begun, the phone rang. It was Luis Garon.

"Mr. Sellars."

"Yes, that's me."

"My name is Luis Garon." There was a hint of accent in his pronunciation of the last name. "I am with The Crane Corporation. I'm in town today."

"Uh-huh." Jacob wondered whether Garon had made the trip to Boston just to see him.

"I understand that you are doing an article."

"I'm with *The New York News*. That's what I do. I write a lot of articles."

"I'm talking about your piece on The Crane Corporation." There was a note of irritation in his voice.

"Well, I did cover the funeral here and the gathering in Nantucket. That story should appear in tomorrow's paper. At the moment, I'm not doing anything on the company, but I do expect to be writing an in-depth piece on the family. Joshua's death is important news, and the family is certainly an interesting one." Thinking fast, Jacob had decided to take the risk of revealing at least a hint of his intent. They would find out sooner or later, and better it came from him.

"Are you?" The tone became testier. "Well, my role here at Crane is in the area of security. The company is in many countries, and the world is not, uh, a friendly place. So I am naturally interested in any publicity on the company or the family. I talked to a Mr. Shanahan of your office. I take it that you are the reporter who will be, uh, specializing in this subject. He suggested that I give you a call. I would enjoy very much the chance to meet with you and offer my, uh, help and guidance. How about lunch just to get acquainted?" All this was very smooth after the initial moment of irritation.

Garon's call had come at an opportune time, giving Jacob an early chance to test the waters. "Sure, how about lunch today? I'm only here a few days."

"Oh, ah, let's see." He paused, obviously caught off guard. But it was also apparent that he, too, was in a hurry. "Can you hold on a minute?"

"Sure."

A minute later, Garon came back on the line. "That would be fine. Meet me at the Carlton at one." Then as an afterthought, he asked, "Is that good for you?"

"It's okay."

"On Arlington Street. If you are not familiar, it's only a short walk from your hotel."

"Fine, see you there at one."

Jacob hung up, excited about the sudden development. This was his chance to see just how cooperative or, more likely, obstructive the company might be.

Booting up his laptop, he worked his way through the rest of his notes, adding initial impressions of Amos and the questions he had raised. Having neglected to ask Shanahan on the phone, he sent a brief e-mail to the *News* business desk asking for any background information they have on Garon. Then he showered, shaved, and put on a clean shirt and tie for his lunch at the hotel, which he remembered had a dining room dress code.

To clear his head, he decided to take advantage of the crisp, sunny morning and walk through the Public Garden. He hoped to work up an appetite because his late breakfast was still rumbling in his gut.

Jacob got to the Carlton a little ahead of time and wandered around admiring the recently new decor. The lobby had been entirely refurnished. He peeked in at the bar where he had drinks with another reporter from the *Globe* a few years earlier when he had come to Boston to do a story on Senator Kerry. It, too, had been redecorated. It seemed to Jacob that the twenty-first century had brought with it a restless need for change just for the sake of change. It reminded him of his trips to the Hamptons. Few houses in hot areas there were left standing after purchase by the new owner. It was either a teardown or total rehab. The rich were richer and needed to spend more. The houses were huge.

"Mr. Sellars." It came from behind him, interrupting his thoughts.

Startled, Jacob turned to greet a small but stocky, rather dark-complexioned man in his fifties. His bulky neck and shoulders suggested that he might lift weights. He offered an outstretched hand.

"And you must be Luis Garon." Jacob went right to first names. It seemed to loosen communication. "You recognized me?" Jacob was impressed. It was doubtful that anyone knew him at the Carlton.

Garon waved a scrap of newsprint. "Your picture?"

"Oh, yeah, I forgot that." It was an old byline column he had written a few years ago on summer celebrities on Fire Island. It was not one of Jacob's proudest accomplishments. "That was awhile ago."

"You haven't changed much." His handshake was oddly light and tentative. "Why don't we lunch in the upstairs dining room? It's a little quieter than the grill."

Jacob mused—a lot more expensive, too. "Okay." They climbed the staircase in silence, Jacob wondering whether the upgrade was intended to impress. Garon led the way, allowing Jacob a chance to give him a better once-over. The suit was probably European, as were the thin-soled shoes. The hair was clipped short, and he had the erect posture of a military man and moved with a slightly muscle-bound gait, confirming his time in the gym. When they were seated, Garon ordered a bottle of wine without asking for a preference from his guest. Jacob noted Garon was not well schooled on amenities.

"This has been a difficult period for the company and the family—I mean to lose a leader the stature of Joshua Crane." Garon didn't waste time on small talk. "And I must say it is a pity that the publicity about a man who has contributed so much to the energy business has become so stridently hostile." He folded his hands on the table. Jacob felt as if he, himself, was being scolded. Garon shook his head sadly. "These innuendoes, I just don't know where they come from." He gazed meaningfully at Jacob.

"If you're talking about the obituary in the *Times,* I'm sure the fact check is the same as ours and other papers. You don't just make this stuff up. It's corroborated, usually by at least two sources."

"Hmm, yes, I understand that is the practice. But much of what was said was mere supposition and rumor. In fact, the *Times* has acknowledged to me that some of what they have is from leaks by outsiders—hostile political sources who have their own agendas."

"That could be true, but you know insiders are not above doing a little leaking themselves." Jacob doubted that the *Times* had made such admissions and was disappointed in the very standard nature of Garon's claims. Most people accused of wrongdoing in official Washington make similar assertions—denials, leaks, foes with an agenda, rumor, unfounded fact. It was often a smoke screen sent up to cover tracks or derail the truth. You didn't even have to be a cynic to recognize this. Then Jacob suggested, "Think some of it might come from the company—you know, leaks?"

"That's impossible," Garon replied.

"Security that tight, huh?"

Their conversation was interrupted by the waiter, and they ordered lunch. Before Garon could add any more clichés, Jacob asked, "So what can I do for you?"

Garon seemed taken aback a little by the frontal question but recovered smoothly.

"Mr. Sellars, I am not asking you to do anything. We have a free press in this country." He smiled mirthlessly. "You know that better than I do. No, I'm not asking for anything," he repeated. "I am confident you will do an accurate story, and I am—on behalf of the company, of course—offering my help and guidance." He refolded his hands.

"Well, Luis," Jacob began, pretty sure the use of his first name so soon would irritate Garon. It was his favorite ploy in opening up interviews with the arrogant notables. "I'd appreciate the company's help in filling the blanks, but I try to do my own research first." By the dark look that began to spread across Garon's face, Jacob knew that he had succeeded in unsettling him. "But your offer to help is generous and, I must say, an unusual one. I'll definitely take advantage of it."

Garon brightened. "Good. Then that's understood. And I fully realize that you need to do your own work first—the independent media and all that." The dismissive tone showed little evidence of any respect for the press.

But Jacob was not quite finished with the subject. "And along those lines, I can't, of course, take you up on what you call 'guidance.' For obvious reasons, we don't let the public write our stories."

"Of course. I understand. I'm afraid my suggestion was inartfully put. All I really meant was that we would try to be helpful."

For the rest of the meal, Garon steered the conversation to other subjects. He said how much he enjoyed visiting Boston, but liked New York better and asked whether Jacob had grown up there. Surprised that it was instead the Midwest, he admitted that he had never seen much of that part of the country, except from the air on a flight to the coast. Jacob was puzzled that Garon did not have more to say about the company or Joshua. In the privacy of the hallway as they left the dining room, however, Garon paused to offer a final comment.

"Mr. Sellars, I must warn you that The Crane Corporation is involved in some very significant, ah, national security matters with the federal government. I hope you understand that there will be things we are unable to discuss with you. These are matters you should avoid. And needless to say, the Patriot Act—which I'm sure you are familiar with—could involve, ah, certain risks for you personally. We would not want anything to happen like that." He put his hand a little too heavily on Jacob's arm.

"I appreciate the advice." This was more like Jacob had expected. "I'll keep it in mind." He did not react to the surprising acknowledgment that Crane was involved in national security matters. Garon did not realize how helpful he was being.

"And one last thing I must tell you." The thought was interrupted by their passage through the revolving door leading to the sidewalk. "Mr. Crane's daughter." He paused until he had passed well beyond the lurking doorman whose offer of a cab he turned down politely.

"What about her?"

"She's got some problems. She's a little unstable. It's been tough for the family." He sighed sympathetically. "Joshua is trying to get some counseling for her."

"Yeah, I met her at the Nantucket reception. She's pretty, uh, outspoken, I guess." Jacob smiled at his own understatement. "But otherwise she seems to be just a spoiled rich girl." He decided not to mention what he had heard about her radical side.

Garon stopped walking and turned to Jacob. "Stay away from her, Mr. Sellars. Interviews with her are off-limits. That goes for Mr. Crane's sister Emily, as well." This was the first hint of an ugly side. Jacob was surprised by the forbidding tone of the warning. He realized that there was a thug beneath the polished veneer he projected. "If you need information, Mr. Crane will be happy to meet with you."

"Thanks. I'll make a note of that." They shook hands and parted. Jacob was reminded of another Hispanic tough he couldn't place. Then it came to him— Manuel Noriega, the pockmarked strongman who briefly led Panama—a spitting image, as they said on the farm.

As he walked back to his hotel, he reflected that Garon had certainly saved the best part for the end. He suspected that his last warnings were the whole purpose of the visit—to discourage any investigation, particularly any effort to see the outspoken Yvonne or Emily. Jacob decided that Yvonne had to be his next stop. Obviously, she was considered important enough to account for the special mention. As Amos had told him, she knew things.

Jacob related this encounter to Mitch at dinner later that same day and urged him to help arrange a meeting with Emily and Yvonne before Garon had a chance to set up roadblocks. "Yeah, we could do that." But Mitch looked doubt-ful. "It'll be tricky—maybe a meeting at some neutral place." They ate in silence while Jacob let Mitch think about it. "You know, I've only heard about that guy, Garon, and none of it is good. I'm sure his meeting with you was carefully planned—but not a smart way to deal with the press." He smiled. "I can see that the warning is just whetting your appetite."

"Could be just bluster." Jacob had not told Mitch about Garon's claim to national security. He had little doubt that Garon was using the company's gov-ernment contracts to raise the national security issue. "I doubt they'll bother us."

"Yeah. You know what I'm thinking?"

"What?"

"It may irritate you."

"Go ahead, for God's sake."

"Well, I bet Garon has assumed that you are not an experienced investigative reporter and probably thinks you're in over your head. So they're going to take advantage of that by intimidating you. They think you are a political flack trying to do an investigative story and they can scare you into doing a piece of pap."

Jacob could feel his face flush with anger. He remembered Rachel's impa-tience with him and her accusations of indifference and lack of ambition. "You're right, of course, as much as I hate you for telling me." Jacob smiled sheepishly. "I suppose I deserve that. I've been kind of drifting these past years."

"I don't mean that at all, Jacob. I'm just saying it's a perception." He reached across the table, uncertain what to grab and then withdrew his hand. "They don't know you—all that crime reporting in Chicago. You're hardly a soft touch. They have no idea what a cynic you are and how good you are about seeing through phoniness. You haven't missed much while you're, uh, drifting, or whatever you want to call it. They're making a big mistake. But it may be in your favor."

Jacob studied his hands. "Mitch, I am inexperienced at this. I don't even know where to turn next. Maybe it's a waste of time even trying to see Emily and Yvonne."

"Come on, Jacoby, quit feeling sorry for yourself. You're a damn good reporter, and your next stop should be the girls." He smiled broadly. "Just stay out of Yvy's panties."

Jacob smiled in spite of himself. "That's kinda crude. She's just a kid."

"Yeah, so is Marilyn."

"Seriously, I need to think of other sources." He decided to ignore the refer-ence to the Coffin girl. "With this new wrinkle, I probably should make a trip to D.C." He was thinking aloud.

"Sure. I can help there, too. Our paper has covered the family and the company for years. You need to look at it."

"And, of course, the investigative guys on my own paper can help. We need to find out whether Crane has a government connection. Until we know more, we should keep this line of inquiry confidential for the time being."

"My lips are sealed."

"Good." It was clear to Jacob that he would need help from Mitch.

"In the meantime, there are stories on the Internet. *Democracy Now,* that program on Pacifica Radio, has had some good stuff on Crane. I just heard recently that Halliburton dealt out a real nice subcontract to Crane in Iraq. And you know, Cheney's back there as a consultant now. That could be another source of the government linkage. We need to meet with some of the people at Pacifica, too. You do have to be careful, though. You've got to take Garon seriously. These new national security laws are very broad. Some of it even covers U.S. citizens now. A new amendment—I forget the title—can put you in jail without any trial for revealing stuff that is classified. You're at risk for writing anything that touches security as they define it."

"Yeah, Garon mentioned it. Sounds like that would be unconstitutional. But the Constitution doesn't seem to matter anymore. The only power that seems to count now is the Presidency. He's got it all. That's not how I was taught, even in grade school. Bush set it up, and it seems to have stuck. What's happened to us, Mitch?" Jacob was for the first time getting worked up about his subject. Garon's threat had been offensive, and Jacob's anger had been simmering since lunch. In the past, he had resisted the alarms of civil liberty handwringers. As a Midwesterner, he was genetically conservative and suspicious of the left side of the Democratic party. But the extreme right-wingers in this new administration, as in the previous one, were still setting rules of personal conduct, foreign policy, and snooping, without Congressional oversight or the courts. He was beginning to appreciate some of Rachel's ranting. He should have listened to her more attentively.

"Hey, you're waking up, old chap. That's what I've been telling you all these years. The Bush era set some dangerous precedents, and the American people still haven't wised up. Or maybe they just don't care."

"We can't fix the country, but we can do our job and explain what's happening."

"Right on. And your story about Crane could be an important start, Jacoby."

"Do you think you could set it up—I mean, with Yvonne and Emily?"

"I hope so. I'll have to think about it, though. I probably should update Emily about Garon's warning."

"I think she already knows. I heard from her this morning."

"Oh, yeah? Then let her make the decision. My guess is she will see us." He gazed intently at Jacob for a moment as if a new thought had come to him. He smiled. "I'm wondering whether there's another reason why you're so anxious to make a date with Emily." His smile bordered on being a leer.

"No, there isn't," Jacob said with an edge of irritation. His friend had hit a sensitive nerve. "It's just that I'm here, and it seems the right time to do it. And the fact that Garon was so touchy on that subject." He paused to think about Garon's gratuitous doubts about Yvonne. "Do you think Yvy's got mental problems?"

"Of course not. What Garon told you was a bunch of crap. She's a problem for Joshua because at Harvard she became a lefty liberal and a major critic of the administration." They were interrupted by the arrival of coffee and dessert. Mitch lowered his voice. "Recently, she has even become a rather vocal critic of The Crane Corporation. I have no idea how she reconciles her attacks with family loyalty."

"I guess that would be difficult for her."

Mitch glanced at him, with that same smile. "So you are interested—a little? I mean beyond professional?" he asked, trying to play it straight.

"Maybe. How could I not be? After all, she slapped me." It was meant as a joke, but Jacob was half serious.

CHAPTER 7

At the end of a long hall, there was a door labeled "Security Office." The door was always kept locked, and computer card keys were available only to a select few. The codes were changed every month.

Luis Garon, Director of Security, thought of himself as a spy on three levels—within the company to prevent leaks and disloyalty, outside the company to protect the interests and safety of the Crane family, and finally, to provide intelligence on terrorist activity that might affect company operations. He was also a skilled infighter looking after his own interests, and he had a loyal staff to help him. One oil company executive had already been kidnapped by a shadowy group that called itself "Defenders of Islam." Garon did not want that to happen at Crane on his watch. Unlike the government, he knew the territory and had the contacts. His men were all battle hardened, drawn largely from retired Army Special Ops, retired intelligence agents, and a few well-placed Arab informants. Garon regarded most of these men as trustworthy, less apt to gossip about the work, and willing to play rough if necessary. They were distributed throughout company operations. His top assistant was a trusted colleague from Mexico. Because Crane operations were multinational, Garon and his men spent a good deal of time flying about to the other offices—in Mexico City, Baku, and Dubai. He had cultivated allies everywhere.

He went to work for the Cranes immediately after retiring from the Mexican military Secret Service, starting at the office in Mexico City and gradually working his way up. He was noticed by old Joshua for his intelligence background and loyalty and eventually moved to the New York office, the nerve center of the company. As the elder Joshua gradually delegated authority to his son, Garon feared that his fortunes at Crane might be in jeopardy. He had a history with the old man but not with Joshua, Jr. He felt that the younger man did not like or trust him. As a youth, Junior, as he was often called behind his back, had been caught in an indiscretion with a young Mexican woman while working in Mexico. It was Garon who first caught on to the girl. Young Joshua had become involved in an affair and was used by his lover unwittingly as a courier. On several occasions the company jet was used to smuggle cocaine and heroin into the States. Crane had long had an arrangement with Customs in the States to bypass border checkpoints and fly directly to company landing strips in Texas and New Mexico—an arrangement irresistible when discovered by the girlfriend. Joshua, only in his early twenties then, was yanked out of Mexico and severely punished by his father. Garon's role in this was a well-kept secret, but he suspected that somehow Joshua had learned of his involvement.

Because Garon knew all the skeletons, the transition after Joshua, Sr.'s, death had gone smoothly so far. Garon knew that he had an edge and that Joshua had no alternative but to rely on him—at least for the time being. But Garon realized that he had to watch his back, so to speak.

The secure phone shuddered with high-tech intensity. "Luis, we should talk. You had your meeting with that newspaper fellow, ah, Seltzer?" Joshua asked.

"Jacob Sellars, yes." Luis smiled at Joshua's error. Junior was not good at names, particularly of those he didn't like.

"Let's discuss it. Now is as good a time as any."

"I'll be up." Garon enjoyed trips to the posh executive floor. It gave him the feeling of belonging. He regretted that it was too early for a lunch in the private dining room. He took the nonstop, paneled executive elevator to the twenty-fifth floor. The air whistled in the speedy ascent, plugging Garon's ears with the pressure.

Joshua had already moved into his father's spacious office overlooking New York Harbor and the Statue of Liberty in the morning mist. The old man had been one of the first to move back to the neighborhood after September 11, 2001. In a press interview, he had said he would not be "intimidated by a bunch of hoodlums in dresses." Garon smiled with pride at the memory.

"Come in, Luis." Joshua's tone was friendly enough.

Garon had to squint at first in the sunlight that poured in. The sweep of the view always astonished him. The glint of the new Freedom Tower was almost blinding.

"Sit here." Joshua rose, indicating a plush couch against the wall, and then sat across from him in a leather chair. Garon noted that he himself sank low into the cushion at a level beneath Joshua's gaze. "This young man, Sellars, I believe is a political writer who only recently came out of City Hall and the precincts to do the national scene." He smiled. "Inexperienced and perhaps malleable?"

"We need to talk about him, Joshua." Garon had always addressed the younger Crane by his first name, and so far Joshua had not called him on it. But he chose not to disagree with this inaccurate characterization of the reporter, at least directly. In fact, after their lunch together, Garon was worried that he had badly underestimated Sellars.

"He has been writing about national politics for some time and recently during the election. He's done a pretty good job, too, according to his editors."

"You spoke to them?" Joshua seemed wary.

"I wanted to find out how much of a story they planned. You know, in the spirit of cooperation. The guy I talked to was pleasant enough, but didn't give me much. Apparently, the story coming out this week will be a personality piece on the chairman." That's what Garon always called Joshua, Sr. It pleased the old man, and the irony satisfied Garon. The Mao Tse-tung connection was never made. The obscure reference amused Garon, who, as a young man, had been a secret Marxist himself. "Needless to say, we need to follow this closely. With the clamor of other news, Sellars's work could metastasize into trouble."

Joshua cleared his throat. "A graphic way to put it, I must say."

"Sorry." The needle found its target. Joshua had recently experienced a scare about prostate cancer.

"What can we do?"

"Sir, I took the liberty of advising Sellars to stay away from Yvonne—not do interviews with her."

"Whatever for?"

"As you are no doubt aware, sir, she has been, well, getting involved with left-wing people at Harvard and elsewhere. She is talking against the administration and promoting antiwar demonstrations here and abroad. And as you know, she's also critical of the energy industry—even Crane."

Joshua laughed uneasily. "She's been on this kick ever since she got out of college. This is just a phase. We all went through it when we were young."

Garon doubted very much that Joshua had ever been interested in liberal causes during his years at Yale or any other time. In fact, he knew a good deal about Joshua's undistinguished record at college. "That may be true, but there's no point in giving her an audience right now. Come to think of it, that goes for Emily, too."

"I couldn't agree more on Emily," Joshua said with irritation. "That woman needs to be muzzled." He softened. "I mean, she's my flesh and blood, but she's a, uh, she's an embarrassment to the family, parading around in public—among our friends with that, that butch with the chopped-off hair. She's the danger here, not Yvonne. I just found out that she's joined some trouble-making minority shareholders' group. They're gearing up to raise a ruckus at the annual meeting in June."

"I'm following that, Joshua." He smiled. "I've arranged to have an independent group organized to discredit them. We've developed some interesting dossiers on her friends. I think we can handle it."

"Okay, that's good. But how do we keep Sellars away from Emily?"

"And Yvonne," Garon added. "I've put a watch on the situation."

"You mean you've got one of your boys tailing Sellars?"

Garon just stared at him.

"Yeah, I know, deniability and all that. I don't want to know anything about it."

"Good." Garon rose and walked to the windows. "Fantastic view, Joshua."

Joshua resented this familiarity, posturing that would never have taken place with his father. "Tell me more about this guy, uh, Sellars," he continued, not without a trace of irritation.

"He may be more dangerous than I first thought," said Garon, turning away from the vista. "I sense that he will not be a pushover."

"Sense? How so?"

"By his style. He's pushy." Garon's tone was impatient. "It's not what he says so much as how he says it. He's cocky. I doubt we will be able to control his story. We can only hope that it comes out as an innocuous family piece on a back page."

"We are powerless?"

"Well, the press is supposed to be free." Garon chose another chair to sit in to get the sun out of his eyes. "We'll watch and wait, and I'll let you know if there is anything to worry about." Garon got up, wanting to be the one to end their meeting.

"Keep me posted on this, Luis. If things get out of hand, I can always talk to Allen Brown." Joshua returned to his desk and opened some files. "Before you go, Luis, will you be making a trip to Washington soon?"

"No plans at the moment." Garon remembered that Allen Brown, a member of the Crane board, was also on the board of directors of the *News*. He had to admit that was good thinking on Joshua's part.

"Then perhaps you should make one and visit with Jim Hazelton at the agency and just keep him up to date on our, uh, relations with the press. Get some advice from him. They are holding off the press all the time. He might have some ideas. You should alert him to the possibility that Sellars, or someone from his paper, could begin asking questions down there. You know—our government contracts, the CIA. This fellow could get lucky and, ah, uncover something."

Joshua's shrewdness took Garon by surprise. Why hadn't he himself thought of this? "Yeah, I plan to do that," he said quickly. "I'm not sure they'd get much from the agency, but they might well go to the Hill and talk to the Democratic staff of the Intelligence Committee."

"Yeah, maybe we should touch base there too, among our friends. You can get some help from our government relations people. Talk to Ron."

"Yeah, I'll do that, and we'll get right on it." Garon headed for the door, pleased that Joshua seemed to be paying more attention to security than he had anticipated. He may have underestimated the kid.

"And one other thing, Luis. You should know that it was Henry Mitchel who brought Sellars to Nantucket. He's close to Emily. They are two of a kind, as you probably know. Mitch and Sellars are longtime friends, but Sellars himself is not gay."

"Mitchel brought Sellars to the party?"

"It was not a party, Luis. It was a, uh, a memorial gathering for my father." He said it sharply. He had caught Garon in an indiscretion.

Even Garon's dark skin flushed with embarrassment at his faux pas. "Of course. So that's how Sellars got in."

"Didn't you have one of your people there?" Joshua loved catching Garon like this.

"I did. But apparently, he didn't make the connection."

"It occurs to me that Mitchel may be helping Sellars with family connections. It's just something you should be aware of." Joshua returned to his papers, signifying their meeting was over, satisfied that he had gained the upper hand with Garon. Joshua thought this kind of employee had to be put down when the chance presented itself. He didn't like Garon and was already looking for a way to replace him.

That same night, Jacob called Rachel again. They were having a somewhat inconclusive chat when his phone began to blink with a message. Jacob promised to call her back, but she said not to bother. It was too late.

"Jacob," Mitch rasped. "Have you noticed anyone following you?"

"For heaven's sake, no. Why do you ask?" Jacob was astonished at the question.

"Emily called me, when she couldn't reach you. You got her message?"

"I did. That was early this morning. She wanted to tell me I'd be hearing from Garon. It was a heads up."

"She had more to say to me but didn't want to leave it on your voice mail. She thinks Garon has put a tail on you. I don't know how she knows this, but she has her own spies inside the company. She says they always tail her—or at least they do from time to time. They aren't very smart though. She loses them easily." He chuckled. "She doesn't use her car. She just hops a subway car or a cab and shakes the guy. Anyway, we've got to be careful. Emily agrees we should not meet at her place and has suggested a friend's house on Beacon Hill, which isn't far from your hotel. Tomorrow for lunch, okay?"

"Sure." Jacob was picturing himself as a spy in a foreign country, skulking around in a trench coat. The thought was both worrisome and exciting. "This is getting to be like James Bond."

"Yeah, sort of," Mitch said sourly. "I'll pick you up. I'll show you some tricks. It will be a good test of whether you're being followed."

"Why would they be tailing me?"

"I can only guess that they are very sensitive about your talking to the family—you know, like Garon said."

"And if I do?"

"They can't do much about Emily except discredit her. Yvonne they can spirit away."

"Would she go?"

"Only if her father tempted her with a nice trip—like to Paris, which she loves. But I really don't know what they'd do. It's not out of the question that they would complain to your editor that you were stalking Yvonne, or something like that. Or they might even get the government involved."

"They would do that, go that far?" Jacob was astounded at the idea. Much later, he would learn that Mitch's speculation was not so bizarre.

"Well, maybe. Seems to me they may have something to hide, don't you think?"

Jacob pondered the possibilities. If Mitch was right, it must be something major. The idea of lurking figures under streetlights was disconcerting. "Maybe I'll walk around a little before it gets too late. You know, see if there is someone following me now. Of course, I could just look out the window. I can see the front door from my room."

Mitch began to laugh. "Don't play James Bond. You won't find out that way. Just wait until tomorrow. We'll know soon enough. See you at noon. I'll ring your room."

Jacob felt his heart beating a little faster than normal. What had he gotten himself into? He glanced at his watch. It was just eleven. He needed a walk anyway.

A cold east wind chilled and dampened the air in the empty streets. There was no sign of anyone lingering. So Jacob began to walk down Boylston Street, normally busy but now quiet except for a stray pedestrian or two and an occasional car drifting by. He stopped and looked in store windows like he had seen them do in the movies, glancing back to check. But there was no one and no idling car. It was probably too late. If there had been someone, he had gone home to his wife and children. For Jacob, that was a comforting thought—to think of the tail as a benign family man.

The next morning, Jacob puttered around his room, making notes on his computer and washing out socks and underwear. On his trips he always packed light, and if he was gone too long, he rotated clothes to the bathroom sink. It was an old travel habit. Mitch arrived at noon as promised, and they walked out of the hotel together, both watchful, but trying not to be obvious about it. As they crossed the street, Mitch noticed a dark overcoat keeping pace on the opposite sidewalk. Recrossing several times, the overcoat always chose the other side but followed relentlessly. They had their man. Mitch thought he saw a second man, but this one turned a corner and was gone.

"The subway station is just ahead," Mitch warned quietly. "I'll lead the way. I have our fare cards. Come on!" He sprinted ahead. "We've got to be quick."

Crossing at the next corner, Mitch ducked down the covered stairway to the underground and Jacob followed. Mitch knew his way, and they moved fast, passing through the turnstiles and catching a trolley that was already stopped in the station. As the car began to roll, Jacob caught a glimpse of the dark overcoat running down the narrow platform.

"We did it!" cried Mitch. "Did you see him?"

"Yeah, I think so—chasing the train?" Jacob was out of breath, more from the excitement than the chase.

"Yeah, but he missed it." They took a seat near the front. "We'll get off at the Museum and take a train back in the other direction. It'll take us to Beacon, close to where we're going." He slapped Jacob on the knee, pleased with himself. The reverse ride was a short one.

They descended Beacon Hill from the stop at Park Street until they reached a red-brick row house halfway down the hill. "This is it. Come on."

Mitch rang the bell, and they were admitted by an aproned black lady whose face was beaming. "Land sakes, Mr. Mitch, you sure are a stranger 'round here. Ain't seen you in a long time. Let me take your coats. Miss Emily is upstairs waitin' on you." She eyed Jacob. "You must be Mr. Seldon."

"Sellars," Jacob corrected. "Jacob Sellars." Jacob was amazed at finding such a relic of a servant—shiny black dress and lacy apron. It was a vision from the past—certainly not his past, but a storybook past, and not even of Boston—more likely Charleston. But this was the home of abolition he reminded himself.

They had been ushered into an English basement of the old-fashioned townhouse. The living spaces were on the upper floors. They climbed the staircase and were met by Emily at the top. She greeted them warmly.

"It's good to see you two troublemakers again. Hope you weren't followed. Come in and have a glass of wine." She turned to Jacob. "Do you like red or white?"

"There was one of Garon's apes, but we lost him," Mitch interjected. "I'll take white."

"Oh, good." She glanced at Jacob expectantly.

"White would be fine." Another maid, this one very "old country," took their orders. This was an equal opportunity household, Jacob mused wryly.

"Yvonne is late, of course." She took a seat on an ornate old couch from another era, as was the rest of the decor. With a sweep of her hand, she invited them to sit. "So, you were followed." She looked troubled.

"Yeah, but we took your tack and lost him easily."

"I don't think they know about this place. But just the same, I wish she'd get here soon." There was a commotion downstairs. "Ah, here she is now."

Jacob could feel the tension in his chest. The "she" turned out to be Yvonne. He was surprised at his own excitement. Materializing from a side door and still in her coat, she announced, "I'm cold. Don't they ever turn up the heat? Can we light a fire in that thing?" She pointed at the darkened fireplace, which had been laid with a layer of cordwood. Emily rose regally and greeted her. "Yvonne, where are your manners? We have guests, as you know."

Yvonne was wearing a long black coat, which she hugged around herself. "Hi," she said, offering a cold hand to Jacob. Then smiling, she continued, "I think I owe you an apology. I wasn't exactly cool the last time we met."

Jacob took her hand and held it for a moment. "No, you weren't. But then I wasn't either." She took her hand back and shrugged out of her coat. She was more striking than Jacob had remembered—a model's slender, long-limbed figure. Her jet-black hair was straight and swept back into a generous ponytail, which she flung about as she got out of her coat. Her dark skin was luminous, and her big, flashing eyes, with only a hint of makeup, were widely set in an expression that suggested a free spirit. A prominent nose and high cheekbones added an austere look. But when she smiled, it was that same crooked smile, and her expression softened, giving her an innocence of someone younger than her age. Jacob couldn't decide which parent she favored.

"Want me to light the damn fire?" she asked, not waiting for a reply. "Ah, there's a Cape Cod lighter. That makes it easy." She lifted the brass-handled stone from the kerosene, and Jacob bent to light it. He could smell her perfume and feel the attraction of her presence. Yvonne placed the flame under the logs, and the fire began to crackle immediately. Straightening up, she gazed at him intently with slightly raised eyebrows. "Thanks."

Jacob had to look away. "The fire's a nice idea."

"Yeah, it's an idea that has been around a long time, Jacob." He was pleased that she had remembered his name. "It nourishes our primitive side."

Emily asked that lunch be served, and the maid brought trays of soup and delicate sandwiches to the large dining room. They sat informally around the mahogany table bantering about mundane matters and getting to know one another. Jacob was impressed with the quiet elegance of the setting.

Emily picked at her food while guiding casual conversation through the weather and questions about Jacob's life on the farm. After lunch, they adjourned to the living room where coffee was served. Done with the luncheon amenities, Emily got down to business.

"Well, we have serious matters to discuss with you, Mr. Sellars," said Emily. "I would like to start this off with some background." Mitch left the table and stood at a large bay window, where he surveyed the street below. Yvonne flopped down on a billowy antique couch.

"I need plenty of that," Jacob said agreeably, taking the far end of the same couch. Emily and Mitch moved to the wingback chairs, which, along with a handsome sideboard, completed the rather austere decor of the large room.

"Look, Jacob—may I call you that?"

"By all means. I've been called a lot worse."

"We Cranes—we are a family in the glare of unwanted publicity, for better or worse." Emily's expression was grave. "Joshua is dead, and the scavengers in the press—no insult intended, Jacob—are out looking for news, as they should be. They are going to find out things about us, about the company. After a lot of soul-searching, I've decided—Yvonne and I have decided—that the best way to save the family is to tell our side of the story first. Joshua, Jr., won't do that. He has chosen, ah, to just hunker down and ride out the storm. We can't reach him now. He won't talk to us. He has all the power but doesn't know what to do with it. And, unfortunately, he's getting bad advice. Most of all we are worried about his involvement with the government, particularly the one we have now.

"Let's begin by making one thing clear. Joshua Crane was a great builder but was impatient with rules. He was careless of the law and took risks to build big. Unlike others—the people at Enron and Tyco, for example—he was not greedy. This may sound strange to you, but Father didn't care about money much. He just wanted to be the biggest and the best at finding oil, getting it out of the ground, and moving it to market. He liked the rough-and-tumble of discovery and drilling. He was an oil man in the truest sense. A bit of an anachronism today. Maybe it was the whaling in his genes. That was a dangerous game, too. He made deals and accommodations he shouldn't have. Unfortunately, he died before he had finished his plans." She turned to Yvonne. "Yvy, you should jump in anytime you want to."

"No, you're doing fine."

Jacob thought of Ahab. Was the pursuit of this kind of oil also an obsession? Was the oil itself the evil, destroying countries and spreading poison around the world? The comparison seemed appropriate.

"Sitting by watching has become very difficult for us. But your arrival on the scene got us thinking. You have given us an opportunity to tell our story, maybe change things. But we want it told with dignity." For a moment she studied him. "Mitch has given us hope that we can trust you." She took a deep breath. "Unfortunately, we are not without our own, ah, foibles and will be attacked by the media personally. You already know that I am gay. I don't hide it. Both Yvonne and I have been active in some left-wing causes, and we have been openly critical of the company and the oil industry in general. We're serious people, Jacob. No matter what you may have heard, Yvonne is not a party girl. She is a fighter." She glanced at her niece.

"Sadly, we are also outsiders in our own family. My brother is alienated. We have been shut out. Our father had the old-fashioned idea that women didn't belong in offices. So, he chose Josh to be the one to take over the company. We suspect that Josh is just beginning to realize that he may not be up to the job. We see this in his vindictiveness and anger—mostly with us. Frankly, I think Father, himself, had doubts about him as a leader. And it is a tragedy that he left things as he did. He just dumped the entire family wealth and responsibility in Josh's hands. With our father dead, Joshua cannot control the people working for him. We are getting troublesome reports from our friends. We're concerned that a few bad sorts—some of them outsiders—have taken effective control over some aspects of the company. They are devious and secretive, and their adventures and schemes will ultimately destroy the company. One of them you have already met—that scoundrel, Luis Garon. He is a minor player, but he has entirely too much power. We don't have the votes to stop him. He has become Josh's Iago," she added. "Our only recourse is to go public with our story." She paused, obviously emotional about the path she had chosen. "If in the process Josh gets hurt, it is regrettable. But it may be the only way to save the family and the company." She folded her hands in her lap and studied Jacob and then Mitch. "So, where do we begin? You are the writer. We have the story for you. Now it's up to you."

Jacob cleared his throat, not really sure of where to go. His small article in the personality section had suddenly grown insignificant, irrelevant. These people were putting their lives in his hands. But she really hadn't told him much. What were these devious unnamed company and outside officials trying to accomplish? Was there a government connection? He could feel Mitch staring at him expectantly. He needed answers. But he needed their confidence first, to make them comfortable with him as their voice.

"Well, it's a little hard to evaluate the concept without the details, but I have some thoughts on how we might approach the story. My assignment was to write a short profile of the family and the company. It is not an investigative job. As a matter of fact, I already did a piece on the funeral." Returning to his original proposal to Emily, Jacob continued, "That kind of fluff won't help you at all. What you are suggesting, I assume, is a much more ambitious project. It would take time to put together. I'd need a lot of facts. And even then, I'm not sure it will accomplish what you have in mind. What you are asking me to do is—and I hate the term—an exposé. That's a big deal in journalism—I mean to do an exposé in the best tradition of that genre in the media. The facts must be reliable and the story credible."

"That's exactly what I want, but a credible one, as you say. And I like the idea of your doing this on your own instead of for the paper. I just want it done with dignity for the family. We're prepared to handle the consequences. I realize that it involves some serious risks for you. You don't have to come up with a plan now. All I need to know is whether this is a feasible idea."

"It may be," Jacob said, not without some doubts. "I'll have to think about that. It's something I can do, but I need information from people who have firsthand knowledge of what is going on. If they're all hostile, it will be difficult. It can't be a 'he said, she said' kind of thing."

"They are not all hostile," Emily said with emphasis. "Some will help us."

"That may be critical."

Jacob glanced at Yvonne, whose eyes were fixed on him. "What about you, Yvonne? Is this what you want, too?"

"Of course. I agree with Emily. We've discussed it."

"From what you say, Emily, we can expect problems with your brother. I've been asked specifically not to interview family members, particularly you, Yvonne. You know they're watching me closely." Jacob smiled. "For example, your father might just send you away—say, to France."

Yvonne looked surprised. "What makes you say that?"

"It was mentioned."

"I wouldn't go anywhere I didn't want to," she scoffed angrily.

"You'd refuse to go?" Jacob asked doubtfully.

"Yes. I would," she said. "Unless I wanted to anyway." His questions had clearly irritated her. "What difference would it make where I was? I can't be muzzled. Hey, are you stalling?" she asked with a faint smile, maybe just teasing.

"Yvy," crooned Emily soothingly. "Calm down. Jacob has not refused."

"He's stalling."

"You're being uncool again, Yvonne." Jacob tried to coax her smile back. But there was no softening her. "Mitch thinks they might accuse me of stalking you."

"That's absurd," she said, laughing in spite of herself. "I have strong feelings about our company, our family, and this country. I find it all disturbing, over the top." Yvonne eyed him and smiled slyly. "Stalking me, huh. That's rich." The diversion had cooled her off.

"Okay, can either of you tell me any of what is going on—at the company?" Ignoring Yvonne's last comment, Jacob turned to Emily. "Like, who is taking over and why? Even if it is just suspicion."

This time, Yvonne answered. "It's pretty simple, actually." It seemed like a put-down. "The Crane Corporation has become part of the defense establishment—that's what's happening. It's become politicized. It's like they are getting private enterprise to do government work. I just found out that the administration has been using the Boeing aircraft manufacturer for those CIA torture flights—you know, when they fly suspected terrorists to other countries to be tortured. They call it rendition. Then there are the private security companies that send their goons to protect the oil fields and provide security for Iraqi leaders. There's no accountability for any of this. It's obscene!

"And now Crane has set up an affiliate in the Middle East that is a front for the CIA. Ostensibly, it is brokering the sale of Iraqi oil. But a lot of those oil profits are being diverted to other purposes—we don't know what. Hundreds of millions—billions—have just disappeared. That's even been in the press. Crane makes money on the sales, of course. We are pretty sure this money is held in the company accounts. It has a lot of cash built up. Company people, like Garon and his goons, snoop around trying to find insurgents and outside terrorists and, at the same time, spy on the local governments. Crane has been used in the past as a government stooge in Mexico. It's the American way of controlling the oil supply. That's what the Iraqi invasion was all about—oil." She shook her head with disgust. Her animated anger made her even more alluring. "Crane has become a tool in all this. It's our name, and it stinks." Overcome with emotion, she paused and then added, "You know, oil has corrupted this family. Oil corrupts everyone it touches. It's much worse than drugs. It corrupts every country that has it. Eventually, it will corrupt the world. What we need is a war on oil before there is a war for oil."

"Can you prove any of this—I mean, The Crane Corporation's being used by the government?" Jacob was taken aback by the jumble of claims and how much these two knew, or had guessed.

"We can't prove anything in the courtroom sense. No one has volunteered to be a witness. Anyway, when it does come up, everyone trots out national security—'it's top secret; you can't touch it.' Ask Amos Coffin. He'll tell you how it all started years ago in Mexico and Cuba. He'll tell you. That's where it started."

"He did, in a way."

"You've seen him? You've talked to him?"

"Yes, a little."

"You move fast, Sellars."

Jacob couldn't tell whether this was meant as a compliment or not. "He's pretty reticent about the past, I'm afraid—at least with me. Anyway, he's leaving soon to sail around the world. He won't be available."

Yvonne turned to Emily. "He knows a lot, doesn't he, Emily?" There was a hint of uncertainty in her question.

"Maybe," Emily said. "Amos knows some interesting things, but that all happened years ago. Things have changed since then. A few in the company have come to us with concerns. In all honesty, Jacob, we don't really know for sure what's going on. The things Yvonne has told you have come to us as angry accusations. We can't be sure what the motives are behind the stories. And as Yvy says, when we ask for specifics, everything is blocked by 'national security.'

Joshua certainly won't help. He doesn't want to rock the boat. Management isn't going to open its own Pandora's box. I suppose we could make our claims to you based on this flimsy stuff, go on the record, and just get out the facts as we know them, as we have been told. Let them attack us in the courts, in the press, and maybe it all comes out. They would have to address our contentions openly." Jacob guessed Emily had thought this through, possibly with a lawyer. But he thought it necessary to add some caution.

"The trouble is if there are no facts, it's just speculation and hearsay until you have witnesses or can document your claims. Your opponents would attack you personally. It could get very ugly. And then there's the security issue. You may run into problems under the law, as you say, with the Patriot Act. There are some nasty amendments. Even Garon has warned us, or me, at least." Jacob reminded himself that he needed to educate himself on the amendments. "I think Mitch is more up on the Patriot Act than I am."

"Well, I know this much," Mitch said. "For the first time in our history, it will limit the extent to which citizens can speak out against government policy on national security matters. It gives the Attorney General all kinds of powers to stop opposition, disclosure—even criticism. People can be wiretapped and detained without access to an attorney, even without any specific charges being made. It's awful and should be unconstitutional under normal circumstances—but not now. It's getting to be like martial law."

Yvonne cursed. "That's what I'm talking about. This country is a police state."

Mitch laughed. "Not quite, Yvy, but we're getting there."

"It isn't funny, Mitch."

The quieter voice of Emily intervened. "Jacob, we know about the risks, and we are willing to take them. Whatever the price is, we need to do this—for the family."

"Let me ask an unpleasant question," Jacob interjected. "There has also been talk—more rumors than anything else—about bribery of foreign governments and the like. These kinds of charges are beyond national security. They are statutory crimes. Can this be documented by anyone in the company—on the record?"

"In the past, J. C. did some of those things," Emily explained. "He broke the law for Crane to make it the largest in its field. A big powerful corporation with global interests was to be his legacy to us. The morals of his forebears were no better when they traded in slaves." She allowed herself to become wistful for a moment. "Anyway," she continued, "anything illegal now would, as we've said, be classified as secret. I'm guessing that the company's reputation for this kind of behavior has been useful to the government."

Jacob was impressed with her argument. But Luis Garon, his arrogance, self-importance, and the veiled threats made him angry. He thought about the people assigned to follow him around town, the intimidation tactics. The threatened strong-arm tactics were repugnant. He was beginning to feel like an alien in his own country. There was something very un-American about all this. His caution began to slip away. He was moved by the intense pride of this old New England family.

"Look, this might be perfect as a magazine story, as a sort of memorial to your father and an important exposé at the same time. If we can get some facts, we could build the story of Crane around a theme. I'll try to rough it out as a history of the family, with whaling and the slave trade as background and Joshua, Sr., as a heroic character in today's world. Living dangerously is an American trait, but selling out is not. Our thesis should be that your father was a patriot who trusted his country and would never sell out the Crane name. That kind of behavior just does not fit his image. It was the administration which was abusing that trust for its own cheap political ends. That's a rough idea of how this could be presented—very rough, of course. If we can get backup for what we say, I can think of several publications that would go for it—even if it is, well, lightly corroborated. But we will need the people who you are in contact with to come forward, or we'll have to find other sources. We need facts. I hate the term, but 'a smoking gun' is what I mean. It's going to take some research."

"It's a good approach. I like it," Emily said with a pleased smile. "I hope we can fit into that ambitious mold. We'll just have to see." Her voice trailed off in uncertainty. "And I worry about the bad things. We can't sugarcoat too much. Joshua Crane was not an angel, you know."

"But your father was very American. Entrepreneurial escapades, even immoral ones, are part of our history—the robber barons, remember? We forgive trespasses in the pursuit of enterprise in this country. In fact, we take pride in them. Think about building the railroads, the start of the steel industry, the oil industry—they were all pirates, and we love to read about them. Nothing is more American!" Jacob was getting caught up in his own rhetoric. "It immediately gets the readers on your side. And remember, many Americans don't think that Ken Lay or Martha Stewart should have been punished. And America loves mea culpas. This could be a silver lining to the story, with the government as the true villain."

"I'm not as proud as you are of what you call American ways," Yvonne said, unable to hold back her crooked smile. "You are clever. But I'm not as pleased by U.S. history as you seem to be. It has been so dressed up and misrepresented that Americans know little about their past—like our own holocaust in wiping out a whole race of Native Americans with our smallpox and violence, Polk's invasion of Mexico, our rape of the Philippines, and on and on. Anyway, I like your approach." Her first positive comment pleased Jacob.

"Why don't we all sleep on this," Emily said, "think it over, and write down our thoughts. We'll consider your approach, Jacob, talk to our friends in the company, and then see where we are. We can meet again. I don't think we should be deterred by Josh's spies either. If they want to follow us around, let them do it. It is better that we are open about meeting. So far, they don't have spies who can tell them what we are planning. Even if they were to find out, perhaps it will slow them down a bit. Who knows?"

Jacob admired Emily's courage as well as her judgment. "Okay. Sounds good. I'll need time, whatever it takes, to get a better idea of what the article will look like and do some digging on my own. And when we're ready, we can explore our options with magazines. I'll have some ideas on that. In the meantime, try to convince your contacts to talk facts."

Emily stood to indicate the meeting was over. She offered her hand. "Thank you, Jacob. It's been good of you to listen to us. I do hope that we can work something out." They shook hands. She signaled the maid to bring their coats. "Mitch, please stay on a bit. I want to chat with you," Emily said.

Yvonne led the way down the stairs to the front door, and she and Jacob left. The sun had fallen behind the buildings, and the air had turned crisp. They walked in silence down the rest of Beacon Hill. Being with her made him tongue-tied, like a first date. It was silly—and at his age! But his mind was blanked out. Suddenly she broke the spell. "See that hotel?"

A red awning was coming into view a few blocks ahead. Jacob could just make out the name. He had to clear his throat to respond. "Yeah, the Hampshire House?"

"It's famous. You know what was filmed there?"

"No."

"*Cheers.* Remember the show, many years ago?" She gave him a pat on the back. "Maybe before your time."

"Very funny. You mean the TV show?"

"It's a neat place. Want to look in? I'm starving. It was a puny lunch."

"I should be getting back to see if my office has called."

"Can't they call you on your cell?"

"I didn't bring it."

"That was dumb." She laced her arm into his and steered him into the hotel. He went along reluctantly. "I have a lot to tell you—a lot to get off my chest, if we are going to do business together."

"Okay," he agreed, not trying very hard to resist. Shanahan could wait. He did wonder how he would break the news about his project. He was sure that a freelance job would not go down well. But he knew that he had to disclose his intent soon. In any event, it was better to put it off until he could come up with some ideas Emily liked. When they all had agreed, he'd call Shanahan.

Yvonne headed in without waiting for the maitre d'. The decor of the place was more on the elegant side, not at all like the singles bar of the television show and obviously updated several times since then. They slipped in on opposite sides of a plush booth. "Let's have some wine. That pallid white of Emily's friend Gloria was shit."

"I thought it was pretty good."

She ignored the comment and ordered a bottle of Merlot and some snacks. "Now tell me, are you really from the Midwest?"

"Born and raised in Appleton, Illinois. Went to college at the University of Illinois."

"My God."

"It's not that bad."

She examined him critically. "Well, you do look kinda corn-fed, the picture of health and self-righteousness."

"You know, keep this up and you might get to slap me again." Jacob laughed.

"Only if you are scathingly insulting."

"Is that what I was the last time?"

"Yes, you were."

"You can dish it out but you can't take it?"

"How old are you?"

"None of your business."

"It's my business if you work for me—for us."

"I'm not going to work for you. I am a journalist."

"Okay. Gotta be independent. I understand."

"I appreciate that. I'm thirty-six. And you?"

"I'm twenty-four, but people tell me I'm old for my age."

"What's this radical stuff I hear about you?"

"I'll tell you. But first you tell me—do you really believe in what you say in some of your columns about the Constitution being corrupted by this government and the last one?"

"I'd write it only if I believed it." He was pleased that she had actually read his turgid political prose.

She studied him. "Do you believe what we're telling you?"

"I do. When it comes to our government and oil, it doesn't take much to make me a believer. However, there is something unique about your grandfather's life, unique to America. His story has an appealing entrepreneurial quality. I meant what I said. He came late to the energy business and had to fight his way up, against all the established titans of the industry. That's gutsy. As I said, it's a great American story."

"My God, you're an idealist?"

"Probably."

"What are you—what are your politics?"

"Golly, am I defined by my politics?"

"Yes. So what are you?"

"You mean what party?"

"You're being evasive."

"And you're aggressive."

"Republican or Democrat?"

"I don't know, Yvy—you don't mind if I call you that?"

"No. You don't vote with a party?"

"I think the last time I registered I put down Independent."

"God. I can't believe it. You probably voted for that asshole Perot."

Jacob laughed. "I don't think I was voting when he ran."

"So, are you apolitical?" she asked, disapprovingly.

"Yes. I'm afraid I am. Agnostic, too. Now, how about answering my question. How did a rich girl like you get hooked on left-wing causes?

"Being rich and a girl, as you call me, do not preclude me from supporting liberal principles."

She ignored the rest of his question and, fumbling around in her purse, found a crumpled newspaper clipping. She smoothed it out on the table. "This is your article on the funeral. It's nice. You write well." She gazed at him. "You left out our little scene."

"Disappointed?"

"No. I'm glad you did. In fact, you treated me a lot better than I deserved."

"Back to the left-wing causes," Jacob insisted. "Why a liberal? What does that mean to you?"

"It's a label that doesn't mean much anymore. Maybe, the old-fashioned rebel is better." She became thoughtful. "I believe—and thank God I'm not alone—that our country is making big mistakes which will change the shape of the world for years to come. And I feel really strongly about it. It bothers me that we, the Crane family and our company, are part of it."

"You're talking about the Iraq war?"

"More than that. But since you brought it up, it wasn't a war. We invaded a weak, defenseless, third-world country—in violation of international law. We did it with the largest, most expensive military in the world—and all for a lie. That's not a war. It was an ugly pushover. Then Bush, dressed up in his little ballbuster flight suit, announced on the staged aircraft carrier, 'Hey, mission accomplished! I did what my daddy couldn't do.' Great! It turns out that there were no weapons of any kind of mass destruction. It was more like mass deception. In fact, Iraq was not even a threat in its own neighborhood. Bush and his people lied about nuclear stuff like centrifuge tubes and yellow-cake uranium, flying drones that could carry nukes to this country, mobile labs to make poison gas—it all turned out to be lies, outright, barefaced lies. And we've now lost almost eight thousand young people—and tens of thousands wounded, maimed horribly. A lot of Iraqis have died too, maybe as many as half a million. And the entire Middle East is on fire with hatred and vengeance. We've concocted a dangerous policy that will let us do this again and again. And if we don't do it, our client state, Israel, is ready to go with an army supplied by us. Any country we say is a threat to our oil supply, true or not, we just invade them and change the government by installing our stooges. We make it our banana republic. That's the way we're going to protect our oil for greedy Americans who consume 30 percent of the world's oil with only 5 percent of the population.

"You know, we couldn't have helped bin Laden and other jihad radicals more. America is their best ally. In fact, people don't even remember that al Qaeda was encouraged and armed by the U.S. to fight the Russians in Afghanistan. After that little war, bin Laden started to mobilize a jihad against his own country. He didn't like the way Saudi Arabia was occupied by the U.S. and became a toady of the oilmen. He wanted them kicked out and not much else to start with. So he blew up the U.S. Army barracks there.

"Right after the World Trade Center went down, much of the Islamic world was sympathetic to the U.S. The invasion turned them all against us. Be careful what you wish for. All that phony talk before the invasion about Iraq's becoming a hotbed of terror. It came true. Bush made it come true."

"A lot of people agree with you now, Yvy." He was amazed at how informed she was.

"Yeah, but too late. Before the invasion, there was credible intelligence that weapons did not exist in Iraq. The inspections had worked. There was also a lot of advice inside the government that an invasion would be disastrous. So Cheney and others ignored it all and made up their own fairy tales. And sure, now there's a bunch of intelligence reports, books galore that tell the story." She sipped at her wine. "These Bush neocons had no sense of history."

"You have time to read history?" It was a kidding remark, but it didn't stop her.

"Some, yes. Enough to know the difference between Sunnis and Shiites—a distinction that the neocon brains never had much curiosity about. And if they'd taken the time to learn a little about that part of the world, it would have given them more than a hint of what might come after the invasion."

He racked his own memory for a reconstruction of the early split in Islam. "You mean the schism after Mohammed's death, the murders?"

"Yeah, as a matter of fact, that's where it starts."

He could tell that he had surprised her. Jacob smiled and admitted, "But I can't remember all the permutations of that history, except that it was complicated. All I do know is that the Shiites' favorite guy was offed by people who turned out to be Sunnis."

Yvonne beamed. "God, Sellars, I'm impressed. At least you're curious."

"But I'm not sure how it's relevant today."

"It is. Go back and read about it again."

Jacob laughed. "I don't have time."

She ignored his comment and continued on another angle. "And the most shocking thing is most Americans think that it's okay to be ignorant. The propaganda of the administration is so effective that people are easily led to believe lies—like most thought that it was Iraq and Iraqis who brought down the World Trade Center. Say it often enough and they'll believe it. Preposterous! That's how Hitler deceived the German people during World War II. We have a history of the same kind of arrogance. But this is the worst. It's doubly bad because we're losing democracy here at home. We can't even vote them out of office. If they're threatened, they manipulate the vote by cheating at the polls with high-tech manipulations. And if they lose, they get their Supreme Court to fix the election."

"Well, you can't fool the people forever. It looks like the country is catching on."

"No, they're not—not at all. Voting has become a useless exercise, a distraction. The corporate media controls what is said. Corporate money controls what is done. The oil, drug, insurance, banks, and chemical companies, along with the military-industrial complex, pay for and own the government, even the press. The voting public is told how to vote and what to think by what amounts to a government propaganda office—right there in the White House. People are lazy and don't seem to mind. Only half the people even bother to vote. Can you believe that at a time like this? Even poor countries get better turnouts."

"Sadly, that's true."

"Glad you agree."

"But I think the press is not so happy these days. They're feeling they've been had. That's what I meant about catching on. It's mainly happening in the press. It's a start."

"Yeah, it should be a wake-up call. Still, the press is easily intimidated. When a newspaper does print stories about illegal things the administration is doing, like snooping or torture, flunkies in the White House trot out the national security flag and accuse the press of helping the enemy. The White House reporters are cowed, and Congress is just a great big cheering section."

Her picture seemed overly bleak to Jacob. "Both parties are talking of withdrawal now. There seems to be a growing consensus. And don't forget, the Democrats even tried to impeach Bush and Cheney."

"And they paid dearly for it, didn't they? They lost the election. Now, they're being *so* cautious. This president has built up a 70 percent approval rating and continues to trot out the old bullshit line 'if you don't agree, you're unpatriotic.' And, yeah, there is a lot of talk about withdrawal of the troops. But, you know, we'll never pull out completely. We've spent huge sums on building military bases in Iraq. Oh, we'll get our troops out of the big cities, and some will come home, but the occupation will go on—for years. It's just a new kind of colonialism—all in the name of U.S. security. And the funny thing is the Democrats want these bases, too."

She didn't even stop to take a breath. "They're so busy making America safer they're overlooking what makes it a target. No one is attacking their premise." She sighed and sat back, finally worn out by her own screed.

"Do you ever share these thoughts with your father?" Jacob asked.

"I try, and he's beginning to listen. But he says he can't get into this stuff right now. And you know why? They've got him. At least, he thinks he's trapped."

Then, shifting gears abruptly, she asked, "Have you heard of the Berkeley Group?"

"Yeah. They're part of some kind of military enterprise fund, aren't they?"

"They own interests in those kinds of companies. A lot of insiders sit on the board. It's a very powerful lobby. They have their hands all over the reconstruction of Iraq. Well, Berkeley has bought stock in Crane—just all of a sudden. Right after that, Emily heard gossip that one of the Crane subsidiaries is a front for the CIA, spying on the Middle East countries not in the fold. Of course, they can't do much about Iran. The idea is to pick off a regime with mercenaries and then use the resources of the country to pay for oil and gas development, using mostly U.S. contractors. I'm afraid Crane may be into that. Maybe it's an exaggeration. I hope so."

"This story gets more and more elaborate." Jacob was beginning to wonder whether Emily and Yvonne were making this stuff up. "I don't suppose there's any proof of this either?"

"Is that sarcasm?"

"No, it's the reporter asking."

"We're telling you what we've heard." She sniffed in exasperation.

She paused while the waitress replenished their canapés. She picked at the crackers and sipped her wine, but she couldn't stop herself. "Did you know that the second-largest force in Iraq right now is the private American army of mercenaries, the private security companies? Crane could be among them. These guys have no accountability. The biggest one is Blackwater Corporation. The government pays them hundreds of millions each year for the jobs soldiers should be doing. And the army could do it a lot cheaper. As private contractors, they aren't even subject to Iraqi laws. Most of these guys are former military, special-ops guys." She paused to catch her breath. "This is the kind of thing Emily and I are worried about Crane's being drawn into. It's why we need you. People come to us from the company. They e-mail us, they phone us—all secretly." She shrugged. "Maybe they're all lying—I don't know."

She sighed with resignation and smiled weakly. "I've talked too much. This whole country is just a humongous mess, Jacob. The system feeds on itself. It's self-perpetuating. We just can't let our name be dragged into it." She drained her glass and poured more wine for them both.

"You paint a pretty dreadful picture. But on your point about Crane, why would the government choose Crane?"

"Because it's not a big name. By comparison, Crane is small and malleable. It has problems from the past. So, it is also vulnerable. And the company knows the business and has contacts. That's why it's a perfect tool."

"This is pretty extreme stuff, Yvy."

"Yeah, well, it fits into the strategy like a glove. And it gets worse. Crane's Russian oil interests in the Sakhalin fields could be used for an attack on North Korea."

"Good heavens, Yvonne, aren't you going a little overboard?"

"Maybe," she sighed. "But I have a lot of friends who don't think so."

"You mean the people at Crane?"

"No. The people we're talking to are from these countries. There is a group … I can't tell you much about it."

"You've asked for my help."

"I know. But this is off-limits. Anyway, I'm only on the outside looking in. And I actually don't know that much about them. I just hear about it, you know, what they're saying."

"Okay." She had insinuated her little bombshell but would not share. "What can we talk about?" It was hard to conceal his irritation.

"You're angry."

"A little. Look at it from my point of view. Here's a young graduate student making extravagant, grandiose assertions of international intrigue and telling me that she can't reveal her sources. She wants me to save her family from future threats described by people who are anonymous. That's a pretty untenable situation for a journalist."

"I've talked too much. It's my fault. It's true I can't prove any of this to you." She spread her hands on the table in frustration and then gave Jacob that engaging crooked smile. "You'll have to provide the facts, be an investigative reporter. There has to be something to back me up. Like you say, there must be a smoking gun. It's all homegrown, Jacob. The bad stuff does not come from foreigners. It's driven by Washington, people who call themselves neocons. They impressed Dick Cheney with their tough talk, which was an easy sell to a shallow, incurious president. They must have left a trail.

"All these guys are followers of Leo Strauss, the dead professor from the University of Chicago. I tried to read his last book, *Natural Rights and Democracy*, but gave up halfway into it." She shook her head in wonder. "Very heavy reading. But the neocons found something in Strauss they liked, and they ran with it. He preached the virtues of democracy for the world, but not at the end of an assault rifle. After the riots of the 1960s, Strauss's views were interpreted—most say distorted—to support the rejection of liberals and what he calls their moral relativism—you know, permissiveness, compromise, that kind of thing. He thought natural rights were absolute—inalienable, like the Constitution says. But so did John Rawls, the Harvard philosopher, in his *Law of the People*. I guess Strauss worked better for the neocons, and of course, it fit right into the Christian-right stuff Bush picked up in Texas to fill his empty mind—and get him sober. Until Iraq, they were on the sidelines in think tanks, just panting for power. In their warped minds, anyone who doesn't think like them is weak. And all we have to do is make democracies out of these countries. Regime change—that's the key. Kick 'em out and manufacture a democracy, like we do washer-dryers. Cheney was their inside man.

"The current crop of neocons wants a change of regime in Iran. The screwup in Iraq wasn't enough." Yvonne snorted with scorn. "Democracy has a special meaning for these guys. It means subservience to the U.S.—or client states. It's empire and oil. For them, things are only black or white, pun intended. For them, all of Islam falls into the black category, mostly black with oceans of oil."

Her mood turned more thoughtful. "You know, many of these neocons are sympathetic to Israel. It wouldn't surprise me a bit if they used Iraq to bring in U.S. power to play tough with Israel's enemies. And they'd have plenty of help from AIPAC." She glanced at Jacob. "Oh, you can't say this out loud because then you're accused of anti-Semitism."

After another gulp of wine, she returned doggedly to her diatribe. "But it goes beyond that. We've turned the whole Muslim world into enemies—from the Philippines, through Indonesia and Malaysia in the East, to Turkey in the West—and even the ones who live in our midst. Bush gave the neocons a blank check. They fed his messianic view of himself. He even called it a crusade at first." She paused, puzzling over a new thought.

"Good heavens! Such erudition."

"I went to Harvard."

"Yeah, I get that. And now your neocons have moved on. They probably won't even be held accountable," Jacob added, thinking of Wolfowitz, Rumsfeld, Feith, and others. Yvonne's knowledge was an eye-opener for him. She seemed to have done some serious reading.

"Yeah, you're absolutely right. And it makes my blood boil. To think that after 9/11, we squandered all the world support that flooded in and in the process have managed to make the world a much more dangerous place. And nobody pays."

"Well, you have to admit that this country has gotten off lightly since 9/11," suggested Jacob, playing devil's advocate. "No major terror."

"But for how much longer? You hear stuff everywhere."

"Your friends again, or reality?"

"Very funny." She studied him for a moment. "You remind me of a story I read back when Bush was president. A reporter once asked a White House official—unnamed, of course—why the administration couldn't own up to the reality that Iraq was making a real mess of the world. You know what his answer was?" She didn't wait for Jacob's reply. "He said you don't understand. This is world empire. We have the power. And we don't think in those terms anymore. We create our own reality."

"He actually verbalized that?" Jacob found this hard to believe.

"Yeah. I may not have the exact quote right, but that was the gist. My own reality is that more attacks are on the way."

"Your friends believe that, I suppose?"

"Some do, yes."

"I wish I could meet these friends."

"I told you they are not really friends, Jacob."

"You make it a little difficult for me with all your secrets. But this—I mean what we've been talking about, you've been talking about mostly—is not going to be in our little project. The Crane Corporation is our focus and, of course, your family. If we can find in the process that the government is doing illegal things, vis-à-vis Crane, we'll tell about it. Agreed?"

"Sure, I just wanted to tell you what I know about the larger picture." She smiled. "I thought it might motivate you. Sometimes you seem, well, detached." She glanced at him as she sipped a little wine. "And it gave me a chance to show off."

Her ability to make fun of herself pleased Jacob. He picked absently at the canapés. While he had always managed to stay out of the heated polemics of politics, the angry division of the country bothered him. The Christian right was playing an important role in this. They reminded him of his father. They took their Christianity literally, but only the words that suited their purpose. They were an abrasive, aggressive bunch who seemed intent on dividing America with issues such as abortion, gay marriage, and flag burning. Strident patriotism had become particularly offensive. He resented all the buttonhole flags worn as Republican totems. It became the focus of dinner party conversation and barroom arguments in which any critic would be charged with lack of patriotism and lack of support for "our fighting boys." In fact, Jacob had never seen America like this.

He envied Rachel, who, like Yvy, seemed to have a clear idea of where she fit. But the poisoned atmosphere of politics had turned him off. Only recently, the ugliness had begun to suck him into the controversy. He was angry at the conservative press—including his own paper—for their selectivity in reporting only one side of the conflict and unwillingness to oppose Washington. Of course, they were intimidated by the endless polls. If you disagreed with the administration—Yvonne was quite right—you would be accused of being unpatriotic.

He remembered with some bitterness television reporters saying that our military could not be criticized at any level after the troops crossed the border in the initial invasion of Iraq. Jacob never understood from where that rule had come. It certainly wasn't in the Constitution.

Yvonne pushed the canapé plate over to his side. "No soggers?"

"No thanks."

"I've talked too much."

"And I'm enthralled."

"Are you making fun of me?"

"Certainly not. These are troubled times, and it's hard to get hold of the big picture with all the recriminations and personal sniping. You're well-informed and thoughtful, if a bit over the top. But I'm impressed." He gazed at her, smiling, and asked, "Are you as, uh, wild as they say?"

"Wilder," she whispered. "But don't let it get around."

"I'm afraid it already has."

Her sly smile faded, and she became serious. "Is it really bad to be an extremist these days? The people with Bush, they were the real extremists." She ate another cracker. "At the risk of boring you with more, have you followed these new security companies, the mercenaries we are spreading around the world?"

"Yeah. I've read about them. It's the old revolving-door syndrome. Former officials and ex-military getting into the business with government contracts."

"Oh, it's worse than that."

"Like?"

Distracted from her mercenaries, she followed his point. There was no stopping her. "You're right about the revolving door. From the outside, they lobby Homeland Security. It's an icky title." She made a face. "Incestuous relationships between the department and private interests are everywhere you look. And we haven't even talked about domestic problems, such as tax cuts for the rich, corrupt drug companies, and, recently, the Federal Trade Commission's changing its rules to favor the takeover of the media by big conglomerates. This in the guise of better service and lower costs for consumers?" Her tone rose to make it a question. "There is so much wrong. It may be too late to change things." She paused in an effort to collect her thoughts once more. "What they are really trying to do is dismantle the federal government by a huge transfer of wealth and influence to their supporters. The deficits don't faze them because they want to scrap all the safety nets. They don't want Social Security, and they're trying to kill Medicare while most countries have long had universal coverage. They care little about the consumer or the environment. And they continue to give away all the money to their friends in tax cuts so nothing is left to pay for these programs. The media likes to call it privatizing, but it's not. It's dismantling—destroying—the federal government. Someday … in the future, you might just have anarchy—like an uprising—when people catch on. Ironically," she added, "that is when things will start to change."

"Well, you certainly have covered it all." Jacob was surprised how worked up she had become. "I hope we don't resort to violence, though." There was something very appealing in her excitement—even sensuous.

"Why? It may be the only way to stop these people. We need to reexamine our methods of protest. Nonviolence may be a thing of the past. In fact, I'm sure it is. Where are the people who should be in the streets and down on the mall in DC? Maybe America needs another revolution."

"You don't mean that literally, Yvonne."

"Yes, I do." But the thought seemed to exhaust her finally.

"Is this why I am writing about The Crane Corporation?" Were there others like Yvonne? Was this the "movement" she talked about? Was he being used? The last question bothered him.

"In a way." She shrugged. "It's all we can do. Still, it would only be an old-fashioned nonviolent response, wouldn't it?"

"I suppose it would." They sat for awhile without talking. Jacob noticed that while she had talked, they had drained the bottle of wine.

"Maybe we should talk about other things—more placid," Yvonne suggested. "So, you have a girlfriend?"

"That's not placid."

"Sure, it is. Well, do you?"

"I told you. I have a friend who happens to be a woman, if that's what you mean."

"Oh, that's right. You don't sleep with her?"

"I didn't say that."

"You do sleep with her."

Jacob was feeling too mellow to get angry at her impertinence. "What would you expect?"

Yvonne frowned into her glass. "I'm jealous."

"Why should you be?"

She untied the ponytail and let her hair fall, running her fingers through the luxurious mane to comb it back behind her ears. "I don't know." She was even more stunning with her hair down. "Mitch says you're a bright guy, but lazy."

"He said that?" She was able to change focus abruptly, like her entire generation brought up on computer games.

"Yes."

"He doesn't know me well enough."

"He says he does." She eyed him oddly.

"Yvonne, I am not gay."

"No. I didn't think you were. But you're not very macho either. I like that. You seem gentler and more comfortable in your skin."

"Good heavens—how do you know all that?"

"A woman's instinct."

"You're doing pop psychology."

"No, it's instinct, as I said. So, you don't love her?"

"Who?"

"The friend who happens to be a woman whom you occasionally sleep with."

"Probably not. But why are we talking about this?"

"Because you seemed to want to talk about other things—you know, more placid than war and stuff."

"It's not a placid subject." For a moment, she seemed very young, more like her age.

"Love is not placid?"

"Of course not."

"No, it isn't, I guess." She laughed, becoming almost girlish. "I don't love anyone," she declared. "It would interfere with my work."

"And your work is?"

"Graduate school first, of course, but then there's the movement."

"The movement, does it have a capital 'M'? Would that be about violent protest?"

"Maybe. But the first action is nonviolent—your article. So, we still have to work on that."

"We're doing that." Jacob was dazzled by her abrupt changes of pace.

"Yes, we're beginning to." She tossed off the rest of her wine and eyed the empty bottle. "God, it's gone." She signaled the waitress for another.

"You're going to get me drunk. I've had enough."

"Sometimes people are more open when they drink." But she waved off the waitress and asked for a check.

"Tell me this. Do you have any friends who happen to be men?" Jacob asked casually.

"Of course. Lots."

"How many of them do you sleep with?"

She didn't miss a beat. "A few."

"A few? How many is that?"

"I don't remember."

"Hmmm," Jacob murmured, unwilling to pursue the issue.

They sat quietly for a moment, each with their own thoughts. Breaking the silence, she said, "I'll walk you back to your hotel. Maybe we can find some other placid things to explore."

They collected their coats, and Jacob paid the check. She took his arm and squeezed. "Thanks for the wine and the conversation."

CHAPTER 8

Feeling a little fuzzy from the wine, Jacob was pleased with her suggestion that they walk through the Public Gardens and air out their heads. He was surprised that it was almost dark. They didn't talk much, each no doubt appraising the situation. Yvonne stopped at a bench and sat down, pulling him to a seat beside her.

"I don't need any more to drink," she said with a sigh. She took a deep breath.

"Actually, I could use some coffee."

"Me, too." She took his hand absently. "But let's sit a minute more. This is nice." Jacob wondered what was going through her mind. He shivered in the crisp evening air, more nervous than cold, as he mulled over his feelings for her.

"You're cold. Let's go to your hotel. Coffee's a good idea."

The cafe at Jacob's hotel was closed, and the lights in the bar had been lowered for the evening crowd by the time they arrived. Only a handful of patrons were scattered through the paneled lounge. They found a secluded booth and ordered coffee. Jacob realized that his resistance was eroding. She seemed to be able to sap his caution at every turn. She was more mature than he expected and certainly more self-possessed and confident. As he sat staring at his hands on the table, afraid to look at her directly, the vision of Christy returned, mingling with the outraged image of his father—memories he couldn't shake. Was it because he was still fuzzy-headed from the wine? Could he be tempted with Yvonne? He knew the answer to the second question was a resounding "yes." He could feel the heat of her presence even from across the table. He thought he knew what was coming.

"What are you thinking about?" she asked from the shadows. Her voice seemed eerily disembodied. "I can't even see you. Come over here and sit beside me."

Her question startled him. He couldn't think of an answer. He considered her proposal for a moment. Why not? He slid in beside her with barely enough room for two. He could feel the warmth of her body against his.

"Ah, now I can see." She laughed. "You want something to eat?"

"I thought it was going to be coffee. We've eaten and drunk enough, don't you think?" He signaled a waiter and ordered two coffees.

As soon as the waiter left, she persisted. "Now, what were you thinking about? You looked so solemn."

"Nothing."

"It was not nothing. You're lying to me."

"That's a pretty strong way to put it."

"Okay, what?"

"I was thinking about moral relativism," he said, trying to finesse her query. "Isn't that what you called it?"

"Oh, that's clever. Can't you be serious?"

"We've been serious all afternoon."

"Then what about moral relativism?"

"I like the concept. I was trying to make it fit."

"So life is not black or white."

"No, but sometimes there's right or wrong. I was brought up in a very religious family—you know, work and God is all there is in life. And you are judged by, well, being good, not doing or even thinking evil things. Forgiveness is not big on the list of what this God offers." He gazed at her a moment. "I've always been fascinated by *Moby Dick,* a story of moral absolutism. Ahab had a pretty good fix on evil."

"He was sick—a pathetic psychopath."

"Well, it sort of fit my upbringing. The lines were quite clear between good and evil. I don't think my parents were psychopaths." His voice betrayed doubts.

"I guess that's hard to admit when it's your parents."

"Belief keeps some straight."

"You are an agnostic, you told me. What kept you straight?"

"I don't know," said Jacob, unnerved at her sudden question. "I guess I didn't succeed."

"How come?"

"I just didn't, that's all. I slipped a long time ago and more since I left home— God, it's now more than how many years? I can't even remember."

"So, what was the first slip?" Yvonne had a way of zeroing right in on the leading question. She would have made a good lawyer. But he knew what she was doing.

"It's a long story, not worth telling."

"Okay. You don't have to tell me." Then she reconsidered and added, "But it would be good for you to let it go instead of obsessing about it."

"Maybe. Anyway, I try not to talk about that part of my life," Jacob added hollowly.

He took a gulp of coffee and thought again of Christy. He could not look at Yvonne, so he just stared into his cup.

"But you should tell someone. How about your friend?"

"Who's that?"

"The friend who happens to be the woman you sleep with."

"There are some things you can't share," he said, surprised by her persistence. But he had told Rachel in a weak moment, and he was sorry he had.

"You can't just lose your history. It's part of you. But you can get it in better perspective and not be ruled by it." She studied him. "You should tell me about your life on the farm sometime. I'd like to hear it." She put her hand on his arm. They sipped their coffees in silence, both thoughtful. For them, it was a long silence.

She looked at her watch. "Hey, I've got to go."

Again, she had ambushed him.

"A late date?"

She seemed flustered in her rush to leave. "No, I mean yes, sort of." She laughed as if it was all a joke on him.

"One of your male friends whom you sleep with?"

"That's none of your business." She smiled as she stood to pull on her coat.

"I thought we were being open with each other." Jacob smiled slyly. "If we are going to work together, this is the kind of thing I need to know," he added, mimicking her earlier comment.

She gasped in mock surprise, "You are incredible!" She threw her arm around his shoulders and kissed him on the cheek—a chaste kiss. "You'll never know," she said mischievously. With a toss of her head and sweep of long hair, she walked out, calling back, "Talk to you tomorrow."

Mystified by her abrupt departure, Jacob sat back and sipped the last of his coffee. She certainly was full of surprises. He realized that he was disappointed.

Later that night, he got a call from Rachel. It was unfortunate timing for him, still brooding about Yvonne.

"Hi, what's up?" was her greeting.

"Well, it's kind of a long story."

"Hey, I got nothing but time for you, dreamboat."

"For starters, I met with a guy from Crane—a company watchdog, their security man, and a spy of sorts. He's put a tail on me."

"Really?"

"That was after he warned me not to interview the family—at least not without him knowing. He offered to provide whatever information I needed. Hah! He even offered to write the article."

"Sounds like they may have things to hide. Or maybe they just didn't like your article on the funeral and your comments on the posthumous fund-raising. It was a rather scathing comment—quite funny actually."

"Thanks." Jacob wasn't sure it was meant as a compliment. "Then I met with Emily. Yvonne came, too. They had a pretty interesting proposal for me."

"Yvonne. That's the bad seed?"

"No, not really bad, just very smart, very left-wing, and very up on what's going on in the world."

"Okay, tell me about it."

He related the whole story of the meeting and Yvonne's diatribe over drinks. There was a long silence, just Rachel's breathing.

"I've been telling you that stuff for years."

"I know."

"And after the drinks?" she asked suggestively.

"God, Rachel, aren't you even interested in what's going on here?"

"Yeah, I am. So, after the bar?"

"You're impossible. What do you think, after the bar? After the bar, nothing. She went home. I came back to the hotel and am now talking to you." Jacob was exasperated with her but was reminded again of his disappointment at Yvonne's sudden departure.

After another long silence, Rachel changed the subject.

"Do you think—by any stretch—they are using you? I mean does Emily have her own agenda like getting back at her brother for not handing out enough goodies to her?"

"No, it seems like they've given this a lot of thought," Jacob said, trying to explain away her suspicion—a suspicion which had not occurred to him.

"Sure they have." She paused. "It just has a phony ring to it, this exposé on Crane and the accusation that the Feds are taking over the company as cover for their own nefarious purposes. Maybe this guy Garon is just protecting his rich employers. Can't blame him for his loyalty."

"You don't really believe that, do you, about using me just to get the money?"

"I don't know. I didn't meet the people. But it's as good an explanation for Emily's motive as any other."

"Emily's brother admitted that he was being used."

"That's only what she says he said. It's hearsay. Do you think it might be a hoax to get you involved?"

Rachel's observations were alarming. "Of course not. They tell me that they can corroborate this stuff." An exaggeration, he admitted to himself. "People in the company are talking to them."

"They could just be malcontents."

"I doubt it. You know the government has set up other dummies as subsidiaries of public behemoths like Halliburton. You remember Bechtel, for example, and its affiliate in Saudi Arabia. They train Saudis to fight. And they provide security."

"Yeah, but it was a legit business."

"Maybe." Jacob wondered whether he had been influenced by his interest in Yvonne. "But this is on a much grander scale and pretty remote from anything legitimate. This guy, Garon … well, he resembles Noriega. He's tough and probably nasty."

"That's unpleasant. I'm just raising a little caution here. If you're right about this, it will be a very big story. But be careful. If you're wrong, you could get yourself in trouble—like jail time. That's what they do to renegade reporters these days. Or worse," she chortled, "you could lose your press card."

"I'd rather go to jail," Jacob said, going along with her little joke.

"Seriously, Jacob, look it over carefully before you make any commitments. It's a dangerous game you're playing. And you'll be on your own because the *News,* or any paper in town, wouldn't touch it with a ten-foot pole. I know the *Times* wouldn't."

"I'll be doing some research first."

"Okay. That's a good way to start. I'm just sorry I can't help—in fact, I can't get anywhere near it. How does your friend Mitch feel?"

"He was at our meeting, too. He apparently goes along with it."

"That's a good sign because he could be taking the same risk himself."

"Yeah, but I'm not sure whether he's going to be a participant."

"You don't need him."

There was a brief silence.

"Do you like the girl?"

"She's interesting."

"Is that a yes?"

Jacob didn't like being put on the spot by Rachel. "No. It's not anything. I don't know what you're implying."

"I didn't think I was implying anything. I was asking whether you had taken a liking to this girl, that's all."

"She's interesting."

"You said that. I take it as a yes."

"Well, you're wrong."

"Okay, let's drop it. Call me when you get back to town."

Her nosy questions had focused him on his real feelings. He knew he was attracted to Yvonne. In fact, her abrupt leave-taking tonight had bothered him more than he liked to admit. He had badly misjudged her. The idea of a tryst in his hotel room had, of course, occurred to him. Now that presumption was an embarrassment. After all, she was younger—by about twelve years. The thought was unsettling. He certainly didn't want to resurrect all the baggage of his past.

The conversation with Rachel had left him with a muddle of conflicting thoughts. He stretched out on the bed and watched the news for awhile, mostly as a distraction. Another terror alert was announced by Homeland Security. The silly color code had been raised once again to the level red in New York and Washington. There was still little intelligence basis beyond the NSA's listening in on volumes of miscellaneous clutter and an ambiguous television appearance by bin Laden and his henchmen with yet another warning to Americans. Jacob turned it off in disgust and decided to begin writing a draft of the article Emily and Yvonne wanted, plugging in facts he had gleaned from them and filling the gaps with suppositions and inventions of his own. His purpose was to create the structure of the story rather than the substance. He kept at it far into the night until he had finished laying out a design with which he was happy.

Then he watched the start of a late movie until his eyes drooped, finally succumbing to sleep at 3:00 AM. He woke at nine with a start, certain that he had heard Yvonne's voice—so certain that he got up and checked the living room just to make sure. He was not being cool. His imagination was out of control. Without opening the curtains, he flopped down on the bed and began to ponder loose ends from the previous night. His story needed a focus—a specific wrongdoing, crime, or fraud—that ubiquitous smoking gun. Why was Crane cooperating with the government? Who benefited and how? Why was the company so anxious to keep it all secret? It was answers to these questions that might give him a story. Jacob hoped he could get some of what he needed from contacts through his own paper. Failing that, he was counting on Mitch for a local investigation. He could expect little or nothing from the company itself.

After his breakfast, he called Mitch, hoping to find him at his office.

"I thought our little séance with Emily and Yvonne was interesting," was Mitch's first observation. "A nice twist for your story, eh?"

"I've roughed something out. I'd like to have you take a look at it." Jacob needed Mitch and at the same time, he knew that Mitch might want a part in it. All Jacob needed at this point was access to the archives of Mitch's paper. The Boston paper was likely to have more on the Crane family than he could find in New York. "Maybe we could get together," he suggested.

It didn't take any persuasion. "Great. Come on down. You know our files on Crane are among the best in the country. Joshua is a favorite son. You say you've got a draft?"

"Yeah, it's just a very rough draft at this point."

Mitch whistled. "God, how impressive. You just wrote all night, I bet. I thought you might have been busy with, ah, other things last night."

Ignoring the implications of this suggestion, Jacob said, "Part of the night, Mitch. Just part. She's a very interesting young lady."

"She is that." There was a short silence as Mitch tried to decipher Jacob's reply. "Okay, I'll see you soon?"

"I'll get my stuff together."

"I'm on the tenth floor."

"Moving up in the world," Jacob said, remembering that when he had last visited Mitch, his office was on the third floor. Before leaving, Jacob gave his papers a last once-over, made a few changes, and burned the file on a disc.

The morning was crisp and clear, and he decided to walk across the park to get the late-night cobwebs out. As he strolled through the pastoral landscape of the Public Gardens, he felt the warmth of the mid-morning sun. It was one of those days in winter that was a tantalizing reminder of spring, still weeks away. On the pond, where swan boats were available for pedaling in the summer, there were a few ducks swimming in a patch of water where the ice had melted. He watched a pair of mallards set their wings for a landing. Jacob was reminded of television shots of jets with noses high, ready to set down on a carrier deck. He paused for a moment on a footbridge, waiting to see whether more would follow, but none did. As he continued his walk, he fantasized about a chance encounter with

Yvonne and realized he was anxious to see her again. In several reviews of the previous night, he had speculated about whether she would have stayed longer if he had asked. An odd awkwardness with her had blocked out any plausible invitation. At thirty-six, he still didn't feel cool with women, particularly this woman.

Crossing a downtown street heading to Mitch's office, he thought a tall figure with long dark hair falling beneath her winter hat might be Yvonne. But when he overtook her, he was disappointed. What was the matter with him? Was this rich girl becoming a fixation? He needed to regain some composure. It wasn't until then that he remembered to look for one of Garon's men. He glanced around instinctively. But he knew it was too late for evasion. They knew about Mitch anyway.

Jacob spent most of that day at the *Globe* using Mitch's password to search through the archives for stories on the Cranes and the corporation. He made notes on the few leads that were of interest to him. Leaving Mitch with a pared-down version of his draft, he worked through the files relentlessly. In two hours of searching under "Crane" as a key, Jacob had turned up nothing unusual. He then tried "Halliburton," but the files were bloated with stories of company overcharges and other accounting problems in Iraq with no references to Crane. "Bechtel" produced more of the same. Finally, he tried Iraq-related topics, but these, too, were unrewarding. Almost ready to give up, he googled "White House" as a key phrase and clicked on "Freedom of Information." Jacob scrolled the list back in time, trying to look for items that might be of interest. One of these caught his eye—a White House denial of a story in a local journal called *Disclosure*. The denial caught Jacob's attention because it grew out of a lawsuit under the Freedom of Information Act to get the names of defense contractors who allegedly met with the transition team of the new president-elect. The dateline was December, 2008. Jacob made a quick search of *Disclosure* and found a reference to the story of the meeting. The Web site stated that the publication had gone out of business.

After a tedious search of an archive file for *Disclosure*, Jacob found the article in question. It was just a couple of paragraphs in a comment section of the magazine. Jacob scanned the brief text with mounting excitement. According to a government source, the meeting was attended by a gathering of big government contractors, including all the names you might expect, and also the major oil companies—including The Crane Corporation! The subject of the meeting and the participants had been leaked—at least that was the claim of *Disclosure*. It asserted the White House was lining up contractors to "formulate plans to rebuild the Iraqi oil industry and then market the oil." The Defense Department had asked the companies to come up with their own security forces to prevent terrorist attacks by the insurgency and get the wells operating to full capacity.

Disclosure alleged that part of the plan was to assure U.S. control over oil revenues, suggesting that it might use private companies to conceal some of these funds either by laundering them into other identities or by transferring them to foreign bank accounts. The funds would not be wasted in Iraq but made available for later use to support covert actions to destabilize regimes in other hostile Middle East countries such as Syria and Iran. The word "wasted" in this context struck Jacob as shockingly cynical. Was the reconstruction of Iraq a waste? He swallowed hard and continued reading. To facilitate control, detailed plans for protecting the Iraqi Oil Ministry and its assets were discussed with private contractors. It was not clear whether all of these allegations came out of the same meeting. The claims of diverting oil revenues struck Jacob as a startling idea—shades of Iran-Contra. It made Yvonne's extravagant story seem tame by comparison.

More research revealed only a few back-page, follow-up stories in the larger media which were uniformly discounted by the corporate media as outrageous gossip with no substantiation. In fact, the harsh allegations of journalistic abuse and breach of national security that followed ultimately led to the closing of the magazine. Of course, the war on terror was in such high gear that no claims of this kind could survive the intensity of patriotism. Lawsuits against the owners of *Disclosure* were threatened. The spin doctors had been vigilant.

Later, when Mitch and Jacob had a chance to review this record, even Mitch thought that the plan to divert funds in this manner seemed implausible to the extreme. If the United States was in control, why the need to conceal anything? Indeed, the United States was in control with only the merest excuse for a coalition—even the British had long since abandoned Iraq. Of course, the United States could not count on being able to ignore the pressure of world opinion if this was ever revealed. So, Jacob argued, the story had to be squelched.

"It does seem outlandish, Mitch. But the U.S. never learns from its mistakes. You're right. It's Iran-Contra all over again."

"I agree." Mitch smiled wickedly. "If it's true, what a story we'd have!"

"We'd have to be right though—real right."

"We need at least another source before we can even think about it." He caught himself. "Before you go with it, I mean."

"My neck, not yours?"

"Yeah, your neck, Jacob. This is really dangerous ground. To be honest, Jacoby, I can't get involved with this. I'd risk all my TV contacts." Mitch studied his friend. "You sure this isn't all for beautiful Yvy?"

Jacob couldn't resist a smile at Mitch's somber-faced concern. "You're being silly, Mitch. Can't you get off that subject?"

"No, I can't," he said earnestly. "It's a dangerous risk for you. I shouldn't be kidding about this."

"I'm going to follow up on this gem, do something for the good of human-kind for a change."

"Yes, it would be that." Mitch's expression became grave. "I'm worried about Yvy, Jacob. I'm telling you that you should be careful—about getting yourself involved. She's got her own agenda. She's not much of a romantic. Don't let her fool you on that. I don't know how to say this, but I know the family, the his-tory—her history. And I say she could be using you. She's beyond Emily on this. When she's done with you, she'll dump you. You'll never be part of her life, Jacoby, and you'll get hurt."

"How in the world do you know all that?" He paused and reconsidered, remembering Rachel's similar comments. "Anyway, who said I was involved with her?"

"You did—it's all over your face."

Jacob had no answer. It was true. He was fascinated by Yvonne. He had already subconsciously admitted that to himself. She had captured his imagina-tion. Had she blinded him, too?

"But thanks for the advice, Mitch. I mean it. I appreciate the heads-up. I'm a grown-up now, too old for her anyway. You don't have to worry about that."

"Not too old, Jacob. Maybe not old enough. Anyway, forewarned is fore-armed. Right?"

"Right," he agreed, but Jacob was eager to move on. "You know, in the group invited to that meeting at the White House, the one that sticks out as not really belonging in that rarefied bunch is Crane."

"Yeah, that's right. You wonder why they were included," Mitch mused.

"There is a disconnect between the obituary story and Crane's involvement with the government. Why would a company with a record of breaking the law be included? One good reason would be that it gives the government an edge. Here's a company in trouble, needing help. In less respectable circles, it might be called blackmail."

"I guess that could be." Mitch looked pleased. "That's a clever way to put it."

Ignoring the comment, Jacob added, "It gives the government a chance to ask something extra from Crane that they wouldn't be comfortable asking of others—like holding an oil slush fund for covert operations hidden from Congress."

"Good. Now all you have to do is find the fund and a set of instructions." Mitch laughed at the absurdity of his own suggestion.

"Well, maybe not that. But, as you said, just confirmation of some kind of a plan."

"But even the press finally discounted the charges made by *Disclosure.*"

"Could the answer be that big news media were warned off the story for security reasons?" Jacob paused, trying to recall another incident he had read about. "Do you remember the story about a massacre in northern Afghanistan while we were chasing bin Laden?"

"Vaguely. Was it near that town where there was a lot of the fighting, uh, Mazar a-Sharif? And the Defense Department denied it."

"Yes, and there was the statement by the guy, a Brit I think, who broke the story, claiming that the Defense Department told him they had warned the media to stay away from it—national security. I think his exact quote from Defense intelligence was 'that will never be in print, even if it is true.'"

"I don't remember that part."

"It came out in a *Democracy Now!* program. I hung onto a reference to it." A sudden thought occurred to him. "Rachel has a copy of the film report! And, of course, there's the huge failure of the press in revealing the weaknesses in evidence of WMDs. Different, I admit, but still a cover-up and the same failure by the press to tell the story. Again, it was intimidation under the phony guise of national security."

Out of the blue, Mitch asked, "Does Rachel know about Yvonne?" It was an effective ambush.

"What about her, Mitch?" Jacob asked, with undisguised irritation at Mitch's obsessing about Yvonne. "What on earth does that have to do with this?"

"Okay, forget it. I don't want to lose a good friend." He smiled sheepishly. "The question just popped into my mind."

Edging around the Yvonne issue for the rest of the afternoon, they reviewed Jacob's draft and planned their next steps. They agreed to meet again before Jacob left town.

It was already dark when Jacob caught a cab back to his hotel. The red alert on his phone blinked urgently in his room as he groped for the light.

CHAPTER 9

There were two messages. Jacob listened to the first impatiently as Shanahan ranted about another story and a new "drop-dead" date "or else." The second took him by surprise. Instead of another call from Rachel as he expected, it was Yvonne. Jacob didn't recognize her voice immediately. The tone was urgent and the message brief.

"I need to see you. Something new has come up." She spoke quickly. "I don't have time to call again. I'll meet you at your hotel at eight. You better be there." Her last words seemed foreboding.

Instinctively, Jacob glanced at his watch. It was 7:30 PM already. He booted up his computer and sent Shanahan an e-mail, buying time until the next day or so. Often the editor checked his e-mail at night, and Jacob didn't want to get a callback, so he said he would be out most of the evening at a meeting with an important source. Well, it was true; he would be seeing Yvonne.

The curtains were still wide open, and the panorama of the city twinkled with nightlife. Jacob stood before the scene and daydreamed about Yvonne and worried about getting better control over his fascination for her. But he was avoiding the real issue. It was hard to ignore. What he wanted to do was express his feelings for her—hold her, kiss her, and to … He didn't even want to put the thought in words. He was, however, very sure that he was powerfully attracted to her, and he was feeling it physically. He distracted himself with the view of Newbury Street, fifteen stories below. From his vantage point, he could just see the sidewalk entrance. Could he watch her arrive? There were two entrances, so he had a fifty-fifty chance of catching a glimpse of her. As he was keeping his lookout, there was a knock at the door. His heart beat a little faster. She was ten minutes early. He opened the door to the maid, wanting to turn down his bed. He greeted her and stood aside to let her in. How timely he thought, smiling at the unexpected foiling of his overheated anticipation.

It wasn't until an hour later that Yvonne called from the lobby.

"God, I'm glad you're here. Meet me in the bar."

"You can come up here, if you like. It would be quieter."

"No. I don't like hotel rooms." She hung up. He felt rebuffed again.

When Jacob walked into the lounge where they had been the night before, it had been darkened for the evening hours. Yvonne stood in the shadows inside the entrance talking to a man. As soon as he approached, they separated and he left. Yvonne saw Jacob and rushed to give him a tentative hug.

"Oh, hi."

Jacob couldn't tell whether she was guilty or excited. "Did I interrupt something?"

"No. Not at all." She seemed nervous. "Let's grab a seat," she said, ignoring the approaching maitre d'. Yvonne was still very much the privileged rich kid who got her way. While Jacob disliked this kind of pushy behavior in most people, he rather admired it in Yvonne. Her brassy self-possession displaced her youth and made her seem more world-weary than collegiate. She guided him to a remote banquette, and he slid in across from her.

"Listen, I've got something for you." She seemed edgy. Jacob had not yet seen her so wound up. "Our contact at the company got hold of a Pentagon memorandum. I think it's important. It's happening in this administration, and it's all about a plan to siphon off profits from Iraqi oil sales for a secret fund to finance undercover activities in the Middle East. I know you'll have questions about it," she added guardedly, but still breathless. "But guess what? The author is none other than ..." She stopped. "I better be careful. I'm so worried about bugs. That's why I didn't want to tell you this in your room."

Naturally, Jacob's first reaction was disbelief. Had he just confirmed his own discovery? If so, it would be a monumental coincidence. But then the doubts came. Rachel and Mitch had seeded them well. For the first time, Jacob began to distrust his own judgment. His initial excitement about Yvonne's discovery was tempered by new suspicions. He couldn't help himself. Was it all too good to be true? Finding the *Disclosure* allegation about a secret fund and then the same day Yvonne's coming up with a Pentagon paper about the plan was too much. Yet, Jacob did not think that the *Disclosure* story was a fake. He had made his discovery only after endless searching. He tried to put his fears aside, realizing that the guilt about his feelings for Yvonne could be affecting him.

"What's the matter?" She grabbed his arm. "Aren't you excited?"

"Sure. On its face, this would be a big story."

"On its face? What's that supposed to mean?"

"I meant superficially. You know, without authentication." He wanted to test her.

"It has authentication. It's a Pentagon memo. A smoking gun, for God's sake!"

"It could be faked or forged."

"My God! I can't believe what I'm hearing. But I guess I should have expected it."

"Where's the paper?"

His questions had disconcerted her. "I … I don't, uh, actually have it."

"Well, where is it?"

"Jacob, do you think I'm lying to you?"

"Of course not. I just need to see the paper."

"You're going to. Emily and I just heard about its existence today."

"Ah, so you haven't read it."

"No. It was read or summarized anyway—on the phone."

"Summarized? Who wrote it?"

She lowered her voice. "We just don't know. But we have our suspicions."

"You see, those things are important. If we are going to make blockbuster assertions like these, we've got to be very sure of the source. If it was as you say from outside, was it ever connected to the inside?" He wanted to believe her.

"It has official fingerprints all over it. That's what we've been told."

"I need to see it."

"And you shall. I thought we were going to take some risks here, that you were willing to stick out your neck."

"I'm just saying this needs to be tied up—verified somehow." Jacob had other worries—the Patriot Act. "Taking a risk is not the same as being a fool."

She gazed at him and then smiled. "No, Jacob. I wouldn't ever expect you to be a fool—about anything," she said with mocking kindness, dripping with sarcasm. It was disarming. "We'll get the copy for you. If you don't like it, we don't have to use it. Obviously, we have to be careful. It just makes me so mad that the government can get away with things like this." Her tone was tense and challenging. "Haven't you ever been reckless in your life, Jacob?"

"I have. I told you."

"But you haven't really told me."

"I told you that I had made mistakes."

"Ah, yes—mistakes. That's not much to go on, is it?" She leaned across the table and laid her hand on his. "I want to go to your room now. And I think you do, too." She stood up, just as a waiter arrived to take their order. Jacob was caught totally off guard by her impulsiveness. "Something has come up, waiter. We have to leave."

Jacob was stunned. This girl was off the wall!

The waiter looked at them both doubtfully. Jacob could feel his face flush. "Well, fine. Hope you can come back," he suggested pleasantly.

Yvonne led the way out of the lounge, and Jacob followed in a haze of indecision. Yvonne's moods changed so abruptly.

"You said you didn't like hotel rooms."

"I don't."

He was oddly afraid of her, of her powers over him. Then as the elevator door closed, she kissed him on the mouth, moving her arms beneath his coat and circling his waist suggestively. It seemed natural to respond to the embrace. As fifteen short floors passed, Jacob's doubts had been eclipsed by his passion. They were still on the same kiss as the doors opened to his floor.

The next minutes in the privacy of his room were like a dream in slow motion for him. Under her guiding hands, they moved from stage to stage as if in a trance, tearing at their clothes and at the same time kissing, sometimes awkwardly amidst the activity. Touching tentatively as they stood naked, they embraced lightly and kissed. She pulled him onto the turned-down bed, and they lay beside each other.

"Be reckless, Jacob—take a chance," she murmured.

Accepting the invitation, he gently pushed her over onto her back and rose to his knees between her legs. Slowly, he let himself down, and they were joined. They kept looking at each other as they moved. Then each of them succumbed to the passion and lost control. When it was over and the fervor had subsided, Jacob looked into her eyes, trying to find a meaning in what they had done.

"I love you, Yvonne." He regretted the admission almost as he said it.

She didn't answer; she just gazed at him and then kissed him gently.

"You are a passionate guy, Jacob." She smiled. "I still can't get over that name."

Jacob rolled away and lay on his back, studying the contours of the ceiling. There was a period of silence. Then Yvonne snuggled closer and said, "Hey, I heard you. I just don't know how to answer that." Her voice was hoarse with sex. "I made love with you, didn't I?"

They lay this way for a long time. He finally spoke. "I guess it wasn't fair for me to say that."

"Say what?" she asked teasingly.

He couldn't repeat it. As their passions cooled, he wished he hadn't revealed such an intimate part of himself.

"That you love me?"

"Yes, that."

She pulled at his shoulder. "Here, turn this way so I can see you." She studied him for a moment. "But I liked what you said."

"Good."

"I think you wanted me to say that I love you?"

"Not unless you mean it."

She hesitated. "I really don't know how I feel about you, Jacob. You bother me. I'm very attracted to you. But we are so very different." She lifted herself onto an elbow, baring a breast without shame. "I made love with you because I wanted to. And I want to make love again and again after that."

Jacob smiled. "That's only three."

"Seriously, Jacob. You do something to me. I haven't met anyone like you before ... and ... I want to love you." She drew him close and chastely kissed his cheek. "I need time, time to understand myself. I, uh, I find it hard to love," she admitted finally.

Jacob thought, so do I, and wondered why he had said it. Even lying close, he felt strangely remote, detached from her. His suspicions returned. Maybe, he should have listened more willingly to Mitch. Yvonne was indeed different. What was her agenda? And where did he fit in?

They dressed slowly without talking. There seemed to be a tacit understanding between them that no more could be said. She straightened up the bed—an uncharacteristically feminine gesture—but he liked it nonetheless. They walked down the hall to the elevator, arms loosely around each other. The maitre d' greeted them at the door of the bar.

"Here you are again," he said cheerfully. The guy's tact was amazing. Without further comment he sat them at the same banquette and took a drink order. Their evening continued as if nothing had happened. Yvonne began to discuss her plan for follow-up on the Pentagon memo. She promised she'd get a copy for him. He told her that he would probably be returning to New York the next day and gave her his phone number. She promised to stay in touch. Jacob decided not to tell her about finding the *Disclosure* article. Later, they kissed good night at the hotel entrance, and she walked off into the darkness. Standing outside in the chill of the evening, Jacob watched her until she turned a corner. He suddenly felt very alone and empty—as if the spirit had been drained from his body.

Escorted by the Saudi intelligence agent who met him at the gate, Garon was led around security checkpoints at the King Khaled International Airport in Riyadh, using side doors and underground passageways. In a secure garage, they were met by a large, white SUV with darkened windows and were whisked away to the Ministry of Security. After bypassing layers of more security presided over by men in traditional white robes and *ghutras*, Garon was ushered into a cool waiting area and asked politely to wait until summoned. Without warning, Garon had been visited at his office in New York by a representative from the Pentagon who identified himself as a member of a unit called Special Projects, a new group set up after the election which reported directly to the Secretary of Defense. The agent had directed him to fly to Riyadh to receive new instructions for the company's security apparatus. Crane was aware of and had okayed the trip, according to the Pentagon representative. After his visitor had departed, Garon immediately double-checked with Joshua, who confirmed his approval of the assignment.

"Yes, Luis, I am aware of this. It is part of our obligation under our contract, and I trust you to use discretion." Garon smiled at this. Discretion indeed. Weeks before the trip, he had been called to Washington and briefed on a new plan for The Crane Corporation. Informed by the government that he was no longer working directly for the company, he was told that he would be paid out of a fund reserved for covert action. Joshua had approved the change. The arrangement reminded him of his experience with the PRI in Mexico many years ago under the corrupt Salinas government. The role pleased Garon because it put him in a position of power over Joshua and his meddling rich family. He would now have support in getting rid of the leakers who were passing Emily inside information. This plan had been hatched in the Special Projects office, and Garon had received assurances that the potential whistle-blowers would soon be controlled.

A dark-suited, burly Arab with a state-of-the-art receiver plugged into his ear appeared. "Ah, Mr. Garon, please follow me, sir," he said, gesturing toward an open doorway. Garon followed down a long hallway of unmarked doors. Finally, they paused at one. His guide inserted his key card, and the door clicked open.

Garon entered the small conference room where six men were seated around a shiny oval table.

"Luis, welcome. Good to see you again. Please have a seat so we can get started. I hope your flight was comfortable?" The tone was like honey, but the eyes were hard. Garon had worked with him previously on company security matters.

Garon noted that only two of the men were dressed in Arab attire—the checked headscarf and white robe. All the men seemed to be Saudis. Garon felt comfortable in the Middle East, having dark skin himself. He took the seat his host indicated.

"I'm so glad you could come on such short notice, Luis. Let's get right to it," he said, with a distinct British accent. "We have a little problem at Crane. It seems there has been a leak of a document that could mean trouble—serious trouble."

"Leak?" he repeated nervously. Luis felt his stomach knot. What had he missed? "And what would that document be, Mamoud?" Garon asked, surprised at the unexpected development, but trying hard to be as smooth as his host.

"A paper, a very sensitive memorandum that outlines plans for, ah, handling funds—certain oil revenues—has been leaked or purloined from our files. It has, of course, information that could be embarrassing to both Saudi Arabia and the U.S. It is most unfortunate. Its publication would cause chaos for us." He frowned. "We have reason to believe it was taken from us here. So, the Pentagon has, uh, asked that we be the ones to get it back. The matter has been very awkward for us."

"It came from here?" For the moment, Garon breathed a sigh of relief.

"It appears so, my friend—at least that is our understanding. We are having a problem with security. It seems there is, uh, a mole among us. We must protect the Pentagon. I should tell you that the paper was highly classified. A copy was entrusted to us." He stared at Luis without expression, as if responsibility lay with Garon himself. "If the story does get out, deniability is of utmost importance. There must be no connection made to Saudi Arabia. That is paramount."

"How is the company involved?"

"We're not sure, but probably someone in your foreign operations relayed the document to outsiders. They're the ones who have been talking to our Special Intelligence, and they seem to be the only ones who had access to the memorandum. It has been tightly held, and there are only two copies, numbered and indexed. They cannot be reproduced—something about the ink being vulnerable to bright light. It fades to nothing. One copy has gone missing—apparently obtained by one of your employees in New York."

"Ah, I think I know who it might be," Garon growled, trying to appear in control. "I'll alert my office at once."

"But you see, Luis, it is too late. They have already let it out."

"Really. To whom? Do we know?" But Garon thought he knew the answer to his question, too.

"That is what you must find out." He paused and smiled again, but without humor. "Luis, I cannot emphasize enough the importance of preventing embarrassment to us." He swept his hand around the table. "Measures must be taken immediately ... whatever needs to be done." He stood and moved to the door, signifying the meeting was over. "On your way out, stop by my office, and you will be given a copy of the title page for identification purposes only."

Garon got up and took the soft hand offered. "It is now your responsibility, Luis." Mamoud's ominous implications were clear. Garon left the room unsettled and astounded at the unhappy turn of events. A receptionist directed him to his next meeting with the security staff on the more routine matters he had come to Saudi Arabia to discuss. Later, that same evening back in his hotel room, he called the office and alerted one of his men to the problem. They talked for about twenty minutes, planning a strategy. Emily would be the principal suspect. It was too late to do anything about the leaker, but steps had to be taken to stop Emily from giving the memorandum to the newsman. Garon couldn't remember his name.

"Sellars—Jacob Sellars, **Luis**," his assistant prompted.

"Yes, that's it. He's staying at the Copley Square Hotel in Boston. You need to call Emily—warn her of the, uh, serious nature of this—you know, national security at the highest levels. **See** whether she will cooperate. If not, we will have to take more drastic measures. Remember, we do have the advantage that the paper cannot be copied. So, there is only one to find." He paused, wondering where this would lead. "Sellars must not leave town until I get back. Do you understand? Use any measures you need. But be careful. We must not do anything which alerts local authorities."

"I understand, Luis."

His aide would know what to do.

The next morning, Jacob decided to return to New York where he could more easily keep Shanahan happy. It was important to soften up his editor with some good material before he surprised him with his freelance ambitions. But it concerned him that he would be leaving town without Yvonne's secret document. The intense experience with her had distracted him from his purpose. The encounter was bothering him in ways he hadn't yet figured out. Rachel's warning that he might be a dupe for the Crane family still rankled him. Yvonne's offering herself so readily had brought back that suspicion. In fact, he realized that his involvement might be blinding him. He considered what message he should leave her. He didn't trust himself to speak to her, so he left a note with the hotel front desk. The message simply said that he was summoned back to his office and he would be in touch. Then he hastily worked up another story for Shanahan, leaving later than he wanted.

The three-hour train ride left time for further thoughts about his predicament. He wanted badly to carry out his plan to tell the Crane story. What difference would it make if he was being used? He was in control. It would be in his words, his story. Finding the *Disclosure* article just before Yvonne's revelation of the Pentagon memorandum had to be pure coincidence. Any connection was very unlikely. Of course, he realized the missing Pentagon paper would not go unnoticed by Garon or the government. If national security was only a bluff before, it certainly was not now. Garon would no doubt come after the document once the leak was discovered. As these thoughts tumbled through his mind, Jacob made a few notes on his laptop. Finally, the train bored into the tunnel to Penn Station, and Jacob gathered his belongings for arrival.

The familiarity of his apartment was a welcome change from the hotel. Far from Boston and back in his own surroundings, his concerns seemed less critical. The wall of books, some read, some unread, was reassuring. The thrum of traffic noise in the streets made him feel secure. He opened the curtains in his living room and viewed the landscape of lower Manhattan in the mid-winter afternoon, deciding for the umpteenth time that he would never live elsewhere. The big picture window was his painting. He had no other artwork. In daylight, the scene was hard-edged and intense and demanding participation. At night, it was softer and suggestive, the twinkling lights beckoning. As he watched the flow of street activity below and listened to the endless honking and occasional siren, a feeling of unease returned. The jangle of his phone startled him. He picked up, hoping it was Yvonne.

"Hallo, is this Mister Sellars?" The woman's accent was distinctive but not overpowering. Jacob could not identify it.

"Yeah, that's me, who's this?"

"Mister Sellars, my name is Natasha Zilenko. I am wife of Joshua Crane—I should say, late Joshua Crane."

"Yes, I remember." He was only just able to conceal the initial shock of hearing from her. "I'm so sorry for your loss."

"Thank you." There was a pause. "You are just getting back from Boston, I believe."

Her knowledge of his movements put him off. "You're certainly well-informed."

"Nothing sinister," she said with a smile in her voice. "Yvy called and told me you were coming back and gave me your number. I would like to meet you. I understand you will be writing something about family, the company. Is that right?"

"I'm considering it, yes."

"Good. We should talk—you and me. Is possible, yes?"

"Sure."

"Can we talk over dinner tomorrow? I would like to meet you."

"Uh, let's see." He felt put on the spot, but this was an important contact. He did not want her to slip away. Rachel would have to wait. "Okay, tomorrow's fine."

"Good. Come to Carlyle Hotel at eight-thirty. I meet you in lobby. You don't know me?" She laughed. It was a tinkly, musical laugh. "I mean, look like. I wear bright-red scarf for you, eh?"

"Fine, I'll see you then."

"Until then, good-bye," she said, with European formality.

An extraordinary development. All of a sudden, she's back in the United States after a prolonged and mysterious absence. The obituary in the *Times* had made it seem as if she had disappeared for good. But here she was now, calling him. What role was she playing in this? The realization that Shanahan was looking over his shoulder postponed any further speculations.

He booted up his desktop and tinkered with his story for Shanahan. Then he printed the notes he had made on the laptop and wove these into the draft, leaving the polishing work for later.

Jacob watched the network news and stewed about Yvonne between segments. After a shower, he settled in and watched CNN for awhile with a glass of wine. After a second glass to fortify himself, he called Rachel at her office. She was on a late assignment, so he left a message that he would be out and about and would call again. Then he tried Shanahan, feeling somewhat more relaxed for this ordeal.

"You're back. So where's my story?" Shanahan was always frontal in his approach. "The Crane stories are getting a lot of ink. The *Los Angeles Times* has already run a piece raising some serious questions about the old man's dealings with the government. They claim he was involved in some undercover stuff to help out the Ruskies and maybe even financed arms deals. And then there's a lot of unrelated chatter about trouble from Saudi Arabia—you know, terror in the oil fields. The Crane name keeps coming up. No one has been able to pin down what's going on here. Damn it, Jake, the *L.A. Times* may have an edge on us. I hope you have a story." He laughed boisterously. "You better have something after all that time up there in Beantown."

Great, he was on the spot. Shanahan was a sloppy thinker, but he had a nose for chicanery. "Look, Tom, I have to be open with you." Jacob had decided it was time to bite the bullet.

"Yeah," he said warily. "You better be."

"A few members of the family are asking me to do a, uh, story on the company. They don't want to be involved with any newspaper." He was ready to blunder ahead with his blockbuster. "I'm thinking about doing something for them on my own—you know, on a freelance basis. I would have to take a sabbatical."

"Goddamn, you are a cheeky bastard. Sabbatical, hell, the boss will fire yer ass. That's what'll happen. You're going to destroy your career." Then with second thoughts about the threats, he asked, "What have you got, Jake?" Jacob knew that Shanahan liked and respected him.

"Off the record, Tom?"

"I suppose," he agreed after some hesitation.

"Crane may be a lot more closely connected to the government than I had expected. The *L.A. Times* may be on to something. But the stuff you're hearing on Russia is probably a diversion. In fact, all this flack about arms deals in the obit may be a big red herring. There is a story here, Tom, and I believe in the people I'm talking to." He had to swallow hard at his last comment.

"Why don't you write your story for us? Good for you and good for the paper."

"Because the Cranes don't trust the press. They won't deal unless I do it their way. Anyway, first, the facts have to pan out—there's got to be a story."

"What facts?"

"That's all I'm saying now."

"Well, I'll talk it over with the boss, but I have to warn you, he's going to be pretty hot about you bailing out on us this way. You know his politics. Need I say more? If it's going to be an attack on the administration, it better be good—a very hard sell here."

"I know, but I have no choice, Tom. And besides, it's an opportunity for me—I'm sure you can understand that."

"It could be, if you don't stumble. You know, Jake, you've never done something like this. You'll be in a very different game. Can you trust these people?"

"Yes." The question was unsettling.

"Care to tell me who your distaffers in the family are? I can guess."

"I'm sure you can, Tom, but it won't come from me." Jacob had to be cautious even though he knew that Shanahan did not fully share the politics of his boss.

"I'll call you tomorrow. Don't count on much, uh, generosity from this end."

He'd done it. His job was probably lost, but there was relief in knowing that he could now work full-time on the story. He would finally be "standing out from the pack." He was beginning to hate the metaphor. Feeling too spacey with anticipation for any more work, he flopped down on the couch, shedding his shoes and drifting into a light sleep. The racket seemed subliminal at first until he was able to identify it as an urgent knocking. Suddenly wide-awake, he bounded for the door and flung it open.

"God, I thought ... I thought something was wrong," Rachel cried, pushing her way in and looking around. "Your hotel in Boston said you checked out."

Jacob knuckled the sleep out of his eyes. "That's what you get for not calling first."

"I did call—more than once." She pecked him on the cheek. "Anyway, I'm glad you're home."

Jacob was alert now. "Didn't you get my message at the office?"

"I never got back there."

"Well, your loss."

"I was worried when you didn't answer tonight ... with all your talk about being tailed and stuff up there ... I thought something might have happened." Embarrassed, she stopped herself.

Jacob stared at her in disbelief. "I'm fine, I'm just fine." He looked at his stocking feet, following Rachel's glance.

Pointing to the shoes, she said, "That girl in Boston hasn't converted you to Islam, has she?"

Laughing, he put his arm around her and closed the door. "Very funny. I'm glad to see you."

She twisted out of his grasp and sashayed into the living room. "Are you?"

"Of course, I am."

"Have you fallen for her?"

"Who?"

"The little rich kid in Boston."

"You keep asking that silly question. I'm not even going to dignify it with a reply."

"You certainly spent enough time with her."

"And her aunt."

She studied him. "Does either of them know anything?"

"Sure, quite a lot. Yvonne's an unusual kid. You'd like her yourself. She's left-wing and very well-informed. I'm going to write their article—for her and her aunt. It could be a big one. It might be the opportunity I've been looking for. I told Shanahan today I was quitting to do this. Actually, I asked for some time off." As he was talking, he knew very well what else was driving him. It wasn't just the opportunity. It was also Yvonne, his growing obsession—and it was making him do things that he knew were out of character.

"You've fallen for these ladies' spiel to quit your job and put all your chips on one story? This isn't like you, Jacob. You're more sensible than that. Why don't you just tell me what's going on—from the beginning. Before you do, though, let's get one thing straight. I don't think I'd like this girl, partly because I want you for myself, but also because I don't trust her." She took hold of his shoulders roughly. "I should tell you, Jacob, I care about you, your future—not daffy, crazy caring or anything like that, but more like, uh, a big sister, you know." She seemed embarrassed by her own words. "So, you write your article—it could help your career however it turns out—play with your girlfriend, and when you are finished, we'll talk again—see whether I still care about you." She dropped her hands.

"Like a sister, huh?" Jacob asked, picking up on the odd characterization. "That's the first time I've heard that one from you."

"You're taking big risks here."

"Like a sister?" He repeated aloud in disbelief. "You don't have sex with your sister. That's incest." He enjoyed teasing her like this.

"Jacob, come off it. I said what I said. Have your little joke if you must."

"I take your caring, as you say, pretty seriously." But he was smiling.

She flopped into the one chair in the room, avoiding the couch they usually shared. "Tell me the whole story."

Trying to subdue the confusion of his loyalties and passions, he began to outline his entire experience in Boston, except, of course, his intimacy with Yvonne. For the most part, she let him talk, interrupting only occasionally for clarifications in his muddled tale. Finally, he told her of his call from Natasha Zilenko and her dinner invitation. When he had finished, she went to the kitchen and poured herself a drink.

"Mind if I help myself?" she called from the kitchen. "I don't think you need one. You're already intoxicated enough."

Rachel amused him. She was acting like a big sister. But the thought was somewhere between irritating and comforting. He watched her as she walked back to her chair. He needed her objectivity.

"You've got to get that Pentagon memorandum—if it exists."

"You have doubts?"

"Sure—don't you?"

"Yeah, I guess," he had to admit. "But I worry mostly about its authenticity."

"You need to lean on them for that. Are you tough enough?"

"I think they intend to give it to me—if that's what you're asking."

"Yvonne's promise, I bet."

"Right." Her use of the name startled him. "The company people might be slow to give it up. But she'll get a copy."

"You know, some of these top-secret government documents are fixed so they can't be run through copy machines. That could be a problem."

"Gosh, that's right." He cursed himself for not remembering this. "I'll mention it." Jacob tried to avoid her critical look.

She looked at her watch. "Oh, I've got to go." She got up and grabbed her purse. "Call me tomorrow—after your dinner. It should be interesting." She leaned over and pecked him on the cheek. "Are you okay?"

Jacob's uneasy mood must have shown. He walked her to the door, putting his arm around her waist loosely. "I'm fine." After she had gone, he leaned his head on the closed door, feeling slightly desperate. Was he fine? He was overlooking important things. Rachel's doubts had shaken his confidence. Yvonne's image loomed behind his closed eyes. Still Yvonne. He could almost feel her naked body at the ends of his fingers. Shaking his head in an effort to clear the memory, he poured himself a glass of wine and then regretted it. Because it was easier to drink it than pour it back into the bottle, he polished it off in two long swallows. Then he went to bed.

The next day, he rose early and continued work on his draft, expanding it and making changes here and there. He spent most of the day writing and rewriting. He was pleased about the way it was shaping up. His enthusiasm, if not his confidence, in the project was returning. If he could get hold of the Pentagon memo for just a day, he would begin to fill in the blank spots in what could well become a sensational piece of journalism. But there was still one thing missing—a better understanding of the late Joshua Crane. The picture of the venerable old sailor giving in to an invasive government just didn't add up. After all, Joshua was a proudly independent New Englander. The words of Father Mapple's sermon came back—"the opening maw of hell, with endless pains and sorrows there; which none but they that feel can tell." Was Joshua fighting off big government or falling deeper into a trap? Jacob was reminded of the slave-trading Cranes. These pious New England merchants were a contradiction. He puzzled over the thought and made more notes.

As he gazed into the undulating screen saver, Yvonne's image appeared again and again. He shut the computer down, and she vanished. From the comfort of his unmade bed, he watched the early evening television news. It was mostly about the continuing chaos in the Middle East. The violence between Palestine and Israel was escalating again. Bombs were going off in Saudi Arabia and now in Egypt. Turkey was threatening the Kurds. It was all pretty depressing. As his eyes drooped, he mused idly whether peace would come to the region only if the United States disavowed its relationship with Israel.

Pulling himself together, Jacob dressed for dinner, choosing one of his two suits—the dark one. After all, it was the Carlyle. He tied his necktie, hating the feel of it. His eyes burned from spending most of the day at the computer. A glance at the clock told him he was still early, so he amused himself browsing through the stack of unread magazines he had found in his mail. Many articles focused on the political campaigns for control of Congress. Polls were showing that Republicans were going to hold the majority in both houses.

Before leaving for dinner, he checked the weather from his window. The pavement in the street below had just begun to glisten with a light rain. He grabbed his raincoat and headed for the elevator, giving himself a quick once-over in the hallway mirror. He thought he looked pretty dapper in his one-of-two suits and clean white shirt. Leaving the warmth of the front lobby, he was greeted by a damp drizzle and quickly buttoned up his coat. Even the wet air felt good. He rejected the doorman's whistle for a cab and walked briskly across town to Twenty-ninth Street and Park. There, he caught a cab going north.

In the lobby of the Carlyle, he searched for a flash of red. A light touch from behind startled him. He turned to find an exceptionally beautiful woman at his side. She looked to be in her late fifties. There was not a fleck of gray in her dark hair, which framed a very ethnic, oval face with wide-set eyes and high cheekbones. There was a red scarf at her neck. For a fleeting moment, she reminded him of Yvonne. The fine lines around her eyes crinkled with an off-center smile.

"Mister Sellars, I believe." She offered a hand and took his with a firm grip. "I think I found you first."

Jacob would not have missed the flash of red at her neck. "And you are Natasha Zilenko. Madam, it is a pleasure to meet you."

"Come, we can go into dining room now." She took his arm in the old-fashioned style. "We can have drink there. I don't like noise and crowds in bar. Do you mind?" In the typical Russian way with English, she used few articles.

"Of course not." Jacob escorted her, although it felt more like she was leading him, through the lobby to the entrance of the fancy Dumonet Room, where they were greeted by the maitre d' dressed in tails and a white tie. Still a farm boy at the root, Jacob was always impressed with the opulence of upscale New York. In subdued light from chandeliers dripping with glass, dark walls with dimly lighted portraits of floral displays rose to the high ceiling. To complement the artwork, the restaurant was ablaze with cut flower arrangements everywhere. Luxurious as it was, the place exuded a surprising warmth and friendliness. All the help seemed to be smiling at the same time. It was obvious that Natasha was well known here. Once they were seated with all the usual flourishes of pulled-out chairs, waved napkins, and carefully placed menus, Natasha ordered a brand of vodka Jacob didn't recognize, neat with lemon. Jacob did the same, promising himself to drink cautiously.

"You like our national obsession?" she asked mischievously.

"Yes, I do. But I've never tried this one."

"Well, Mr. Sellars …"—her long eyelashes fluttered theatrically—"it is nice to have opportunity to meet you. Yvonne has said such nice things. Let me say, I support what she and Emily are doing. And Joshua would approve. He was very proud of this girl." She smoothed the tablecloth with her long fingers. "He loved her, her spirit."

What was this woman to Yvonne? A doting babushka or more?

"Tell me about yourself—may I call you Jacob?"

"Of course."

"You work for *News* here in New York?"

"Yes."

"Yvonne tells me you are of Midwest, a farm."

"Yes, in Illinois." Jacob was eager to get started with questions of his own but restrained himself.

"You are far from home. Do you miss it?"

"I love living in New York, but I guess some part of me will always be a farm boy." He tried to make it sound casual and not sentimental. Obviously, Yvonne had provided a biography—he hoped without too much ridicule. He could feel his color rise at the thought.

"An interesting background. I, too, was brought up on farm, in Georgia outside of Tbilisi near where Stalin was born. Do you know it?"

"Yes, vaguely."

She sighed, turning her palms up in resignation. "Alas, it is mess now, with still terrible troubles in Chechnya. But now I'm staying in Baku—I'm sure you know where that is. It is almost American city, but full of intrigue and sinister plots and oil." This last she said with a wink and a certain relish, taking small sips of her vodka. Raising her glass slightly above the table, she asked, "What do you think of it? It is very Russian, this vodka."

Jacob took a sip. "It's, uh, more tasty than most. I like it." Actually, Jacob thought all vodka tasted the same—like pure alcohol.

"I know you have questions for me, but I want to tell some things first—some important things." She took a delicate bite of the smoked salmon canapé that had appeared with the drinks. "The stories about Joshua being involved with bad things of, how do you say it, cleaning money. This is untrue, silly. And we, Joshua and I, were not strange as was said." Jacob assumed she meant "estranged" but didn't correct her. "Such things are personal and troublemaking." She said this with disgust. "Some stories even talk about arms-selling. False! Made up by oligarchs who could not do deals with Joshua they wanted. They were blackmailing him, and your government was blackmailing him, too. They are using company today. I think you already know why." A shadow of profound sorrow clouded her face. The candlelight seemed to deepen the lines around her eyes. "The company has lost reputation, position, and is now losing wealth also. It has become joke in Baku. The Bush Company, they call it now, behind their hands. Cruel things are said about my Joshua." Her eyes glistened with emotion, but there was a hardness about her, revealed beneath the Slavic warmth.

Sensing that she might be finding it difficult to go on, Jacob filled in. "I understand how difficult this must be for you to talk about your husband under such circumstances. I want to expose these schemes, but I need better information. Contrary to what you suggest, I don't really know why the government is using Crane or what they hope to accomplish. This is where I need help."

"But you know about Pentagon paper."

"I hear one exists. I haven't seen it yet. And I need to verify its authenticity."

"Yvonne is bringing it."

"Here, tonight?" Jacob's heart skipped a beat, but not about the paper.

"Yes, here—tonight, soon." She glanced at the gold watch on her slender wrist. "She should be here now."

Hoping to probe a little deeper before Yvonne arrived, Jacob raised a question that had been bothering him since her unexpected call. "May I ask you a personal question?"

"Yes." She looked surprised.

"You are a bit of a mystery to our press. Joshua's obituary said that you and he had separated. You say that is not true." Her expression did not change. "I should think that you are the kind of woman a man would always want to have with him." Jacob was trying to sweeten the unpleasant implications.

She sighed. "It is fair question. We had some differences. Yes. But they are about my independence. I wanted to pursue my interests—in art, as collector. Russian art I knew best. I was gathering works for a show which would travel first around Europe, later America. Joshua resented my frequent travels." She raised her arms in exasperation. "So I got place in Paris. We often met there."

"But you live in Baku, in Azerbaijan?"

"No, not live, visit. I am in Paris more. I go to Baku because of all this, the bad publishes—what we are talking about, the guns, the influence. There are people there who know what is going on. I talk to them. They tell me much, which I am now telling you. I am trying to help Yvonne and Emily to find truth and make things right."

"I see," Jacob said, wondering whether this was one of Yvonne's mysterious sources. "You have visited Baku since Joshua's death?"

"Yes, of course. I need to find things. Oligarchs now tell me there is blackmail and more."

"Like what?"

"Russia has understanding with U.S. to get help in Chechnya and other Muslim republics to wipe out uprisings and weaken Taliban who are spreading into these countries. Iran, too. Maybe go back into Afghanistan. It threatens oil and Russian power, you see."

"And money would be transferred to Crane and maybe others for safekeeping and be available for covert activities by both your country and mine. Is that the gist of it?"

She smiled. "As Yvonne says, you are quick learner. Yes, we think that is part of plan. It is what oligarchs tell me."

"And Joshua, your husband—did he know about this plan?" Jacob was struck by the ironies of his country and Russia joining together to dominate the world. What a ridiculous culmination of the Cold War.

"Yes. That is disagreement we had. I wanted him to fight it—to reveal all. But he kept telling me not now. The promise of more oil contracts, pipelines, and digging wells in Russia was his hope, and Americans encouraged him, promising big benefits. Young Joshua has same hopes, but he is not so stubborn. He does listen."

"Really." This positive comment on Joshua surprised Jacob. Maybe there was hope for his ultimate cooperation. "So you still have an interest, yourself, in the company—I mean a financial interest?"

"Of course."

Jacob was digesting the import of her story and its value as news, if true, when Yvonne appeared. He first caught sight of her pausing at the entrance to engage the maitre d' briefly and then following his nod in the direction of Natasha's table. She waved quickly and smiled. Refusing help with a coat draped over one arm, she made her way through the large room, pausing at several tables to greet friends as if she were a politician. She wore a simple black dress at knee length with spaghetti straps. She flung her hair to the side as she leaned over to greet and kiss a cheek or two at other tables. She was very poised and quite at home in the fancy setting. Jacob totally lost his train of thought as he watched her. He was mesmerized.

"She is beautiful, no?" Natasha's comment startled him.

"Yes, she is." As Yvonne approached the table, he noticed that she held a par-tially concealed envelope beneath the coat. He suspected this was the notorious Pentagon memo.

Flouncing into the chair offered by the attentive maitre d', she said, "Have you two solved the world's problems?" Her luminous skin glowed in the light cast by the candles on the tables. Jacob studied them both, searching for clues of a relationship. The possibilities intrigued him. Yes, this dark beauty could be Rus-sian.

Yvonne ordered a Perrier with lemon and slipped the envelope into Jacob's lap. "That's the memo. We'll discuss it later." She pulled her chair in closer to the table and leaned forward. "I've been followed since I left Boston. I can't get rid of him." She glanced over toward the entrance. "I don't see him now. He's probably in the lobby."

"You were followed all the way from Boston? How did you come?" Jacob asked dumbfounded.

"On the new bullet train—and yes, all the way from Boston."

"You see, Jacob," Natasha said, "these people will stop at nothing. I am very worried for Yvonne's safety. They are bad lot."

While it all seemed Hollywood and extreme, Jacob began to doubt his own suspicions. He and Mitch had been tailed in Boston. He had seen the guy follow-ing them and then chasing the underground streetcar. Garon was himself quite real. Still, Jacob could not shake entirely the uneasiness sown by Rachel, who was very street-smart and had plenty of experience.

"Natasha has told you what she has learned from the oligarchs?" Yvonne asked.

"Yes. It's not a pretty picture."

Turning to Natasha, Yvonne said, "Jacob is still a doubting Thomas, I'm afraid. He always has to verify, authenticate, or whatever." She glanced at him. "I think you should start to write." Her tone had a friendly warmth despite the critical assertion.

"I already have. And as a journalist, I should be verifying everything. It's routine. You should understand that."

She reached for his hand. "Oh, I do. I just want to get you on our side."

"I am on your side, for heaven's sake. What's your hurry? We're not talking about a long delay here. I've quit my ... I mean ... I've taken a sabbatical from the *News* to do this full-time. I just want to be sure we tell a credible story. Readers are suspicious of the press now, way more skeptical. Because this will be a high-profile story, it'll get a lot of scrutiny. We should be ready for it."

"I agree with him, Yvonne," Natasha said. "We must take his advice."

"We will, *Maman*. We will." Yvonne eased her petulance, still holding Jacob's hand and gazing at him meaningfully.

Jacob was startled by the term of endearment. Was *maman* like "mother"?

"You probably already know, Jacob," said Natasha, returning to the subject, "that Iraq is quite good oil for your government. Country has several billion barrels under its land. It could when healthy put out five million barrels a day in production. It will be money-raiser and important supplier. Crane Corporation was going to be part of this, until government came."

"I thought Crane oil exploration was mostly in the U.S. and Mexico." Jacob was trying to recall the obituary history of the company.

"That's true, but company is important middleman, broker of oil sales and shipment in Middle East. It is also pipeline builder. Iraqi oil presents opportunities in all areas, very lucrative opportunities. Maybe gone now."

Jacob was impressed with Natasha's knowledge of the business. "Why would it be gone now?"

"Because Crane is now perceived as agent of U.S.—government no one trusts anymore. Russia and your country trusted by no one. Europeans want to put Iraqi oil reserves under international controls. And China wants oil, too. Of course, U.S. opposes. Crane is left in middle with black reputation for conniving with America and Russia. Other countries, especially Europe, do not trust. Bad things happen when oil goes over one hundred euros a barrel. It will corrupt everyone."

Jacob was beginning to understand. "You want to free Crane from this, ah, relationship? A bargain with the devil, so to speak." He liked the cliché, but he would not use it.

"I'm not sure we can. We just want to tell truth."

"The article would do that." Jacob wanted agreement from Natasha and confirmation that she was part of the team.

She smiled. "We hope so. Crane family should be ones to expose this."

"But if the U.S. stays in control of the oil, as they are likely to, Crane is left out anyway. You win nothing."

"Yes, that is risk we will be taking." She turned to Yvonne. "Your Mr. Sellars is very wise."

"Now do you see why I am so anxious?" Yvonne asked Jacob.

They ordered dinner, and Natasha continued with her stories from Baku, some of which seemed little more than gossip, but other comments suggested much harder information about America's complicity with Russia to capture Iraqi oil and other Mideast reserves for their shady activities. Natasha had good reasons for wanting him to tell their story—both wealth and pride. He guessed Yvonne was in it mostly for pride. He decided against further probing. So he just listened, making scribbled notes and trying to be subtle about it. His story was beginning to take shape.

During the rest of the evening Natasha dominated the discussion, but he could feel Yvonne watching him intently. She drank very little and was uncharacteristically silent. Jacob realized that she was slightly in awe of this interesting and impressive woman, whom she had oddly addressed as *maman* earlier. They seemed to know and trust each other and revealed an unusual closeness. Jacob wondered when they had opportunities to meet, with Natasha living abroad most of the time. Then he remembered that Yvonne liked her trips to Paris.

"Now, I'm going to leave you two," Natasha said, looking at her watch. "It is late, and I am old woman." She smiled wearily at them. "I need my beauty sleep."

Yvonne took her arm as they both stood. "And you're not an old woman." She hugged her fondly. Yvonne's tenderness was real.

He started to get up. "Yeah, it is kind of late. I better get going, too."

Yvonne shoved him down firmly. "No you don't. Stay put. I'll be right back."

"You better sit, Jacob," Natasha said. "She'll be angry if you don't. And let me say good night. I want to thank you for listening. You and Yvonne can take over from here. I'll be in town for week or so, and if I can help, Yvonne can reach me." She held out her hand in a way that Jacob thought a European man would be prompted to kiss it. However, Jacob just accepted her hand in his.

"Good night, Natasha, if I may call you that. I've enjoyed meeting you and hearing your fascinating story. I'm so glad we could get together. I hope we can do it again." They walked out slowly, leaving Jacob in awe of this astonishing woman.

For his few moments alone, he allowed himself to indulge his muses. Here he was far from the sweeping cornfields of southern Illinois, where Jacob had lived with influences quite alien to his life now. Many of the country roads in Appleton were still dirt, throwing up huge clouds of dust with every passing pickup truck. The Amish farmed with horses and hand tools and rode to town in their horse-drawn, black buggies. Some of these families were related to his father, and they often met in the feed store for conversation and farm talk. His roots seemed strange and oddly foreign to the perspective of the dining room at the Carlyle—his Russian visitor and the descendants of a whaling family trying to save their oil company.

Beyond the doors of the Carlyle spread Manhattan, the restless, raucous city of international proportions, bearing little relationship to anything American. The new, if temporary, elite of the city included super-rich Arabs, lavishing their oil wealth on every part of upscale life. They competed with the mostly homegrown hedge fund operators and takeover artists. This strange city had changed Jacob, probably forever. But there were certain influences he could not shake.

Not until after he had left home for good did he recognize the overwhelming influence his father had exercised in his life. He was a moody, religious man, not articulate, and given to long periods of mental detachment from the family. He had urged his son to learn the wholesome disciplines of farming. Under penalties of stiff punishment, Jacob was required to do his share of the daily chores. Weighing on daily life was always the fear of his father's wrath. It wasn't as if Jacob didn't know what the inviolable limits were. He had heard them every Sunday from the pulpit. The preachments were not unlike those resonating in Father Mapple's chapel.

His mother had allowed the old man to fulminate, quietly managing the household in silent submission. Actually, his parents were so unlike one another that Jacob wondered why they had married. His mother was of mixed heritage, mostly English and Dutch, and his father was German—just German. They were not demonstrative in their fondness. Looking back, Jacob doubted that they had ever had an intimate life together. Any natural warmth between them had long been stifled by biblical taboos. His mother was unable or unwilling to express her differences, if she had any. This environment had left something out of Jacob's life. He had always felt abandoned by her in the violent scenes with his father. He resented this at the time. He didn't know why, but he felt that his mother's failings were somehow related to his attraction to Christy. He knew that Christy had confessed her experience with him, and he suspected that the families had met to discuss the transgression. Nothing had come of it, but the episode had left its mark, like a scar on his soul.

"Hey, did you miss me?" Yvonne suddenly materialized across from him. "Deep in thought again? And what was it this time?"

"Oh, nothing important. Just a bit of reminiscing."

"About what?"

"You're too nosy. Just the ironies of life."

"I guess that's better than moral relativism," she suggested teasingly. "Maybe you think too much, Jacob."

"It isn't that interesting."

"Okay, not to press. Let's get out of here."

"Where to? I need to get home."

"I want to see where you live. Take me. We can read that memo together. And I can leave it with you, if you like." She got up and offered her hand in encouragement. Was she also offering bait?

"Really, it's late." Jacob was stalling, worried about Rachel's waiting to hear from him. He glanced at his watch. It was past eleven. He was pretty sure it wasn't reading that Yvonne had in mind. He was wary of her—what she was doing to him. "Maybe we could do it in the morning."

"Does your building have parietal rules?" She smiled impishly. It was moments like this that Jacob was reminded of how young she was.

"Gosh, I hope not." He played along with her joke. "I've never had problems before."

"Now, you're bragging." She tugged at his hand. "Are we going or not?"

Reluctantly, but with a shudder of excitement and trepidation passing through his body, he relented and followed her out. She reached the curb first and jumped into a cab, exposing a flash of her long thighs. Joining her, he gave his address, and they were off. As the driver careened through still-busy streets, she rubbed Jacob's leg suggestively and kissed him lightly on the cheek, whispering, "Jacob, I really do like you." It was a surprised tone, as if she had just made a new discovery.

"That's a relief. And you haven't had a thing to drink." He put his arm around her, and she snuggled in closer as his heart thumped. Jacob watched the turbaned driver's eyes shift in the mirror, wondering whether he disapproved.

"This is cute," she said as Jacob turned on a few lights in his small apartment. "It's very you, spare and all boy colors." She snooped around, taking a quick inventory of his bookshelves. "Wow, have you read all this stuff?"

"No. But I'm working on it."

"A lot of fiction." She paused and pulled out a tome. "And Freud?" She studied him. "You got hang-ups?"

"Some."

"That's right, you mentioned that."

She replaced the book without more comment and studied several publicity photos on display at one end of the bookcase. Picking up one of the frames and waving it in his direction, she asked, "Who are you with here?"

"A Chicago detective."

"You did crime work?"

"I'm afraid so."

"Wow. And in Chicago. It's a tough town." She continued her search. "No family pictures—your mom and dad, siblings?"

"No."

She glanced at him quizzically.

It was becoming difficult to chatter on with the tension that was mounting within him. He suspected that she was feeling the same. "Do you want to talk or …"

"Fuck?"

"That's kind of crude, Yvy."

"That's nice, you called me Yvy. I like that. It makes me feel, ah, close." She stood with her hands on her hips, challenging him. "So what are you going to do about it?"

It wasn't difficult for him to be aggressive this time. She was irresistible, and he was burning up with desire. Like the first time, their clothes were flung off, dropping in a trail to the bedroom. Embracing as they moved and not letting go as they lay together, they began the ritual they were both possessed by. The intensity of desire became almost unbearable for Jacob as they began to explore each other's bodies on his king-size bed. Jacob felt devoured by his own passions as well as hers, as if his identity was being sucked out of him. They used their hands and mouths until there was nothing left untouched. Now and then they would stop, as if some signal had reached them simultaneously, and gaze at one another, eyes blazing with desire. Then they would return to their madness, rolling into successive positions as they shared their fervor. Finally, in one of their pauses, she spoke in a husky voice. "Now, Jacob—I want you now."

She pushed him roughly onto his back and knelt astride him, lifting her arms and gathering her hair. A smile lingered on her lips for just a moment as she looked down on him mockingly. Her exhibition worked. Tipping her over on her back while fighting her tentative resistance, Jacob pinned her arms and possessed her as his own. They both cried out in the union of their bodies, joined in every way nature had planned. Moving together as if they were also one in mind and spirit, they drew from each other what they needed in the final surge of their passion.

When it was over, they lay together panting heavily and looking blankly at the ceiling. "Oh God, Jacob." She turned and peered at him through the shadows of reflected light from the hallway. Her eyes had become liquid pools of soft innocence. "Where did that come from?" Then she frowned. "How many women have you been like that with?"

"None." Jacob looked away, embarrassed. He wanted to tell her again he loved her, but this time, he restrained himself.

"Something the matter?" She rolled closer to him, running her hand down his stomach until she touched him. "I'm still feeling sexy. You really got me going. Is that what you learned on the farm?" Her play became more assertive. When he seemed to resist, she asked, "Are you okay?"

He didn't move away from her; he couldn't. He was still under her spell. "I'm fine." He looked at her as he felt himself becoming aroused again. "You're making me fine." He smiled and gave in. They made love again, this time slowly, trying to keep their ardor under control until the last moment. Yvonne was less patient, more demanding. Holding onto himself as long as he could, Jacob finally took her with the same intensity as before—lost in an overwhelming knot of emotions. Afterward, he held her in his arms, hiding his face in her neck, trying to keep his feelings in check. He wanted to tell her that he would never leave her but realized that was for him, not her. He couldn't bear the thought of losing her. Instead, he said, "It gets better each time." He turned away from her, still catching his breath, and they rested quietly in silence until she dozed off. Jacob crept out of bed and retrieved his trousers from the floor. Smiling to himself at his neatness, he gathered up their discarded clothes, leaving hers in the bedroom. Standing at the window, he watched the light traffic pass in the streets below, his favorite occupation when he couldn't sleep. It was half-past two. To his relief, Rachel had not called. The twinkling lights of the city created a glow against a patchy cloud cover that was moving east. He realized that he was completely mesmerized by Yvonne. Was it the sex? Or had he fallen in love? The difference didn't really matter. Either way, he was hooked. She had occupied his thoughts full-time since they had first met on Nantucket. It was too late for caution. Feeling drained, he stretched out on the couch but didn't close his eyes.

Later, still wrestling with his feelings, he was surprised by her sudden appearance, fully dressed. In the dim light of the room, she could have been a dream. She moved toward him noiselessly. He felt the brush of her lips on his cheek.

"I've got to go, Jacob." She sat on the edge of the couch, the bodice of her stylish black dress gapped in front, exposing her breasts. Jacob could feel himself respond. "You read that memo and then let's talk." She was all business now. "We have a lot to do. Call me in Boston." She wrote a number on a scrap of paper.

"Leaving town so soon?" Jacob heard himself almost pleading.

"I plan to fly back early this afternoon." She stood, impatient to go. "I'll let myself out."

"I should come with you," he suggested, thinking of the hour and the dearth of cabs. "Maybe you were followed here." He started to get up.

"It's okay. I already ordered a car on my cell. They're probably out there now." She leaned over and kissed him again, this time on his mouth. "Thanks for a delicious evening." And then she was gone.

Her abrupt departure left him with a panoply of doubts and hopes. He remembered Mitch's words as if they were etched in his brain. "She's not a romantic … she's using you … you will never be part of her life … you'll get hurt." The words seemed so wrong now. Their lovemaking had turned him into a believer.

CHAPTER 10

Smoke filled the air in the small conference room tucked away in the basement of a waterfront warehouse, scheduled to be razed. Modern high rises surrounded the old stone building, which had not quite made the cut in the historic preservation list. Luis Garon sat with four other men at a big glass-topped table requisitioned from Crane's Boston office across the street. Each of the burly foursome had a distinctive button in a lapel and a device in one ear for communication—government issue. With shaved heads and blocky builds, they looked as if they would be more comfortable in military fatigues than in the business suits they wore. Each had a copy of an official-appearing document before him. They sat in silence reading. After a reasonable interval, Garon spoke.

"This document is a first-page copy of the memo in question. It's been digitally scanned by a special software. It's marked top secret. The cover sheet will help you identify what we are looking for. I don't have to tell you how sensitive it is. The one we're looking for has been treated to prevent any kind of photocopies from being made. There should only be the one copy out there. That's the good news." He smiled, smug with his insider's knowledge. "The bad news is we can't be sure who has it. We need to find it and soon." He glanced meaningfully at each man. Garon felt confident with his "government-issue" troops. He paused to emphasize the urgency. "You will note that the directive authorizes me to take, and I quote, 'all steps necessary' to prevent dissemination. Someone we don't like could still scan it digitally. 'All steps' includes detaining any who are uncooperative—by force, if necessary." There was a restless fidgeting following this remark. "The culprit can be held indefinitely under the Patriot Act, probably outside the country with no access to the press or lawyers. It would be quite legal. Of course, if they resist …"

"Are we going to whack anyone or not, Luis? Or do we just put 'em in Gitmo?"

"I hope neither will be necessary." Garon was enjoying his role as leader. "This is serious business. If the press finds out what's in the memo, the political consequences could be disastrous for national security." He paused again to let the importance of their mission sink in.

"I see you've listed a couple of names here. One is that Crane girl. Could she have the paper?"

"Yes, I think she had it, but she may have passed it on to a reporter she met up with in New York. They had dinner together last night at the Carlyle Hotel, where they were observed."

"Think? May have? Or what?" It was the same questioner, the ringleader of the bunch. "We don't want to make mistakes here."

The cocky independence of some of the newer staff was irritating. Garon realized he had to regain control.

"We don't do guesswork here. The reporter, Sellars, has it." He hoped he was right. "He was seen leaving the hotel with the Crane girl. We are sure she left it with him. They were together late in his apartment." Garon paused, improvising his strategy. "Her Russian stepmother … you know, the wife of the old man … had dinner with them. She's been a troublemaker for the Russian government. But she is beyond our mission. Leave her alone."

"What if the girl still has it?"

"It's unlikely."

"Okay, so do we go after the reporter?"

"No, not yet. There are others we need to watch in case digital copies have been made. The new technology may be out there. We must find out how big our problem is. Mitchel, Henry Mitchel—as you know, he's a reporter with the *Globe*. He's probably at least read the memo." He paused, folding his hands before him. "We need to find out how much he knows, whether he scanned it, who he is talking to. I've arranged to have a tap on his phone and a hold on his cell records. Hank, you stay in touch with our guy at NSA. He'll keep you up to date on Mitchel. We don't want this guy to blab to other media people either." Garon pointed to another of his men. "And then, Norm, there is Joshua's sister, Emily Crane."

"The lez?"

"Yes. We need to follow her, see who she is in contact with. Same goes for her telephone records."

"Well, what do the rest of us do?" The men seemed eager to get started.

"I am anticipating one or more of these people will try to leave the country. We want to prevent that. If we suspect, uh, an unscheduled trip for any of them, you should be ready to get on the road. And we'll need you all for that." He closed his file. "Now, a word of caution. Follow these two, Mitchel and the lez, with discretion. No rough stuff. If necessary, you can interview them. Identify yourself as a government agent and just talk. Impress upon them that they need to tell us what is going on with this paper, talk about national security, et cetera, and find out whether they have shared the information. I want to know what Sellars is planning before he does it." He dropped the file into his briefcase and stood. "The memo will be all you need for now, names and addresses, phones to tap if you need to. I will take care of Sellars. And if I want help, I'll be in touch. We may have to move fast." He studied his men, meeting the eye of each, a technique he had found to be effective in Mexico. "Let me warn each of you again— be careful how you do this. No rough stuff. Mitchel and Emily Crane are well-known figures. Joshua will be watching, too—so will the media." Signaling the meeting was over, he added, "Thank you, gentlemen. Let me know if you hear anything."

"Is there time to catch up with the reporter?"

"Yes, and hopefully before he gets wind of this and runs for cover."

"Keep the big fish for yourself, eh, Luis?" That got a laugh from his men as they filed out in military order. "Be the hero." Garon did not appreciate the sarcasm but said nothing. He would have to be watching his back with these agency types.

He sat for a moment staring at the bare walls. The project had been set in motion. The rapid response would impress his Arab friends, as well as the Feds. The turncoats at Crane would be apprehended, and the troublesome Pentagon memo would soon be under control. And yes, he would be a hero. He allowed himself to dream of a large corner office on the executive floor of Crane headquarters in New York—or even a big job at the CIA. He glanced at his watch. He had an hour before his flight back to the city. Sellars would not be expecting a visit. Garon looked forward to it.

Jacob wrote all day and into the night. It was almost midnight when he got the call from Mitch.

"I'm glad I got you. We have a problem." He sounded very tense.

"A new one? I've read the memo. It's a blockbuster. It could spell big trouble for the administration. I'd say it's they who have the problem. I hope you're not going to tell me that the memo is a fake."

"No, but they're fighting back. Joshua is beginning to wake up. He says he is no longer in control of the situation. It's too complicated to go into details now. But he's telling Emily she better make herself scarce, and Yvonne, too."

"Scarce? What does that mean?"

"Run."

"Run? Where? Why?"

"Run, because we may end up in Guantanamo Bay or a place just like it. What we're doing may be a crime under the new Patriot Act. Possession of this paper is a violation of the Act. They want it back and will detain anyone who's read it until they can figure out damage control."

"I can't believe it. This is America, Mitch."

"But this is the way it is, like it or not."

"Yvonne? She's just a kid, for heaven's sake." Jacob wondered why he said this.

"Doesn't make any difference. Anyway, she's an adult, not a kid."

"Where is she? Is she okay?"

"She's fine."

"And Emily?"

"Okay, too."

"So, where are they—Yvonne and Emily?"

"I'm not going to get into that, Jacob. We don't have a secure phone line. These guys are all over. You can't believe their reach, using the NSA. My point in calling is to tell you to get lost yourself—and fast. They probably know about you," he added cryptically.

"Get lost? Where?"

"Come on, Jacob—you're smarter than that. I haven't got time to discuss this. I have to go. Just make yourself invisible until this gets straightened out."

"How will that happen?"

"You're impossible! They've already grabbed a guy in the company. He's disappeared. I've said enough. Get going." Mitch hung up abruptly.

Jacob sat in disbelief. Run from the law when he hadn't done anything? Run from his government? He'd surely be guilty then. But Mitch had a point. The new Patriot Act was insanity. An indefinite sojourn in Cuba didn't seem very appetizing. Instinctively, he began throwing clothes into a suitcase. A call to Rachel now was out of the question. If he disappeared, she would worry—maybe even call the police. She didn't know enough to be in any trouble herself. Jacob hoped the government wasn't tracking her, too. He continued packing, still finding it all difficult to believe. Then the phone rang again.

"Mr. Sellars, this is Luis Garon. We need to talk. It's important. I'm in New York on business. I have some information for you. When can we meet?"

"What kind of information, Luis?" Jacob was thinking fast.

"I'd rather not say now."

"Uh, how about tomorrow morning?"

"That would be fine. How about 9:30 at your office?"

"So early? Must be important."

"I think it will be of interest. I'll tell you then."

"Okay, see you at 9:30." Jacob hung up quickly, his heart beating fast.

This was bad news, real bad news. Mitch's warning had come almost too late. He wondered whether his apartment was being watched already. Continuing to stuff a small suitcase, he folded the memo in among his clothes. Hastily packing up his laptop, he left his apartment without even checking for surveillance, keeping his eyes straight ahead. Walking fast, but not too fast, he ducked down into the subway at Twenty-third Street and caught an express train downtown. At Fulton Street, he got off and raced to the nearest stairway, ignoring the escalator option. When he got to the street, he grabbed a cab he saw waiting at the curb. It all went very smoothly. He was sure he had eluded his follower if there had been one.

As the cab headed across the Fifty-ninth Street Bridge to La Guardia, he looked back several times, but in the heavy traffic, it was a useless effort. Finally, he relaxed a little and took stock of his situation. Where had Yvonne gone? Options began rolling through his head. Paris, her favorite destination? She probably had friends there. Was that where she got involved with left-wing causes and anti-American concerns—the Movement? But it was a wild guess and an expensive one, if he followed her. In a sudden inspiration, he decided to fly to Chicago, a familiar town in which he could "get lost" for awhile. He would call a friend from his old newspaper. Phil Ross was a stalwart left-wing Democrat with views similar to those of Rachel. Jacob would be safe there for the time being. If Ross was not around, he could take a hotel room until his friend got back. The casual plan did not feel reassuring. Once on the plane, he found himself constantly on the lookout, not for terrorists, but for government agents. It was a nerve-racking trip.

It turned out that Phil was at home and happy to see his old friend. Jacob quickly told him of Mitch's warning and his precarious status as a possible fugitive. The story did not seem to shock Phil, who was a legal reporter and familiar with powers of the Justice Department under the new laws dealing with terrorist threats.

"I knew the press would be the first to be caught in this! What a disaster!"

He generously offered sanctuary for as long as necessary. Jacob also heard a vigorous critique of the administration's threats to attack Iran. Phil insisted on sending out for pizza instead of chancing a restaurant. After settling Jacob into his digs in a rather spartan second bedroom, Phil proudly produced several bottles of vintage Bordeaux and with a flourish opened the earliest date and poured two glasses. "I always serve French wine to piss off my critics." It was the same old Phil. They ate and drank and talked into the wee hours of morning about the Crane family and his freelance project. Phil expressed concern that Jacob might lose his job at the *News*. Jacob hadn't yet faced up to his bad career choice. After his friend went to bed, Jacob lay awake in the thrall of Bordeaux, wondering whether the whole experience was a bad dream. Before he slept, the image of Yvonne appeared in a variety of incarnations, creating an instant longing.

Just before dawn, he was pulled from a drugged sleep by the chime of his cell phone. He had the presence of mind to place it on the night table before collapsing into bed. Even so, it took him awhile to identify the sound and find the phone.

"Jacob," Mitch's voice was edgy. "I've been trying you for hours. Where are you, for God's sake? Some guy answered at your apartment, and I was scared to death that they had taken you in. Are you okay?"

"I'm fine, Mitch, fine. Just tired." But he feared for the havoc being wrought to his belongings. "I'm in … are we secure?"

"Don't say it. It could be risky."

"My lips are sealed." Jacob was beginning to think he was playing a movie role.

Mitch said, "For the moment, we have things under control—in a friendlier environment."

Jacob assumed that this was intended as a hint. Were they all in Paris? "That's reassuring. And the others?" He wanted to ask about Yvonne.

"As I said, fine. What about you?"

"I am for awhile."

"You better be out of New York." Mitch's tone made it urgent.

"I am."

"Good." Mitch paused. There was a chatter of background conversation while Mitch covered the phone. Then he was back. "We've gotten hold of a reporter who will help with your story and get it placed, uh, in the foreign press. The guy is really thrilled about what you've found. Can you fly to London?" Not waiting for an answer, he asked. "You got your passport with you?"

"Yes, I always have it." The sudden suggestion of London confused Jacob, and the involvement of another newsman was unsettling.

"Listen, I need another day to set things up. I'm assuming you're still in the U.S." There was another pause and a muffled phone. "I'll have a plan for you then. At the moment, we are a little disorganized."

"London it is, and I'll wait for a call."

"So you better get on your way. Can you manage? Surveillance will be pretty tight, so be careful. Okay?"

"Yeah, sure." An odd choice, Jacob thought. The Brits were hand in glove with U.S. intel.

"Okay, I'll call you tomorrow or the next day." The connection went dead.

Jacob rolled over, still in a haze of the night's wine and the early hour. Mitch's uncertainty was disturbing, but at this point Jacob had no alternative. London? Was that where Mitch was? Or was it just a cover? He glanced at his watch. It was 5:30 AM. As he lay on his back studying the cracked ceiling, a gauzy image of Yvonne floated for a moment among the splotched paint cover-up attempts and then dissolved. With increasing regret, he reconstructed the evening with Phil and his revelations about his article. Phil had probably drunk enough to have forgotten any details which may have slipped out. At least, Jacob was sure he had kept mum about the content of the Pentagon memo. His concerns gradually let go, and he fell back into a deep sleep, until he was aroused by tentative taps at his door. The shape of Phil came gradually into focus.

"Hey, I gotta go to work, buddy. You okay?"

"Yeah, I'm … sorry. I'm a little hung over."

Phil grinned. "Me, too." He made a face. "There's some coffee made, and I got some bagels—if you want a bite. Sorry, it's kind of slim pickins. I'll be back in the afternoon. Gotta make an appearance at least."

Jacob sat up. "I need to get going, Phil. I should fly to Canada, the quickest way out of the U.S."

He stared at Jacob in disbelief. "When did you decide this?"

"I got a call early this morning on my cell."

"From where?"

"I'm not sure yet—Europe, London." Jacob was intentionally vague.

"I'm impressed. Someone's looking after you, huh?"

"Something like that. They want me to join them as soon as possible."

"Where?"

"I don't know yet."

Phil shook his head. "Sounds pretty weird."

Feeling the need to get started, Jacob struggled out of bed. "So I'll be gone when you get back." He stuck his hand out. "You've been a real help to me, and I appreciate it. I'll keep you posted."

"Yeah, I'll be looking for your story. We'll try to get it in the paper here, too. Serve them right." He shook Jacob's hand vigorously. "They can't fault us for just reporting about what we copy. Hah!" He clapped his hands.

"Well, we'll see what happens. I've got to get there first."

Phil became serious. "Oh, damn! Hold on! What about the fugitive thing?" He sat down on Jacob's bed. "You know, they'll be looking for you by now. The airports are crawling with Homeland Security types anyway." He became thoughtful. "You should rent a car and drive to Canada—you know, an easy border exit, like Windsor. It's only about a five-hour drive. Then fly wherever you have to. I could rent the car. It would give you a head start. You can pay me back later." He grinned impishly. "God, this is exciting." He rubbed his hands together. "I'll just put it on my plastic. Your name won't even come up. I kinda like being part of this."

Jacob considered the idea for a moment. "That's probably a good idea. But I don't want to get you in trouble. We shouldn't underestimate these guys. They're a bad lot."

"Hey, man, I'm just a bystander. I don't know anything." He smiled, miming innocence. "If they ask, I'll tell 'em what little I know. By that time, you'll be long gone."

"Sounds like a plan, I guess."

"So hang here until I get back. I'll bring the car. We'll get you off to a safe start. Agreed?"

"Okay." They shook hands again. "This really helps, Phil. On the car, I'll give you a check to cover it."

"Whatever. Gotta go—bye. Now, stay put." He shook a finger at Jacob.

That night, under the cover of darkness, Jacob drove out of the city in a rental car, after having had an early dinner with Phil, who had continued to make attempts at prying out more details on the Crane family and the project. It was a forgivable curiosity thought Jacob, as he sped down I-90 toward the Indiana state line, keeping a watchful eye for police cars. He and Phil had been close friends in Jacob's Chicago days, and it seemed natural to share some of his ideas. He smiled to himself at old memories of Phil's and his clumsy efforts to meet women in the glitzy nightlife of Rush Street. They had both been brought up on a farm.

During his drive, several coffee stops were needed to stay awake. Mesmerized by the unfolding lane of black tar ahead, his overactive mind flashed to the image of his father's florid face as he swung his big open hand to strike Jacob's mother. Bad memories came back at night—probably stirred up by the stimulus of strong coffee. Jacob had watched her crumple under the impact of the blow. She had been trying ineffectually to defend him against his father's wrath about the trouble over Christy. The violence had left him frozen with fear, unable to act. His heart pounded as he relived the moment. The blow was her punishment for her tentative defense of him. Fearful of being next, Jacob had cringed in the corner of the room, avoiding the inert heap of his mother on the floor and the looming hulk of his messianic father. But the attack on him never came. Instead, the withering words tumbled from the big man's wet lips. "Pedophile, pervert, sodomist!" he had roared in the deep baritone of an evangelical preacher. They were words he had hurled at Jacob before. Jacob shook his head violently to rid himself of the image and those which might follow. Then he pulled off the road and stopped, closing his eyes tightly as if to squeeze the ugly memory back into his subconscious. It was one of many episodes of his father's violence that haunted him.

First light began to brighten the eastern sky as he crossed into Michigan and headed across the state to Detroit and the border crossing at Windsor. Daylight helped him regain his composure. When his eyes started drooping in the warmth of the rising sun, he decided to stop again for coffee. A Denny's would have to do. The graphic pictures of their big breakfast choices on the menu made him a little sick. Juice for his dry throat and coffee to stay awake were all he needed.

Crossing the Ambassador Bridge over the Detroit River into Windsor, he approached the busy border station. Jacob's stomach lurched with the dread of being caught. Trucks were lined up ahead of him. He tried to calm himself with reassurances that the Feds had no way of tracing the rented car to his name, and it was doubtful that they had time to generate the information necessary to ID him. He worried about Phil, however. Would they trace his cell phone? Belatedly, he regretted involving his friend.

Jacob thought the guards on the Canadian side peered at him suspiciously. But didn't they always do that? Flashing his passport and press card, he was waved through after only the most routine questions. He picked up speed as soon as he found his next route. A careful study of maps at the coffee stop paid off in an easy transition to the highway system of Canada. He passed reassuring signs for Montreal and drove east. His next worry was the airport.

He breathed a deep sigh of relief as the lumbering Airbus roared down the runway. He smiled with satisfaction at his success in eluding Garon. While Jacob had nervously cooled his heels in the waiting lounge at the airport, Mitch had called again to confirm the flight number to London and advise him to wait for further instructions the next day. Jacob had been able to book a flight on Air Canada using his credit card. The purchase of his ticket and check-in had gone without a hitch. Air Canada had even upgraded him to first class. Mitch had reminded him that cell phone calls could be tracked. The NSA had that capability, and he warned him to be alert. Stewing over this after the call, Jacob had phoned in a reservation for a flight to Paris later that afternoon, hoping the double booking would not be caught in any airline security web. He used his *News* company credit card this time instead of his own. Garon would be expecting Paris as a destination. Jacob was pretty sure of that. The extravagance would sow confusion and buy time.

There was still a long, dangerous trip ahead. The uncertainty of it all made him restless, but eventually he managed to nap.

Luis was frustrated. Sellars had slipped out of his grasp. But everything had been set in motion for pursuit. Sellars must be stopped—at any cost! The document was still out there. The Cranes had made a fool of him by sneaking the copy to Sellars and then running, probably to Paris. He had received several angry calls from his Pentagon bosses. He had to admit, however, that the government had acted quickly to put out an alert at all U.S. airports, with a picture ID they had demanded from the *News*. Intelligence had been arranged for the French to look out for Sellars at Orly, just in case he made it out of the country. But Luis's men had been alert and had traced the fugitive to Chicago. Again with the help of the *News,* they were able to identify Jacob's friend, Phil Ross. Pleased with himself that he had bypassed the Pentagon, he easily tracked down Ross. With a little persuasion, the reporter admitted that he had used his credit card to rent a car so Sellars could drive to Canada, but that was all he seemed to know. Garon hoped that his men's strong-armed tactics had left Ross intact. Their official credentials had apparently been effective in convincing Ross that it would be useless to contact the local police.

In a makeshift office at FBI headquarters in Chicago, Garon fretted with impatience. He had not heard from customs at Windsor yet and feared that Sellars might have already sneaked across the border. Then his phone jangled. He shouted his name into the receiver.

"Luis, we have his flight. He's on his way to Paris—Air France." His man was sounding very smug until Garon responded.

"Of course, he's going to Paris, you fool. Why haven't you stopped him?"

There was a long pause. "Well, we just didn't see him at the gate. There was no one who matched his description." The last words were in a plaintive tone.

"Don't tell me, I know. You lost him."

"Well, we could have. Or maybe he didn't show." The caller was becoming more doubtful.

"Damn!"

"Like I said, he just wasn't there, Luis. Couldn't do a thing about it. But we know the flight, and we can check it out at the other end. It stops at Heathrow first and then Paris. We'll be on a flight direct to Paris. Gets in two hours ahead. If he's there, can we take him our way? Can you authorize it?"

"Absolutely, of course. But don't mess up. We don't want to lose him again," he warned pointedly. "Take him to the safe house and call me. You know how to do this without noise."

"I understand. We'll do it."

"What flight are you on?"

The caller was ready with a flight number and schedule. They hung up. Luis glanced at his watch. His men apparently had phoned from the plane because it was a couple of minutes past departure time. He felt better. The plane was probably already taxiing down the runway as they spoke. Garon was tempted to report his success to Washington but decided to wait until he was certain, when his men had both Sellars and the document. But there was a lingering doubt about what had happened in Montreal. Had Sellars outwitted him again? Garon had an uncomfortable feeling about the words "he just wasn't there."

CHAPTER 11

Back in New York, Garon spent the day in his office making calls to allies in London, alerting them—just in case Sellars tried to slip away at Heathrow. This was the best place to grab him. MI-5 would be cooperative, if he needed them. Still, bothered by the possibility that Sellars was not even on the flight, he began to think of other options.

He had just finished a call to London when his secure phone to the Pentagon shrilled its ugly alert. He let it ring. He had no answers. He couldn't even be sure where Sellars was headed.

A loud clattering woke Jacob from a sound sleep. As he rubbed his eyes, he was jolted by violent bumps and lurches of the plane. The seat belt warning chimed, and the pilot came on.

"Hi, folks. We've run into some turbulence. 'Fraid I can't do much about it. There's a big North Atlantic storm brewing. We'll try and go around it, but this baby is a big one. We had hoped to beat the weather before it got organized. Obviously, we didn't. We're planning to head for an alternate airport—maybe Glasgow—if it stays open long enough. Not to worry, though. Just a little unpleasantness from Mother Nature. We'll do our best to get you to your destination. Keep your belts fastened and stay in your seats. We're going north a ways and see if we can find some smoother air. We'll keep you posted. Thanks for your patience."

"Damn!" Jacob said aloud to no one in particular—because he had no seatmate. He was sure that by now Garon knew something about his plans. With the help of all his intelligence resources, he might even know Jacob was on this flight rather than the one to Paris. Landing at Glasgow might be a blessing. If customs went smoothly, as expected, he might be able to lose himself at a hotel and wait for Mitch's call. He hoped that Garon and his men were still behind in their information. There was a chance that rerouting the flight could be helpful. A smile flicked across Jacob's lips as he remembered his mother's pet phrase for finding good in bad luck—"Maybe God has a plan." But it didn't make him feel any better.

As the air began to smooth out, his thoughts turned again to Yvonne. It was doubtful that she was part of "God's plan." So what was she to him? A compelling sexual experience? Or much more? Images of her cascaded through his mind. Jacob found himself wanting to possess her, to make her part of him. Sleeping with her wasn't enough. Yet, she was elusive, indefinable, and unknowable. Thoughts of her eclipsed all others—the article, Garon, his job, his safety. Jacob felt he was being driven by an irresistible force. Beyond the sensual, he was dazzled by her mind, her self-possession, her unattainability. He was obsessed with her. This kind of thing had never happened to him before.

He needed to control himself, look at her rationally. Was she offering herself only as a sop to keep him involved? And what about other men? Was she just an oversexed, spoiled rich girl? Jacob didn't care. He had already rejected Mitch's warnings against an involvement. As he muddled his insecurities, he was reminded of his father's ugly words. The old guilt began to resurface. His father's dreadful accusations rang in his head, over and over, until his brow became wet. He ordered a vodka from the flight attendant—hoping to purge the memory—and then a quick second, under her disapproving glance. A third drink finally settled him down. But he could not shake thoughts of Yvonne. He imagined a conversation—after sex—about his feeling for her, asking her whether she loved him. In the daydream, she said, "Yes, I do, Jacob," and to prove it, she kissed him tenderly. He gazed out the window at the grayness of breaking dawn and smiled ruefully. This was probably not the reality.

Later, the pilot announced that they would be landing at Glasgow, and alternate transportation would be provided to London. Connections would be missed, but Air Canada would assure all conveniences during any layover. The flight time to Glasgow was one hour plus. High winds were buffeting the plane again, tossing it around as if it were a toy. Out the window, Jacob watched the wings trembling in the turbid murk of first light. He was not a nervous flier, but the violence of this storm made him uncomfortable. His active imagination began spinning out scenarios. "Fugitive Lost in North Atlantic Crash" was one headline. Others came to mind, until Jacob pulled down the shade and tried to ignore the violent yawing.

After awhile, the seat belt warning chimed, and the plane rocked and bumped in its final approach. The green landscape of Scotland suddenly broke through the fast-moving scud. It was raining hard, the windows running with streaks as the flaps came down. The motion became even more violent in the last moments before the plane slammed onto the runway. Jacob took a deep breath of relief as they taxied to the gate—"not this time," he muttered, thinking again of imagined obituaries.

Jacob's small suitcase and laptop made it through customs easily with his press credentials. He had hesitated to use them, but he decided that he had nothing to lose, since his name would have been enough to alert local authorities if they had been advised in time. Luckily, his notoriety had not preceded him. The cabbie recommended the Royalton Hotel as "pretty posh," and "a lot o' lasses in shaart skirts roonin' around." He checked in, but at that early hour, there were no "shaart skirts" in evidence. A room was not available until later, so he had breakfast at the small cafe in the hotel and lingered over coffee, hoping his cell phone would work in this environment. He was anxious to talk to Mitch. Later, he found a secluded spot in a small library off the lobby and waited for a call. When it came, the muffled ring under his coat startled him. After a series of transfers, patching through other systems, there was advice in French and English that published tariffs would be charged to his account.

"Mitch?"

"Yeah, it's me. Where are you? I've been worried sick."

"In Glasgow. We got diverted from London because of a storm."

"We've had a devilish time getting any information. I'm glad you're safe. That storm is very bad." There was a long pause. "Okay, now listen to me. We should make this quick. We have a plan. But I need to make a couple more calls. Where are you staying?"

Jacob told him the hotel and a room number.

"Okay, fine. But don't settle in. We gotta keep you moving. You should be ready to leave when I call you back. I'll call your room in two hours. I won't use your cell this time. Got it?"

"Yes, but ..."

"Gotta go." There was a click, and he was gone.

Jacob hoped he could get into his room in time for the call. He made his way to the desk, trying to think of a good excuse for his urgent need of a room. But as he approached the desk, the clerk was smiling broadly.

"Your room is ready, Mr. Sellars." The formally attired, young clerk seemed pleased with himself. "We sent your bag up." He whacked the bell for an attendant who magically appeared out of nowhere and took the key handed to him. "Enjoy your stay with us, sir," the clerk called, as Jacob followed his guide to the elevators. The subdued elegance of English, or in this case Scottish, hotels was a refreshing change from the crass hustle of American hotels.

The room smelled of being recently cleaned. It had a starchy look and smelled faintly of a pleasant freshener. After the attendant had left, Jacob opened the French doors to a small protected balcony. The air was damp, and a fine drizzle was blown sideways by a gusty wind. He thought of Amos Coffin alone at sea in a storm. He smiled, remembering their talk.

He closed the doors against the weather and carefully turned the bedspread to the foot. Stretched out to rest, he quickly dozed off in a daze of jet lag. It was not long afterward that the hotel phone woke him. It was Mitch, calling back as promised.

"Okay, here's the deal. You're leaving Glasgow—now. Garon's people might know where you are. We have to expect the worst. Get the first train you can to London. Get one that goes to Victoria Station. I think most of them do. Wait there—there's a waiting room off the main concourse. Someone will pick you up. They'll find you. Got it?"

"How do you know—I mean about Garon, what he knows?"

"Get moving," Mitch said, before hanging up abruptly. For a moment, Jacob's head spun with questions he knew could not be answered. Meet whom? And how? Where would he be going from London? He realized that Mitch was getting off the line quickly to avoid a trace. He pulled himself together and collected his things. On the elevator ride down, he decided it was better not to stop at the desk. The clerk had already swiped his credit card. He crossed the lobby quickly and caught a taxi at the entrance.

At the Glasgow station, he found that trains were delayed by equipment dislocations caused by the bad weather conditions to the south. Advising that things would soon straighten out, the clerk sold him a ticket for a first-class compartment on the next scheduled departure. Pacing the marble floors and window-shopping, Jacob worried about the delay and the possibility that Luis's men might catch up with him. Every casual passerby was a potential threat. He constantly changed his pattern of browsing to check whether he was being shadowed. His suspicions were exhausting him, so he found a seat and gave up his search. In spite of his lack of sleep, he tried not to doze off, each time catching himself. Finally, the announcement of his London train jolted him into alertness. It wasn't one of those high-speed trains with fancy names the English were famous for, but just an express to London's Victoria Station. Jacob was one of the first to board and found his compartment unoccupied. After what seemed like a long delay, the train began to roll out of the station, picking up speed quickly as it crossed noisy switches in the rain-soaked yards and then smoothing out on a right-of-way, racing through the rural landscape of Scotland. The click of the rails and gentle motion lulled him into a stupor almost immediately. He had now been more than thirty hours without meaningful sleep. Still, this was not to be a restful one. It was full of fearful dreams, nightmares about his father, about Luis, and, of course, about Yvonne. He woke himself with his own outcry in the darkness of the compartment, which was still empty. He turned the light on, hoping to avoid any more dreams. The black windows, reflecting only his troubled image, were streaming with water. Now and then he could feel the car being buffeted by the wind. It had become a wild, stormy night of heavy weather. The train had slowed down to a crawl. After dousing his face with water in the nearby WC, he returned to the compartment and allowed himself to rest. He didn't sleep this time but watched the passing scene of darkness and the occasional lights of a sodden town.

Later, in the cavernous London station, he found the waiting room with old wooden benches and staked out a position from which he could watch the two entrances, waiting for his mysterious contact. The trip had taken ten hours. He hoped Mitch's plan had accounted for delay. Two hours ticked by, and Jacob began to worry. Then he saw her—Natasha! Dressed in a black raincoat that brushed the floor, she was shaking an umbrella. It took her only a moment to recognize him.

"Jacob, so glad you are safe." She squeezed his arm. "Come," she said. "We must hurry." She escorted him into the rain and popped her inadequate umbrella, the sharing of which got them both soaked. Her remote opened the doors of a black Mercedes coupe. "Get in," she ordered. "We must go quickly."

Once seated, Jacob brushed some of the wetness off his pants. He had many questions, but he thought better of pressing her. "What a pleasure to see you again, Natasha. Are you going to save us?" It was a feeble effort, but by this time he was feeling punchy.

"I hope so." She flashed a smile and started the car, pulling out of her parking place into the puddled street. "We are going to try Chunnel. It will be safest, maybe least expected—I hope."

"I'm impressed with how well organized you all are. You and Mitch and Yvonne. I assume they arranged this."

"Yes," she replied without elaboration. "Thank God, Emily and Yvonne have loyal spies in company. They have been following—spying on—Garon quite

effectively. His computer, his phones are all being watched—I mean listened to."
She smiled again. "I just hope nothing has been missed." Natasha was a fast
driver, threading her way through the traffic and finding the highway to
Southampton. They didn't talk much. Driving was difficult. The weather was
still quite bad, windy with persistent downpours.

Jacob broke a long silence as the first signs for the Chunnel route to France
began to appear. "Is the tunnel closely watched?" His anxieties had returned.

"Not so much going this way as coming back. French aren't so paranoid." She
touched his knee. "I think we'll make it."

"Have you seen Yvonne?"

"Yes. She is safe." She seemed uncomfortable with the question. "You know
Yvy. She's been seeing much of her friends, plotting and planning. And she has
plans for your article." She laughed. "She's busy girl. Of course, she's looking forward to getting into print." She paused. "But she is so impatient."

"Mitch told me a little." Jacob wondered about the plotting and planning but
was afraid to ask. "What kind of plans? I understand there is another journalist?"

"Yes, I think so. But I don't know very much about that. You have, uh,
paper—Pentagon paper."

"I do. And my article."

"Good. Her idea is to publish abroad—get it out fast. No more delays."

"I guess that's a good idea."

"You have doubts?"

"No, not really." But Jacob did have his worries. He wanted the article for
himself—to control the story. A pride of authorship had taken hold of him.

Luis stubbed out a large Cuban cigar. He was angry. Sellars had escaped him
in both Glasgow and London. Obviously, he was getting help. Garon was puzzled how they had eluded his every plan. He feared there was a leak at the home
office. Those responsible would pay dearly.

His men in Paris had called off their interception effort. Garon assumed that
Sellars's contacts in Paris were getting information from New York and relaying
it to him. He tried to imagine what they might do next. It dawned on him, like a
flash. The damn Chunnel! Avoid the airports. That is what they would do—drive
Sellars to Paris! But how? In a rented car? Unlikely. Probably a contact in
England had been set up to meet Sellars and drive him. But who? Who was in
London? He picked up the phone and called the company, asking for the travel
office. One of his spies was employed there.

"Conrad, I need your help." He made an effort to subdue his voice. "Any recent intel on the Cranes? No? Are you sure? Think again, man." Garon listened, his eyes blinking rapidly. "Yes, yes. Zilenko? From New York? I don't care how long the trip was planned. When did she go? Yes. Yes." He scribbled notes on a pad. "Good, that's what I need. Now, keep this to yourself. There are leaks in the office. Do you understand? This is top secret." He banged the phone down in his renewed excitement. That was it—Natasha Zilenko! She was up to her ears in plots against the government and up to no good in the Caucasus.

He called his idle crew in Paris and alerted them. "Watch the roads to the north if you can't get to the Chunnel exit in time. We must get him before he gets to Paris. It will be our only chance. Otherwise we will lose him in the city." When he hung up, he decided that he had to go to Paris. He did not expect his men to intercept Natasha Zilenko and Sellars. There was not enough time in the bad weather. Many routes to Paris were flooded. It was probably pointless even to try. The raging storm had slowed traffic everywhere. Garon knew Yvonne's haunts in Paris. He had once been sent along with her as a bodyguard. But his information was badly out of date. He'd have to communicate immediately with his spies in Paris. He hoped the local police would help.

Natasha proposed a stop before they reached the Chunnel and Sellars agreed, but not without concern about delay. There had been reports on the radio of roads in the north of France being closed or impassable. The weather had deteriorated, and the rain had increased so much it was hard to see the road. Improvements were forecast for the morning. They found an inn and had an early supper. Natasha was very gracious and insisted on treating Sellars. Jacob's head began to spin with the wine at dinner and the effect of the cognac. He tried hard to focus on their conversation when it turned to Yvonne.

"You must love her very much, Jacob," Natasha said, out of the blue. "I mean to do all this for her. You are risking career, maybe even your life. These are dangerous people."

Jacob laughed at her dramatic suggestion of violence. "I think they just want their document back. They're not interested in me. When I'm finished, I'll return it." Jacob ignored the love comment.

"I think is more serious. Garon and his men are evil. They are responsible to no one. They are contract killers. Pentagon has put them beyond law. Same is done in Russia. That's where Americans learned such nasty business."

"You worried about Yvonne?" He tried to make it casual.

"She is safe. They know she does not have document they want. They won't bother her for now." Natasha gazed at him for a moment. "You know, she is probably ..."

"She is what, Natasha?"

"You should know something about her." She placed a hand on his arm and gazed at him sympathetically. "She is, uh, right now not for—for any man. She has no time for serious relationship, Jacob. She doesn't want to settle down." She sipped at her drink, choosing her words carefully. "She is very ... very unusual young lady." She chuckled wryly. "As you know already, she is extraordinary." She took Jacob's hand. "You cannot count on her, Jacob. She has no time for love." She squeezed his hand. "I know is hard for you to hear. But have your time with her, if you must, but move on. You should have nice girl, someone who can love you."

Jacob smiled, he hoped convincingly because he was not happy at all. "I don't know what you mean." He took his hand back as she released her hold. He couldn't deny his involvement, but he certainly would not confess it. Her earnest comments, even though familiar, shook him. He felt angry. Was Natasha pushing Yvonne into a life of intrigue? Was she being used by fanatics? "Is that the way you want it, Natasha?"

She looked at Jacob sadly, not reacting to his hostile charge. "No, Jacob. I don't control Yvonne. No one does. She does as she wants."

He decided not to pursue the subject further. He needed to cool off. He politely excused himself, admitting that he needed to get a good night's rest. As they parted, Natasha gave him a motherly peck on the cheek.

"Sleep well, my friend. Pleasant dreams. I'm afraid I've talked too much. Anyway, darling, how should I know what that girl feels about you? Maybe you are one to capture her heart." She touched his arm. "We must leave early, six o'clock." She turned and left him.

Her conciliatory remarks were not reassuring. He trudged up the dimly lit stairs of the old inn, feeling desperate and unable to accept the advice, now twice given. As he got ready for bed, he wondered what Natasha's relationship to Yvonne really was. Were they coconspirators, or did some deeper relationship exist? Mercifully, these were his last thoughts of the night.

CHAPTER 12

They started early as planned, after a continental breakfast of coffee and sweets. There was no further discussion of Yvonne. The weather had improved. As Natasha predicted, the border crossing at the French side of the Chunnel went smoothly. Natasha's fluent French was a help. She carried a French passport, which eased the customs inspection and questions. As she opened her purse, Jacob noticed that she furtively sorted through several passports to find the right one. He showed his own with the press credentials, and the official seemed satisfied. By late afternoon, they reached the outskirts of Paris. Natasha threaded her way through the streets of Paris like a native. "I'm going to take you directly to house Emily has arranged. It is older family place. My Joshua bought it when we first met. No one knows about it in company. Mitchel's place is not safe for you." She smiled. "Anyway, his apartment is mess—always."

Jacob could only imagine what kind of mess. Unmade beds or party clutter? A roommate? "That's fine. I assume he knows where I will be."

"Oh, yes. He does." She signaled a left turn and zoomed down a broad boulevard Jacob did not recognize. Paris was not totally strange to him. He had been to the city on assignment several times covering traveling politicos. Natasha glanced at him, catching him trying to read street signs. "Do you know Paris?"

"A little. I've been here a few times."

"We are going to *Arrondissement Deuxieme*, near *Le Sacré-Coeur*. Do you know it?"

"Yes. I think I stayed in that neighborhood once—nice views of the city, as I recall." He liked her rich pronunciation of French. She was fluent in the language.

"Spectacular! … ah," she exclaimed, taking a sharp left down a narrow street lined with small shops. "Here we are!" She swept her hand in a little circle. "Is

Montmartre!" She drove her Mercedes like the sports car it was. "Here we are." She swerved into the curb, scuffing the tires with abandon. "This is place. Come, I'll introduce you to concierge."

The building showed its age but projected old-world dignity in the bustling modern neighborhood, giving it a sense of timelessness in contrast to the trendy storefronts. Jacob followed Natasha through an iron-gate entrance to a brick patio shaded by a few scruffy trees but otherwise unadorned with greenery. A casual effort had been made to garden at one time, but the gardener had given up several seasons past. Unswept leaves rattled in a cold northerly wind that was slowly clearing out the storm. The late afternoon sun cast a pallid patch of light on one side of the building surrounding the patio. Ornate iron balconies in need of a paint job ringed the open promenades, and external stairs connected each level. Doors opened onto the balconies. They found the concierge on a stairway. He was a dumpy, taciturn French stereotype of the kind Jacob might have expected. Recognizing Natasha, he grunted an acknowledgment to her introduction with a faint smile creasing his puffy, veined face and walked on, waving a casual hand in approval. The apartment Jacob would be using was on the second floor. The place turned out to be nicer than the exterior suggested. There were two bedrooms—the larger one with slightly tarnished but still fashionable queen-sized brass beds, mahogany bureaus, and other Victorian-style furniture. In an abrupt shift of decor, the living room and a modest kitchen were furnished mostly in Skan-style—somewhat spare, but slickly modern. The mismatched layout reminded him of his own New York apartment.

He set his modest luggage aside and laid his computer case on a desk in the living room. "Nice," he said, for something to say.

Natasha laughed. "It isn't nice at all. Is vile. I don't know why Joshua keep it all these years. We did not use it. Of course, when Joshua bought it years ago, it was rather grand." She flashed a forced smile. "It will be safe for you." She pecked him on the cheek. "I must go now. It is okay to use telephone. Call whomever you wish. It is taken care of. And I think there is something in refridge to start you out." She turned to leave. "Oh, yes—Mitch can show you how to hook up computer to service. I don't know much about those things." She paused at the door. "And call girlfriend in New York, please. I'm sure she is worried about you." Then she left.

Jacob guessed that Natasha had learned of the girlfriend from Yvonne. The thought depressed him. How much had Yvonne told her? He opened a window to get rid of the musty smell of disuse and made a cursory tour of the apartment—looked in closets, inspected the refrigerator, tested one of the beds, and made a pass at looking into the bureaus—empty. There was a wall of bookcases in the living room. When he had finished browsing the titles—mostly in French—he drew the curtains for privacy. There were the makings of a small dinner in the fridge, purchased, no doubt, at a French cousin of New York's Barefoot Contessa—pâté, cheese, salads, wild rice, and salmon. One of the chilled bottles of *Montrachet* seemed like a good place to start. A quick search of kitchen drawers scored a corkscrew. He chose a wedge of *Pont l'Evêque* and settled in the living room with his wine and cheese like any self-respecting Frenchman would do. As he finished his first glass, he could feel the fatigue return. His head ached slightly with the swirl of events of the last twenty-four hours. Jet lag added to his listless feeling. He toyed with the idea of calling Rachel just to see if she was okay. Did Garon's men know about her? Would her phone be tapped? Unless they had found her name in his apartment, there was no other reason why Garon would have even heard of her. With the assurances Natasha had given him, he was pretty sure that Garon could not know where he was—not yet. On a sudden impulse brought on by the second glass of wine, he looked up the international codes in the directory, punched in the numbers, and waited nervously. After four rings, he was rewarded with her unmistakably low-register, rather gruff "Hullo."

"Hi, it's Jacob," he said.

"Who?"

"Jacob."

"I'm afraid I don't know any Jacob."

"Come on, Rachel. This is long distance. Are you all right?"

There was a lengthy silence. "I really should hang up."

"Please don't. I have to tell you, uh, what has happened."

"Where are you?" she demanded, not softening at all.

"I can't say."

"Oh, great. So, why are we talking? Why are you bothering me?"

"Because I, uh, owe you a call." It was a lame excuse. Of course, it was Natasha's reminder that made him call. Another silence.

"Damn you." Her voice was hoarse with anger.

"I … I had to leave in a hurry."

"Tell me something I don't know, Jacob."

"They were going to arrest me. I have the top-secret document. They want it."

"Top-secret document? Arrest? Is this about that Crane business? What in God's name have you gotten yourself into mooning over this spoiled rich girl?"

Jacob was relieved that she seemed so far to have been untouched by Garon and his men. "I'm not mooning, as you say, over anyone. As a matter of fact, I am being hounded by our own government." But she was partly right.

"This is too much."

"Look, you must remember the Pentagon memo I told you about. Well, it does exist, and I have a hard copy. It's a bombshell. No one would touch it in the U.S. So we're going to publish it, uh, elsewhere …" He stopped himself.

"You've left the country?" she exclaimed. "My God! And why are you running?"

"I think I've broken the law." He had already said too much, but he went on anyway. "You were right about the Patriot Act, you know."

"I'm not surprised." Her tone was only slightly sweet. "Let's go back a little in this conversation. The government is hounding you, not just that goon you tangled with in Boston? Did I hear that part of it right?"

"Yes, you did."

"It's a lot to swallow. Sounds kind of fishy." There was a long pause. Jacob was afraid she might hang up. "Is there another part of it? Has the girl gone to your head?"

He let her question pass. In his eagerness to explain his sudden disappearance, Jacob had dug himself into a hole. He needed to know whether she had been contacted by anyone, but she wouldn't let up.

"It's sick. You're just proving something to that perverted old man who you don't even think is your real father. That son-of-a-bitch has emasculated you, Jacob. You're letting him take over your life." She paused. "I don't think I have time for a sickie. If you had any guts, you'd get a DNA test and prove to yourself once and for all that he's an imposter. But you'd rather gallivant around the world chasing a will-o-the-wisp wet dream."

The sudden barrage was an unpleasant surprise, to say the least. Her angry words rang in his head. All he could think of to say was, "I'm sorry I didn't call. That's what I'm trying to tell you."

"And that's tacky. It doesn't work for me. You know what I think? This girl, this Crane kid, has brought back some old hang-ups. It's like a replay of your life. But you don't get second chances, Jacob." Her tone became ironic, tinged with bitterness. "Face it. You're trying to break away from your father by fucking another little girl and thumbing your nose at him. Is that about right, Jacob? You should be calling your father, not me."

"You're over the top, Rachel. That's … that's nonsense. I don't even understand you."

"You will someday, after you crash and burn. I hope it won't be too late. But I can't let myself worry about you anymore. You're in over your head. These people—the Cranes—are dangerous, and you're going to be left holding the bag, an empty bag, and a criminal record." He could hear her catching her breath. "I just can't afford you emotionally, Jacob. I can't watch you destroy yourself. And this I am sorry about, for myself as much as you. Good luck, honey. Gotta go. And don't call until you get yourself straightened out." The line went dead.

He sat, stunned by her harsh reaction. Her candor depressed him. The truth of his predicament had been obscured by his own infatuation. Rachel had seen through him but had missed the point. Yvonne was only a part of his interest. Something much more serious was bothering him. U.S. policy was being driven by a few rogue officials who were working outside the law. They had to be stopped. Accountability had to be reestablished. As a journalist, all Jacob could do was reveal what was going on. It was his responsibility to do so quickly. The problem was now much larger than the Crane family reputation.

Rachel was right about his attraction to Yvonne. She had always read him accurately. The thought made him uncomfortable. The dreams were bad enough, but her icy comment about another "little girl" hit home. He set aside his wine and decided he needed some fresh air to clear his head. He was too roiled up to sleep. He wanted to escape the ringing warnings and cautions against his single-minded effort to possess Yvonne—shut out the layers of doubt and suspicion.

Peering from the window into the night, he saw a brightly lit street beckoning with its row of cafes just beginning to get busy. He hoped the distraction of nightlife might be a welcome change. At least, he had reassured himself that no one had contacted Rachel. She would have told him.

The chilly air helped push Rachel's reproaches out of his mind—or as Mitch once suggested, down into his subconscious. It was glib, but accurate enough. He took a side street down steps into a small square of shops and eateries with windows steamed up by the activity inside. A few hardy souls sipped espressos at outside tables. Jacob envied a happy young couple walking arm in arm along the narrow street. A small cafe with a bright-red awning caught his attention. Candlelight projected from the windows. He wasn't hungry, but he needed the distraction of other people, whether he talked to them or not—just to have them around. On the awning, *La Mer* was printed in black and again in gold letters on the window, giving an upscale impression.

Inside, the air was redolent with the rich garlic aromas of dinner. It was a noisy mixed-age crowd, many of whom seemed to know each other, talking back and forth across tables—obviously a neighborhood meeting place. He took a seat at the bar and ordered a Pernod in a liquid salute to all expatriates. Served neat without ice, it was clear as water. The sweet licorice odor wafted up from the glass. On the rocks, the oily liquid turned into an unappetizing milky color. Jacob preferred it neat. He stared at his image in the mirror, seeing signs of fatigue from his ordeal and an aging that surprised him. He dropped his eyes quickly. Girls in high school had said that he looked like the movie star Ben Affleck. He suspected they were just teasing him. It had taken him awhile to discover that his looks did attract the opposite sex. It was not until much later that he realized this. His style had been awkward as a teenager, and excessive shyness in conversation had made girls feel uncomfortable around him. He smiled at the memory of his bumbling experiences, Sylvia included. He was smoother now. He glanced back at the mirror. As if his thoughts had somehow been revealed at that moment, a young woman whose image was reflected caught his eye and smiled. She was sitting nearby, only an empty stool separating them. He swiveled around and faced her.

"You are American?" She spoke first. Her English was heavily accented, but her voice was warm and pleasant.

"I didn't know it showed." He laughed. He wondered whether she belonged to that breed of Parisians who hated America.

She toyed with her empty glass. "Oh, yes. It does. You come from California?" She pronounced each syllable carefully.

"No, the Midwest originally."

"Bad guess, eh?"

After his humbling by Rachel, her smile was reassuring. He noticed her glass was empty. "Can I offer you a drink?"

"Well, *mai oui. Merci.*"

Jacob felt oddly relieved by her easy acceptance. "What are you drinking?"

"White wine, Chablis, please."

He ordered one and got another Pernod for himself.

"Chicago, perhaps?" she tried again.

Jacob was surprised by the good guess. "Close. And I spent time in that city, yes." Her questions seemed sincere, and she projected an innocence without design. "Actually, I was brought up on a farm south of Chicago," he admitted, taking a better look at her. She wasn't a knockout exactly, but appealing—blond hair, large blue eyes, translucent skin, and, from what Jacob could see of her on the stool, a trim figure. He always marveled at how French women seemed to make the best of themselves. "But now I live in New York City." He hoped this improved on the farm.

"*Ah, oui*, the Beeg Apple?"

"Yeah, I work for a newspaper there."

"Ah, interesting job for a farmer," she said, smiling and eyes twinkling with humor. "Do you speak French?" She swirled her refilled glass of wine and studied the effect.

"Very little."

"Ah, New York City," she sighed. "I love New York City—maybe better than Paris." Most of her conversation had been directed to her glass, with only an occasional glance his way. Jacob wondered whether the shyness was a pose.

"Then you've been there?"

"Yes, often, with my parents years ago. My father went on business." She swiveled her stool around and finally met his gaze. "So, what brings you to Paree?"

"I'm doing a story."

"Ah, of course—a story, a story for your newspaper, yes?" She met his eye, for a lingering moment.

"Yes, but not for my paper." Jacob had to be cautious. It would be foolish of him to talk too much—to anyone.

She shrugged. "For what then? I mean for who, whom." She was struggling with the language.

"It's complicated. I, uh, can't really say more."

She peered into her glass again, embarrassed by her own forwardness. "I am sorry to make so many questions." The flush that colored her smooth cheek made her seem more like a schoolgirl, although she was probably close to Jacob's age. "Anyway …," she said, as she turned and faced him again. He felt he was being sized up. "You Americans are so secret." She paused for a moment thoughtfully. "You know, many of us here are disappointed in your country. We like your people, but not much the leaders."

Jacob had been expecting this. It was as if she had already guessed that his work involved something political. She became more serious. "There is this American woman who often comes to Paris—I don't remember her name—but she speaks at the university. I go to some of the meetings. She hates her country. She is very critical, even more so than French. She talks against America and the government. She spoke last night at *La Sorbonne*, about Iraq. I heard her. She knows a lot. It was interesting. She said that Americans would steal the oil." Jacob felt he was being accused personally. Then she softened a little in admiration. "She spoke French like a *Parisienne*." She took a sip of her wine, glancing at Jacob to see his reaction. "I bet she is—how do you say—expatriate? Maybe you have heard of her. She must be famous in America. Do you call it unfamous when it is the wrong kind?"

"Infamous, I think you mean. What's her name?" Her story reminded him of Yvonne—another firebrand. "Did you say that she talked about Americans stealing Iraqi oil?"

"Well, yes. But it was complicated, maybe a little crazy. I didn't understand it all." She paused, her eyes lingering on his a little longer. "I don't know her name. I couldn't stay to the end."

"What did she look like?"

She smiled. "Oh, very pretty, long black hair—like a model, I think. You know her?"

"Maybe. Sounds like someone I've heard about." Jacob's stomach lurched at the possibility. Could it be Yvonne?

"I knew it. She is famous—I mean, in famous." She pronounced it as two words. Then she asked, "You are famous, too? Or in famous?" She laughed.

"Heavens, no. Neither." But he was not so sure about the latter.

"You are modest, maybe." She was becoming easier with him, taking stock of him, looking into his eyes.

"No, not even that. I'm just a journalist." He was fascinated by the possibility that she might have actually seen Yvonne. More likely, it was just a coincidence. It would be too risky for her to make such an appearance.

"Can I ask you your name—just the first? Sorry, if I'm being, ah, what do you say, too forward?"

"Well, my first name is Jacob. How about yours?" Jacob decided this woman was no ordinary cafe pickup. She was a cut way above anyone like that.

"Lynnette, with two n's and two t's."

As if to prove the query was not intended to prolong the evening, she reached for her coat and got up. "Anyway, now I must go," she announced, looking at her watch. Even in the dim lighting, he could see that she was flushed with embarrassment.

"Well, Lynnette, I've enjoyed talking to you." Her sudden decision to go disappointed him. He was just becoming interested in her. "I'll have to track down this American you heard speak. Sounds like a good story." He paid the check quickly and stood beside her.

Lynnette gathered her purse and, with Jacob's help, shrugged into her stylish coat. "*Merci*." Her blue eyes flashed his way as she turned.

Following her out, he noticed that she had a shapely figure, swinging her hips slightly as she threaded her way through the crowd, which had now thinned. A few friends waved to her. Jacob was tempted to prolong the evening but rejected the idea by the time they reached the sidewalk.

"I hope we can, uh, talk again," Jacob stammered. "I enjoyed it."

"*Moi aussi*. I come here after work sometimes. It is a nice place."

Jacob could think of nothing further to say as they shook hands rather formally and parted, leaving in opposite directions. At the steps leading up to his street, he looked back at her receding shape. He wondered whether he'd ever see her again.

Back in the apartment, the unpleasant memory of his conversation with Rachel returned. Her accusations flooded into his mind and with them another memory of his father and mother—the last time he had seen them. The ugly scene was a festering wound that wouldn't heal. He had gone home for Christmas just before he had moved to New York. It was almost six years ago, but it was as vivid as yesterday. His parents had been more distant with each other on this visit than ever before. On the second night, they were in the kitchen having supper when his father began haranguing his mother about something she had neglected. He was working himself into a rage. Out of the blue, he accused her of infidelity. Jacob didn't know whether it was a recent event or just an old issue. At first, it didn't faze his mother. Her stolid expression didn't change. Apparently, it was an accusation she'd heard before. But it was the first time his father had been open about his suspicions in front of Jacob. The bitterness seemed to overflow in the slow burn of his mood.

"You're like your son, corrupt to the gizzard," he lashed out. "Using your bodies to gratify, like prostitutes. Jacob had no idea what was going on. His father threw up his arms as he raved, a grotesque, leering grimace knotting into his face. "My son's a pedophile," he roared, "and my wife's a whore. How's that for a Christian family?" Then he broke down, big watery tears rolling down his ruddy cheeks. Suddenly, one of those long powerful arms swung across the table and caught Jacob's mother in the mouth, almost knocking her off her chair. It was the second time Jacob had witnessed his striking her. She grabbed the table to steady herself, blood trickling from her mouth. Something ruptured inside Jacob. Without thinking, he took his plate and smashed it against his father's head. More blood flowed. Then Jacob came to his senses and rushed to his mother with towels to stem the bleeding and comfort her. While he was dabbing gently at her thin lips, she never took her eyes off his father, who now towered above them. She was not crying. There was more hate than fear in her stony gaze. Then the old man stormed out of the house and roared down the driveway in his truck.

After a time, the bleeding stopped, and she absently fingered a tooth which had loosened. She was unable to talk. Every time Jacob asked her if she was okay she held a hand up as a barrier against conversation. Finally, with cold dignity, she excused herself and disappeared upstairs for the rest of the night. Stunned by what had taken place, Jacob sat at the kitchen table waiting for the trembling to stop.

The next morning before breakfast she asked Jacob to leave, saying that she didn't want him to see her like this, that she would take care of the matter and would see him another time when things are different. Her face was swollen and bruised. The sight made Jacob sick with sadness. Apologizing for the dreadful Christmas Eve, she kissed him on the cheek and firmly told him to go. Later in a letter, she wrote him that she had moved into town and taken a small apartment and suggested that it was better that he stay away from Appleton until things were sorted out. "Someday," she wrote, "I will sit down with you and try to tell you the whole story. I am not ready to yet, but I promise that I will in time, God willing."

Other letters from her followed. They were newsy and motherly, like nothing had happened, except that she was still living alone and quite content in her solitude. He wondered whether the whole story would be about the neighbor, Mr. Baum. In a way, Jacob didn't want to hear the truth. If this cruel man was not his real father, Jacob was afraid of the hate he felt. It was only a fantasy, but the gun in his hand was as cold as his heart, as he pulled the trigger and watched the old man's face come apart.

Luis had just received new instructions. Forget about Sellars. We can pick him up later. If a story gets out, the memo can be discredited as disinformation planted by terrorists and a few disgruntled CIA agents.

It is the girl who must be watched. She may be involved with a cell of terrorists backed by a Saudi prince. She must be detained. It is preferable that she be taken with the prince so the connection can be made. That way the cover story—that she is a spy for terrorists—will have credibility. You can have all the help you need from intelligence and from the Saudis. Use any means, legal or otherwise. But do it fast. We need this to happen before the election. Garon was surprised how quickly priorities had changed. It was hard to believe that the girl had become so important and the missing document was now irrelevant.

With the help of a lucky break, Garon had finally located Sellars. An off-duty special agent of the French police had identified him in a bar and followed him to his quarters. The police had alerted the French intelligence people, who then informed his men in Paris. Luis smiled smugly as he remembered the surprise in Washington when he told them he had accomplished what they had been unable to do themselves. The response had been, "Of course, it would be helpful to get the document from Sellars. Just don't let it interfere with getting the girl and her Arab friend." Garon had developed a strong dislike for the newspaperman and resolved to pay him a visit anyway and extract the memo.

He had made first-class reservations on a flight to Paris and was at this moment waiting for his driver to take him to the airport. He preferred traveling commercial instead of on those dreadful military planes with bucket seats and military rations.

The next morning Jacob left his apartment early to find a cafe for coffee and a pastry. On the way, he bought a paper to catch up on the news. He wondered whether he was imagining that his place was being watched. As he headed down the narrow street, he noticed a slouching figure that seemed to be waiting for someone. At first, he was relieved by the fact that the man did not follow him. But as he sat with his coffee, the same man appeared, loitering nearby. Was it just his overworked imagination? He had to find out. Jacob paid and left the cafe, unsure of what to do. Without an objective, he strode up the street and headed for the *Sacré-Coeur Basilica* at the top of *Montmartre*, one of his favorite spots in Paris.

He was out of breath when he reached the top of the hill from where the dramatic cathedral watched over the city. Entering quickly without looking back, he headed for the stairway to the tower. After a few false starts, he found the steps and began climbing. When he reached the first parapets, he stopped, pretending to enjoy the spectacular view. Damn! There he was! The same man had stationed himself at the entrance, and for a moment, their gazes met. Now Jacob was sure. The signature trench coat was a giveaway. Wandering casually to one of the outdoor kiosks that sold water and colas, the man bought himself a drink and coolly sat on a bench, apparently unconcerned that he had probably been discovered. What arrogance!

It dawned on Jacob that his apartment might have been broken into and rifled for the secret paper. He decided that he should ignore his shadow and return at once. He smiled as he walked out, catching the man by surprise. Jacob decided the guy wasn't very smart after all. Retracing his steps to make sure he didn't miss his way, he returned to his street and clanged the gate shut at the entrance to his building. His heart thumped as he raced up the stairs to his apartment. But nothing was disturbed. A light was blinking on the answering machine. It was a message from Mitch, warning that Jacob's whereabouts might have been discovered. Jacob smiled. The warning was a little late. Breathless and dramatic as only Mitch could be, he rattled off a set of instructions to meet him in the late afternoon. It was complicated, but Jacob was able to follow it, after confirming the location on a map he had found in the apartment. Before leaving, he stuffed the Pentagon memo into a pocket.

Taking several buses and then transferring to the Metro, Jacob followed Mitch's instructions and managed to elude the stranger in the trench coat. Mitch's directions had been surprisingly effective. By the time he arrived at the rendezvous, a cafe on *La Rive Gauche*, the sky had darkened prematurely into a cloudy dusk. Mitch was watching for him at a table just inside the door with his big hug at the ready. This time Jacob welcomed it.

"God, I'm glad to see you. Were you followed?" Mitch glanced up and down the street.

"Yes, I think so, but I lost him. Your directions worked very well."

"Good." He motioned Jacob to a chair. "We have a lot to discuss."

Jacob could not contain himself. "Before we do that, tell me about Yvonne and Emily." He tried to be cool. "Is she, are they here?"

"You mean in the restaurant?" Mitch smirked.

"No, dummy. I mean in Paris."

Mitch studied Jacob for a moment. "Jacoby," he began ominously. "You really need to, uh, ease up."

"Ease up? What do you mean?" But Jacob knew exactly what he meant. "Is she okay?" He really wanted to know a lot more. Natasha had already sown suspicion with her mysterious comments about Yvonne's activities.

"She's fine." Then he reconsidered. "Actually, I should tell you what's going on."

"Like what?" Jacob didn't like Mitch's implications.

Mitch measured his words carefully. "Yvy has a friend here in Paris. He's some sort of a Saudi prince. And I don't know whether it's the blandishments of royalty, the Movement, or just the man himself." He gazed into his glass of wine. "I don't think there's a relationship, you know, sex or anything like that. He's married. The guy is a radical Muslim, critical of the Saudi government. He wants to make changes, clean up the corruption, and do more for the people, you know, like an Arab populist." Then smiling brightly, Mitch asked, "How about a glass of this? It's a great Rhone. Full of body and …"

"Are they …?" He ignored Mitch's diversion. An Arab prince? He hadn't realized how much he had taken for granted—how he had assumed that Yvonne would be waiting for him. His only doubt had been about convincing her that they should be lovers. The word "lover" was like a stab in the gut. "A prince, huh?" His imagination began to fill in the blanks.

Mitch glanced at Jacob quizzically. "Don't jump to conclusions, Jacoby. It's just politics. He's married, for God's sake," he added. "Most of her male friends seem to be political."

"She never told me about a prince." He was already picturing her in the arms of a turbaned sheik. Remembering her casual admission of intimacies, he persisted, "She's sleeping with this terrorist." It was an assertion, not a question. "How could she?"

"Jacob, take it easy. I don't know that. She could never be your girl, anyway. I told you that in the beginning. Yvy sees a lot of guys ... 'compadres.' She is loyal to the cause. And this prince doesn't much like the Royal Family. But he's no bin Laden, no terrorist." He shook his head slowly. "I'm worried about her. This guy is playing a dangerous game. For him, all sides are enemies. Yvonne could get herself tangled up in it. She's taking risks."

Jacob was becoming dizzy with conflicted emotions—jealousy, humiliation, and his own misguided passions.

"Consider yourself lucky, Jacoby. She'd have driven you nuts with all her fervor for revolution."

Jacob didn't have to tell Mitch that he was already driven nuts. His wine came, and he drank it quickly, sorry he hadn't ordered a whiskey instead. Until now, he hadn't realized how close he was to losing control of himself.

"Anyway, you should cool it." He realized Jacob was on the edge. "Yvy will be joining us in few minutes."

The sudden revelation stunned Jacob. He was hardly prepared for an encounter. "Here, now—coming here? With her prince?"

"No, alone."

"I ... I don't know whether I can handle that," he admitted. "I mean ... this prince ... and ... I don't know what the fuck I mean."

Mitch laughed, trying to ease the building tension. "God, I shouldn't have mentioned all this stuff." He put his hand lightly on Jacob's arm. "Just relax, please."

Obviously, Mitch did not appreciate the extent of his friend's feelings for Yvonne. Under Mitch's disapproving eye-roll, he ordered a scotch.

Mitch glanced toward the door and waved. "Here she is. Now, take it easy." He patted Jacob's arm. "Okay?"

Jacob withdrew his arm and sat bolt upright. "I'm fine," he said stoically and then repeated with irritation, "just fine." In his imagination, he was unfairly linking Mitch with a conspiracy against him.

Yvonne flounced in. She looked radiantly beautiful without any makeup and with a scarf on her head in the style affected by many secular Arab women. Jacob ached to embrace her, tell her he loved her. At the same time he hated her.

"Well, Jacob, you're a sight for sore eyes!" She bent down and kissed him lightly on the cheek, rubbing his shoulder. He could feel himself stiffen. Pulling up a chair, she signaled a waiter and ordered a drink—cognac. "I need two, actually." She sighed and flashed a smile, gazing at Jacob. "So, tell me about your trip. It must have been hairy."

"Not really. It was pretty easy. Natasha put me in what was supposed to be a safe house." He paused, searching for the persona he wanted to project. "But Mitch tells me they know where I am anyway. And I've got a guy tailing me. Not much of a safe house. Natasha assured me—"

"She isn't up to date," Yvonne broke in. "A lot has happened, just in the last few hours." Yvonne was breathless with excitement. "The whole picture has changed, Jacob." Her drinks came, and she took several quick sips. "There's been a bombing of the U.S. headquarters in the Green Zone in Iraq. It just happened. They did a job on the embassy this time." She took several more quick sips. "A bunch of Congressmen and Saudis were visiting. I feel really bad for people who had to die. But, damn it, it's our corrupt government's fault! They thought a few more troops could tame Islam and turn Iraq into a democracy. Ha!"

"What bombing? I haven't heard that," Mitch interjected.

"They—we don't know exactly who yet—managed to get Humvees loaded with explosives into the compound and blow them up in front of the embassy. I guess the Shiites didn't like the Saudis interfering." She suppressed the flash of a smile. "Humvees, no less—that silly, overstuffed, gas-guzzling symbol of U.S. power in the Middle East. There's an irony in that, huh? Amazing!"

"How'd they get in, for God's sake?"

"Because the guys looked like they were military. They even had IDs. The army has clammed up totally. The coalition authority is trying to control the press, but we ... Al Jazeera was first with the news."

"God, how awful!" Mitch exclaimed. "How much ... how extensive was the damage?"

"I don't know, but there was a lot to hit there. It's the largest embassy we have in the world—over two thousand people. Can you believe it—in tiny Iraq? They must have been targeting the Saudis."

"You mean your prince and his friends told you." Mitch wrung his hands at the possibility. "God, Yvy, you'd better be careful. You're keeping dangerous company these days."

"Oh, crap, Mitch. There's no risk in what I'm doing. Ali tells me very little anyway. And he certainly wouldn't have anything to do with this, if that's what you're suggesting." She paused and sipped her cognac. "I'll tell you this, it's all clear to me now. The only way to stop the corrupt dictatorship in America is to make it fail in Iraq—that's what the whole world expects."

Overcome with resentment and a sudden burst of patriotism, Jacob could feel her studying him as he stared into his glass, realizing that she was a lost cause for him.

She went on, but Jacob wasn't listening.

Finally, he couldn't help himself and interrupted angrily, "This, ah, prince—is he part of the Movement you told me about?" Jacob asked, seething. "Your boyfriend, the prince." There was an obvious sneer in his tone. "And he's living it up on all that oil money—takes the filthy lucre from the Royal Family with one hand and stabs them in the back with the other. Kind of a hypocrite, isn't he?"

She eyed Jacob, and he could feel her contempt. "Ali Sandar Ibn Saud is his name, Jacob. And yes, he is a prince in his country. But that's not how it is at all." She gazed at him with a smile flickering on her lips. "I think you're jealous."

He could feel the heat come to his face. His fury bubbled over. "Not at all," he said, with false assurance, trying to laugh but not quite bringing it off. Unable to hold back his mounting anger any longer, he lashed out. "I'm sure your loyalty to the prince includes fucking him. Would it be like a royal fuck, as the saying goes? How does it work with all his wives? Are you first in line, or do you just get seconds?" He knew he had gone over the top.

Yvonne stared at him in disbelief. "That's disgusting! I've never heard you talk so crudely, Jacob. I'll tell you one thing, Mister Smartass—he's a better man than you are. At least he knows who he is." She, too, was getting wound up now. "You're still looking." Her last words had a special poignancy for Jacob. They cut deep. She knew him better than he had realized.

"Oh, come on. You know what? You're still only the spoiled little rich girl I met in Nantucket."

Yvonne was on the verge of tears. "I was going to be glad to see you." She was trying not to fall apart. "But you've ruined everything." She took a last slug from her glass and stood up, looking down on him. "I came to tell you that we don't need you or the silly Pentagon memo anymore." She tossed her luxurious hair. "We have other plans. We, at least, know what we have to do." She flung out her arms in frustration. "Oh, shit, you wouldn't understand anyway." She stepped back away from the table so others could hear and added in a louder voice, "You need to get a life, Jacob Sellars. Did you think one night let you own me?" Tears were now running down her flushed cheeks, but Jacob didn't notice.

Still boiling, Jacob felt beaten and demoralized. "It was two nights, Yvonne. And yes, I thought you … we …" He couldn't finish.

"We didn't. It was a diversion. And you don't even know the difference." She turned to Mitch abruptly. "Catch up with you later, Mitch. I may have a new idea for you," she added mysteriously, casting a glance in Jacob's direction. Then she was gone. Jacob could feel the impact of every word in the hollow silence that followed. He became aware that he was the focus of attention of others in the cafe. Then, as if from far away, he heard Mitch's voice.

"You lost it, Jacoby. I'd hoped you could play it cool," he said, lowering his voice. Shaking his head sadly, he added, "God, you are beyond hung up."

"I'm sorry, Mitch. I acted like a fool. But I did have feelings for her—once." It was an absurd thing to say. He could still feel the sharp pain of her words. In desperation, he clung to the hope of another chance.

"You're a bigger dunce than I thought. No one will ever have Yvy, in the sense that you have a wife or a lover. She's unpossessable—even for a prince."

"Is he really a prince?" Jacob, a little calmer now, managed a sick smile.

"Sure. In Saudi Arabia, they're a dime a dozen. Incest is state policy. They're all related. If one is part of the Royal Family and a man, he's a prince." He snapped his fingers. "Just like that. Trouble is half of them are more loyal to bin Laden than they are to the king. And they're all corrupt, conniving, and very rich. I'll tell you what. Yvy won't take long to find out that women don't count in that country. She thinks Ali is different. We'll see." He sniggered wickedly. "I give it two weeks."

"Then there is … a relationship?" The word came hard.

Mitch ignored the question. "I told you there isn't. It's what she's doing that has me really worried."

"Helping al Qaeda?"

"She might be."

"How?"

"I don't know. All I do know is that she's no longer interested in the Pentagon story. She seems to be on a different kick—very excited. But both she and Emily are secretive about it. Yvonne is spending a lot of time with the prince and his cronies, and it worries me. They refuse to clue me in." He shook his head in disbelief. "Emily did tell me this much—there's something big brewing." Mitch shivered. "It's so exciting, all this intrigue." He became more serious. "But what are we going to do about you, Jacob? What you need is another woman—an exciting one. Hmm. Let's see. It's Paris. We'll find you a hot one. I have contacts." It was an obvious attempt to distract him.

"Slow down. I've had my fill of hot ones, Mitch." Oddly, he still desperately wanted Yvonne. He could not leave Paris without seeing her again—confronting her with his feelings and apologizing for the scene. At the very least, he could end it that way—if it had to end.

"But first, we have a problem. Your security. You can't very well go back to your apartment. That dreadful man Garon is sure to come after you. He'll kill you, Jacob. He could actually do that, you know. He answers to no one. You'll have to stay with me." He frowned. "I'll get rid of my roommate. He's just temporary anyway."

"No, I'm going back. I'm tired of being chased. I'll give Garon his stupid memo, if Yvonne doesn't want it, and it will be over." He wasn't as sure as he sounded. "They've got to be careful with journalists."

"Yeah, what about the Reuters guy and a bunch of others? They were journalists."

"But I'm American. They won't touch me."

"I wouldn't count on it."

"I'll be all right." Jacob wanted very much to be alone with his thoughts. He gave Mitch several euros for the check and got up, patting him on the back. He did not want to alienate his friend and hoped his refusal of help wouldn't be misunderstood. "Thanks for the offer, but I should head back."

"You worry me, Jacoby. Please call me when you get to your apartment. I'll be sick if I don't hear from you." He scribbled a note and handed Jacob the number. "If you don't call, I'll be over—with help. Emily has security, if you can call it that. They're a bunch of Algerian thugs." He grunted in disgust. "But effective."

"Okay. If you don't hear, send in the thugs." He laughed and was relieved to be out of the cafe, away from Yvonne's still-ringing words.

CHAPTER 13

His stomach knotted when he found the door to his apartment ajar. The acrid smell of cigar smoke burned his nostrils. He was deciding on whether to run or stay when the door swung open and a large swarthy figure appeared and pulled him roughly into the room, uttering something like a curse in what he knew to be Spanish. Then he spotted Garon sitting on the couch enjoying a big cigar. A partly separated six-pack of beer had left a puddle of sweat on the glass coffee table.

"Ah, the elusive Mr. Sellars. Come, join me for a beer." He pushed a can away from the others.

Taking in the scene quickly, Jacob noticed that the room had been thoroughly ransacked—drawers allowed to fall where they opened, tables overturned, pillows thrown about. He shuddered to think of what the other rooms might look like. Then he was struck from behind, a blow to the head just hard enough to make the blood flow and dim his mind. When his head cleared, he found himself on the floor in a sitting position, drops of blood beginning to collect on the carpet beside him.

The words came from a distance. "Ticci! You're too rough on our boy." Luis was making a phony show of disapproval of his man's action. "Give him a rag or something. I can't stand the sight of blood." A dish towel materialized in Jacob's lap, and he made an ineffectual effort to mop up the pool of blood. "No, no. It's for you. Just press it hard on your head. That will stop the blood." Garon smirked. "Heads always bleed a lot even at the slightest nick. While Ticci gets rid of the mess on the rug, you can make it easy by telling me where our memo is— you know, the one you shouldn't have."

The goon leaned in close to take a swipe at the blood, jamming his hand into Jacob's crotch. Jacob summoned enough energy to swing at his face. It wasn't much. The man straightened up and delivered a painful kick to the spine, which Jacob thought might have temporarily paralyzed him from the legs down. Pictures of Iraqi prisoners at Abu Ghraib began flashing through his dulled brain. He tried to roll to his knees but couldn't make his extremities work. The pain was too intense. When he opened his eyes, he saw noticed Garon's open hand under his chin. "Where is it?" His voice was no longer pleasant, and the smile was more of a sneer. "I can't always control my friend Ticci." The ugly smile faded. "You know, you have caused me all kinds of grief, you little *chochona*. He pulled out a small revolver and cocked it. "You know the word 'chochona'? It's a faggot. You want to be a faggot like your friend Mitchel? He got down and knelt beside Jacob, jamming the gun roughly into his groin. Jacob bent double with the pain. The nice-guy pose was over. "I could pull the trigger and shoot them off." He laughed and so did Ticci. "No one will care. You are scum to your country." Another jam in the groin with the pistol. "Make you like Mitchel, your *amiga*?"

Jacob managed to point to his coat. He didn't care anymore. There was that smile again and one more jam in the groin before Garon pulled the envelope from the inside pocket of Jacob's jacket. "Good. You're a smart boy. I wouldn't have guessed you'd be so stupid and carry it around." He ripped it open to make sure it was the real thing. "Now you can go home and face the charges against you—as a traitor. You're lucky you still got your balls." He laughed loudly at his little joke. "Of course, I might change my mind, eh, Ticci?" To emphasize the possibility, he slammed the muzzle of the pistol into Jacob's groin one more time. Jacob groaned and rolled over on his side, trying to ease the pain. There was one more halfhearted kick in the back and then silence. Jacob did not move, partly because he was unable to and partly to avoid any new blows. This was the position that Mitch and his Algerians found him in when they burst in like a posse.

It wasn't until the next day that he was awakened by the sun slanting through a window. Small experimental moves produced too much pain for more than a turn of his head. He was in bed under a heap of blankets, and someone had bandaged his head. His groin ached dully, and a sharp pain in his back was the response to any movement but the slightest.

"How are you, Jacoby?" Mitch's familiar voice seemed far away.

Jacob cocked an eye to locate his friend, whose shape materialized beside him. "How do I look?" he managed to croak.

"Pretty black and blue, old boy. The bastards kicked you around quite a bit, and your … ah, equipment is messed up." He touched the bandage on the back of Jacob's head lightly. "A doctor patched your head pretty well. Put in a few stitches—the disappearing kind. They did a job on your back, too. Lucky the apes didn't break it." He presented a glass of water with one hand and two pills with the other. "Here, take these. They'll ease the pain. You need to rest more. That's the best medicine right now. But before I lose you again, I have a message from Yvonne. She says she's sorry for the way she treated you and wants to stop by in a few days. She seemed really repentant." He patted Jacob gently on the shoulder. "I just wish you had stayed with me."

Jacob tried to answer but could not mouth the words.

"Yvonne is working on a new idea and wants to get your advice."

"Yeah? Great." He found his voice. "I don't need any more of her ideas. She's just using me. I'm sick of the whole Crane family." He smiled weakly and tried to turn over but gave up. There was too much pain everywhere, and he was feeling sorry for himself. "She's a user, Mitch. She's using her prince, she uses you and Emily, and she certainly has used me. Except for her, uh, overheated ideology and sex, she's a ... cold, calculating ..." Jacob was losing the thread of his point.

"I know, I know. All that and she's still got you," said Mitch, smiling down at his now sleeping friend, adjusting the cover like a doting nurse. "Get some sleep," he added uselessly because Jacob was already out cold.

Luis Garon didn't speak French well, but he was learning to get by. He hated the snotty Parisians and their bad Spanish. Of course, because of his dark color, Garon was often mistaken for an Algerian. That added insult to injury. He could tell that the chief inspector general looked upon him with suspicion and disdain but realized that he could not function effectively without the cooperation of the French police. They had already helped identify the Saudi prince with whom the girl had a relationship. They had documentation on the source of the funds to which he had access. Millions had been laundered into euros and forwarded to Muslim groups in Paris and elsewhere. Luis had also learned that the prince might be directing money to the Sunnis in Iraq and to Hamas in Palestine. The inspector cautioned, however, that they had not been able to find any hard evidence of this latter connection. It was only a suspicion. Of course, the prince could be just one of the many radical-leaning Saudis trying to oust the corrupt Royal Family. But worst of all would be a regime change in Saudi Arabia that could shut off the oil supply.

Garon had dutifully reported what he'd learned to his bosses at the Pentagon, but without the inspector's caveats, and added his own groundless assumption that the prince was in fact an al Qaeda operative. He purposely exaggerated the connection. It was payback for their dismissing his capture of the Pentagon document as "too late." He was still nursing the insult. The Defense intelligence chief had told Garon that a directive would be sent through the embassy asking the French police to pick up the girl for questioning. Another insult. Garon frowned with dissatisfaction, knowing that under this latest order, he would be frozen out of any interrogations. She was a sexy little *puta*.

He resolved to find the girl himself by simply staking out Sellars's place. Neither the French nor Washington could stop him. He still had friends in high places. To get the jump on the local police, Garon had already stationed a watcher at Sellars's apartment, hoping to nab the girl before anyone else could.

With the help of an attentive Mitch, playing the role of Florence Nightingale to the hilt, Jacob had his first meal in four days. His head no longer hurt, and the swelling and bruising of his genitals had calmed down. The only residual pain was in his back, which was still stiff and sore to the touch. As he took a second soak of the day in the small bathroom tub, his thoughts returned to Yvonne. He was mildly curious about her visit, but the ugly memory of their encounter in the cafe lingered. Mitch had taken a call from Yvonne earlier asking whether Jacob was up to a visit. Jacob had reluctantly agreed, surprising even himself.

He dried off slowly, stretching to test his condition. The bruises were fading, and the swelling was down. He studied his reflected image, still wiry but leaner now. His naked form evoked the memory of Yvonne and their overheated encounters. Unsettled but reassured by his brief arousal, he turned away and briskly finished drying. With Yvonne, he had lost his inhibitions entirely. The things they did together had left him feeling liberated but at the same time guilty of the pleasure the liaisons had brought him. Painfully, he dressed for the first time in four days.

Yvonne arrived late, as usual, coming in with a burst of the damp Paris night at her back. More girl than woman this time, her cheeks were tinged pink by the chill, and her hair fell untamed. Jacob didn't resist the quick embrace. There was that familiar brusqueness about her which usually preceded a new direction. He was wary and unsure of how to present himself.

"My God, you're up. I was so worried about you!" she exclaimed, focusing on his bruised features. "You're a mess! What did they do to you?"

"Thanks." Jacob tried a grin, but it hurt his head. "You should see the other parts."

"Are you in pain?" she asked, ignoring his suggestive comment.

"Actually, I'm a lot better."

She sat across from him. "I feel so responsible."

"Well, you aren't. Mitch warned me not to come back here."

She continued to study him. Her voice softening, she said, "I get so mad at you because ..." Standing suddenly, she threw up her hands in frustration. "I don't know ... you always seem so, well, superior and above it all." Jacob was surprised to see tears glistening in her eyes. "But, but ..." Her voice trailed off as she gave up and collapsed back in the chair. "God, they could have killed you. No one would even know." She paused and gazed at him through her bleary eyes. "That's what Garon does—and so do the others." Jacob noticed her trembling.

"Hey, take it easy," Jacob interjected, stunned by her show of emotion. In spite of himself, he could not conceal a smile. "I'm alive." He gazed at her for a moment. "So how's the prince?" He couldn't resist the dig.

"Ali's just a friend, Jacob. You must believe that."

"I must?" She always seemed able to redeem herself.

"Yes, you must because it's true. He loves his wife, for God's sake. I, uh, care ... about you."

"Sure didn't sound like it the other day."

She stood quickly. "You were disgusting. And you know it."

Yvonne began to pace around the room, occasionally glancing at Jacob. "But I want us to get past that."

Here it comes thought Jacob—another proposition.

"Listen, I have a new idea, or at least Ali Sandar does. It might appeal to you—that is, if you can get him out of your mind as my, uh, lover."

Jacob winced a little at the jocular comment, ruing the scene he had created in the cafe. "So, what is it?"

She came and sat down on the couch beside him. "He's been talking to some guys who are in touch with al Qaeda."

"Uh-oh," Jacob interjected.

"They have a message from bin Laden," she continued, frowning at the look of incredulity that spread over Jacob's face.

He tried to control what he feared would come across as a smirk. "And you say this guy, your prince, is not one of them?" He resisted the temptation to snipe. "Okay, let's just stipulate the good faith, for now."

"See! You're such a cynic."

"Can you blame me?"

"They are hoping you would be willing to carry a message to your paper."

"Of course, you know, I don't control what goes into the *News*. All I can do is report it, particularly when it's third-level hearsay like this. I'm not even sure I have a job there anymore. I left it to write your story, remember?"

"Yeah, but if you do report this, they'll have to print it." She didn't wait for an answer but laid her hand on Jacob's outstretched arm. "Please, Jacob, hear me out. We could be onto something big—I mean maybe we could do some good—without violence." She looked away, obviously unsure of herself. "And I'm sorry about your job."

"Okay, okay. Let's have it."

"They want to make a deal, Jacob. The terrorists—at least al Qaeda—want to talk." She swallowed hard. He could see that she was trying to find the right words to make her case compelling.

"What kind of a deal? Talk about what? The three thousand people who died in New York?"

"No. It's about the future, not the past."

"I bet it is," Jacob said sardonically.

"Just bear with me, please." Finally, the full proposal bubbled out of her all at once. "Al Qaeda wants you to write in your paper that bin Laden has offered to help stop the violence and encourage others to do the same if the people in the U.S. will vote against this new administration and put it out of office—like the Spanish did once, remember?" She began to pace, nervous about his reaction. "The American people have to reject this crusade against Islam. Al Qaeda wants to see some movement in the new Congress to reject this president. They think that the Democrats could win Congress back this time. Some Democrats even talk of impeachment. It's what they should have done with Bush. But it's not too late for this president." She paused, a cloud of doubts beginning to dampen her enthusiasm. "I can just tell from your expression you think this is crazy ... but ..."

Jacob stopped her. "I sure do. It's off the fucking wall, Yvonne. And it sounds like blackmail. And it's offensive to the voting public. They don't want some Arab terrorist guy who has killed a lot of Americans to be telling Congress what to do. It's a dumb idea, Yvonne. And I wonder if it even came from bin Laden. I can't believe you've fallen for this." He paused to sort out his disbelief. "Anyway, we're not like Spain, we can't just choose the time we decide to kick out our government. It's an absurd idea."

She straightened her back, taking the insult in stride but ready to fight for her point. She kept her anger in check. "I expected this reaction. But don't you see, America can take the Congress back and make life miserable for this little Napoleon in the White House. There is a chance to do that now. And it's not blackmail. It's an expression of a sentiment held by most of the world, particularly our allies. This president wants permanent military bases in Iraq. Iraqis don't want that—Americans don't want it either. Polls disapprove by wide margins. You've seen them I'm sure. So it's not a dumb idea. I agree that it is troublemaking and manipulative coming from bin Laden. But coming from him, it is also very persuasive. It will get America's attention—and the Europeans, too. Everyone wants to see an end to the threats of terror. This would be a start. Let the people decide." She was getting herself revved up again. "Of course, bin Laden wants more, but not as part of this deal. He will wait for a new Congress, a new president if necessary. This should pique the interest of all Americans." She had finally run out of persuasion. "It's all in a letter … or will be if you agree to get it to the people who matter—in a press release."

Jacob had to smile as he thought of the disruptive effect such statements would have on the upcoming election. The American people, suffering with security burdens everywhere they turned, were yearning for a magic bullet that would return them to a normal existence.

"Why doesn't he put it out on one of the Arab networks, like he usually does?"

"Because it won't get the same attention or trust. Being in the American media makes a much bigger deal of it. It won't be easy to ignore. And after all, it is the American people who are at risk. You know, if there is one more big attack—like an airliner hijacked or some kind of dirty bomb in New York—it could destroy the economy. This is serious stuff, Jacob. Maybe we'd never recover from it."

"It is a bizarre idea, Yvonne." But Jacob began to appreciate the implications. It was certainly timely. The administration was becoming more belligerent, threatening Iran again and sending even more troops into the Middle East and Afghanistan. The press seemed increasingly impotent in their ability to mount an effective critique of the administration or Congress. Yet, public opinion was beginning to harden against foreign entanglements. The administration was on the defensive, pumping up the propaganda machine and escalating fear tactics. Nevertheless, Democrats were still wary of going on the offensive. They needed a major boost. Polls were turning around, but not fast enough. Yvonne's proposal would certainly throw a monkey wrench into the Congressional election, no doubt about that. "It would be the mother of all October surprises." Jacob laughed. "It is the craziest idea I've ever heard, Yvy, but I'll admit it has a sick appeal."

"Will you do it?" she asked excitedly.

"I'll think about it."

"That's all I ask." She squeezed his hand.

"Why not wait until 2012, when we'll be electing a new president?"

"It's too long to wait. Things are moving too fast. People are dying."

"Maybe the proposal should go directly to the leadership in Congress?"

"It would be smothered. You know that."

"Yeah, I suppose so." Jacob was trying to convince himself that the idea was flawed. "But why me? People in better positions than I am could do this for you."

"I've told Ali about you, why you're here, and he knows about the Pentagon memo. He thinks you are a credible guy. They've promised to protect you from Garon's thugs. And they mean business. I can tell you that." She bent over to kiss him, but he turned away. "And they trust me."

"Well, I guess that clinches it," he said, not with the degree of sarcasm he wanted. An uneasy silence fell between them.

"You and I need to …" He couldn't find the words he wanted. "If I do this—and I'm not committing to anything yet—I think we should keep this on a …"

"Strictly business?"

"Something like that. I'd only be a conduit, not an advocate."

"That's good enough."

"Okay."

There was another long silence broken only by the tick of a mantelpiece clock.

"I am fond of you, Jacob. But I'm afraid that you think I'm just …"

"Using me? Yes, I do."

"No, I haven't been using you. But I have been pretty lousy. And you have a way of aggravating me, as I said—acting so high and mighty, like you did the first time we met. It gets to me, and I react." She paused after this critique. "I'm really sorry about how I behaved in the cafe. It was, I admit, nasty and mean." She smiled. "God, I even slapped you the first time we met." She shook her head. "That was pretty awful, too." She touched him again. "I don't know how you stand me."

Jacob laughed. "Sometimes I don't either."

"You know, you're different. Others piss me off, too. But it doesn't get to me like it does with you."

"Maybe I'm just a good lay?"

She tossed her head to clear a hank of hair that had fallen over her forehead again and smiled. It was a self-conscious gesture. "Yes. You certainly are that, I guess."

"You guess?"

"No, I'm sure." She stood up. "I gotta go—Mr. Conduit, remember?"

"I do." Jacob could not stop the smile. At that moment, he felt sorry for Yvonne, caught up in worldly issues, having to grow up too fast, missing all the normal things a girl of her age would be doing.

"Please think about my idea, Jacob, seriously." At the door she turned and said, "When this is all over, I hope we can, uh, try again, Jacob. I …," she was groping for the right words, "I need you." A smile lurked in the corners of her mouth. "Anyway, I hear you have been a man about town—I mean, before Garon." She turned and tossed her head in a last defiant, knowing glance. Not waiting for questions, she slammed the door behind her.

Well, as usual, she had the last word, but he had no idea what she was talking about with her "man about town" parting shot. Jacob closed his eyes, recapturing her smile as she walked out. He found her mood strange. She had lost some of her characteristic combativeness and seemed almost wistful about her feelings toward him. The new personality surprised him. But he was still wary of her motives. Yvonne was always, above all, manipulative. She had put him on the spot with her outrageous proposal. It was an intriguing idea. But how believable was her prince? How truthful was she about her relationship with Ali?

Fatigued by the visit, he stretched out on the couch and lapsed into a sort of daydreamy detachment, visualizing himself proposing the idea to a skeptical Tom Shanahan. In his imagination, he laid out all the arguments in magical perfection. Shanahan's skepticism gave way to curiosity and then to exhilaration. "Yes, yes, brilliant, Jake! We'll do it. The boss will love it! It will be a huge story for the *News*." In the euphoria of the unreal moment, Jacob fell asleep.

The phone woke him abruptly. The first light of dawn was beginning to brighten the curtains, which were still closed. He had slept the whole night away. He was surprised to find himself fully dressed, except for his shoes. Then he remembered Yvonne's proposition.

"Jacob, did I wake you?" Mitch asked softly.

"What do you think?" Jacob had to clear the hoarseness from his voice.

"Sorry, old man. I guess I did. How are you feeling?"

"Better, thanks."

"Some big news for you. I heard it late last night but thought it too late to call. Garon's been shot, one right between the eyes, like an execution!" he said excitedly. "What do you think of that?"

"Garon shot?" Jacob had difficulty concentrating on the thought. "Yvonne? Did she have anything to do with it?"

"I don't know." Mitch paused. "She did visit you last night?"

"Yeah, for awhile. You seem to be up on things."

"You've got bodyguards now."

"I do?"

"She wants to save you."

"For a purpose—there's always a purpose, Mitch." The news of Garon's death was beginning to worry him.

"You know what I'm thinking?"

"I never know what you're thinking, Mitch."

"Well, she seems to be truly fond of you—ever since you told her off in the cafe. Then you got roughed up, and she began to think about another person, for once in her life." He paused. "I might have been wrong about her before."

Jacob considered that for a moment and then said, "I doubt it. She's just thought of another way to use me."

"Yeah, how's that?"

"I thought you knew."

"Knew what?" There was a touch of irritation in his tone. "You mean other than the article?"

Mitch didn't seem to know about the prince's most recent idea.

"It's just that the prince keeps feeding her insatiable appetite for excitement." He was purposely vague.

"Jacob, you need to get over that guy. He's just a glimpse into a different world for her, nothing more." He paused. "So what's the prince come up with this time?"

"I bet you thought there was a relationship between them, too," he said, avoiding the question. Now it was clear. Mitch had been left out of this plan.

"That was before I met the wife—and there is only one, by the way. She knows all about Yvy and likes her. Both view her as sort of a daughter, if you can believe that. They read the Koran together. Yvy's kind of spellbound by them. What makes it spicier for her is that the prince and his wife are at odds with the Royal Family."

"Really? You think the prince is sympathetic to the wayward cousin?"

"You mean bin Laden?"

"I was afraid to mention the name. But yes."

"I have no idea. But I doubt it. The prince doesn't seem that radical—just a lonely liberal among all the conservatives. Anyway, since you are now under the protection of the prince, all you have to worry about is Saudi intelligence." After a pause, Jacob could almost anticipate Mitch's curiosity spinning back to "start." "So, what's this new thing with the prince?"

"Ah, nothing specific." Jacob was reluctant to share Yvy's most recent proposal. He knew Mitch would knock it down as harebrained—as it most certainly was. Gossip that he was, Mitch might spread it around among his friends with the admonition of silence, which would be ignored. Jacob would be the laughing-stock of the entire press community. If the idea was pursued at all, it had to be done carefully after a case was developed to sell it. "She just wants me to meet some of her friends. You know—listen to their side. She doesn't care much about the Pentagon memo anymore. But I still think it's a powerful indictment of the administration." He hoped this would be enough to divert Mitch's curiosity.

"Yeah, I agree. But Yvy seems to have something else up her sleeve. She's being very cozy about it." He seemed satisfied with Jacob's explanation. "I have a copy of that memo, if you want it. I had it scanned, and it worked."

"Good thinking, Mitch—that's great!"

"Go ahead and write your story, old boy. It's a good one. You've got all the corroboration you need." Jacob could tell that Mitch was anxious to get off the line—probably to try to find out about Yvy's new venture. "I guess you'll be sticking around for awhile. Keep me posted on your plans."

"I will, Mitch. We should get together soon, though, and rehash this thing about the Pentagon memo—how to let it out and when. But I must tell you, I'm a little worried about the repercussions from Garon's, uh, execution. It could complicate things. I certainly don't want to be pulled into that."

"Me neither. There'll be an investigation, for sure."

"I hope not a serious one. Stay in touch."

"Will do."

Jacob decided to shave and bathe. He needed to test himself—check out his various aches and pains. He'd spent a lot of time in bed and was unsure of his condition. After his cleanup, he found the energy flowing back into his body. The hot water had soaked out much of his soreness, and he felt almost normal again. Rummaging in the refrigerator, he found some juice and poured a large glass and then another.

Stretching out on the couch to ease the pains, his thoughts turned to Yvonne. The effect of her visit had been less than expected. Yes, she was sexy and appealing. Yes, he would sleep with her again if the opportunity came around. But he realized that he was losing the intensity of his feelings. He didn't know why, but he speculated that his beating might have changed him somehow, given him a better perspective on his priorities. At one point in the ugly encounter, he was certain that Garon would kill him.

He was willing to accept the reality that Yvonne had been manipulating him all along. She had filled him with all this guff about having fond feelings for him. She had even conned Mitch. This was just part of the setup for her next manipulation. He would have to make his own decision about the offer she proposed. There was no point in talking to Emily or Natasha. They would likely be parties to the scheme. It would be his decision and his decision alone, whether to run with the idea.

As the day faded into evening, Jacob developed the urge to get out of the apartment—free himself of his four walls and try out his sore back. Before he left, he grabbed a file of the drafts he'd been working on, thinking he might review them if he had dinner. Outside, the crisp air cleared his head as he set off down the bustling street. The roar of the city reminded him of New York. He walked several blocks at a fast clip until the soreness in his back muscles returned. Retracing his steps, he found *La Mer*, the little cafe he had visited his first night in town. He needed to sit down. Inside, the aromas of cooking reminded him that he hadn't eaten a real meal for a few days. Choosing a table in the back, he shed his coat and first ordered a coffee, then changed his mind and asked for tea. He sipped it slowly and watched the crowd arrive. The babble of French mesmerized Jacob. Relaxing finally, he amused himself by tuning into random chatter and tried, with little success, to decode what was being said. Words and phrases were the best he could do, but it was a nice distraction. The tea was strong and bitter, with a smoky taste. He liked it. Closing his eyes seemed to help his feeble translation effort. He recognized some of the conversation as a discussion of the wars in Iraq and Afghanistan and often critical remarks about familiar American politicos. His concentration was broken by a rustling nearby. When he opened his eyes, he found he had company. It was Lynnette, the woman he had met on his previous visit.

"Hello," she said, eyeing the open file on the table. "Are you working?"

It seemed like ages since he had last seen her. "No, people-watching. The papers are just for cover. I'm eavesdropping—not having much luck, I'm afraid." He closed the file and got up to greet her. "How nice to see you again." He had quite forgotten her in the heat of his recent ordeals. "Lynnette, it is, with two n's and two t's."

"*Ah, oui*, you remembered." She looked pleased.

"Of course I remember."

"May I join you?"

"By all means." He offered to take her coat and gestured to the opposite seat. He wondered whether this was, after all, a subconscious reason for his returning to *La Mer*. Then he admitted aloud, "I could use some company."

"*Ah, tres bien ...*" She sighed and slipped out of her coat. Her bright-red cashmere sweater over a simple flared skirt revealed an even nicer figure than he had remembered. Her wavy blond hair gave her a glamorous appearance, but nothing about her seemed contrived. Suddenly, she did a double take. "*Mon Dieu!* What happened to your head?"

Jacob instinctively reached up and touched the spot. "Nothing, just a bad bump—a kitchen cabinet."

"A pretty big bump."

"It's okay." He wanted to avoid the subject. "What would you like?" he asked.

She glanced at his cup and the accompanying pot. "The same as you." She sat and folded her hands on the table and gazed up at him. "So, we meet again?"

"Yes, we do, we have." He sat down across from her.

"So, you are still working on the story?" She glanced again at the file.

"Well, I'm taking a breather at the moment."

"You are not working, then."

"No." Jacob smiled agreeably.

"Okay, *c'est bon*. We can—how do you say it—gab a little."

Jacob laughed, amused by her little attempt at American slang. "Would you like something to eat?"

She flashed a tense little smile. "Let's just talk." Her tea arrived, and she took a sip. "This is very English, having, ah, afternoon tea—late tea." She raised her cup and glanced at Jacob. "You remember the girl I told you about—the American who gave the radical lecture?"

Jacob swallowed and nodded, uncomfortable with this new direction. He was already pretty sure about the identity of the American girl.

"Well, I met her the other day. She's interesting. I just happened to mention to her that I had met an American newspaperman, and she knew you! Isn't that amazing?" She eyed him meaningfully. "You didn't tell me you know her." She dropped her eyes. "Of course, I told her I just had a drink with you." She looked up and smiled innocently. "But is she a girlfriend—I mean—you know, important?"

Her revelation cleared up Yvonne's parting comment the day before about his being a "man about town." "No, not at all. I'm doing a story on her family, who own a big oil company. They are famously rich and important." He regretted the description before the words were out. "I mean, I had no idea that it was her when you first mentioned it to me."

"Famous? How?"

"Maybe not so famous, but important—in my country and abroad. Anyway, let's get away from my work." Jacob wanted very much to change the subject.

"She is very beautiful." Lynnette clearly had other questions but hesitated, uncertain whether to proceed. Her eyes downcast, she finally asked softly, "Is she, eh, more than a friend?"

"No. I'm just doing the story." Then for some reason he could not fathom, he said, "It's you I'm interested in." The minute he said it he regretted it. It was probably the intensity of her blue eyes that elicited this.

She frowned, flustered by his sudden declaration. "What? You don't even know me." But it didn't stop her from persisting one more time. "Then not a lover?" Her probing eyes searched his face.

"No."

She sipped her tea, glancing at him over the rim. "And the other part?"

"You mean being interested in you?"

"Yes, that." She nodded.

"Yes, I am. I meant it." Unsure of his own intentions, he tried to say it with conviction. He had dug himself a little hole.

"That's so American. You know nothing about me."

"We've met twice now. You went to New York with your parents, uh, years ago." He smiled brightly to ease the tension he had created. "And you like New York City. We have that in common."

"You remembered that?" She relaxed a little in spite of her doubts. "But that isn't knowing me."

"I want to learn more about you. You see, I'm interested enough to be curious." Jacob was discovering things about himself. He was beginning to enjoy her company. "Why don't we have some dinner? Then we'll both learn more about each other." He reached across the table and touched her hand. "Please."

She thought about his proposal for a moment and then accepted. "Okay. An early one. That sounds nice."

"It's a deal then."

"I remember one thing about you. You are a farmer."

Jacob laughed. "No, I'm a writer. I was brought up on a farm."

"*Ah, oui*—that's what I meant, brought up. Now you work for a newspaper."

"Not any more. I got canned."

"Canned?"

"Yes, fired, lost my job."

"*Mon dieu!* What did you do?"

"Actually, I quit. I just wanted to do my own thing, my own story, maybe even a book."

"About what?"

"About how oil corrupts the world." He felt bad about having to shade the story. She seemed so trusting.

"How interesting. Then you were not, ah, as you say, canned. That's good."

"I'm afraid it amounts to the same thing."

She laughed. "Well, can you afford to take me to dinner?"

"Of course—I invited you."

"I hope you get your job back."

Jacob tried to divert the conversation. "You know, I think I came here hoping I might find you. It was in the back of my mind."

"You did? *C'est vrai?*" The idea disarmed her completely.

"Yes, it's true."

As they finished their tea, he got her to talk about herself. She had a doctorate in modern French literature and hoped for a professorship at *La Sorbonne*. She was now an assistant professor assigned to advanced undergraduates who wanted to write theses on her subject. She helped them with reading sources and guided their writing efforts. He learned that she was thirty-four years old and lived nearby in an apartment.

She looked at her watch. "We better eat. We have talked already too much about me."

"And you know all about me. So, now we know each other—at least a little. That's good. You choose the spot, Lynnette. It's your town."

"Okay, but you can call me Lynne—it's shorter." She gazed up at him as they stood to go. "I like the name Jacob. It's so, so ..."

"Don't say biblical, please."

She frowned. "I wasn't. I was going to say old-fashioned, but that didn't sound right. I guess I mean it is a reassuring name, if you can understand that. There is a word in French for what I mean. It translates into something like dependable—but that sounds boring, and you are not a bore."

"Enough. Let's go."

He helped her with her coat and felt her delicate shoulders as he rested his hands there for a moment. It was a conscious intimacy he allowed himself. They walked out arm in arm.

"This way," she directed. "It's not far." They moved comfortably in step, silently wondering what the other was thinking. She squeezed his arm and said in a tiny cloud of her own breath, "But we don't really know each other yet."

He squeezed back and conceded, "Okay, not yet."

CHAPTER 14

Later that same night, Jacob reread his article and decided it was too good to give up on, even though Yvonne and her aunt might no longer be interested. He rewrote it as a chronology of his investigation, working into it developments he had not yet included like Garon's roughing up and later execution, the prince's proposal, and the more recent comments of Mitch about the prince's political sympathies. When Jacob felt that he had filled in most of the gaps, he set it aside and made himself a snack before going to bed. As he ate, he realized his work had just begun. The story would now have to be shaped into the wide-ranging exposé he had originally planned. Of course, it would be more about government scheming than the Cranes. He considered himself to be free of any obligations to Emily and Yvonne. Still, the catchy title, "Whale Oil to Crude Oil," intrigued him.

As the night quieted the city, his thoughts returned to Lynnette. He tried to remember all the words that passed between them—her questions about Yvonne, his denials and then his spontaneous admission of interest in Lynnette, the touch of her hand, the feel of her slender shoulders, her figure beneath the sweater, and, most of all, the warmth he felt for her. Dinner had seemed to pass too quickly. Afterward, they had walked and walked, covering a myriad of subjects—war, terrorism, the world, and then their own lives and dreams, revealing much about themselves. She was easy to talk to, quietly smart and informed and, above all, open and sincere—not manipulative like Yvonne, nor calculating like Rachel.

As they talked themselves out, Jacob noticed her pace slowing. Then she stopped on a corner and gestured, "*Voila!* My home!" She pointed to one of the older buildings across the street.

"So soon." He toyed with the idea of asking her to let him visit. He was disappointed at having to leave her. He glanced at his watch, wondering whether it was too late to ask himself in.

She had anticipated this. "It's still early, and I can get some work done."

"Okay. That's good, I suppose."

She put a hand on his arm. "Thank you for supper. I enjoyed our time together." She gave him a tentative squeeze and then pulled out her keys.

"I enjoyed it, too."

"I hope we can do this again. You know—what do you call it—a date?" Keys in hand, she started to cross the street. He followed her to her door. She turned and smiled. "You will call me?"

"Of course." He took her hand in his. "Could we have dinner again?"

"I'd love to."

"How do I call you?"

"Here, I'll give it to you." She scribbled a note on a scrap of paper and handed it to him.

He watched as she unlocked the door and slipped inside without a look back.

Jacob lay awake for awhile, wondering why he was suddenly so smitten by his new friend. Maybe his interest in her was just a reaction to his having given up on Yvy. He remembered the schoolboy talk about the dangers of a romance on the rebound. Surely he was too old for this sort of behavior. The possibility that this was just a dalliance on his part made him feel uncomfortable. Was another relationship a good idea? There could be little future in it for either of them—with him in New York and her in Paris three thousand miles away. He had to fly home soon in any event. He needed to resolve his job and complete his story. There was much to do. Finally, he gave in to his drooping eyelids and fell asleep.

The next morning his first thoughts were of Lynnette. She had given him her number at the university and said it was okay to call—best in the afternoon when she had finished her seminars. Eventually, he made a pot of coffee and popped a croissant into the toaster oven. Out his window, the street below was still busy in the late-morning rush hour. While he munched on the pastry, Yvonne called, prodding him on her proposal.

"What's your decision? Are you going to help us?"

"Maybe."

"Well, I've talked to Ali."

"And what exactly am I being asked to do?"

"I already told you." A noisy sigh of frustration blew into the receiver. "Pass the idea on to your editor. See whether your paper is willing to run it as an exclusive. I can't believe they won't be interested."

"Can your prince and his friends put this bizarro thing in writing? That would help a lot. And I'll need some names—beyond the generic."

There was a pause of uncertainty. "Okay. I understand. I'll have to get back to you on the names part."

"Good."

"So how are you doing? Are the aches and pains better? I miss you."

"I'm almost back to normal."

There was a long pause. "You sound cool. Are you still mad at me?"

"No, Yvy. I'm just preoccupied."

"Nothing wrong, I hope?"

"I'll tell you what's bothering me. As you know, I may no longer have a job at the *News*. I don't know how welcoming my editor will be to anything that comes from me. I left to do my own thing on a subject that my boss thinks the paper has a proprietary interest in—your story. Editors get pretty upset when that happens. I'm not sure I have much goodwill left at the *News*—maybe anyplace else either."

"You're blaming me, aren't you? I'm not surprised. We did cut the rug out from under you. But, look, this should put you back in their good graces. It's a great scoop. Anyway, I still do want you to do our story. I never did want to give up on it. This other thing just got in the way."

"Get me something in writing, with a source, first. Then we'll see."

"I will. I'll do my best." Another pause. "Do you miss me, Jacob?"

"Remember, Yvy, this is strictly business now. You agreed."

"Yeah, okay. But I do hope we can get back to our business. I need to hold you."

"Business, Yvy."

"You bastard. You're insufferable!"

They hung up.

He had to smile with satisfaction. It was Yvy's ego at work, not her interest in him. While the remnants of his attraction to her were still there, he had awakened to the less promising reality of the relationship. Yvy would probably never love anyone but herself. Sadly, he had allowed himself to become infatuated with her physically and had confused his feelings with love. Jacob wasn't sure what had changed him. The scene in the cafe had left him with serious doubts. Then an odd epiphany occurred in their last meeting at his bedside when her undisguised opportunism again revealed itself. The foundation for his disillusionment had been growing for some time. He just hadn't recognized it. The disenchantment had come quickly. It was as if a blazing light had transformed a darkened room, bringing with it a sense of relief.

An envelope appeared under the door sometime during the next few days. It was not from the prince. An indecipherable signature was the only identity shown. The paper was of high quality, and it showed that a copy had gone to Yvonne. The meticulously typewritten proposal took the form of an open letter to the American people agreeing to stop the attacks by al Qaeda if the Congress did the proper thing and "initiated impeachment proceedings against the president for breaking rules of international law by continuing the military occupation of Iraq." The letter described the American crusaders as "a government within a government with no accountability." The author pointed out that impeachment could succeed only if the American people threw the Republican crusaders out of Congress.

It was a patent effort to influence public opinion in the coming Congressional elections. A lengthy list of trade-offs followed, including assurance of security for America. There was an offer to arrange for an emissary to meet with the Democratic leadership at an agreed-upon location to show good faith. It was a dramatic idea—with the most troublesome implications. At worst, it was an arrogant interference with the voting process, a despicable attempt to manipulate public opinion. But it was also a publicity stunt of major proportions, guaranteed to sell newspapers and likely to influence a fearful country yearning for peace of mind. Could any editor reject the opportunity? Shanahan? The publisher? Jacob decided to sleep on it. The decision to take the plunge was his to make.

He smiled. What would Rachel think—if she was still speaking to him? "Take a chance, Jacob, for once in your life. For God's sake, take a chance, be daring." Is that what she would say? Or would it be, "You're a fool if you even touch this." He was tempted to call her. But he rejected the idea. It would be unfair to put her on the spot. He began to pace around the room. There was another reason not to make the call. He wanted to do this on his own—mark his own territory. Yes, it was a defining moment. The realization scared him a little, but he knew he would take the chance. He would e-mail Shanahan in the morning. Better not to do it by phone. An e-mail message could be placed in the *News*'s protected file, which was secure from prying. That much privacy was crucial.

He slept uneasily, dreaming of one frustration after another, waking in a sweat, then forgetting and falling asleep again. Drugged by the poor night, he slept through the morning. After a late coffee and a bagel, he went online and pulled up the *News*'s file and wrote his message, summarizing the al Qaeda proposal and promising to provide a hard copy of the letter. If the editors were interested, he would hear back quickly. Verification of the source could come later. Of course, without it, Shanahan probably could not publish the story. He paused before sending the e-mail and took a deep breath.

"Well, here we go," he said aloud. He clicked the send button with a flourish and sat back, his heart thumping with anticipation.

Later, after puttering around tidying up the apartment and taking care of other housekeeping chores, he decided to take a walk to ease his nerves. He walked until dusk, agonizing over the ramifications of his decision. A negative reaction from Shanahan would stymie the plan. Then there was the risk that he would be charged with a crime for consorting with Arabs under some provision of the Patriot Act. The gang-like execution of Garon could present further problems. The papers were now saying that Luis was a U.S. intelligence operative. He dreaded what answer he might find on his computer.

Stirred from these unsettling thoughts by the ominous tolling of bells at a nearby basilica, he decided to take a break in a little cafe. Sipping an American coffee, his thoughts turned back to Lynnette. The picture of Yvonne kept popping up to interfere. In exasperation, he ordered a light dinner and ate it slowly. It was late when he slipped the key into his lock, remembering Garon's painful visit. There was a message on his phone from Yvonne pressing him again for a decision and the dreaded e-mail from Shanahan. He went to bed without opening it.

Waking early, he decided it was silly to wait any longer, so he booted up and read Shanahan's letter.

> Jacob, I was pleased to hear from you—until, that is, I read your message. I don't know what you've gotten yourself into over there, but you better run from it as fast as you can. You are flirting with dynamite. I am attaching a copy of the relevant parts of the Patriot III Act, as signed by the president. I urge you to come home soon so we can talk about your job here. If you play your cards right, I might be able to get you back in good graces here. Burn the Arab's letter and make a plane reservation. Tom.

Jacob opened the attachment, which turned out to be amendments recently passed. It was full of wordy language about what constituted "acts of disloyalty" to the United States. He wasn't sure it would apply to anything he had done so far. It wasn't even clear that making the letter public would be covered by the Act, unless his purpose was "subversive," whatever that meant. Shanahan had not included any definitions. Nonetheless, the new law was a forbidding document.

Shanahan's reaction was discouraging but not unexpected. A reply would need some thought. Jacob knew that another newspaper might be interested. He toyed with the idea of just sending the whole text of the letter to the *Times* and seeing what happened. It would risk his proprietary interest, but it surely would get attention. He knew Yvonne would be calling again soon and considered how much he would tell her about Shanahan's reply. He planned to stall her so she wouldn't go elsewhere with her idea. He had to admit that he was hooked on the concept. "Damn Yvonne," he said aloud. He wondered again why she and the prince hadn't just made the calls themselves. It was likely that he didn't want his fingerprints on al Qaeda's involvement. It would cause him serious problems with the Saudi authorities.

A sudden pang of hunger made him think of lunch. He glanced at his watch and then hurried to get away before Yvy could call. Returning to *La Mer* hoping he might run into Lynnette, he chose the same table. He needed a diversion. The waitress took his order, and he settled back with his thoughts. Disappointed that Lynnette didn't appear, he found the note she had given him. The cafe was almost empty, so he could talk in some privacy. He punched out her office number and waited expectantly through five rings.

"*L'office de Mademoiselle Fouché.*" The French startled him. He had expected her to answer.

"Uh, yes. Is Lynnette in?"

"*Oui, Monsieur.* One moment," the secretary answered in heavily accented English. "Who is calling, please?"

Jacob told her, carefully spelling just his first name.

"Jacob," Lynnette said warmly. "I have been hoping you would call. It's so nice to hear from you."

"I'm here at *La Mer* having lunch and was thinking about you."

"*Ah, c'est bon.* This is good timing. There is a concert tonight, some early French folk music. Would you like to go?"

"Well ... sure."

"It is not a long one—just an hour." Then she added for more appeal, "Old instruments are used—you know, like they had in the Middle Ages. It should be interesting. We could have some dinner afterward."

"I'd love to. It sounds wonderful," he said, warming to the idea.

She described to him where they should meet, and he made careful notes. "I will be pleased to see you again." Her tone was formal, and Jacob guessed it was because of the office environment and maybe a curious secretary. "See you at seven." She hung up before Jacob could say more.

Excited about the prospect of seeing her again, he paid the check and returned to his apartment. The first thing he did was check his e-mail. He was surprised to see another message from Shanahan.

Jacob. On second thought, send your letter. Tom

There was no explanation for the change. Stunned, he stared at the words on the screen. What was going on? It could only be one thing. Newcomb, the publisher, had overruled Shanahan! It was likely that Newcomb had decided to do something with the proposal. Knowing Newcomb to be a loyal supporter of the administration, he worried about motives. The story was a bombshell, of course. In the hands of another paper—like the *Times* or *The Washington Post*—there would be a clear editorial purpose. The eagerness of the *News* to get their hands on it first was probably impetuous. Jacob dialed up Yvonne and unfortunately got her answering machine. He waited for the tone and left a message for her to call as soon as possible.

For the rest of the afternoon, Jacob worked on his exposé, fashioning it into a more polished narrative. As he wrote his own story, he became more convinced that publication of the prince's proposal was anything but subversive. Instead, it was an effort, albeit a clumsy one, to make peace.

In the process of writing, he decided that he needed to emphasize the dangers of the Pentagon document to the foreign policy of the United States. The story could be his best defense against any retribution under the Patriot Act. He spent the rest of the afternoon working furiously. In the intensity of his composition, it was only the chime of six at the cathedral that reminded him of the time. He had to dress hastily.

Jacob was looking forward to his dinner with Lynnette. It made sitting through the concert worthwhile. He had decided to put on some better clothes for his appearance at the university, exchanging blue jeans for cotton trousers and a decent shirt and jacket. Glancing in the mirror, he noticed for the first time flecks of gray hair and wondered whether the tensions of his recent days had aged him. The pulse of the telephone distracted him from these thoughts, and not surprisingly, it turned out to be Yvonne.

"Hi. Got your call." She was a little out of breath. "What's going on? Have you lined things up yet—I mean have you been in touch with your paper?"

"A bit pushy, aren't we?"

"Sorry. Let me begin again. So how are you, your bruises and pains?"

"I'm fine," he said, laughing at her transparent recovery.

"You got the letter—hand delivered?"

"Yes. It came. I read it."

There was a short silence. He made her wait. Finally, she said, "You called me."

"I did talk to the paper. Their first reaction was … it wasn't a good one. Disbelief, to put it mildly."

"They thought it was a bad idea or a hoax?"

"Probably the first—and disbelief that I could bring them such a preposterous idea." He wanted her to suffer a bit.

"You called to tell me that?" Her feigned sweetness dried up. "You said it was a first reaction?"

"That's right."

"Yeah, and what else? There was a second?"

"My editor wrote back. He seems to have changed his tune. Maybe his boss overruled him. I'm a little suspicious about motive here. He wants the letter or statement—whatever there is in writing. I assume the one slipped under the door is all we can get."

"Yes, it is. So why didn't you say this in the first place?" She was still edgy. "Your paper wants to do it then?"

"You should have the full picture, Yvy. Your story is pretty incredible for anyone to take seriously. Anyway, I'm not sure what is going on here—I mean at the *News*. I don't trust the publisher."

"Apparently he thinks it's credible."

"We'll see. First, I've got to have better sources. The signature I have is illegible. I need names and relationships. That's the first thing they will ask for."

"I can get that. It may take awhile."

"Well, don't jerk me around on this. I'm out on a limb. Since your Arabs agreed to a meeting, there should be names."

There was a long pause. "I know, Jacob. I know. I'll do my best. I promise. But I also want to see you. I really miss you." Another pause. "I can make it up to you," she said suggestively.

"You could do that." He tried to suppress any response to the obvious sensuality of her implication. "But for now, it's business—remember?"

"I wish you'd stop reminding me."

"Get the info—the names. Like who is the intermediary. No newspaper will use this kind of explosive stuff if it's a blank check."

"I will. I'll get it all." And before she hung up, she added, "And they're not my Arabs, by the way."

Their conversation unsettled him. Even the sound of her voice turned him on. He could still feel her pull on his emotions.

Following Lynnette's directions, he found her cramped office in the Fine Arts building. Her desk was stacked with what appeared to be manuscripts and test papers, piled like blocks. If she had been seated, he never would have known that she was there. But she had risen to greet him.

"It's a little late, so we should hurry." She glanced at her watch and grabbed an oversized purse, slinging it onto her shoulder. "Let's go." She took his arm.

"Gosh, I thought I was right on time."

"You were. I made a mistake. It starts a little earlier than I told you." She squeezed his arm. "Anyway, they always tune up first."

The concert auditorium was in a building nearby, so they held hands like two teenagers and hustled across a grassy courtyard. They were in time to find seats in the back as the small orchestra began its concert. The music was pleasant and medieval in sound, or at least what Jacob assumed early music should sound like. Classical music had not been a part of his education. He did own a modest stereo system in his apartment, mostly because Rachel had insisted he get one. She had bought him a starter set of Mozart CDs. He had never bought another and rarely played what he had, except when Rachel was visiting.

After the concert, Lynnette insisted that they stay for refreshments. Jacob met a few of her associates. They were an intense lot, and the discussions were more of literature than music. Before they could get away, a coterie of devoted students gathered around Lynnette, eyeing Jacob and shooting questions at her. He was impressed by their respect and apparent fondness for her. Their French was rapid-fire and unintelligible, leaving Jacob on the sidelines with an occasional translation by Lynnette. He was glad to escape to the restaurant.

All through dinner, he stewed about the e-mail from Shanahan. He found it hard to concentrate on what Lynnette was saying. Several times, she asked whether something was bothering him. He apologized and admitted that it was an office thing. They parted again at her apartment door, without either of them making any suggestion about extending the evening, although they lingered longer over a still-chaste good night. He had the feeling that he might have let her down—not performed as expected. After he'd left her, he wandered off without direction in total confusion. It was not a satisfactory evening, but he was not quite sure why. Had he insulted her by not being more focused? Trying to improve his mood, he fantasized about holding Lynnette in his arms. But it didn't help to shake his worries about Shanahan. As a distraction, he stopped at a bar and ordered a scotch.

In another part of town, Yvonne was having dinner with her prince alone at the *Hotel Place de Concorde*. True to his word, the prince had brought another letter, and they were arguing about the name used. The signature was that of the diplomatic representative of the organization, a well-known figure who had often appeared on Arab television networks. The prince was very reluctant to reach for a higher authority. Yvonne was worried that a letter without bigger names might be considered just another ploy. Their discussion became animated and angry. Yvonne was impatient. The prince had just said, "Yvonne, go back to your friend and tell him it is impossible. He'll have to use it with the name we have."

She was crying. "I can't let him down again. I ... I ..."

"I know," he said soothingly. "I know you love him. You've told me over and over tonight. And I'm so happy for you. But if he loves you, he will understand."

She sniffed. "No, he won't. I'll lose him. I know I will." She got up from the table. "I'm going to lose him. The only man I ever—"

At that moment, there was a huge explosion. It shook the earth and was felt for miles. A huge fireball engulfed the hotel as it disintegrated. When the dust had cleared enough to see, there was little left of the ornate structure that once was one of the favorite watering spots of Arabs in Paris. Yvonne survived only long enough to feel the first weight of the concussion. After the blast, there were minutes of eerie silence. Then the wail of sirens shrieked through the night.

Jacob felt the blast as a large window at the entrance of the bar shattered, showering the customers with shards. Blood ran down his head. He had been cut in several places by flying glass. The bartender, who had ducked behind the bar and seemed untouched, handed him a towel.

"Here, use this." He was American, with a tinge of Brooklyn in his accent. "You'll be okay. Heads bleed a lot. Just press the towel on the cut and keep it there." After checking on other casualties, he helped Jacob cover the wound. The few who had been in the rear of the bar seemed to be unscathed. "Just take it easy for awhile. Don't move." Jacob noticed that the man's hand was trembling.

"Was that a bomb?" Jacob asked, shaking his head in disbelief. "I wonder where it hit." Then, still numb from the shock, he said to no one in particular, "God, another 9/11, right here in Paris."

The bartender returned after checking other patrons. "Yeah, everyone seems to be okay. Thank Gawd."

In spite of the situation, Jacob managed a smile. "You from New York?"

"Oh, yeah."

"When the Trade Center went down?"

He cleared his throat. "Yeah, I was in it."

"My God, how awful!"

"It was. And so's this, I betcha." He brought a clean towel and opened a first aid kit. He took cotton from a box and poured vodka into a glass, dipping it in and dabbing Jacob's forehead. He squeezed a tube of ointment onto an oversized Band-Aid and stuck it to the cut. "There, you should be okay, pal."

Jacob had a million questions, but the guy was too busy helping people flooding into the bar seeking shelter from the dust. They were covered with grime and chattering so loudly that Jacob could not make heads or tails of the conversations. "What happened?" he called to the bartender, who apparently understood the French chatter.

"It was the *Concorde*, just down the block."

"A hotel?" Jacob only vaguely recognized the name.

"Yeah. That's what they're sayin'." He was offering towels and booze to the new arrivals, moving like a man possessed. "A big-deal luxury hotel," he shouted. Between making drinks for others, he poured himself a vodka and took a big slug. Returning to check on Jacob, he elaborated on his story of 9/11. "Yeah, I got outta New Yawk after the World Trade Centah went down." He pressed another vodka-soaked rag to Jacob's forehead. "I was workin' there, got caught in that shit—the dust, the bodies jumpin'. It was sumpthin' I'll never fugget." He coughed as if to prove it. In fact, the musty smell of concrete dust was beginning to filter into the bar. "This is the same damn thing." He coughed again. "I wish someone would throw a bomb at that son-of-a-bitch Bush and his rich cronies. They didn't give a nickel to New Yawk. Said it was safe to breathe when it wasn't. And then that phony war ... and nine years later, nothin's changed."

Jacob listened to these familiar words, smiling and nodding in agreement as he pushed his way through the crowd to the street. The air was filled with clouds of grit and ash. Sirens were coming from every direction. A stiff breeze was helpful, blowing dust away from the immediate area. He kept one of the damp bar towels over his mouth as he hurried toward his apartment. The air slowly cleared as he put more distance between himself and the blast. But even when he got to his own neighborhood, an acrid stench lingered in the air, and flecks of debris floated on the breeze.

Remembering the toxic effect of September 11, he showered thoroughly and poured a glass of wine for himself to clear the coppery taste in his mouth. His hand shook as he held the bottle. Television was running replays of the chaos, and speculation was rampant. In the background, Jacob could still hear the shrill two-toned sirens on television and echoing through the closed windows of the apartment. It was unnerving. Of course, every announcer was on the same subject. "Al Qaeda" was cited over and over. The French was repeated enough so Jacob could get some of what was being said. While he watched the television, he flipped on the clock radio and found a BBC station. An Egyptian terrorist group, not al Qaeda, was taking credit for the bombing. So far, nothing was heard from al Qaeda. When the radio became repetitive, he focused on television, trying to learn more. Jacob kept sipping glasses of wine and watching until he lost track of time. The speculation was endless. The hotel was a favorite of foreign visitors, particularly powerful Saudis who kept lavish apartments year-round. The size and explosive force of the bomb suggested the touch of a professional. It was a thorough job. No one could have survived the blast.

Successive glasses of wine were dulling Jacob's ability to make sense of the rapid-fire French, when an announcer began to speak English. Jacob was snapped out of his haze when he heard the familiar name.

"The Russian wife of Joshua Crane, the famous oil baron, who only recently died, has been staying at the *Concorde* for the past few days." Then the announcer went on to other notables who might have been guests. "My God!" Jacob cried. He immediately picked up the telephone and called Mitch. There was no answer, so he left an urgent message to call. With the television chattering on, Jacob paced around the room trying to ignore his empty glass, which he had been refilling until he had drained the bottle. Occasionally, he would peer out the window as if he were expecting a visitor. Finally, the story ran dry of new information, and the repetition grew monotonous. At two in the morning, he gave up and turned off the set and collapsed on the couch, drugged by the combined effect of trauma and wine. It was a dead, dreamless sleep until a call woke him. It took a few minutes for Jacob to drag himself out of a near-comatose state. The noise of the phone was insistent and alarming. He collected himself enough to get up and grab it.

"Jacob? Jacoby? Are you there? Jacob!" It was Mitch.

He glanced outside where the sky was just beginning to show the light of dawn. The pavements were wet with a drizzling rain. "Yeah, yeah, I'm here."

"Oh, thank God you're okay! Do you want to call me back? You sound awful."

"No, no, I'm fine," Jacob said quickly, not wanting to lose him. "The bomb at the *Concorde* ..." The whole nightmare resurfaced. "And Natasha, was she there?"

"I'm afraid so. Emily, too. We all had dinner earlier, and I left them there. I spent most of the night at the big hospital, *Jeanne d'Arc*. That's where a lot of the people went, the lucky ones, the injured—you know, bystanders and people going to and from the hotel. Unfortunately, it was early enough so people were still out and about." Mitch was very emotional and keyed up. "I haven't slept a wink. Emily just arrived in town last night." It sounded as if Mitch dropped the phone. There was fumbling and banging in the background. Jacob could hear him curse. "It was so horrible to see all those people cut up, some burned, and the dead ones …"

"Okay, take it easy, Mitch." Jacob wanted to keep him talking. "But you haven't actually heard anything specific—no report about them. Could Natasha have gone to visit Yvonne at her place?" He feared the answer. "They're very close." He knew he was grasping at straws.

"No. I've been calling Yvonne all night. Damn! She makes me so mad. Choosing this night, of all nights, to be out gallivanting with that prince of hers." His voice was breaking into a sob.

"How do you know that?"

"She had some kind of business meeting with him. She told me that there was going to be an important gathering, but I'm not sure of the night. She's been so sneaky recently."

"Can we call the prince?"

"I don't have a number."

Jacob was confused. "Would this meeting go that late?"

"I'm not even sure it was last night. But the meeting would have been finished early. She's probably holed up in a boyfriend's house." There was a pause. "Oh God, Jacob, I'm sorry. I didn't mean to be crass. I'm just a mess right now."

"Why don't you get some sleep, Mitch, and give me a call later."

"I couldn't possibly sleep. I have a better idea. I could use a little support, and I'm hungry. I think most places are closed now. Um, let me look." Jacob could hear him rummaging around. "Ah, here it is. There is a *petite auberge* in your neighborhood—*L'Oiseau de Paix*—great name for the times, isn't it? I'll tell you how to find it." He gave directions in some detail. "It's well marked. I hope they're open this early. Maybe we can get coffee and sweets. Cross your fingers. A lot of places will probably close today. Better that we just show up than call. Even if it's closed, they'd open for me. The owner lives upstairs."

"Sounds good. I'll be there."

Jacob decided to shave, mostly to wake up. The hot water and aftershave helped. He also took care of the three cuts on his face with peroxide and a fresh Band-Aid on the deeper one.

The smell of the blast still lingered in the soggy morning air when he left. The streets were empty. He found the inn with little trouble and was greeted by the proprietor, who pulled a long, doleful face but agreed to bring coffee and sweets, if he could find any. He complained that his baker had not shown up, so the choice was limited. Jacob picked up a discarded newspaper and glanced quickly at a headline story about the explosion, but the edition was an early one and didn't add to what he already knew. The owner reappeared with coffee and in heavily accented English babbled on about the disaster. It was all too familiar a litany. More than 400 were killed. The only good thing was that they got some Arabs. They deserved it! So, al Qaeda did it again! He glanced at Jacob for approval and then noticed the Band-Aid. "But you are hurt, *Monsieur?*"

"Just a few scratches. I was too near a window."

"Well," he spread out his arms as if he might hug Jacob, "you Americans know all about this—this kind of thing, September 11. So many died—*tres triste!*" He pulled up a chair in a show of comradeship. "Have you been to New York?"

"Yes, I live in Manhattan."

"Oh, *mon Dieu!* You were there!"

"Yes, but uptown, a couple of miles away."

Mitch appeared, looking haggard. "The hotel was wired cleverly like a demolition—the building just disappeared," he announced, without waiting for greetings. "A very professional job. Had to be those devils in al Qaeda." He stood in a daze without bothering to shed his coat. "My God, you're cut!" Beneath a flush of sudden color, Mitch looked tired and strained.

"It's nothing, just scratches."

"Thank God." Mitch slumped into the nearest chair. "I'm devastated."

The proprietor jumped aside to make room for Mitch and stood wringing his hands helplessly. "*Monsieur* Mitchel!"

"Any word on Yvy?" Jacob asked.

"No." Mitch glanced expectantly at the owner. "Coffee?"

"*Ah, oui, deux cafés—un moment.*"

It was enough to send the man scurrying. Mitch sighed, shaking his head. "Emily, gone. I can't believe it. Just in a cloud of dust, Natasha, too." Tears brimmed in his eyes. "What a god-awful waste. Was it glass?" he asked, inspecting Jacob's facial cuts again.

"Yes, I was at a bar when it happened. I was lucky."

"This is the saddest day of my life, Jacoby. I loved Emily. I think she was truly fond of me. Natasha I knew only a little, but she was a very, very unusual woman." He held his head and began to sob. "So horrible." He sniffed and looked at Jacob mournfully. "I can't believe either one is gone. They were wonderful, brave women."

"Do we know for sure about Emily? I heard only about Natasha on the TV."

"Oh, yes." Mitch was sobbing. "I had just left them." He choked up with emotion. "I was close by when it happened. The smoke was so unbearable. I ran into an office building. It was packed. Everyone was crying. It was a nightmare." He collapsed with his head on the table. "And then the hospital …" He couldn't go on.

Jacob waited until Mitch had collected himself. The owner reappeared with the coffee and a few pastries. He placed a hand on Mitch's back and rolled his eyes upward, muttering, "*Sacré bleu*," and then retreated to the kitchen.

Mitch sipped coffee and sat back. "Sorry to fall apart. I'm not good with this sort of thing."

"No one is." Jacob reached for his hand. "Try to eat something. And we'll take a time out."

After sitting quietly until Mitch seemed to regain his composure, Jacob asked as gently as he could, "And Yvy, how else can we check on her?"

"I don't know. She hasn't answered her phone all night." He sipped his coffee and absently fingered one of the pastries. "I'm not very hungry, but you're right, I should have something. I don't remember when I last ate. Dinner, I guess," he mused sadly. "Actually, I feel a bit nauseated." He pushed away the sweet. "Maybe, I should have tea instead."

"But you said Yvy was with the prince?" Jacob felt uncomfortable pressing Mitch.

"I'm not really sure, Jacob. I called her apartment just before coming here. There was no answer. She should be home." He glanced at Jacob sheepishly. "Even if she did stay out late." Looking down, he added, "Sorry, I just don't know any more. I can't explain her not being home."

The owner reappeared with toast. "Would you bring me a cup of black tea—any kind you have." Mitch touched his cup. "Do you have your cell, Jacob? My battery is dead." Jacob set his on the table. "I'll try her again." Mitch punched in the number. Jacob watched expectantly, hoping—praying—there would be an answer. After a few moments, Mitch gave up and handed the phone back.

"Nothing," he said unnecessarily. "This isn't like her." He shook a bag of sugar vigorously before tearing it open and added the contents to his coffee. "I feel helpless. There really is no way to check on her—I don't even know how to reach the prince, if he's alive." Then he added tentatively, "We could call the Saudi Embassy."

"We could also check her apartment," Jacob suggested. His calmness about her fate surprised him.

"Yeah, but what's the use of that?" When his tea appeared, Mitch looked surprised. "Oh God, thanks so much, Pierre. I'd quite forgotten."

"Maybe there'd be clues—you know, a note or a list of what she was doing or going to do." Jacob was remembering his experience on the crime desk in Chicago. People often left notes or collected mementos that told a story. They had a head start with Yvonne because between them they knew something about her activities in Paris. Jacob couldn't shake the growing feeling of foreboding—that somehow she had been caught by the bomb.

"Maybe you're right. We should go over there, even if she comes home and is furious with us for snooping." He fidgeted with his tea. "We'll have to talk the concierge into letting us in. He's very protective."

"We'll tell him you're a relative of the family and are worried that she might have been hurt in the bombing."

"Okay, we can try." They got up to go, and Mitch left a tip of a few euros on the table. "God, I hope … we're wrong," he said, echoing Jacob's unspoken fear. He put his arm around Jacob's shoulders. "I know you do, too."

They walked at a brisk pace in an uneasy silence of anticipation. It was quite a distance, and the exercise relieved Jacob's anxieties a little. The apartment was in a small courtyard complex at the end of a cul-de-sac. The neighborhood had the feel of understated continental privilege. The building was low-rise and a little on the beaux arts side, with a feeling of "old Europe." There was a uniformed attendant at the door. In perfect French, Mitch explained the situation and asked for the concierge. After a short wait in a plain, mirrored reception hall that had a black-and-white tile floor and a few formal chairs, a middle-aged man appeared, dressed in a rumpled suit and tieless shirt buttoned to the neck. He smiled and shook hands with Mitch, eyeing Jacob with some suspicion. Mitch explained that Jacob was a close friend of the family from New York City. After more discussion, the man's concerns seemed to ease, and he guided them to a small elevator that lifted them to Yvonne's apartment—a private entrance. He unlocked and opened the door and stood aside. At the entry was a small hallway that led into a rather large living room with a fireplace at the end. The furnishings were tasteful without being elegant, and more colonial than continental.

"This was where Natasha and Yvonne spent a lot of time," Mitch explained. "Feels like New England, doesn't it? Joshua and Natasha met here, too. I was invited once for a cocktail party. I think Natasha inherited the place. Garon never knew about it." He rubbed a finger across a table. It was a gesture of fondness. "Joshua added a few touches of Boston wherever he went." Mitch took a deep breath and looked around critically. "It's mighty tidy—shipshape, the old man would call it. Seems like Yvy doesn't dare mess it up." The concierge still lingered at the front door discreetly, giving the two visitors their privacy.

Mitch led the way down a long hall, his hard heels clicking hollowly on the creaky oak flooring. Jacob followed, noting a cozy library tucked in halfway from the end of the hall where there was a small sitting room. Mitch stopped and turned to Jacob.

"I guess we could look around in here. Looks like Yvy uses it." He walked to a desk and picked casually at a few papers strewn around on the top. "Look at this stuff." He lifted a paper and pointed to the title, *The Imperial Bush Administration—a Tragic Legacy*. "This must be where she writes her speeches—look at this—'they stole the U.S. government more completely than Nixon even dreamed about.'" Mitch laughed, breaking the tension that had overtaken them both. "Actually, she's not far off. You know, she often speaks at the university. She's become a female Noam Chomsky."

Leaving Mitch to go through the desk, Jacob continued to explore. So this was where she visited Natasha, her *"maman"*? The unmistakable scent of Yvonne's perfume led him to her bedroom. Jacob could feel her presence everywhere. It was her smell. The room was a mess—clothes tossed around, strewn randomly on the bed, bottles and face creams littering the smudged top of a dressing table. Jacob doubted that she used much of the stuff. The door to a large walk-in closet was wide open. Jacob flipped on the light to reveal designer clothes on satin-padded hangers.

"Yvy isn't much of a housekeeper," Mitch commented as he reappeared. "This is the only messy room in the apartment."

"I guess it is." Jacob glanced into the bathroom, feeling uncomfortable as a voyeur. Just a quick once-over revealed that it, too, was a disaster area—towels on the floor and a few more bottles of lotion scattered across the large sink area, some with their tops missing. Jacob wondered how often a maid came to clean up.

"Hey, Jacob—there's a sticky note on this mirror." Mitch bent over the small dressing table and stripped the note off the glass. "Look, it has a time—7:30, but no date—and the prince's name. Then there's a scribble which looks like '*Concorde*'. Here, see what you think."

Jacob's heart skipped a beat. "I guess I missed it." Mitch handed it to him, and he rubbed a thumb gently across the ink as he read the few words. "It's probably current, but we don't know which night." He studied the note more closely. "It does look like the *Concorde*."

"So, we're left with the question of which night. The night before last, she called me around 9:00 PM. She didn't talk about anything going on then." He carefully restuck the note on the mirror and cleared his throat. "This is not reassuring."

"There's something unreal about this, about the whole thing—the bomb, terror, people dying, and … now …" Jacob couldn't finish. He gazed around Yvy's bedroom. There was so much of her perfume, her aura, her clothes, even the few bits of underwear that seemed familiar. Suddenly, he wanted to leave. "Let's go," he said with a catch in his throat. He turned abruptly and walked down the hall. Mitch caught up with him.

"Listen, we don't know anything except a bomb killed a lot of people, Emily and Natasha included. That's all we know at this point." He grabbed Jacob's arm and stopped him. "But we've got to face it, Yvy could be gone, too. It's almost as if the three of them were targeted." He shook Jacob's arm gently as if to demand attention. "Listen to me. If something did happen to her last night, Jacob, I, uh, am sorry, so sorry for you. I realize how much you were hung up on her. This might sound cruel, Jacoby, but I don't think things would have worked out for you two realistically. Yvy would have owned you, not loved you. That's what the rich do. It's why they're rich." He put an arm around Jacob's shoulder. "If she is gone, we'll both miss her, for different reasons. But you should look at it in real terms, not as some idealized illusion." He dropped his arm. "I hope I said it right."

They continued down the hall slowly. "Yeah, she is different," Jacob said hollowly, unwilling to let her go. "I appreciate your thoughts, Mitch. I, uh, am, uh, was, hung up on her." But he didn't know which was true at the moment. He swallowed hard as the possibility of losing her forever seemed increasingly likely. It was going to be hard to think of Yvy in the past. She was so alive.

Outside, they shook hands. Mitch paused and hugged his friend. "Call me if you need to. Of course, if I hear anything, I'll call you."

Jacob walked away without answering, his mind a jumble of emotions. But on the long walk back to his apartment, Mitch's comments continued to echo in his ears. He had already come to similar conclusions about his relationship with Yvonne. They had used each other. She had used him to create a mea culpa for the family. Their relationship had helped him defy his father. With her, he had found sexual freedom, in spite of his hang-ups. Somehow the admission eased the pain of losing her, if, indeed, she was gone.

That night, still hoping, he called Yvonne's apartment several times, but there was no answer. He drank a heavy scotch and went to bed, tossing and turning with visions of Yvonne, but slept poorly. The last time he remembered looking at his watch, its dull glow showed three-thirty AM.

Waking early, Jacob went out and bought the *Herald Tribune*. He folded the headlines away from his gaze with resolve and returned to his apartment. He made some coffee, and only then could he begin to read the stories of the nightmare in Paris. He searched for names, but it was too soon for that. It was obvious that the paper's press time preceded any developing news. There was much speculation about the perpetrator, but popping up over and over was a plot to kill high-ranking Saudis. The *Tribune* estimated that twenty to thirty Saudi officials were caught in the blast. The Arabs had been in town for a meeting with EEC officials about easing the crisis in oil supplies. Of course, as the paper lamented, many innocents also died in the blast.

CHAPTER 15

To distract himself, Jacob began to write again. Working feverishly, he wrote a redraft of his exposé. His central themes were oil and the Pentagon memo, revealing the government's scheme to use The Crane Corporation to disguise its efforts to control funds from oil production in Iraq, including the strong-arm tactics used to cover it up. It was satisfying to spell out the covert operation—amassing Iraqi oil revenues in a private corporation to fund U.S. actions, destabilizing other unfriendly regimes in the Middle East and perhaps elsewhere—all done off the books. Of course, it was an allegation he could not prove, but he had the memo as a smoking gun. It had to be explained away. In doing so, the government could hang itself.

It was an eerie parallel to Iran-Contra and the use of proceeds from the sale of TOW missiles to get rid of the Ortega government in Nicaragua. Like Iran-Contra, the cost of activities would be off-budget with no accountability. The operations would likely be organized as a so-called black program where only a handful of policy-level officials knew the details. He wrote with particular relish a description of the attempted cover-up by Garon and the uncontrolled operations of his goons as part of the private army. Jacob liked the story better and better. It was indeed an explosive revelation.

Then he got out the letter from the prince and reread the cynical proposition, puzzling over the scribble of a signature. Now, with the visiting prince probably dead, this would be all he'd get. After several tries of fitting the proposal into his story, he gave up, deciding to leave it out for the time being. It was a bombshell, but how could it be used? He was not sure Shanahan was the answer. For the moment, he had no plan. He decided not to make a decision until he returned to New York. Perhaps, he would discuss it with Rachel. Both stories could influence the election. He was comforted by the fact that no paper would touch the prince's proposal without something in writing, and for now, at least, Jacob had the only copy.

His doubts about Yvy's well-being persisted. Each time he had tried to call Mitch, neither his cell nor the phone in the apartment could get service. The lines seemed to be shut down. It was five days after the bombing and still no word on Yvonne. He continued tinkering with his draft and made a list of possible publications he might approach. Two days later, the phone rang. Service was finally restored.

"Yvy's gone, Jacoby. She died in the hotel," were Mitch's first words. He was very emotional. "They found, uh, some evidence or something. There was a problem. I didn't even want to know. I ... and Emily, too, both gone. I couldn't go down there. They'll have to wait for her parents to arrive." Jacob could hear his choked-back sobs. "I just couldn't, as a relative ..." Then as if he had anticipated the questions already on Jacob's mind, he added, "They wanted a family member, a relation—you know, to be a witness. They had trouble with the analysis or something. I just couldn't face all that stuff. They tracked me down. Jacob, I didn't have the heart to call you right away. I was afraid to. Feeling the way you do, it was not where you would have wanted to go."

Jacob wondered what kind of problem there could be, but he said, "That's okay, Mitch. I didn't really belong there."

"I ... I just feel so bad for you, Jacoby."

"I'm okay, Mitch. I've not been counting on much." During his days of extensive rewriting, he had gradually come to accept the probability of her death. The sticky note referring to her date with the prince had convinced him that she had been in the hotel at the wrong time. In a way, he had been expecting the worst.

Prior to the disaster, Jacob had been gradually weaning himself of his obsession. His residual feeling was one of deep sadness for her—so young and vibrant—and yes, there were the sensual memories of intimacies that could be no more. Perhaps more importantly, he would no longer be challenged by her sharp intellect and strongly held beliefs. He would miss that. But he had come to realize that he really didn't know her as a companion. They had never spent time together, like a date. What did she like to do for fun? Did she like movies? Would she be good company for a long weekend trip? He would never find out. As he reflected on the reality of her being gone for good, he remembered his dinner with Natasha and Yvonne at the Carlyle. Was Yvy the child of her parents, or was Natasha the real mother? If so, who was the father? Would there be a DNA problem when her remains were identified? The question that still haunted him was whether she had any real feelings for him. The uncertainty left him with uncomfortable doubts about himself and the depressing apprehension that only disappointments were in his future.

"Are you still there, Jacoby?"

"Yeah. It's a lot to digest."

Mitch sniffed and changed the subject. "So what are your plans?"

"I really haven't made any yet."

"Why don't we fly back together?"

"Sure, we could, I guess. When would that be?"

"Well, the family has asked me to clean up the apartment and organize Yvy's things. They'll be flying here for the inquests and possibly using the place you are in. So, you'll have to move out sooner or later anyway. Of course, there's no need to rush. It'll be at least a week before they get here." He paused. "There's going to be an investigation," he added ominously. "The French, pushed by the Americans I'm sure, suspect Yvy of—I don't know what—but some kind of involvement with bad people. It's absurd, of course."

"It is?" Jacob was remembering Yvy's comment about the Movement.

"You know it is."

"You're probably right." A new thought came to him. The prince's letter—it could be used to protect Yvonne and perhaps clear her of wrongdoing or bad motives—even if she had been talking to terrorists. She and the prince were trying to stop the violence and bring peace. The idea had a special meaning for him. He could do something for her in death that he could not do in life.

"How about next week, say Saturday?" Mitch asked. "Could you be ready to go by then?"

"I can try."

"Look, I'll make the reservations and call you about the details. Okay?"

"That's fine. I'll wait to hear. Thanks, Mitch."

Jacob was pleased with his new idea. The prince's letter could accomplish two things—protect Yvonne and get the prince's proposal out. He just had to figure out how best to pass on the information. It could be an open letter to her family.

Jacob considered the possibility of a condolence letter to Joshua, Jr. He spent the rest of the morning and part of the afternoon composing the letter, first as a condolence and then the bombshell, a copy of the prince's letter. He wrote that Yvonne and the prince were working toward peace with the terrorists and that they were responding to the first constructive overture from al Qaeda sources. Of course, he would not divulge any of the details of his own article, just the fact that there would be a story on the family. When he tired of writing and rewriting, he stretched out on the couch and allowed his mind to reel back through his nights with Yvonne.

When he woke, it was late afternoon. He took a shower and then made himself a drink. He had just settled down, feeling better about himself, when the phone rang. It was Lynnette.

"I was so worried. The bomb." She pronounced both b's. "I haven't heard from you in awhile. I was afraid to call—that you would have gone back to New York or something. And then the phones didn't work. You are all right?"

"Sure, fine," he said. Her call had taken him by surprise. In the emotional haze of the last few days, he had all but forgotten her.

"What an awful thing to happen. New York, now France, again."

"Yes, this one was a real shock."

"I'm so happy you are safe." She paused to give him an opening. When none came, she asked, "What have you been up to?"

"Ah, well," he stammered, unable to shift gears. "Working, writing mostly."

"I would love to see you," she suggested tentatively.

"That would be nice. I'd like that. I've been up to my ears trying to finish the article I'm doing. I need a break." He was glad she called.

"*Bon*—why don't we have dinner tonight? I know it's very short notice, but I have some chicken and a great bottle of *Puligny-Montrachet*. The chicken is already cooked I'm afraid. I hope that doesn't insult you."

"Are you kidding? We won't have to sit and watch it in the oven."

"Okay, seven—is that too soon for you?"

"I'll be there," Jacob said, getting into the mood.

"*Tres bien*. I will see you then. Good-bye for now," she added rather formally.

Jacob sat for a moment thinking it over. Maybe going out would be good for him. But the prospect did trouble him. He was not yet free of his connection with Yvonne. His conflicted emotions were still bothering him. He had another drink. In any event, it was too late. The decision had been made. He wondered about the cooked chicken. Was he a backup plan for some other date that failed? He sighed in resignation. What difference did it make?

It was good to get out. There was a smoky residue of haze lingering in the air. It surprised him because he had not been outside his apartment in four days. Although it was on his route, Jacob chose to avoid the cordoned hole in the ground he had seen on television. Instinctively, he touched the healing cut on his forehead, grateful that he had not lost an eye. The walk to Lynnette's apartment was shorter than he remembered. He poked at the bell tentatively and wondered why he had agreed to another date. She opened the door wide and struck a dramatic pose. She meant it as a joke, but Jacob was struck by her sleek appearance, out of her academic duds. There she stood in a long, slinky black skirt and a high-collared silky top that revealed the soft swells of her breasts. She had transformed herself.

"You look … ah … different," Jacob stammered.

"Only different?" she asked in mock anger. "Jacob Sellars! You can do better than that."

Jacob stepped through the doorway, recovering his cool. He took her hands in his, not quite prepared to go further. "You look beautiful," he managed without much originality and then added impulsively, "and very sexy."

"*Ah, oui!* That's better." She stepped aside to let him pass. "Let me take your coat." He followed her into a large living room at the end of which was a small table set with candles burning. There were pungent aromas of garlic and butter cooking. "That explosion was such a terrible thing to happen. I was just going to bed and I even felt the *comment c'est dire* …?"

"The blast?" Jacob suggested, still appalled by the whole scene.

"No, we heard it—so loud—everyone in Paris did. I meant the bump of it."

"The concussion."

"Yes." Then she noticed his Band-Aid. "You are hurt!" She took his chin gently in her hand and turned him toward the light. She touched his forehead. It was a tender gesture. "How did this happen? Were you near the hotel?"

"Heavens, no. But I was in the neighborhood at a bar having a drink. There was a lot of broken glass from a blown-out window. They're just scratches."

"They look worse than that." She took her hand away. "Now sit, and let me get you a drink." She went to an antique-looking chest and opened two large doors. "You choose—I have everything, scotch, vodka, gin, I think, and I also have wine, of course, red or white."

"I'll take a scotch, but I can make it." This was like a first date, Jacob mused to himself.

"*Ah, oui, bien*, help yourself."

"What are you going to drink?"

"We should have the same. Then our tongues will loosen at the same time." Her laugh was musically pleasant and engaging. Jacob was glad he had come. Tonight, she was alluring and beautiful. She was stunning!

She brought warm canapés from the kitchen, and they sat side by side on a large couch behind a coffee table. "Did you know anyone? I mean in the *Concorde*."

"Well, yes. Unfortunately. Some of the people I am—I was—working for."

"Mon Dieu!" Her eyes widened in disbelief. *"Tragique!"* She laid a hand on his arm. "How awful for you." She looked down and asked almost in a whisper, "And the girl, the beautiful one?"

"She's, uh, gone, dead." The words echoed dully in his brain. He had not yet come to terms with the reality.

"I'm so sorry. I had no idea."

Lynnette's consoling words left Jacob with an empty feeling—a profound sadness that he thought he had put aside. Now, the finality of his loss returned to haunt him. His face must have shown it. "Yes, I heard just today."

She studied him. "She was important to you. I can tell." Then her eyes dropped down to her hands in her lap as she waited for his reaction.

It took Jacob too long to find the right words. "Yes, at one time, she did mean something to me, but when I answered you that first time you asked, the relationship was over." The admission did not come easily. "I did not ... ah, care anymore." He tried to take one of her hands, but she pulled away. "I guess I was less than truthful with you. It wasn't right. I'm sorry."

Still staring into her lap, she said, "You loved her." It wasn't a question. "Why did you lie to me?"

"No, I did not love her. I was infatuated with her. She was brash and foolish—and far too young. We didn't fit at all."

Then she looked at him. "Do we fit, Jacob?"

"What do you mean?" he asked, stunned by the directness of the question.

"I mean ..." She was still focused on her hands. "I mean, Jacob, that I have—or I think I have—fallen in love with you ... and uh, I don't even really know you." Her eyes glistened with tears, and she turned away to hide her emotions. "And now I think I shouldn't be ... in ..." She sniffed and then laughed quietly. "I'm sorry to say this now. It isn't the right time, I know."

"It doesn't matter. She's dead." The raw word was painful.

"But your love goes on."

This time he caught her hand before she could get it away. "This is silly. I don't love her and didn't when we talked about this—probably never did. Now she's gone. It's in the past. You're the present. I like you very much. I liked you the very first time we met. I ... I just am not moving as fast as you are, Lynnette."

She managed a weak smile. "It's okay."

"Give me some time."

Recovering her composure, she said, "So, you like me very much, eh. Like a sister? Like a friend or what?"

"I don't think I have ever been in love, period. It would take me all night and then some to tell you why, or at least what I think about that. Let's not spoil a nice night with either my hang-ups or silly infatuations of the past." On an impulse, he leaned over and kissed her, first on the cheek and then on the lips. She didn't respond, so Jacob stopped.

"I guess I've been a little brash myself," she admitted. "A girl should never be so quick to …"

"To love, or say she does? Why not?" Jacob wondered where his words were coming from. "If you feel that way, say it. It's okay." He remembered ruefully his own declaration to Yvonne.

"But it makes me so vulnerable—it is a way to be hurt." She dropped her eyes demurely. Jacob realized her openness was not a show.

"I don't want to hurt you. I like you, too … and maybe I do …"

She put her hand over his mouth. "Let's not say any more. Just be like you feel. I've already told you I might love you. I've given my hand away. So do with me as you please. I'll say no more." She got up and started for the kitchen. "But now let's eat. I think it's all ready. Come," she called over her shoulder. "You can help."

Jacob followed her, wondering what was meant by "do with me as you please." Was this an awkward translation of a routine thought into English, or something more?

At dinner, they couldn't let go of the subject of the hotel explosion. He questioned her about any breaking news, urging her to tell him everything she knew from the French media. She confirmed that many of those killed were Saudis who had gathered for a meeting. There was speculation about the purpose of the meeting. "There is talk of a move to unseat the king and bring reform to Saudi Arabia. Someone from al Qaeda—I don't remember his name—was on the Arab networks warning Americans to leave the Middle East or suffer the consequences of another September 11. He blamed the bomb on the Royal Family. It was strange to hear him go on. He even had the … whatever you say … to warn the Americans to stop supporting their own corrupt leadership. Hah!" She spread her arms out. "Such chutzpah! That's the word—chutzpah! Our President Sarkozy was very angry. He has said he is with the Americans to stamp out al Qaeda."

"So the Saudis did the bombing?" Jacob felt a little helpless being in a country whose language he didn't understand well enough. He was a journalist after all.

"Ah, yes, that was one of the stories."

"My God! Why the Saudis?"

"Well, it is coming out, as I said, that some in that Saudi group—you know, the ones meeting on oil—it was a clique supporting opposition to the king—to have a coup d'état. They must have been planning something at that meeting."

"So the bomb was to get rid of them?" Jacob immediately thought about the prince's offer on the election. Was this part of the coup d'état?

"Yes, that's what they are saying." She was clearly frustrated. "You can believe no one. There is no truth."

"It's hard to believe the Saudis would do that."

"I agree."

This was such monumental news. Jacob took awhile to assimilate the possibilities. If true, it would have dire implications for the oil supply. There would surely be more violence. Yvonne's bizarre proposal from the prince suddenly loomed more significantly.

After dinner he helped clear the table, watching her move. His head was swimming a little with too much wine. As they sat over coffee, she asked about his future plans.

"You will be leaving Paris?"

"Probably Saturday."

"So soon?"

Jacob didn't answer immediately. Finally, he smiled and met her gaze. "I need a job."

"I thought you worked for the newspaper. Or was that a … just a story, too?"

"No, of course not. Aren't you being a little hard on me, Lynne?" He hoped his use of her name this way might soften her attitude. "Remember, I told you. I lost my job."

"Yes, I do remember now." She sighed.

"I hope I can get it back. But I made some mistakes, and I guess I need to mend some fences. At this point, I just want to tell my story—about the Crane family and how they were being used by our government."

"So, that is what your article is about?"

"Yes. I thought I told you. It will make a lot of people angry. I'm going to expose some pretty bad stuff that my country has done."

"Oh. Will it be dangerous for you?"

"I don't think so."

"But it will be controversial."

"I hope so. Wait till you read it."

"When will that be?"

He reached across the table and took her limp hand. "I'm going to see that you get a copy. Then we can talk, and you can tell me what you think."

"It is all true—the story?"

"God, Lynne, you don't let up, do you?"

"I should do the dishes. Will you wait?"

"Of course. But I'd like to help."

She turned at the kitchen door and smiled. "You go sit, and I'll bring some more coffee."

"I'd rather be with you. And I can dry," he offered." It sounded a little phony, but he meant it. Her face flushed, and her expression softened. She tied on a blue, bibbed apron. A lock of her blond hair fell over one eye. She looked beautiful and fetching.

"Okay. A towel is hanging behind that door."

They stood close to each other, and Jacob had to resist the temptation to take her in his arms. As he reached around her to place the dry dishes on a center block, he watched the movement of her slender body under the slinky skirt. The faint trace of bikini underwear outlined the back of the silky material. He'd had just enough to drink to imagine the visual beneath. What was he doing, he asked himself—trying to replace the lust he had lost? Was it still a case of forbidden love? These questions flowed through his mind like lava, blocking rational thought. Then the bomb went off again in his mind, and the image of Yvonne floated before his eyes. For the first time, he began to doubt his sanity. His mind clouded, and Lynnette became Yvonne standing close to him. The events of the recent weeks began to hit him hard—the escape, the storm, the beating by Garon and his thug, the horrible bomb and awful loss of Yvonne—and the scotch and wine. The cumulative effect had taken its toll. His head was spinning.

Then Lynnette was facing him, her hands on his shoulders. "Are you all right?" Guiding him to a kitchen stool nearby, she said, "You are very pale. Sit, please." Obedient in his stupor, he sat heavily.

"Maybe I drank too much."

"It really wasn't that much. Are you sick, do you think?"

"No, I'm okay. It was only a moment." He felt the need to offer more of an explanation. "Maybe I ate too fast. Happens to me sometimes. Not enough sleep, either." He felt slightly damp all over. To reassure himself, he carefully got to his feet and walked with Lynnette into the living room. The familiar feeling that had overtaken him came as a surprise. He had experienced the same anxieties before, with similar effects.

"You rest, and I'll finish up." From the kitchen she continued, "I'll be just a moment."

Jacob's head gradually cleared. He could tell because he soon recovered, remembering her at the kitchen sink and the bikini outline. He wanted her, needed her. He couldn't tell which.

Then she appeared at the door. "Would you like a brandy? Would that help? Sometimes it does."

He eyed her silhouette. The backlight from the kitchen made the skirt seem sheer, showing the outline of her slender thighs. "Sounds good." She came and stood over him with the glass, which he took. "So, Lynnette, what did you mean when you said do with me as you please? Before dinner."

She laughed. "You are feeling better." Over her shoulder she added, "Let me finish. I like to leave a clean kitchen."

He waited, wondering where this was going to lead.

When she finally joined him, Jacob said, "Let's talk about you."

He asked questions about her life, her job, and her family.

Her mother and father had divorced when she was twelve, an only child. She told of crying alone in bed every night, trying hard to stifle the sounds of her sobs. She adored her father. The split was a great loss to her. Her teenage years were spent shuttling back and forth between two parents, a life imposed on her by a family court. Most of her schooling was in a Swiss private academy for girls tucked away in an Alpine valley. She had hoped her move to boarding school would soften the hostility between her parents. She held herself responsible for the incessant quarrels between them. Despite chronic homesickness and worries about her parents, she did well at school. It was evident from her story that she earned high grades and stood out in her class. But the time sequences in her education gave more away. At sixteen, she entered *La Sorbonne* and was awarded a high degree in three years. The month before she graduated her mother died of cancer. Her father remarried a woman Lynnette didn't like, so the visits she had so relished with him grew less frequent. She found that after graduation she really had no family. Devoting herself to her work, additional years of graduate school earned her a position at the university in the literature department.

After some pressing by Jacob, she acknowledged that she had written several books, gaining some fame for a respected treatise on French existentialist writers—Camus, Sartre, and others. As the brandy loosened her tongue, she told Jacob that she was bored with her life as a teacher. The students were tiresome and interested only in making money. With Jacob's gentle prodding, she confessed that she had dated several men, but no one who interested her. They, too, were interested only in money or position and always tried to impress her with stories of their business conquests. She had come to a crossroads in her life. She was existential enough herself to realize that changes came only by making choices, and any choice was better than none.

"You know—perhaps you know—that nothingness, as Sartre described it, is terrifying." She laughed, as if to make light of an otherwise desperate thought. "One has to make choices. I've toyed with the idea of going to Africa. I could write or teach—anything to bring hope to the hopeless." She folded her hands in her lap. Jacob noticed that she usually did this when she felt she had given too much of herself away—when she was vulnerable, in her words. At that moment, he knew he was really smitten by her.

"Enough about me," she said finally, steering the attention away from herself. "I want to hear about you. Your farm and your family. And the rest."

"No, you don't. We'd never get to bed." The moment he said it, he regretted the way it had come out—the odd disconnect he had bumbled into. All he had really meant was that the evening would go on and on. To her, it must have sounded cheap and aggressive, even though he had not intended it. "I ... I didn't mean it that way at all." She avoided his reach for her hand. "I didn't."

She remained very still. "You didn't mean it?"

"Of course not, not that way."

"Oh," she replied stiffly. "Well, it is late." She got up.

"Wait, Lynne. Do we have a misunderstanding?" He was sure that he had misjudged her, multiplying the insult. "I just didn't mean to make it sound like a ... a proposition. I don't know how else to put it to you."

"I'm glad you came," she said with too much formality. "I have enjoyed our visit." She thrust out her hand. "I hope you have a safe trip home."

At that moment, things were going very wrong for Jacob. He had to stop her from slipping away. He got up and caught her in his arms as she started to unlatch the door. "No, you don't. You can't get rid of me that easily." He kissed her gently on the lips. This time he hoped for a response. "I'm too fond of you. No, that isn't right. I ... this isn't easy for me to say, but I ... I ... I think I am falling in love with you," he blurted out recklessly. The rest just bubbled to the surface as if it had always been in his subconscious. "I want to ... to stay with you. I couldn't bear to go and think that I have made the worst mistake of my life. I can't do that. Please, let me stay."

She looked up at him in surprise, eyes bright with tears, and said with an odd, but endearing, formality, "Yes, I understand. You've been very clear."

Jacob, teasing her, said, "Is that good—that I've been very clear?"

"Yes, oh yes." Then she kissed him, this time giving herself completely. They clung to each other as if they had been lovers long parted. Jacob returned her kisses while they both became less inhibited in their desire for each other. As they embraced, feeling their bodies touch, their ardor was more urgent. Somehow their misunderstanding had brought them closer. They stood, bonded to each other, their hands tentatively exploring. Occasionally, they would look at each other to confirm a silent agreement on every escalation of their desire.

Lynnette's ardor gave way to a strange serenity that Jacob had not seen before—certainly not with Yvonne. It was contagious. In the subdued light of the bedroom, her eyes glistened as she gazed at him while she explored the upper part of his body with her hands. Her calmness and detachment unnerved him. He was almost afraid to touch her—that he might break the spell.

"I love you, Jacob," she murmured. Her gaze pierced his conscience. "Is that too much for you?" Her smile was gentle and forgiving.

"No," he whispered, unable to find his voice. "I … I love …"

She put a finger on his lips. "Don't say it till you mean it. I can wait."

She buried her head in the crease of his neck and said, "Jacob. I'm yours, je t'adore. Now, you can do with me as you please." There was more, all in rapid French, which Jacob could only guess at. But all the uncertainty was gone. He kissed her, first gently and then with more urgency. She responded, but still with the same serenity. It wasn't as if she was passive. She was a full partner in their quest. Responsive to his every touch, she let him lead. He proceeded slowly and gently. As his hands pulled clothing aside, he explored the exposed parts of her body. He could feel her tremble in response.

"I want you, Jacob, so much," she whispered, barely audible. She pulled him onto her, pressing her heels into his buttocks. As they became one, he raised his head and looked at her. She met his gaze and smiled, and they began to move together, first slowly and then more urgently. There wasn't the wild passion Jacob had known before, but a purposeful force, inexorable and beyond control by either of them. It was for her and with her and not just for himself. The intensity was a shared experience. When consummation came, Jacob felt it more deeply than ever before. The effect continued in waves for some time, for both of them. Afterward, as he lay beside her in silence, he wondered whether this was the difference in making love rather than having sex. At that moment, the concept of love seemed very real to Jacob. Could it be that he, Jacob Sellars, had finally found what love meant? This time would there be no dreams of his father, no ugly nightmares?

They lay quietly side by side for some minutes, each deep in thought. "What are you thinking about?" he asked finally.

"Oh, how delicious that was. To be with you. To have you lie beside me, like now. All that and then ..."

"Yes, and then what?"

"I'm trying to find some meaning." She raised herself on one elbow and studied him. "Was it ... was it anything like ...?" She laid back and stared at the ceiling. "I ... I felt very close to you."

He rolled over, partially straddling her with one leg, and kissed her. "I think I just made love to someone for the first time." He let his head rest on her bosom.

"Me, too."

They slept for a time like that, drifting in and out of sleep, waking only enough to be sure it wasn't all a dream. Later he became aware of her hands on him, gently, insistently. He let it happen. They made love again in the dark. The intensity of the experience seemed to increase the second time. Both drained and tired, they slept soundly until the first rays of morning sun peeked through a partly opened curtain.

Lynnette was busy in the kitchen by the time Jacob had pulled himself from the drugged sleep he found difficult to shake off in the still-curtained shadow of the bedroom. It was the smell of bacon that got to him. As he pulled his rumpled clothes together, he could hear the clatter of dishes and smell the aroma of coffee.

"Ah, here you are. Did I wake you?" she asked, when he emerged, tousled with sleep. She had put on a robe over her nakedness.

He took her into his arms and held her. The warmth of her body through the robe seemed right. He kissed her.

She pushed him away gently and adjusted the apron she had tied around her waist. "Look." She swept her arm in the direction of the stove. "Look, I have made an American breakfast." A pile of buttered scrambled eggs and bacon warmed in a pan, and dark coffee brewed on a counter. "I was going to wake you when it was ready. First, I have to make toast, and then we can sit down." A small table was set in the kitchen corner by a window. "You sit." She poured coffee into one of the cups and pointed to a chair. *"Ici."*

After they had eaten and were sipping their coffee, Lynnette reached out with a foot and placed it on his chair between his legs, wiggling her toes. "This is like being married. Does it frighten you?"

"A little, yes."

"Can you imagine it?"

He laughed. "You ask hard questions early in the morning. But yes, I can imagine it."

She gazed at him. "Sorry. My curiosity was partly academic."

"Academic?" he asked, astonished.

"Someday, I want to know all about you. I hope you will tell me, not to explain but … to broaden my human experience. I didn't tell and should have … I have a little secret, too."

"Heavens! What's that? It sounds ominous."

"Well, you know my field is literature. And you know I am bored with teaching. So, what do bored teachers of literature do?"

"Write?"

"*Ah, exactement.* And what do they write?"

"About literature."

"No. Bad answer. I already told you. I did that."

"Novels—fiction, then." He did a double take. "Oh, my God! You're going to write about us?"

"I already have."

"You mean you have been taking notes since we met?"

"No, not at all. I wrote it long before we met. I have been at this book for a number of years. And since I met you, I haven't touched it. I was afraid to."

"I, ah, don't understand."

"Nor do I. The man I wrote about is … is very much you, it turns out. A man I wished for, in an abstract way, but flawed—a man who didn't know he could love." She paused, choosing her words carefully. "When we first met, I thought I recognized my fictional character. It was astounding." She laughed. "But that's enough. Writers shouldn't talk about their work. It's bad luck. I've already told you too much." She got up and started to clear the table.

Jacob found this both surprising and amusing. "Does this mean that all our … were you just using me?" He wasn't really serious, but she took the bait.

She swung around and faced him, her face flushed. "*Mon Dieu!* Who has misused you so! You don't believe in anything—or anyone. Would I bare my soul, my body, to you as a ruse? No! What I told you last night was the way I feel. We made love. I wanted to hear you loved me, but you couldn't say it, so I stopped you from making it up. Jacob, I think you confuse—I think there is a useful word in English, conflate—sex and love, like my character—sadly, like many men. And that is not a new discovery. What interests me is why men are like that—not all men, but so many. Each has a different story to tell. Yes, I would like to use you. I am collecting stories. I want yours. But it doesn't change the way I feel about you, or my character."

Jacob was smiling broadly. "What is his name?"

"Silly question! Ah, you are impossible!" She threw her hands up in exasperation. "He's not even real, you know. And his name is unimportant. I will not tell you anything more about my book. You can read it when it comes out." She turned back to the dishes. She glanced at him with a sly smile and added, "But I'll get to read your article long before that happens."

"Okay, so I'm like the guy in your—novel?"

"Yes, as I've already said, a fiction."

"So there's a story with a character—nameless, for now—who is like me, a sickie about sex and love." Jacob was enjoying himself and finding the subject intriguing. "Is that it? What does he do? Has he got a girl? Is she like you? And let me ask you this—isn't it going to be hard to juggle your real life and your fictional one?" He took her in his arms again.

"I'm not sure I have a real life yet, Jacob. I had given up on that, at least until you appeared. But it has been, ah, how do you say, putting off." She twisted away. "Anyway, you ask too much questions."

"Are you really going to do something different with your life?"

"Maybe, yes. *Mais c'est difficile.*" She smiled. "It is true for other writers and for actors, when you think about it. They have to keep their fictional lives separate."

"But you have already mixed them up."

"Yes, *c'est vrai*. So what am I to do?"

"Are you asking me? I can't answer that until I see your book."

"Someday." She took his hand. "Come with me." She led him to a small hall at the entry. Jacob had not noticed the second door. She opened it, and he followed her into a darkened study lined with books, leaving just enough room for a big desk stacked with neat piles of papers. She pushed these aside and opened a drawer. "*Voila!* That is my novel. It is almost done. Of course, it must be edited, parts rewritten—especially now," she added, laughing.

Jacob leaned over her shoulder, and sure enough, there was a box containing a manuscript about four inches high. On the top page was printed *"L'Histoire."* Reading the term aloud, he asked, "Does that mean a story or more like a biography?" He reached to thumb pages, but she caught his hand. "How do I even know it's yours?" he asked, teasing.

"Because I told you. And it is fiction," she insisted. "I was not lying. And the title is just for now."

He looked around the cramped room, fascinated by the sheer volume of papers and books. On the desk was a laptop, and a larger computer sat on a separate table attached to the desk. He inspected the books, finding French, English, and German titles and two small how-to books in English on writing fiction. "Have you read all this stuff?" He swept his hand around the crowded room.

"Of course, that is my job."

"And these?" He pointed to the two books on fiction-writing.

"I read them both. But they don't help. You can't teach someone to be creative. It must come from inside."

He turned back to the desk and made a show of reaching for the manuscript, and again she caught his arm. "No, Jacob," she said firmly. "Someday, but not now."

"Will you at least tell me his name—the character like me?"

"No. But I should think you'd want to know her name, too."

"Okay, tell me."

She just laughed and led him out of the room and closed the door. "So, now you have seen it. You see, I don't tell stories, Jacob." He followed her back to the kitchen.

Later, when they had washed up and watched the midday news, Jacob was startled to hear his own name. He sat bolt upright. Lynnette increased the volume. It was all in rapid-fire French.

"They are saying that you are wanted for questioning," she translated for him.

"By whom?"

"Shush, I am trying to listen."

Jacob watched the screen with fascination as he heard his name repeated several times along with the FBI. Then he heard Yvonne's name. He was far too upset to follow the nonstop French patter.

"Jacob, they say you are only a person who they want to talk to, not anything bad, I guess—oh, I just don't understand all this stuff. An American agent was murdered." She waved him away, listening intently. "The girl, your friend, has done something very bad, helping the Arabs. Do you know someone called Ali Sandar?"

"I've heard of him, yes."

"He was one of the Arabs lost in the bombing. They are saying that he has contacts with al Qaeda." She turned to him. "Is that true, Jacob?"

"I'm not sure." He wondered whether he should tell her more. "Can I trust you with a secret?"

"I … I don't know. Are you … in trouble?" She became wary. "Have you done something wrong?"

"Maybe, but not what you are thinking. Listen to me, Lynnette." He decided to tell her of the prince's letter. She was a receptive audience with her own doubts about America. A contact in France might be useful to him. Lynnette was plugged into the intellectual world. The connection might even lead to corroboration of possible sources other than the prince. He made his decision. "Listen—you must promise to keep this confidence. Will you?" He didn't want her to doubt him.

"Ah … yes, I suppose so." He held her arms, squeezing with urgency. The doubt slowly cleared from her expression. "*Oui*, I promise," she said solemnly. He knew that she meant it.

He told her about Ali Sandar's proposal involving Congressional elections in the United States and then described generally his own story implicating the administration in the diversion of Iraqi oil profits to fund covert takeovers of certain oil-rich Middle East countries. He assured her that both Yvonne and the prince were opposed to violence anywhere and that they were trying to make a deal with al Qaeda to stop the terror. The bombing of trains in Spain and the London subways and now the *Concorde* in Paris had gotten the attention of the United States. These tragedies had sown fear of another 9/11. At least some voters would be influenced by the deal offered, and if the manipulation of Iraqi oil revenue was also revealed, many voters would be angry.

Lynnette was staggered by the overload of information. "Do you know what you are doing, Jacob? It all sounds very dangerous—the most powerful country is against you, wants you for questioning and would certainly not make a deal with … with those terrorists. Sarkozy would not make such agreement for France, nor would any other European leader." She gazed at him with tears in her eyes. "They will destroy you. You remember what they did to that lovely CIA agent. I forget her name. I believe they ruined her. Their power is frightening."

"Yes, I know the story. It was a cruel thing to do—and it was illegal."

"Oh, Jacob, maybe you are too mixed up in this." She was very tense. "What will you do now? I don't want to lose you." She forced a tight little smile. "I need you for my book." She embraced him firmly. "And I need you for other things." She squeezed a bit more and then pushed him away. "Does this mean you will have to leave sooner?"

"I'm afraid so. I'm going to have to talk to my friend. He's making arrangements." He stood and collected his coat. "I probably should go now. I need to figure things out. I'm sorry. My life is getting complicated." He held her one more time. "I'll be in touch. I promise. I have an investment in you." He put his hands on her shoulders and looked into her eyes, trying to imprint them in his memory.

"Investment? That isn't very romantic." She took his hands and held tight, closing her eyes to contain the tears. "I hate to let go of you." But she did. "Go, but please call me before you leave." She gazed up at him, eyes brimming.

They embraced again. Then gently untangling from her, Jacob left quickly, afraid he might lose his resolve. As he walked, he could feel the tug of her tearful good-bye. The loose ends of their relationship would have to await a sorting-out at a more propitious time. He would try to call her when he had a plan.

Later that same day, Jacob called Mitch and had to leave word. While he waited, he busied himself with packing and straightening up the apartment for the arrival of Yvonne's family. Then he e-mailed Shanahan.

> The Crane women are dead. They were caught in the hotel bombing. My proposal is also dead. Do I still have a job?

His answer came back two hours later.

> Sorry to hear about the women. The boss wants to hear your crazy story first-hand. It is far from dead. Bring any documentation you can lay your hands on. Don't talk to the press over there. The Feds want to talk to you. You have not been charged with anything. You are just a witness. Arrangements have been made for the company plane to fly you back. We have your address in Paris. A car will pick you up tomorrow at 10 AM. Be there. And off the record —you are not in Federal custody only because the boss has vouched for you. Look forward to seeing you. Tom

Jacob was stunned by this ominous confirmation that he was wanted by the FBI. He wondered whether a deal had been made to get him back. Maybe Newcomb planned to block or sanitize his story. Obviously, the publisher had already been in touch with the administration. If Jacob did what Shanahan wanted, his story would certainly be squelched. Newcomb had moved fast. Was Newcomb being pressed by the Feds? Jacob knew he had to get back to New York and avoid talking to anyone for awhile—at least until he could find a place for his story. He did the only thing he could think of—he called Rachel.

"Well, the prodigal son comes to the surface once again!" was her greeting. "Where the hell are you? No, let me guess. Paris, still chasing that rich kid. Am I right?"

"I am still in Paris, yes." He paused, waiting for an attack that didn't come. "But the rich kid is dead, Rachel. So is her aunt."

"Oh, my God! In that bomb?"

"Yes," Jacob said, the sadness coming back in a surge.

"I'm so sorry," she said, softening her tone. "Are you all right?"

"Yes."

"How did you find out—I mean, about the girl?"

"Mitch."

"Her poor parents."

Parents, indeed, he thought. He remembered Mitch's casual reference to the identification problem and with it the haunting sound of Yvonne's open warmth for *"Maman,"* that night at the Carlyle. Jacob had been fascinated by this and had been wrestling with the possibilities. During his writing binge, he had come up with a theory. Natasha had become pregnant before she married Joshua. Then to conceal the paternity, Joshua arranged to have his son secretly adopt the infant. This would explain Yvonne's remarkable resemblance to Natasha as well as her distance from her own family. Yvonne's striking dark hair and features could just as well have been Russian as Mexican. If this were true, her death was even more poignant. Pulling himself back from this speculation, he realized Rachel was talking. Trying to cover this sudden lapse, he said, "What? What did you say? This connection isn't very good."

"I said, aren't you interested in how I guessed you were in Paris?"

"As a matter of fact, yes, I am. I hope you haven't gotten yourself into this."

"I'm too smart for that." She sounded pleased with herself. "After the bomb, I worried—a lot. I finally gave up being coy and called the *News,* but without saying who I was. I got sick of worrying about you. They were pretty tight-lipped but did say you were ... how did the girl put it? Oh yes, you were in Paris on assignment for the paper. They wanted to know who I was. I didn't say. They were a little too insistent. I smelled a rat, so I didn't call again. When are you coming back?"

"I'm not sure. But I don't have time to explain. Look, I'm in a jam again. I have to get back to New York. I need a place to stay—it can't be my apartment." Jacob was relieved that Rachel had not revealed herself to the *News.*

"Are you hot? You know what I mean. Are you in trouble?"

"Yes, I suppose I am. Your place would be good. It wouldn't be for long. I'll explain it all when I see you." It was an awkward position for him, begging this way.

"This is sort of where we left off. Isn't it? I mean when you ran out of town without even calling."

"I had to. I had no choice. It's a long story."

There was a brief silence as she thought it over. "Am I going to be in trouble, too?"

"No," Jacob replied, with certainty outwardly, but with doubts internally. "If you like, we can talk about that too, when I get there. If you are not comfortable, I'll have to find some other place."

"Yeah, okay. Sure, you can hole up here awhile. I have a guest room the last time I looked. It needs to be cleaned. And I'll do that before you get here. By the way, when will that be?"

"As soon as I can figure out how to leave."

"You mean run?"

"I think the FBI wants to talk to me."

"Jacob, what are you talking about? What the hell is going on in your life? What kind of trouble have you gotten into? You know, you're lucky to find me at home. I've been away for a couple of weeks."

Jacob began to worry about the length of the call—if the phone was tapped, they might be able to trace Rachel. Then he'd have no place to hide. "I'll tell you everything later. Got to go now. Not good to talk too much. Thanks. Bye." He hung up the phone quickly and took a deep breath. Now what? It was hard to believe that he had to run again—this time from his own government. But that unpleasant prospect did not shake his confidence that he was doing the right thing.

He would have to leave the apartment quickly. Should he call Mitch? He had probably already made reservations. If he didn't call, his friend would probably make plans anyway, getting seats for them both and expecting to meet him at the airport. The reservation would help him by drawing attention to that flight. Fine. He would leave from another airport—better, another country. Thinking it over, he decided to go by rail to Germany and fly from there. He packed his bag and stuffed in his laptop, hoping to avoid any complications about it. After giving the apartment a quick once-over, he caught a cab to *Gare du Nord*. He took the next train to Frankfurt, a fancy fast one with few stops.

The train raced through the still-wintry countryside. Late storms had left patches of snow, and the few people he saw in passing villages were bundled up against a late cold snap. As he considered his strategy, he envied their simpler lives. Getting on a plane in Germany would probably not be a problem. He would book a flight to Montreal rather than New York, where they might be looking for him. Of course, Mitch would finally call when Jacob did not show up and then would likely just go on alone, assuming that Jacob had changed his plans. He hoped Mitch wouldn't worry too much and be tempted to talk to the authorities. From Montreal, the safer way to New York would be by train. It was a tedious trip, but security would be lighter. His press card would probably work again to get him through any border surveillance. Satisfied that he had a viable plan, he sat back and reviewed his situation.

He wanted to call Lynnette on his cell but decided against risking it. It was not an easy decision. More than anything, he wanted to hear her voice once more. While the evening with her now seemed eclipsed by all that was happening, the tenderness of their night together lingered with him, and would for a long time.

He forced himself to stay focused on his plan. His first objective had to be publication of his Crane story and the document. It would likely make a big splash and could even affect the election. For a moment, he allowed himself to fantasize about the headlines and his own notoriety. It was far too early to count chickens. The process was dangerous for him personally but was worth the risk. For the first time in his life, he had a purpose.

He reviewed the letter of condolence he had written to Joshua, Jr., and enclosed with it the prince's proposal. The tone of his message was perfect. In Frankfurt, he would mail it to the apartment address in Paris. This would accomplish two of his objectives. First, it would get the prince's story out, and second, it might help clear Yvonne of any wrongdoing—and himself as well. He sat back with a deep sigh and wondered whether it could all be sorted out.

At the border stop entering Germany, customs officials boarded the train and in loud German-accented English and poor French began their questions about passports and identity papers. His heart raced as he groped for his press passport, hoping that his name had not reached the border first. But it all went smoothly. The press card seemed to save the day. The guards gave his passport only a cursory glance. Apparently, the fourth estate had more credibility in Europe than in the United States.

CHAPTER 16

An exhausted Jacob struggled out of a cab with his one bag, weighed down by his laptop tucked away at the bottom of a bundle of stuffed clothing. He took a moment to relish the feel of a Manhattan sidewalk. He was home again!

Before each flight, he had been forced to take out the computer and slide it through the X-ray machine to scan for explosives. At least he had been allowed a carry-on. Using Air Canada instead of the train to New York had been a risky venture, but Jacob was so tired and tense from the long journey that he had taken the fastest and easiest way and prayed. He also thought he had a good chance to beat discovery of his elusive travel plans. Throughout the trip, he had been looking over his shoulder for a new version of Garon. Under questioning by the various customs agents, he watched their eyes for any sign of suspicion. His worst moment came on entering Canada when the officer glanced at his passport and picked up the telephone, punching out a three-digit number that Jacob was sure alerted security. However, he was only asking for a lunch break. Jacob had to smile at the memory, relieved that he had apparently outdistanced his pursuers, who would doubtless be concentrating on the empty seat on the flight arriving tomorrow at Kennedy with Mitch.

As he took in the familiar sounds and smells of the city, he felt good to be back in the bustle of traffic noise of the Lower East Side. His own apartment just down the street could just as well have been miles away, if there was a search for him. He was hoping Rachel was still out of the loop.

"Mr. Sellars, let me help you." The doorman at Rachel's building reached for his bag.

"Oh, thanks," Jacob muttered. He had overlooked the possibility of being recognized. As he followed through the revolving door, he groped for a bill in his pocket. His attentive escort was already on the phone announcing his arrival.

"She's expecting you. We can go right up."

Jacob moved toward the elevator, pressing a ten into the man's hand as he recovered his bag. "Thanks, I can make it."

"Oh, thank you, Mr. Sellars. Nice trip?" There was no change of expression suggesting anything unusual about Jacob's sudden appearance.

"Yes, it was." The elevator door slid closed, and the upward motion pressed on his feet as the floors ticked off.

After the muffled ding-dong signal of the doorbell and the rattle of multiple inside locks, the door swung open, framing Rachel as he remembered her, faintly defiant, gaunt, dressed casually in jeans for a day off, and bare feet.

"Well, it's you in the flesh. Let me look." She inspected him from toe to brow and smiled broadly, softening her severe features. "I can't help it—it's good to see you." Without any hesitation, she hugged him and held on. Jacob responded, feeling her skinny body pressed against him. She pushed him away and examined him again. "You have a lot to explain, buster," she chided. "Come in, for God's sake. What are we standing out here for? The neighbors might gossip." Taking his bag, she led the way. "What's happened to your head?" He followed her through a cluttered living room to the extra bedroom, where she dropped his bag pointedly. He winced, thinking of his computer. "This is it," she said, sweeping her arm through a wide arc. It was obvious that the small space had recently been tidied up. Two grimy windows looked out on the blank walls of the building next door. The limited view made him feel secure. A double bed was smoothed out under an old quilt that had seen better days. A light was on in a small adjoining bathroom, also spruced up.

She fingered his forehead lightly. "You tangle with that bomb?"

"It was just glass from the window that nicked me. I was in the neighborhood." He looked around. "This is fine," Jacob said. "It's great of you to put me up."

"I didn't say I would yet, remember? Gotta hear the story first and how much trouble I'm going to be in." She turned to go. "Before anything else, we better talk. Come on. I'll fix you something to eat. You must be starved. I picked up a few things at Gristede's." Jacob followed her to the living room, smiling. Rachel, the consummate New Yorker—he had missed her. "Go sit. I'll put something together." She disappeared into the kitchen and began rattling around.

It felt good to be back in Manhattan.

He browsed around, leafing through old newspapers and gazing out the window at a sliver view of the Empire State Building. She had arranged her narrow railroad-style apartment with an office at a far end. The two bedrooms were lined up on either side with the kitchen wedged in at the side of the living room. Oddly, Jacob was relieved that he would have some privacy at his end.

Being in her apartment was not entirely a novelty. While their few assignations had been at his place, he had spent a couple of nights in her bed. She was sensitive about privacy, and Jacob had always felt a certain reluctance on her part to his staying very late. Usually, she would shoo him out, saying that she was worried about the neighbors. Her rough-hewn independence seemed to have a few sensitive spots.

The place had a cluttered feel. The furniture was sort of an ersatz collection, probably of European origin and inherited from family members who had emigrated to the United States before the war to escape the German pogroms. Rachel's grandparents were Polish Jews, originally from Danzig, and among the few survivors of the Warsaw ghetto. She had shown him family pictures—faded shots of people at parties, of babies, formal portraits, and haunted-looking immigrants on shipboard with a foggy view of the Statue of Liberty in the background.

The foreign feel was reinforced by the presence of a small spinet piano of German make tucked into the end of the living room. Sheet music was arranged on the rack. It was the same collection that had always been there—Mozart, Bach, and a partly revealed Sibelius. Apparently, the pieces had some nostalgic significance for her. Rachel could actually play this stuff. She had played for him only once on a snowy Hanukkah, when her natural reluctance was weakened by wine.

"Snooping?" She appeared, hands on hips, smiling. "That's why I didn't like you here. Men are too curious."

"You didn't want me here because of what the neighbors would say."

"Yeah, well, they talk." She set out a plate of cheese, corned beef, and a toasted bialy, along with a cup of hot tea on the coffee table, pushing aside stacks of old magazines. "That's the best I can do on short notice." She plunked herself down on the worn couch and invited him to dig in. "So now, tell me. What's going on with you?"

"Your pal the doorman—he knows my name."

"I'm not worried. He's not a gossipy type."

"He must be the only one in New York who isn't."

"I've got him trained. Anything he hears, he tells me first." She pulled him down beside her. "Now, talk to me?"

Jacob brought her up to date on his story about the takeover of The Crane Corporation by government intelligence agencies and the revelations of the Pentagon plan to divert oil revenues to fund covert operations in troubled oil-producing countries such as Iran and others in the Mideast to secure oil supplies. Rachel listened to it all intently without interruption.

"My God, you have any proof of all that?" she asked when he had finished.

"Yeah, some. The diversion plan is described in a top-secret memo. It was leaked. But I thought you knew about that. I have a copy of it. But its authorship is obscure," he admitted. "It was scanned—your advice. I don't think they know yet. I found some corroboration in a magazine called *Disclosure*, before it went out of business."

"Yeah, I vaguely remember that mag. Can I see the memo?"

"Sure."

"What are you going to do with it?"

He told her about his last e-mail exchange with Shanahan and the veiled threat of custody.

"They want to block your story. That bastard Alfred Newcomb. He has a love affair with the administration. His television channel makes me sick."

"They'll kill it if they can. It would be too embarrassing, coming up at election time."

"It could be dynamite."

"Which reminds me. There's more." He told her about Yvonne's proposal and the prince's letter suggesting a deal with al Qaeda: Terrorism in the United States will end if the Republican Congress is defeated.

"God! That's preposterous, beyond belief! The epitome of chutzpah. They're onto us, though. Americans want their anxieties about terror to go away. They just believe in any kind of a deal to make that happen." She sat for a moment, intent on her thoughts. "What did you do with this stuff?"

"I sent it with a letter to Joshua Crane."

"What! Why? He'll just hand it over. They'll bury it!"

"I don't think so. Yvonne is suspected of being a traitor and a terrorist. Her father is in Paris now for the inquest. This could help, but only if he goes public with it. Think about it. Yvonne looks like a peacemaker. The prince also comes out looking good. Even Joshua will understand what he has to do. He's dealt with this crowd long enough to know that if he just hands it over, they'll bury it, like you say." Then he told her all about Garon and his ugly tactics.

"Good God! What a story! And they actually beat you up?" She was aghast at the thought, but not shy about probing further. "Like what did they do to you? Burn your feet? Hook up wires to your balls? What?"

Jacob laughed at her reporter's curiosity. "No, none of that, but Garon did jam me in the groin a few times and threatened to shoot them off."

She cuddled up closer and put her arm around him. "You poor thing. Do you … have bruises? Are you black and blue?"

"It was mostly black. But that's gone away." He laughed. "Do you want to see?"

She shoved him away in mock anger. "How can you kid about it?"

"It's easier to kid about it now. Garon was bumped off, execution style, before I left Paris. And that could complicate things more."

"What a colossal mess!"

"So," he said, returning to his subject, "Joshua's letter will get out, one way or another. Even if the Pentagon tries to bottle it up, I'll release it myself. But I think Joshua will insist that it be made public if only in memory of his tragically dead and wrongly accused daughter." An expression of irritation flickered across Rachel's face. Jacob hurried to fill the gap. "I need your help in finding a place to publish my story. It has to get out soon, before they can do damage control."

"Can I ask you something first … it's a little off the point. But I'm curious." She didn't wait for an answer. "What was your relationship … did you actually love that crazy girl?"

"Sure, I was very fond of her, maybe too fond. But it wasn't going to work out. The whole experience was, uh, unfortunate, sad … I was wrong to get involved with her. She was too young, too absorbed in her own interests." He paused. The admission was hard for him. "And she was using me."

She considered his reply for a moment. "I figured as much. Did she dump you?"

Her question unsettled him even more. He had not thought of it that way, never admitting the possibility. "Yes, I guess you could say that." He smiled. "But I'm not sure there was ever much to dump. It was … an infatuation. Maybe it was like Christy." He was sorry that ironic analogy slipped out. "I can't explain it—except as you did in that dreadful telephone conversation we had when I was in Paris."

"Except this one was old enough to know what was going on. It was always pretty obvious to me." She studied him. "Still hooked on her—I mean the idea?"

Her question hit home, but he was ready for it. "Maybe, a little … the memory." He was glad she had asked because, yes, he was getting over it and a lot else, too. He was finally getting control of his history, his guilt, and the bad nights.

His sorrow must have showed because she asked no more about Yvonne.

"I can get you a publisher," she said, obviously wanting to change the subject. "Do you have your story on a disc? I need to read it."

Jacob had no real alternative but to trust her. "Will your computer take an old CD? I'm a bit out-of-date on equipment."

"Yeah, it'll work. Why don't we print it up and look at it together." Then, as if in answer to his uncertainty, she added, "Jacob, you know by this time you can trust me. I know what you're thinking. I will not in any way mess up your story. I'm so proud of what you have done. Let's get it out. I just want to see them squirm. This could be the biggest thing I've seen in a long time. It could change the course of the country." She gazed at him for a moment and added, "Any editor in the country would be proud. You have joined the august ranks of investigative journalists. I knew you had it in you."

Her praise pleased him, but he was cautious. "Let's not get ahead of ourselves. You better read it first." He opened his suitcase and pulled the disc out of its protective envelope. "Here." Any doubts about their working together slipped away.

For the next two days, they labored over the language of Jacob's story, smoothing it out and adding references from the Web. On a break from their work, Rachel called one of the two leftish publications, her favorite for the job, revealing nothing but the general subject. They were interested and willing to read what Jacob had. She quickly accepted and settled on a tentative publication date. Her reputation had clearly clinched the deal.

It was 2:00 AM of the third day when they finished editing a final draft. They had a drink in celebration and then went to bed, this time together, fired by what little adrenaline they had left, and without much passion. It was not successful. Lynnette was too much a presence in Jacob's mind. Afterward, they both slept soundly, suppressing doubts about their strange relationship.

Over coffee and the morning news, Rachel was oddly silent. Finally, she said, "You've changed, Jacob. I could tell last night." She stirred some sugar into her coffee as she reflected. "I don't know, it's a woman's instinct I guess," she added, as if anticipating a response from him. "I liked you better when you were … well, needy. Something's happened to you. You seem distracted and distant. Maybe it's a guy thing. I just can't put my finger on it." She got up abruptly and began to scrub dishes. "You know, you don't have to sleep with me." Addressing the sink, she added, "Oh, hell—I don't know what I'm saying. I just think you've changed, period. And I'm wondering why." Then she added, "But I don't want to talk about it anymore."

Jacob was thinking as she talked. "Maybe it's like you said. I have done something worthwhile for a change." But he knew that she was right. He had changed in other ways. He knew his time with Lynnette was affecting him.

"Maybe. That's a good place to leave it. Sorry I brought it up. It was a good one-night stand."

Jacob allowed this to pass without an answer. He couldn't think of one. There had to be a change of subject. "So, you like the people we chose?"

"Very much. *The National Outlook* is widely read among the people who count. And they were onto the Bush people from the beginning." She seemed as willing as Jacob to avoid further personal discussion. "I'll get a date with the editors for eleven tomorrow morning. Okay with you?"

"Good. Let's do it."

"I have to tell you, Jacob, you've done a magnificent job on this. It will sell easily."

Taken by surprise, Jacob said, "Well, thanks, Rachel. Your opinion means a lot to me."

The next day, Jacob wore his road-weary suit, and Rachel put on a severe tailored skirt with a black turtleneck, making her appear slightly intimidating. For the first time in his life, he had no doubts about himself. He knew his subject inside out. The meeting couldn't have gone better.

In the weeks leading up to publication, Jacob had a series of editing sessions with the magazine's able staff, polishing, filling gaps, and working on a layout. The final product was impressive. If the story broke any laws, it was too late to turn back—and no one seemed very worried anyway. On the day before his article was published, Jacob decided it was safe to return to his apartment, at least to collect his mail and some clean clothes. He timed his arrival in the late evening, but even so ran into a few insistent television reporters who apparently had been staking out his place. He avoided taking questions and with the help of the super managed to leave through a freight entrance into the back alley.

The *Outlook* editors had agreed to take the story after the first reading and were able to fit it into an early issue. The magazine wrote its own sidebar with background supporting material. A few days before release, the print media had gotten wind of the article, and there was a buzz of gossip about Jacob's revelations. The administration had been ominously silent.

The entire media, goaded by the administration, went on its usual feeding frenzy. The main question was, "Who is this guy?" Demands for interviews were coming from all sides. It was only a matter of time before Jacob would have to respond. The *Outlook* was doing a creditable job of holding off the media with bits and pieces of information. Jacob's legal position was uncertain. A further complication of Jacob's life would come with the release of his letter to Joshua.

Fortunately, that had not yet occurred. Jacob would just have to await developments. His editor thought that his detention for any cause now seemed unlikely. The administration would be too busy containing the story. In any event, that was the hope.

On a personal level, it was also an awkward time for Jacob. His live-in relationship with Rachel was falling apart. She was becoming edgy and resentful of sharing her space. He couldn't blame her. It was an unfair arrangement. But it was too soon to return to his apartment. He needed time for the excitement to die down. Rachel made the first move. Her change of heart began a week after they had successfully closed the deal with the *Outlook*. She had suggested dinner at a neighborhood restaurant. Fortified by a couple of drinks, Rachel had returned to the subject of how much Jacob had changed. She had rambled on for awhile incoherently, circling around what was bothering her.

"It's been several weeks now. You're in your room, and I'm in mine. Most of the time you eat out, go out alone, come back alone—it's like having a boarder. I'm just not comfortable with … well, it's awkward, Jacob, in a small apartment." Her plaint was a little out of character, and she knew it. "I've got a life, you know."

He suddenly realized how insensitive he'd been. He was taking advantage of her. He should have seen it sooner. "Gosh, Rach, of course you do. I understand. I should get out of your hair. I can get a hotel room." He reached for her hand, but she pulled it away. It wasn't quite the reaction he was looking for.

Flushed with the embarrassment of her admission, she sat in silence sipping her third drink. "Do what you please."

She had worked herself into a regular snit, and Jacob was at a loss.

"I just don't think we should be living like this—it's as simple as that."

He had not realized that his presence had become that difficult for her. Their discussion didn't seem to be leading anywhere. Anxious to reach a better understanding between them, Jacob decided to level with her about Lynnette. While it seemed off the wall, he felt the moment had come for her to know.

When he had finished, she said, "Well, that makes sense. Now I understand. But you should have told me right off." She was cool and businesslike. "You'll work it out, if it's meant to be. I'm happy for you. I wish you and your new girl luck. She sounds nice."

"Thanks, but I have to admit that it's not much of a romance—she in Paris and me in New York in a mess." Jacob paused. "It doesn't solve our problem, though, does it?"

"No, it doesn't. And yes, I agree, it would be better for you to be in a hotel. You'll have to face the music soon enough. You can't keep avoiding the press. But let me tell you, they won't be nearly as bad as the administration's propaganda machine. It won't be easy for you. They'll attack, and I can't help." Her tone softened. "Anyway, I'm going away for a few days. You can get your stuff moved. We should get back to our own lives." She collected her things and got up to go. Their dinner date had turned out to be just drinks. "Stick with your story, Jacob, and don't lose your confidence. You have a chance to do something for the country." She laid a hand on his shoulder. "If you don't screw it up, you'll have a major accomplishment in your resume. Keep your career on track." Then she left.

Jacob sat for a long time. He still wasn't sure whether he understood what was going on with Rachel. Revealing his romance with Lynnette had seemed to tip the scales in an odd way. It almost seemed that Rachel was relieved. Nevertheless, he had mixed feelings about the way things were left between them. He hoped their fragile relationship had not been compromised.

Jacob's newly discovered confidence was soon to be tested. Rachel's prediction was clairvoyant. It didn't take long for the administration to break its silence— and attack the messenger. How they unearthed all the stuff they came up with was a mystery. The soggy chill of a wetter-than-normal spring seemed almost benign by comparison. The media—both print and television—were filled with it. Jacob had acquired a record of pedophilia, of homosexuality, of stalking. And the victims? The cast of characters was identified, too—Christy, even Marilyn Coffin, and Mitch—and then in a bizarre turn, it was alleged that Jacob had gone to Paris to stalk Yvonne. Lurid details of their relationship were all over the tabloids. The half-truths and innuendoes were in overdrive.

The trashy stuff was repeated everywhere—cable, the networks, the news magazines, radio talk shows. It was saturation. Witnesses? The sources were thin in this department. As if the wild accusations weren't enough, some of the research, unfamiliar even to Jacob, was revealed with gusto. They found out his father had approached the school after the incident with Christy and asked that Jacob be watched. The old man had reported his discovery of the Christy episode and expressed a concern to the school that it might happen again. Apparently, old police records confirmed this. Jacob had been secretly monitored by school authorities for several years. The furor over Christy died, however, when there was no recurrence. Much of this was news to Jacob.

On other subjects, they identified a witness in Nantucket who had seen Jacob and Marilyn Coffin taking the hotel elevator to the rooms upstairs. It was reported that she was drunk, and he had picked her up in the bar. There was a tricked-up photo of Jacob and the Coffin girl together. Capping this story was the suggestion of date rape. A few stories took a different view of Jacob's sexuality. They had seen him and Mitch consorting at odd hours in Boston and at a Nantucket inn—and at a party on the island, witnesses even asserted that Jacob appeared as Mitch's "partner."

Of course, it was never made clear how any of these shenanigans might affect Jacob's credibility as a journalist. But the scorching media coverage did get the focus off his article. To remove any doubts that Jacob was a despicable, unreliable character, they planted ominous suggestions about his patriotism, which boisterous talk show hosts translated into terrorist connections. Despite Jacob's letter to Joshua, finally revealed, explaining the activities of Yvonne and the prince, the right-wing press continued to label the two as terrorists. This was true even after the Justice Department had reluctantly exonerated them. It was typical of the administration's strategy—repeat lies often enough and the people will believe them. The propaganda machine was very effective.

While Jacob remained under investigation "as a person of interest" under the Patriot Act, he was not detained. It was as if they wanted to keep him in the public eye with the innuendo and gossip—at least until after the election. Fortunately, the media had missed Rachel entirely. That was the only shred of good luck.

As an overheated summer gave way to a more moderate September, Jacob moved back into his apartment and began living an open life, going on talk shows, doing interviews on both the networks and cable. The focus on him had been diverted by the onset of a panic atmosphere on global warming. It had been a record hot summer with daily temperatures reaching into the hundreds for weeks, offering increased credibility to the science of carbon dioxide poison fouling the air.

The interviews went on. With only a few exceptions, he was treated well by his hosts and encouraged to tell his own version of events. Even though there was a growing wariness of the administration's hype, Jacob continued to suffer from his notoriety. At first, he had resisted television invitations and the blandishments of talk radio, but under pressure had relented. He even consulted with the staff publicity manager at the *Outlook,* who assured him that the media attention would, in the end, be a benefit.

There were rare moments when Jacob got a masochistic pleasure out of his appearances. But it came at a cost. The dirt was always the first subject covered, not his article. Sadly, some people believed the things that were said about him. His defenses were constantly on guard. He became a recognized figure around town, attracting attention in restaurants and having questions tossed at him even in the streets. Hero to some and a pariah to others, he had to work hard to avoid being overly defensive. The experience was a dreadful one, one for which Jacob was ill prepared. There were times, after a particularly difficult interview, he would have to shake off his own doubts about himself.

Mitch called once or twice to encourage him and invite him to have dinner. Jacob refused. It would only stir up the partner story.

It was now more than six months since he had left Paris. The trees in Central Park were showing their fall colors, and the air was crisp. The seasonal change had its effect on Jacob, too. The winter ahead made his plight seem bleaker. Would the clamor never stop? Sleep didn't come easily at night. But there were no dreams anymore. Real-life issues—a job, his future—and, of course, the drumbeat of scandal were the stuff of every day. The *Outlook* had offered him a part-time job, more as a courtesy than a real opportunity. But to support himself, he needed a full-time position. As he sat grappling with his unwanted fame and new directions, which he often did these days, he began to distract himself from the unpleasantness with thoughts of Lynnette. Finally, late one night, he considered calling her, realizing his long neglect would be awkward to account for. It would be morning in Paris. A good time. He wasn't sure how she would feel, but he hoped they could reconnect. Of course, he would have a lot of explaining to do. It took him an hour of rummaging around to find her number. As he waited for the call to go through, the thought occurred to him that she might be so angry that she wouldn't talk to him.

When they were finally connected, after a few interruptions, she came on the line, surprised and edgy.

"I've been reading about you." She raised her voice as people sometimes do when they talk long distance, as if they need to shout over the miles. "Such bad things they say." She didn't know where to take it and then added, "And I don't hear from you at all."

"Most of that stuff isn't true, Lynnette," he said. "This bunch always attacks the messenger. If he brings the king bad news, kill the messenger. It's an old trick going back to the Middle Ages," he added, trying to make light of it. But he was on the defensive.

"Yes, I suppose. But, but you remember how you didn't tell me about that girl? I … I don't know when to believe you, Jacob. These stories … what the people are saying. There is so much of it."

"Well, I don't know how to answer that without saying you just have to believe in me."

"It is hard for me now. I was … I am … it seems like so long ago, you and me," she stammered helplessly. "Now it is all … confusion. And then I didn't hear from you."

Jacob wished now that he had called her as soon as he returned from Paris. "Well, I thought I would just, uh, call and see how you are. I know I should have called a lot sooner. This whole thing has just swamped me." He wanted to get on a different subject. "Have you seen the article?"

"Yes, it is good. You write well." She seemed preoccupied. "Jacob, I am going to Mozambique. You remember what I told you about doing something different? I am going to Africa to write about the troubles down there."

"I do remember. But why Mozambique?"

"It is French, or it used to be. I can have a base there. Doctors Without Borders. Do you know it?"

"Sure. They're very good people."

"They have hired me to write about health problems—AIDS, malnutrition, the things they are working on all over sub-Saharan Africa. I am so happy." But she didn't sound it. Even with a poor connection, her voice was tremulous.

"That's good." He began to understand what was going on. "And what about us, Lynnette?"

"I am sorry, Jacob. I … I need to do this now."

"Is it because of all the bad stories about me? Are you running away from them, from me?"

"I am not running away," she said angrily. "I am doing what I hoped to do, as I told you when you were here." They were talking at the same time, until they both stopped. The line just hummed in silence. Finally, she came back to what was really bothering her. "Months you didn't call, Jacob, not even when you left Paris. How can you expect …"

"Yes, it was unforgivable to do that. I'm so sorry. I didn't want to hurt you, Lynnette. I did what I did to protect myself. I had no options."

"Yes, I think I understand. But now I must get on with my life."

"I thought we … we …" He forced himself to say what she had not, "I thought we were, uh, fond of each other." He realized that his words must have rung hollowly in light of his being out of touch so long.

"Not even a letter, Jacob. And then all this ugly news." She paused. "I have appointments this morning. I must go. But you are nice to call." Not knowing how to respond he waited, paralyzed, for her to hang up, but she didn't. Instead, in a slightly friendlier tone she added, "Jacob, I am going to Africa to work, to think—about you, us. I don't know whether there is anything left. We'll just have to see." Then she did hang up, after a softer, warmer *"ciao."*

During most of the conversation, she had been stiff and formal—until their last exchange. He realized that he could not penetrate her anger or her doubts, so he had given up. Jacob sat for a time, stewing over the call and how poorly he had handled it. Her plan for Mozambique was likely driven in part by his long silence and then by the nasty smears. Maybe it was all for the best. The prospect of a long-distance romance was probably not workable. And even if they did meet again, wouldn't she always doubt him? Once she left for Africa, he would have no way of contacting her, and she probably would never call him. Was this to be the last time they talked? For a moment he allowed himself to imagine taking her in his arms again. Grasping at straws, he told himself that her warmer "just have to see" held a ray of promise. He felt her body in his arms, but the image faded in the reality of the moment.

CHAPTER 17

Toward the end of October, demands for interviews slowed, and the personal attacks against him tapered off to just an occasional diatribe on Fox TV. But there were no job offers and not a peep from Shanahan. Even Mitch was silent. The administration was still busy defending itself against the charges in Jacob's article. There was a desperate quality to their evasions. While they disclaimed the idea of an oil fund as a scheme of rogue intelligence officials from the previous administration, they did finally admit to diverting some oil revenues to covert operations against certain unfriendly regimes. They argued the actions were necessary to combat the chaos in Iraq caused by outsiders. They insisted the roots of terrorism could only be attacked with the benefit of secrecy and made the stunning argument that funding these efforts openly within the law would not provide the needed security. They asserted lives would be endangered, without any explanation of whose lives were in jeopardy. Of course, the funds would be returned to Iraq ultimately. In the meantime, the apologia continued, the investment in disarming dangerous countries was just as important as rebuilding Iraq. These secret operations were the first phase of that objective—necessary to create a secure climate for reconstructing a stable environment for new democracies in the area. The public did not seem to be buying it. Billions of dollars of oil money were still missing—gone, with no record and no accountability.

The propaganda continued to pour out through the captive media nonstop in an effort to salvage what remained of the new administration's fading credibility. The war against terror had been the centerpiece for the last election. Now, a fresh Congressional judgment could be made, learning from the mixed message of 2008. The notion that a Democratic Congress was needed to contain the administration seemed to be gaining more support than in the 2008 election. The

Democrats had badly squandered their previous chances during the last two years of the Bush administration.

Jacob had a hard time listening to the debates and speeches. Although America was gradually catching on, the polls still showed that the country was sharply divided, before an election that should be a landslide of rejection. While Jacob's story had shaken public confidence, a significant percent of the voters stubbornly clung to their belief that a Republican president and a Republican Congress could better handle security of the nation.

The days passed quickly in the rigorous routine Jacob had set up for himself— breakfast at home, a long power walk, followed by work on his computer, and finally, a quiet dinner at a small restaurant in another neighborhood to avoid the press. Even so, on his walks he was usually followed by a few haggard tabloid regulars, whose breathless questions were always the same after they ran out of substance. And what about the Coffin girl? She won't even talk to us. Did you have sex with her? Are you going to see her again? To all these queries, Jacob replied, "I won't answer any of these questions. So don't hold your breath." But it didn't stop them—even when he added, "What good would it do to comment anyway? You guys will go on writing this stuff. Your readers love it."

Then one day, the phone rang. He didn't get many calls on his new number. He could feel his hand tremble as he reached for the receiver. It could be the beginning of a new onslaught of investigations, a resumption of the spate of crank calls, more death threats, or the warning of his arrest. He had begun to hate the instrument. It never brought good news.

"Hi, Jacob. It's me, Rachel."

"Rachel, how nice of you to call." He sighed a deep breath of relief. He was glad to hear from her.

"I take it you aren't married yet."

"You must be kidding."

"Not really, why?"

"Well, I'm not. Uh, that thing with Lynnette didn't work out."

"No?"

"No."

There was a long pause while Rachel considered the news.

"How come?"

"She dumped me."

"Oh, I'm so sorry," Rachel said gently.

"She didn't like my, uh, biography, I guess. Made her nervous."

"Well, I'm not surprised. Pretty raunchy stuff. But I must admit, interesting. You're quite the scoundrel."

Now Jacob was laughing. "You think so?"

"Listen, I'd really like to see you. I didn't like how we left things. Let me go out on a limb and make a proposal."

"Yeah, okay."

"Let's have dinner. Same place. Is that acceptable?"

"Pretty daring I'd say, even a little outrageous."

"Well, save your outrage until tonight."

"Gosh, so soon? Let me check my calendar."

"Okay, go ahead." She became wary.

"God, Rachel, I'm kidding. There is no calendar. I'm a pariah now. I live like a monk. You're the first person to call in weeks."

"Yeah, I was afraid of that. It's, ah, kind of why I called."

"I'm glad you did."

"So … I'll see you at seven?"

"You bet."

"Bye, then."

Her call was a real surprise, but a welcome one. He had been thinking about her, hoping that she was not gone from his life for good.

He spent the afternoon reading a book, an old pleasure he had returned to in his time of need. It filled the void and was a distraction from his less pleasant world. He looked forward to his dinner with Rachel. He had been thinking a lot about restarting his life—the hows, whens, and wheres. Eventually, he would have to come out of isolation. He needed all the friends he could get. He had come full circle, but finally without the baggage of his father. That seemed to be gone. Jacob was beginning to have some hope for himself. He wanted to turn his life around. His article had at least put him on the map.

He arrived first at their little bistro. The same waiter who had witnessed their breakup greeted him and hovered nearby solicitously, saying that Rachel had chosen the table, a special table, and that she had just called to say that she would be a few minutes late. Usually, Rachel was just late without calling. Jacob ordered a scotch and absently opened a package of crackers from a basket on the table. Having skipped lunch, he was hungry.

Feeling a little lost, he sat back and closed his eyes. Another woman came to mind, a woman he hadn't thought about recently—his mother. He had neglected her, not calling or writing for months. A letter from her had been waiting for him when he had returned to his apartment to collect his things. It was filled with news. She had been seeing Mr. Baum regularly. She wrote that he was a great solace to her, "a good and kind man." She said she hoped Jacob would write soon. A mother shouldn't have to wait so long for her only son to call. She went on to say that she realized that his childhood hadn't been a perfect one, but she had done the best she could. She closed by saying that Mr. Baum missed him and asked, too, that Jacob write real soon. The letter saddened him. His poor mother was the one who had suffered the most. He had gotten out. Her failing was to have submitted to the brutality and abuse of a relationship that almost destroyed both her and her son.

Over the years, Jacob had not been very good at staying in touch. It wasn't because he was lazy. The quintessentially American pull of a mother, Mother's Day, and all the other elements of "momism" had never been part of his life. His mother had gone through marriage fearful and passive. Hers was not the traditional maternal image fostered in American homes, where more often than not matriarchies prevailed. He had regarded her as a pathetic figure. Her inadequacies as a mother had doubtless influenced his own choices of women—usually the opposite, strong and independent, dominant. On the other hand, the lack of nurturing may have accounted for his early attempt to find warmth elsewhere. The violence of an abusive husband was certainly a nightmare for his mother to contend with, but then she didn't seem to make much of an effort to escape it. Jacob sighed with the same resignation he always felt as he remembered his early life. For better or worse, she was his parent. There was a bond, of course, but his image of her was fleeting and sometimes tragic. He promised himself he would not let any more time go by.

"Hey, wake up, Jacob! I'm here."

Embarrassed to be caught woolgathering, Jacob struggled to his feet and awkwardly put his arms around her.

"I wasn't asleep," he mumbled. "Just resting my eyes." He had trouble untangling himself from his troubling thoughts.

"Good." She shrugged out of her coat, revealing a somewhat severe black shirt tucked into a pair of loose tweedy trousers. The only makeup was an exaggerated eye job, reminding Jacob of a female in the Munster family. He wondered whether it was a role she was playing. She dropped into the banquette beside him. "What are you drinking? It looks like scotch."

The waiter materialized from the shadows. "What can I bring you, Miss Kline?"

"The same thing." She pointed to his glass.

When he had left, she said, "It's good to see you, Jacob. I … I acted like an ass the last time. I'm sorry. It was a teenage tantrum. I don't usually do that."

He smiled. "I've forgotten about it."

Her drink came, and she fingered the glass and stared into the amber liquid. "I hope you know that I … I didn't ask you to come just because you broke up with the French girl—you know, like you'd be available."

"It never occurred to me." Was this part of the wardrobe plan?

"No, I guess it wouldn't." A half smile lingered on her lips. "It's very sad about the Crane girl and her aunt. I guess I didn't realize how interesting they were. From what I read, they were very gutsy women."

"I've tried to stay away from the papers."

"Can't blame you." She reached for his hand. "You know, I don't think anyone—anyone who counts—swallows all that stuff about you."

"Lynnette did."

"You think that's why she broke it off?"

"I think so, yes."

"That's hard to believe, Jacob. I've been reading the European press. Pretty uniformly they are saying that these stories about you are lies, like WMDs that were never found. In Europe they are defending you. Your story is catching on. It's making an impact. No one accepts anything that comes from this crowd in Washington, particularly the French."

"Well, that's reassuring. But Lynnette has gone off to Mozambique to do good work."

"Mozambique? My God! What's she running away from?"

"I don't know. Enough about her. Let's talk about you. What's behind this little rapprochement of yours? I smell a motive."

"I told you. I wanted to apologize for my behavior." She lowered her eyes for a moment. "There are some things I need to explain." She cleared her throat.

"I appreciate that. But nothing needs explaining." He gazed at her, smiling.

"I also wanted to give you some moral support. It must be very difficult, living under this barrage of dirty jokes."

"Oh, I've gotten used to it. Not the gay part."

"This kind of stuff isn't relevant to anything, other than making you suffer and discrediting your fine story. Anyway, I know firsthand that you are not gay, and you're not a pedophile." She smiled and withdrew her hand from his. "And now that you mention it, you should know something about me."

Jacob glanced at her quizzically. "Yeah, what?"

"I'm bisexual." She sat back and waited for his reaction. She watched him do a slow double take, and for shock value she added, "Read that as gay."

"You are?" Her sudden off-the-wall admission had clearly startled him. "Is that why we're having dinner tonight?"

"Yes, in a way. I haven't been truthful with you."

"This may sound odd, but I was never too sure what bisexual meant or whether it even exists."

"It does. And it means that I have had relationships with both men and women."

"Sexually?"

"Yes, sexually, of course. That's ... that's why I, ah ... Jacob, I could never be a good lover for you. When we were together the last time, I got confused. I felt rejected by you. It hurt me. I got possessive. Afterward, I was able to admit that it wasn't so much that I wanted you as it was that I didn't want anyone else to have you. I think that's sick." She lowered her eyes and stirred her drink with a finger. "Anyway, I'm certainly not the marrying kind, to anyone. I couldn't do it. I'd be pulled in different directions all the time." She gulped the rest of her scotch and banged the glass down. "The fact is that I've made a mess of things."

"That's silly. There's no mess. You have a good job, and you are a hell of a writer."

"I wasn't talking about that part of my life. It's the personal part that's a mess. Anyway, I had to say this to you."

"Well, you've said it," Jacob said, trying to assimilate her little bombshell.

"And there is one more thing. I care about you, Jacob. You are a very talented, bright guy. You have a future. I don't want you to waste it. I've been talking to some people about you. There's a new magazine coming out, and the publishers want to talk to you. Would you be willing?"

"Of course I would. I don't exactly have to make room on my calendar."

"You came back from Paris changed. I don't mean just the girl, Lynnette. The whole experience taught you a lot. You're a pro now. You've done some terrific work. And you had the guts to take a chance on your own. I think you're ready for a new challenge."

Jacob laughed. "You're embarrassing me, Rachel. It's a wonder what being hounded and beaten up by the government can do for man. Yes, the experience of writing this article was a transforming one for me." He paused thoughtfully. "You might laugh, but Yvonne changed me, too. She was just a kid, and I guess I had a ... was taken with her, ah, attraction ..."

"You mean sex."

"Not entirely. It was her example. Her courage. I was eventually able to pull free of the sex part, but not the standard she set. I've been thinking about her recently. She was a very perceptive person for her age, for any age. The things she had to say when we talked in Boston woke me up. She took her message everywhere. She impressed people. She set the bar pretty high. I had to do something."

"Yeah. Sex and intellect are related. One drives the other?"

"Could be."

"Let's have another drink?"

"Sure." Jacob caught the waiter's eye and ordered.

When the waiter left, Rachel asked, "So how did you meet this ... this Lynnette?"

"I suppose I picked her up in a cafe, or maybe she picked me up."

"You got to like her?"

"I know where this is going."

"No, you don't. I'm not interested in whether you went to bed with her. But I'm going to guess, however, that you didn't regard her as a ... one-night stand."

"You're right."

"It was more serious?"

Her questions began to irritate him. "It's over," he said impatiently.

"Is it?"

"Look, she was more serious or surer than I was, at least at first. But before I left Paris, we became, uh, involved. Then I disappeared, and there was all this lousy publicity. It worried her—too much, I guess. And she was understandably angry that I let five months go by without calling." He studied his hands for awhile. "She's left Paris for heaven's sake, with no forwarding address. I'm afraid it's over," he added with finality.

"I don't want to beat a dead horse here, but you are still hooked, I take it?"

"Yeah, I guess I am."

Rachel dropped the subject, and they ordered dinner. While they ate, Rachel told him more about the new magazine and the people who would own it. She wrote down the names and suggested that he wait for a call. She would set it up. She said it was a good deal and urged him to meet with them. It was not a fly-by-night group. They were determined to succeed and well financed.

As they sipped coffee later, Jacob told her how much he appreciated her help and admitted he was at loose ends and needed an opportunity. They got through the evening amicably enough without returning to personal subjects. When they said good night at her door, she had some parting advice.

"Call Lynnette, Jacob. You can find her if you try. I have a feeling—call it woman's intuition—you should call her and test the waters again. You don't want to miss out on something that might be right for you." She turned to go. "And stay in touch. We're still good friends?" The rise in her voice required an answer.

Jacob leaned in and kissed her cheek. "We are friends, Rachel, of course." He laughed. "You may be the only friend I have."

Before the door closed, she said, "I meant it. Get in touch with the French girl. You know, half the battle is finding someone who wants you."

By the time he had reached the street, it began to rain lightly. He hurried home ahead of the threatening downpour.

The new magazine offered him a job with the title of assistant editor and a salary of more than he had ever earned. The owners were gearing up for the possibility of political changes. Jacob would help run the political side and cover what they all hoped would be a new Congress. He was even given a small staff to do some of the legwork. It had all happened very quickly. He and Rachel had dinner to celebrate. She was bursting with enthusiasm for him and not at all embarrassed to take a little credit herself.

The Congressional election turned out to be a defining moment. The Democrats were returned to both houses of Congress with comfortable majorities. In the endless analysis that followed, Jacob's article was often cited as a turning point. While little was made of the revelation of the al Qaeda peace proposal, Jacob's letter to Joshua did free Yvonne of any stigma under the Patriot Act. It also restored some degree of dignity to the Crane family. But there was to be no peace. The late prince's offer was rejected with a vengeance by the United States. A huge attack was launched on suspected al Qaeda camps in Pakistan, killing many innocent civilians in the process. This turned out to be a sad miscalculation.

In the wee hours of one morning a few weeks after the election, the unexpected ringtone of his cell woke Jacob from a deep sleep. In his haste to get the call, he knocked the phone off the night table and struggled to find it in the dark. When he finally did answer, it was an impatient operator asking him to confirm his number. Then he heard a ringing signal at the other end. Six rings seemed to take forever.

"*Oui*, this is *Mademoiselle Fouché*. What? You have found Mr. Sellars?"

"Lynnette, is that you?" His heart skipped a beat.

"*Oui.* Is it too late? I'm so sorry. It must be an awful hour for you. What time is it?"

He peered at the clock through the haze of sleep in his eyes. "About three-thirty in the morning."

"Oh, *Mon Dieu!*"

"No. It's fine. Are you in Africa?" It wasn't a very good connection.

"No, I am in Paris." There was an encouraging lightness in her tone. "I have been reading about you and thinking about us. I wanted to talk, but I had no idea that they would find you at such an hour." Her husky voice was warm and sexy.

"It's okay. What have they been saying now?"

"Good things. I … I should not have believed all that, ah, gossip. I was such an idiot."

So, Rachel was right. He had been getting better press in Europe. And Rachel was right again that he had not lost her. Damn! That girl was certainly clairvoyant.

"I have been talking to people, too—Americans. They don't believe it either. Many think you are a hero. They are very angry about this president, just like Bush. Your article has brought up bad memories."

"I'm glad to hear I have some support." He was wondering about Africa. "Did you go to, uh, Mozambique, was it?"

"It was a silly idea. No, I stayed home and finished my novel. You remember?"

"The one about me?" He laughed.

"It's not about you. It is fiction, a story. I told you. But it is about a man and a woman—in love, and more. Finishing it helped me sort things out."

"I want to read it."

"Yes, I know, and you will. Look, I'll keep it short. It is very late in New York, and I'm sorry I got you up. I've just been trying so many numbers to find you. You weren't at your old newspaper. I finally found a note with your mobile phone." She was talking very fast. "But I had to tell you. I am coming to New York. I may have a job. I don't know … I am not sure you want to see me again. I wouldn't blame you. But … I am coming anyway next week for a job interview."

"Next week? That's wonderful!" The idea of seeing her again thrilled him.

"You will see me then?"

"Absolutely. Silly question. I'd love to see you. When do you arrive?"

"I'm not sure of the time yet, but on Thursday. Can I call you?"

"Of course." He gave her the other two numbers—the magazine and his apartment.

There was a short break as she wrote them down. "But will you forgive … for judging too quick?"

"There is nothing to forgive, Lynne." Static on the line increased.

"Not believing in you, doubting you, that was wrong of me." She wanted to be sure he had heard her, and she repeated it.

"It doesn't matter. I should warn you. I don't have many friends anymore." He laughed to make light of it.

"I am a friend, still a friend."

"You know, some of the stories you read are true, at least partly." He wanted her to realize that she still might hear bad things.

"I understand. I know. But we all make mistakes. You did something brave and got too much in the, uh, spotlight." She paused and added, "I am now an expert on your life."

"But the gay part is not true," he insisted.

She laughed. "*Ooo-la-la*, I know that."

The allusion to their last night pleased him. "So, you have a job here in New York?"

"No, not yet. But I have a good offer. I will tell you all about it when I see you."

"This is such exciting news. It will be so good to see you. It's this Thursday?"

"Yes. Which number is your house, if I am getting in late?"

He repeated the number for her. "Where are you staying?" he added.

"With a friend—a girlfriend."

"I'll be waiting on tenterhooks for your call all day." Any doubts he had about his feelings toward her were quickly slipping away.

"You are being silly." She laughed again—that familiar musical laugh. "But I like it. And I can't wait to see you. Go back to sleep. *Bon nuit.*"

"Okay, good-bye then."

She hung up, or they were cut off. Jacob couldn't tell which. But it didn't matter. He had found her! She had found him, actually.

Jacob did not go back to sleep. Instead, he spent the rest of the night going over their conversation. Lynnette had obviously made a significant effort to find him. He was immensely happy that he would be seeing her again. He felt relieved that she already knew the worst about him. In the remaining hours before day-break, he turned and tossed with little sleep, but much anticipation.

He was in the office early the next morning before others arrived. Over the weekend, the owners had come into possession of a leaked document. At mid-morning Jim Casey, the working owner and editor in chief, called Jacob into his office. Casey was in his shirtsleeves surrounded by staff.

"Jacob, look at this." He shoved a pile of papers across the desk. It took Jacob only a moment to read the title page: *Minutes of the Emergency Energy Resource Committee*. "It's a move to put Iraqi oil production under the control of a few of our biggest oil companies. This time we have the names. EERC will be writing the oil law that the Iraqi government could never get right."

Jacob couldn't believe it. The implications were devastating. Had they learned nothing from their last attempt to hijack Iraqi oil?

"Yes, it's a secret meeting much like Cheney tried at the outset of the Bush administration, but wrapped in the cloak of national security rather than executive privilege. The oil guys came to the meeting with legislation all drafted."

"Do you know the leaker?" Jacob asked, worried about authenticity.

Casey smiled slyly. "I have no idea. A contact passed it on to us through an intermediary. We're clean, Jacob."

"What about the Patriot Act?"

"What about it?"

"Oil is national security. Can they stop this?"

"Let me introduce you to Leonard Kagan. He's our outside counsel. Tell him, Leonard."

"The leak itself is a big problem, for the leaker. But the First Amendment trumps any action against us. They'll try, of course, but if you get it out fast enough, all there will be is an interesting case that will be in litigation about who said what and when. It'll be too late. And now the Democrats want to repeal Patriot Act lll." He smiled and raised both arms, shrugging.

"With your article and this one, the new Congress will start off with a bang." Casey got up from behind his desk and began to pace. "Jacob, I want you to write the cover story on this. Make it as ... as picturesque as the one you did on the Crane people and the Arabs." He smiled, pleased with himself. "I want your best draft by Thursday morning. Can you do that?"

"Thursday, yeah, that'll work." Perfect timing he thought. "Can I take this?" he asked, pointing to the papers on the desk. "The story fits nicely with mine."

"It's all yours, my boy."

Jacob began to sort the papers into some order and then gave up.

"All right, get going on it." Casey was sounding a little like Shanahan. "We're devoting the whole issue to this. The risk-reward situation here is very much in our favor." He rubbed his hands together with enthusiasm. "Maybe we'll all end up in court—eh, Leonard?"

Jacob hurried off, pleased with the assignment. As he was leaving, he overheard the beginning of Casey's plans for other articles. "We have to cover the whole history of this and show how it hurts the energy business in the country and undermines our security. This is the beginning of the presidential campaign, boys. This …" The door closed. Jacob already had in mind the start of his own article.

Before he started to work, he called Rachel to tell her of the new government plot. She was as astounded as Jacob and encouraged him to write a strong story.

"It's a great opportunity, your second within the year. This doesn't happen very often."

"I know, and I have you to thank for it. I just wanted to say that one more time."

"I appreciate the thought. Good luck with it."

"There's something else." He paused.

"Yeah, what?"

"I heard from Lynnette."

"You did?"

"Yeah, yesterday."

"And?"

"She's coming here—to New York. She's got a job offer."

Rachel was silent until Jacob spoke.

"I know, I know, you told me—woman's intuition."

"Yeah, something like that. I'm very happy for you, Jacob. Now don't flub it with her. Be thoughtful. Get her some flowers. Do something nice for her. When's she coming?"

"Thursday."

"I'm real happy it is working out."

After they hung up, Jacob was glad that he had told her. He needed to share his excitement.

A little after noon, the Airbus lurched into full throttle. Lynnette sat back and clutched the sides of her seat as she always did. Someone had told her that the most dangerous time was takeoff. A fearful flier by nature, she had never forgotten this. She was sorry that she had heard it. Like other flights she had taken, there was no problem, and the lumbering jet began its climb in a few lazy circles.

The roar grew more subdued as the flaps retracted and Orly disappeared in bil-lowy clouds. She felt a touch of excitement as they leveled off and headed west.

She wanted to sleep with Jacob again, and it didn't take much imagination to reprise the sensation. It made her feel tingly all over. To distract herself, she thought about the new job she might be taking. Although her father had always been supportive of her teaching, she knew that he had hoped that she would use her considerable intellect in the law. That profession had never appealed to her. Now, she would be doing something in business—in publishing. Lynnette was hoping to be offered the position of managing editor of a well-known name—St. James Press. Her father would have been proud of her this time. Her knowledge of literature as well as creative writing had gotten the attention of the higher-ups in the big media company. She had made the short list of the headhunting firm and was invited to interview. Her heart beat a little faster imagining the ordeal. But she was up to it. Nothing could be any more intimidating than academia. The tentative offer was very attractive—and who knew, they might even publish her novel.

She took one of the New York newspapers handed out, hoping to find Jacob in it. But there was not a word. A small breakfast was served in first class, an upgrade compliments of the media giant, no doubt to impress her. They did things in a big way. The pilot announced that they expected to arrive in the Big Apple on time. Lynnette thought she could be in her friend's apartment at a rea-sonable hour that afternoon, when she would call Jacob.

The weather was clear, and the endless expanse below just barely showed the fleck of whitecaps. The blue seascape curved submissively as it met the horizon. The infinity of distance and the sense of detachment from the world felt mystical. It gave one perspective. Her life seemed smaller in the power of this vast expanse.

She read for as long as she could keep her eyes open and in the end succumbed to a restive nap. An announcement woke her. She heard only the part about being an hour from landing. Out her window a thick cloud cover had formed, and from the lower altitude, the sea had turned gray and was lined with foamy swells. A ridge of dark, lumpy land appeared ahead. What could it be—Nova Scotia, Labrador? Her geography wasn't that good. An occasional bump inter-rupted what had been a smooth ride so far.

She sat back, anticipating the excitement of the New York skyline. She loved the city, the bustle, horns, sirens, and rush of traffic and people. How long had it been? It seemed like ages since she had last trekked to New York with her parents. On the first visit, she had marveled at the two tall towers at the end of Manhat-tan. In her first view of them from a distance, they seemed oddly out of place and detached, as if floating on the horizon. As they had approached, the distant towers became a city. She had enjoyed the restaurant at the top of the World Trade Center. The view from the window was frightening—more so as she got closer. The drop was dizzying. Now, she could only imagine the terror the people felt, trapped on the floors above the impact of the planes.

Sleepy from her early start and long travel day, she allowed herself to drift beyond daydreams into a light sleep. A sharp bank of the plane woke her abruptly. It was her first hint that something had changed. The plane leveled off again and began to descend rapidly, more rapidly than it should, it seemed to her. A group of men and a woman chatting next to the lavatory dispersed, two hurrying toward the rear and two more stopping at the front of coach class. They all were nicely dressed, clean shaven in business suits, and looked as if they might come from anywhere. The last man and a woman remained at the lavatory. Lynnette thought they might be waiting for it to become free. However, she was very wrong. The two produced small guns with long clips. They moved to the door of the cockpit and seemed to have a key to the security lock. All this Lynnette took in as if it were a dream. It happened so quickly that the flight attendant in the galley had no time to react. As the man and the woman disappeared inside, Lynnette caught a glimpse of the pilot turning around in surprise. The door slammed closed. The plane banked again and tipped over to almost stand on its wing. Lynnette could feel the pressure of the seat belt tugging at her waist as the plane maneuvered wildly. The motion made her queasy. Her stomach lurched at the realization that this was probably the beginning of a hijack. In her panic, she began to grasp for more benign explanations, but none could satisfy the situation. A commotion in the back and then a scream confirmed the worst. Whenever a passenger tried to get up, a dark-suited figure appeared, a can of mace in hand, and roughly pushed the passenger back. The terrorists, as they must be, seemed to multiply. They were everywhere and very menacing. Lynnette thought of trying her cell phone, but they were too vigilant—nothing escaped them. Tears of frustration and anger flooded her eyes as she contemplated her end. She wanted so much to live.

From the cockpit of his F-22, Tomahawk—that was his code name—heard himself identified. He confirmed.

"We have a report that Air France 194 may have been hijacked. Disappeared from radar. It's due at Kennedy in twenty minutes. Pick it up—pronto, Tomahawk. We're sending help. Try to make visual contact."

"Confirm. Air France Flight 194, possible hijack."

It didn't take Tomahawk long to find Flight 194. The silvery Airbus was lumbering along where it shouldn't be at about six thousand feet, no flaps, no gear showing, and closing fast on the city. He reported the location immediately. Tomahawk switched frequency and tried the airliner. No answer. He tried again, while he maneuvered close alongside with the cockpit in view. He could just make out a figure hunched over the controls. It didn't look like an airline pilot. He knew the Airbus was flown with levers and buttons and was surprised that an untrained pilot could guide it. No answer came, and he checked with control. The voice crackled with urgency.

"We have a confirmed hijack. We have orders to shoot down. Repeat, shoot down. Confirm."

"You sure?" Tomahawk asked, far from certain whether he could make himself do what he had been trained for. But he had no choice. God! All those innocent people.

"Affirmative. Affirmative. Order comes from the president. Do it. That is an order. We have to save other lives." Tomahawk watched aghast, as the Airbus approached the edge of Manhattan airspace.

"Confirm. Shoot down 194. Will do."

At that moment, Tomahawk was joined by two other fully loaded F-22s. Out of the corner of his eye he caught the streak of a missile. One of his new companions who had heard the same message had obliged without hesitation. Anticipating the explosion, Tomahawk swung wide and climbed, banking steeply to keep the Airbus in sight. There was a huge orange burst, and the Airbus disappeared. Only a clutter of pieces could be seen spiraling down into the tidal swirl of Hell Gate—very aptly named, thought Tomahawk. His hands shaking in disbelief at what he'd just witnessed, Tomahawk turned and headed back to his base. He realized that his own reaction had been too slow. Still, he was glad it wasn't his missile. He had to keep telling himself over and over again that at least no one suffered, no one suffered. The repetition didn't help.

Sitting in his apartment, planning to spend the rest of the afternoon waiting for her call as he had promised, Jacob heard the boom faintly and wondered what it could be. There were no sirens. That was a good sign. The Big Apple didn't need another disaster, certainly not on the eve of Lynnette's arrival. He had gotten a reprieve on his deadline, but he had finished on time anyway. There would be a good draft on Casey's desk the next morning when he came in. Before he left, he saw to it that Casey's secretary had his article installed on the computer. He took a bus home, mostly out of habit. He could afford a taxi now, but he had always enjoyed his bus rides down Lexington Avenue, watching throngs of commuters heading for the subway stops. Most were leaving the island, leaving behind an emptier city and quieter streets. Manhattan denizens like him could take back their town, at least until morning brought back the crowds. On his walk from the bus stop, he stopped at a florist and bought a dozen roses of mixed colors—one of Rachel's many good ideas.

He was excited about Lynnette's arrival. To distract himself, he made a light drink and flipped on the television. He clicked around while a string of ads ran on his favorite channel. Then he saw it—a bright orange explosion on CNN—in the air framed by the Manhattan skyline. Stunned, he stood before the screen listening. "To repeat, Air France Flight 194 blew up over the East River. The Airbus from Paris was pretty far out of the pattern for Kennedy." Jacob's heart wrenched in his chest when he heard Paris. "There is speculation that it was a terrorist attack. The jet just blew up. But why over the river? This aircraft did not belong at La Guardia. We're trying to put this together to make sense out of it, and we urge our listeners not to jump to the "T" word just yet. Reports are coming in as we speak. A lot of the debris fell … There, we have shots of some activity. The police and Coast Guard are frantically trying to collect as much as they can before it's swept away in the choppy current. For those of you who tuned in late, we'll run the video again. The airliner was caught by our network helicopter out on their evening traffic check—moving very fast. The pictures are graphic— we must warn you. There, the plane is just over Hell Gate. You can see it does not have flaps or gear down, strange … Now, in a moment you'll see the flash of the explosion—there! The fuselage of the Airbus is disintegrating, one wing spinning down with other debris into the river, and the other wing and tail section breaking up over Queens. Eyewitnesses are saying a missile brought it down, but there has been no confirmation of that yet, and we didn't see that on the film."

Jacob left the set on, lowering the volume, and tried to stay cool. It might not have been her plane, of course, but he had to do what he could to check—even though he was sure every line would be busy. Predictably, all he got were recordings. He kept trying for more than an hour, banging the receiver down in frustration between attempts. He realized there was nothing he could do except wait for her call. Haunted by the ugly possibilities and unable to eat, he drank to ease the growing anxiety. Later, he drank more, but it wasn't helping. There was no call that night, and Jacob began to fear the worst. If she had missed her flight, she would have called. Gradually, he lost hope, trying to come to terms with the inevitable. He sat on his couch with his feet up, staring out into the darkened windows of the neighborhood, envying those who slept. His mind was dulled by the dread of reality, pushing him deeper and deeper into a coma-like state, eyes wide open but unseeing. Unable to sleep, he began to pour whiskeys, one after the other—barely aware of what he was doing.

The full story appeared in the morning news, but Jacob missed it. Sometime before dawn, he finally slept. He had never moved from the couch. An empty scotch bottle lay on its side on the coffee table, an equally empty glass beside it. Spots of spilt alcohol had stained the wood. The telephone had rung a number of times, unanswered. Toward dawn, he cracked his eyes just enough to read the time before he fell back into a stupor. Even the banging on the door would not rouse him.

Rachel was beside herself with worry. She had seen the explosion on television, and it got her thinking. She called Jacob's apartment repeatedly from her office, where she was trapped on a project. When she had finished work, it was very late and time to call it a night. Early the next morning, she again got no answer. A little desperate, she took a taxi to his place and banged on his door until the neighbors complained. She no longer had a key. The frustration finally drove her to rouse the super and persuade him to let her in. It took a lot of sweet talk and lies, but she got in. There he was sprawled on the couch, eyes open staring into space. An empty scotch bottle sat on the table. He glanced at her without moving his head and smiled. Rachel suspected that he had been drinking ever since he heard the news. She worried about the quantity and toyed with calling the EMTs.

"I'm drunk, Rach. For the first time in my life I've managed to get myself shit-faced drunk. Whatcha think of that?"

"Predictable."

"Yeah, I s'pose." He gazed at her vacantly.

"I'm going to make some coffee. You've got to get hold of yourself." She marched resolutely into his kitchen and began rattling around.

"That's two of 'em, Rach. Hear me?"

She peered around the door. "I hear you. What on earth are you babbling about? Two of what?"

He rolled over, moaning, "Don'tcha unnerstand?"

"Understand what?"

"My women. Now I've lost two, in sish months—just like that," he said, trying without success to snap his fingers. "Yer next, old Rach. Yer next." He managed a guttural chuckle. "War on terror," he mumbled. "It got me." He mimed a bullet to the heart.

She brought in the coffee and set a cup in front of him. "I was never one of your women, Jacob."

"You weren't? Damn, an' I always thought you were." He struggled to sit up, holding onto his head as if it might fly off. He sniffed at the coffee aroma. "That's better than scotch. After awhile it shmells like puke." He smiled slyly. "But I wasn't sick, Rach. See fer yerself. No puke. I got a drinkin' future or what?"

"Look, let's talk about this later. You're in no condition."

"There's nothin' to talk about."

"Just drink some coffee—then I've got something that will clear your head so you can sleep, and maybe it'll help with the hangover you're gonna have." She inspected his sorry condition. "You could use a shower, too."

He leered at her. "Maybe you'd like to give me one. You've never done that." He sipped the coffee quietly for awhile until a silly smile flitted around his wet lips. "Yeah, I always wanted to do somethin' kinky with you, Rach." His expression changed, and a frown appeared. "Oh, damn. I fergot. Yer a lez."

"That's a cruel word, Jacob," she said evenly without anger. "Did you want to hurt me?"

He reacted to her question as if he had been smacked. Straightening up as much as he could, he reached for her hand unsuccessfully. "Yeah, that wasn't nice. I'm … I'm shorry. I'd like to take it back."

She sighed. "It would help if you tried to get hold of yourself. You have a job to go to and a future to take care of. And, damn it, I recommended you. Don't let me down."

For a moment it seemed that he'd passed out and then he revived. "Rach, do you think God exists?" His eyes were closed tightly as if he were trying to shut out the world.

"I don't know, Jacob. The question is not an important one for me." She smiled and instinctively glanced up—but she might have been just rolling her eyes. "This is not the time for a theological discussion."

"Well, I reject the whole damn myth—Jesus and all that. There's no way to justify this in a heavenly plan." His mother's words of biblical resignation "God has a plan" left a bitter taste.

They didn't talk much after that. He began to sober up little by little. A stray tear or two rolled down his cheek, but there was little emotion left. They were just the vestiges of utter desolation. Rachel administered him a handful of pills with a glass of water and got ready to leave. "Take a shower, Jacob. Are you able to do that? It'll help you sleep. We'll talk later."

"Yeah, sure." He looked up at her with a sick smile. "Thanks for, uh, dropping in."

His puffy face looked tragic and tired. She felt like crying herself.

"You've always been there for me, Rach. I don't deserve you." He dropped his eyes. "Yeah, a shower would be good."

She took a last look at him as she walked out. He'd be okay now, she thought. He was young and resilient. In the hall, she glanced at her watch. Her friend would be worried by now—probably angry and hurt. She hoped the note she had left beside the bed would smooth things over. It was a time Rachel would need a friend to hold her.

Jacob was startled to see that the clock read 10:45 AM when he woke. He had a heavy sense of foreboding. Something was terribly wrong. The curtains were tightly drawn against the morning light. Sitting on the edge of the bed carefully appraising his condition, he tried to figure out what day it was. He mulled over his dilemma for awhile but couldn't come up with the answer. The television, he thought—the answer would be there. Enduring an endless string of ads, he finally got the weather guy's report for Saturday morning. Rain, heavy at times, then clearing for the rest of the weekend. A beautiful Sunday was in store for you, the happy prognosticator said joyfully. That was enough for Jacob. He flipped off the set.

Glancing outside at the gloomy sky, he watched the gray wisps of scud. Wind-driven rain rattled his windows. Only then did it all come back—the orange burst, the disintegrating plane, and Lynnette—like an awful nightmare. The shock of the disaster had been lost temporarily in the fog of his intoxication. He had compartmentalized the horror. Gingerly, he got to his feet and let some light into the room. Other than a faint headache, he was surprised that he felt pretty good. He vaguely remembered Rachel's visit the day before. It seemed like a dream. He found her note and the bottles of pills on his night table. One was a prescription in her name. So she really was here. That would explain his miraculous recovery. He knew that he had drunk a lot. But it wasn't until he inspected the kitchen that he understood how much. He wiped away a tear that came as he read Rachel's note. "Yeah," he announced aloud to the empty scotch bottles on the counter, "I lost her, lost her before I had a chance." He struck the surface with his fist. "Even before we ..." He struck again and again, rolling the bottles into the sink.

After some coffee and a long shower, he felt almost normal—physically anyway. He wondered whether he was hungry. Of course, there wasn't much edible in the fridge, so he decided to go out. He pulled on some clothes, straightened up the living room, and left. Pausing under the awning of the apartment house hoping for a break in the rain, he gave up and made a dash for the deli across the street. Only two tables were occupied. He said a weak hello to the proprietor, Larry, and ordered coffee and a seeded bagel, but with no onions please. The place was heavy with the aroma of fried bacon and eggs. A wave of nausea hit but passed quickly. He slumped into a booth near a steamy window and looked in his coat for his cell, but found that he had left it at home. He was tempted to go back and get it, but he didn't have the energy. Instead, he settled for a used copy of the *Times* that Larry brought him with the coffee. He reminded himself to call Rachel and thank her for playing Florence Nightingale.

A big black headline on the right side of the front page caught his eye: *Tragic End to Terrorist Attack on City!* A smaller headline, *Plan to Control Iraqi Oil Revealed,* was on the left. Not good news for the administration. But the spinners were quickly circling the wagons. An investigation to identify the source of the leak had been set in motion. The well-oiled White House propaganda machine was in high gear. Jacob could not bring himself to read the article on the explosion of Flight 194. After breakfast, he hurried home, expecting a call from his office. Sure enough, Casey had called early that morning, and Jacob, still fuzzy-headed, had failed to check his messages when he got up. Jacob was happy to have the distraction.

He punched out his office number and was immediately transferred to Casey.

"I was afraid you had joined the missing." There was a discernible gentleness in his normally brusque style.

"Yeah, I'm sorry, Jim. I … I had a friend …" He tried hard to keep his voice together. "I had a friend on that flight, the one that went down."

"Rachel told us. And you were, uh, close."

"Yeah. You could say that." Jacob had to reach for control of his emotions. "We were about to find out how close."

"You sure she was on the flight? Some people found that their families didn't make the departure. Have you checked?"

The long night came back to him. "I couldn't get through to a human being. But I'm, uh, pretty sure she was on it." The words came hard. "She would have called."

"Want me to check? I know the folks at the airline. I can get through."

"Sure. That would be good of you. Her name is, uh was, uh, Lynnette Fouché." Jacob could hear his own hollow voice as if from another planet. He already knew the answer.

"Sit tight, and I'll get back to you. And don't worry about the article. Your work was terrific. It's already on the street. We speeded things up yesterday after we got wind of this latest ploy. Have you seen the morning papers?"

"Yeah, I saw the lead. They're getting ready with an attack on the magazine and probably you personally. That's what they do."

"I know, but we'll be there first. Now take it easy. Don't assume anything yet about your lady friend." He hung up.

Jacob sat, unable to move. Why did losing her have this effect on him? In Paris, he hadn't even been sure of his feelings. But she had changed him. He knew that now more than ever. In the days before the crash, after Rachel made her comments about lost opportunities, Lynnette was with him just beneath the surface of his mind. She would come to the top every time he had a solitary moment, particularly at bedtime. There were nights when, after dreaming about her, he'd waken and expect to find her in bed beside him. In the hubbub of the new job, he had tried to shrug this off. *Love's Labour's Lost,* he thought. He had so been counting on seeing her, looking forward to holding her and telling her that yes, he did love her.

As he paced through the rooms of his apartment, he glanced at his watch, dreading Casey's call, hoping for news—the good news he knew wouldn't come.

Finally, he heard.

"Jacob?"

Who else would it be, thought Jacob with irritation. "Yeah."

"I'm afraid she was on that flight. I'm so sorry. How perfectly awful for you. Take all the time you need to deal with this. Don't feel under any pressure. Your job will be here when you are ready. And God bless you. If you want to talk, give me a call at home." All this came out at once, making further conversation unnecessary.

"Thanks, Jim. I really appreciate it." That was it. Casey had tried to make it easy for him. He sat for a moment as if he had received a punch in the stomach. He didn't even bother to blot the tears running from his eyes. He wasn't sure how long it took, trying to sort out his emotions. Finally, he made a decision—a small one. Knowing he would need his friend now as never before, he left word on Rachel's voice mail at home that he wanted to see her. "That's the least I can do after your TLC last night," he said on the message. Then on a whim, he added, "Have dinner with me tonight, Rach. Make it seven-thirty at the usual dump. You don't need to call, unless you can't make it." He knew his words sounded a little gruff and goofy. It was the only way he could keep his emotions in check.

With no specific objective in mind, he decided to take a walk, rain or no rain. He just wanted to see the East River. The weather was easing when he started out, down to just a drizzle. Picking his way north up avenues and east across streets, he finally reached the river and Carl Schurz Park. Exhausted and wet, he sat on a bench watching the oily current slip through Hell Gate. A few workboats were still dealing with wreckage under spotlights on the Queens side. He had always wondered what drew the bereaved to the beaches near where a plane had crashed into the sea or a ship had gone down. Now he understood. It was the last place she had been, and he wanted to be there with her. It was as simple as that. He sat on the bench watching the river until the lights of Queens began to twinkle in the clearing air. Then it was time to catch a cab to meet Rachel. As he made his way across the park to East End Avenue, a wave of loneliness washed over him. Walking crosstown in a haze of memories, he finally found a cab on Third Avenue.

She was waiting for him when he got there. She had dressed up for him. She looked pretty—too pretty to be unavailable. He put the unkind thought out of his mind. She greeted him with a hug and kissed him on the cheek. "This was a nice idea, Jacob." They sat and ordered a bottle of red wine and some canapés. Jacob had tasted enough scotch to last him a long time. He wasn't even sure the wine would go down well. They had a different waiter this time. Maybe the change would bring luck. Jacob shed his coat and slid into the booth. A sense of the old neediness seeped back. But there was something new—a feeling of resolution, of having known real love, probably for the first time. They sat together, saying nothing, until the silence grew too burdensome.

"She's dead. It's confirmed," he announced.

Rachel reached across the table and touched his arm, but said nothing.

The wine came, and he waved off the tasting formality, nodding with approval to the waiter. "Fine," he said, to get rid of him. He gazed at her as they touched glasses and sipped.

"Umm," she intoned. "Good choice."

"You know it was above and beyond what you did for me." He shivered involuntarily as he swallowed.

"Yeah, I guess it was." She set her glass down and smiled. "But it wasn't hard. In a way, it was kind of refreshing to see you all vulnerable again." She was serious, not teasing. "Like you used to be."

"I still feel that way," he admitted.

"No, you don't. You're just dealing with the lousy situation you're in—your loss and being alone again. You need a woman, Jacob. That may sound crass, but you've finally discovered that you could have a good relationship, even a lasting one, and I bet it felt good, natural. Am I on the right track?"

"I suppose." Good old Rach, always the perceptive one. Taking a new direction, he added, "You know, Lynnette wrote a book—a novel."

"Really?"

"Yeah, she did, but it's not published yet." He swallowed to suppress the emotions welling up. "She was going to an interview with a publisher for a job here in town."

"I know."

"You know?"

"Jacob, I have an admission to make."

"What's that?" The numbness of the night before had sapped his imagination.

"Well, I wanted to find out whether she was on that plane. I did some checking around."

"Checking around?"

"I called Paris, the university. Your friend was coming here for a job interview."

"We already said that." Rachel's deviousness was beginning to irk him.

"The job was at St. James Press—they liked her. She was going to get the position, as editor."

"My God! Aren't we the little sleuth?"

"Don't be that way, Jacob. I had the best of motives." She began to tear up. The emotion was intense between them.

"Okay, okay. What else?"

"That's it."

A silence fell between them. Slowly, he reached for her hand. "Thanks." He choked back a surge of emotion.

"What was it about?" Rachel asked after a pause to let him recover. "The novel."

"Maybe about me." He laughed.

"You?"

"Yeah. In a way. I mean a guy like me."

"You mean she made it up—before you came along?"

"That's right. It was almost finished."

"Wow! And she told you the character was like you."

A sheepish grin brightened his face. "Yeah."

"Aren't you curious, for God's sake?"

"Sure. I suppose so. But it's lost now—gone with her." The turn of the conversation was beginning to get to Jacob. "Let's talk about something else. You were saying something about relationships—some hope for me."

"You don't know if the book is gone," she said, ignoring his diversion. "She might have sent it ahead to somebody at St. James."

"Could be."

"Why don't you ask them? Call and talk to the editor. I know people over there."

"I could, I guess."

"Could? No, should, Jacob, *should*. Quit feeling sorry for yourself and do something for her—as a gesture, you know, out of respect—how much you cared about her." She paused. "It would be the decent thing to do and good for you. And then move on with your life." She studied him. "I'm going to give you a name, and you call." She scribbled a note on a scrap of paper and handed it to him. "Here. Now call this guy. Promise me. Get that book published. You owe it to her for giving you a second chance."

He took the note and glanced at the name. "Okay, I will. You're right, of course. I'll follow up. I promise." The darkness of his loss returned as a series of images flowed through his mind—meeting Lynnette in the bar, the first tentative kiss, the awful misunderstanding before they went to bed that first time, the only time … the fireball over the East River shattering their dreams. Could he ever get over it?

"Good. Now, about you." She sipped her neglected wine and looked him in the eye. "You gotta start caring about yourself, Jacob."

"Well, I do," he said, trying to clear the emotion from his voice.

"Not until you start facing up to your demons. There's been some pretty bad stuff in your life. You always try to change the subject."

"Talk away. It doesn't bother me." Jacob sounded edgy.

"You're getting defensive."

"No, I'm not. Look. Everyone in the world knows stuff about me now—true or not. There was a story in every paper. I'm surprised the waiter hasn't mentioned it," he said sarcastically. Then he added, "It doesn't matter. I've accepted it."

She sipped her wine and ignored his bitterness. "That's not what I'm talking about. It's Christy and what that experience did to you."

"What about it?"

"I don't mean what you did with her. That kind of thing happens all over the place. It's the way that father of yours handled it. Jacob, your father was a monster."

"He wasn't my father."

"We've been over that before."

"There was this guy next door. My mother liked him." He felt a little disloyal to his mother admitting this much.

"My God, how classic. Right out of Edith Wharton."

He ignored the literary reference and waited for her to continue.

"You know, I've got it figured out." She paused. "Want me to tell you?"

"Sure," Jacob agreed with resignation. "Go ahead."

"I don't know how you got through life before you came to New York, but when I got to know you, you were so busy running away from something you had no life. Particularly in bed, you seemed to be … I don't know … it was as if you were fighting something or someone while we were … Anyway, you were close to being a basket case. At first, I thought it was just a fear of failure. Uh-uh. You wanted failure."

"Yeah, Rach, I'm beginning to see some of this myself." He sipped his wine. "But it's hard to, uh, discuss—with anyone."

She reached for his hand. "Your old man had you under a spell, Jacob. You *wanted* to get free. It was tough because you had the same drives as any normal guy. But for you, a load of guilt came with sex—guilt mostly about your little séance with Christy and I'm sure other things between you and your father—or whoever he is. He infected everything in your life. And I have a hunch that the guilt trapped you into repeating the Christy experience with others, like the girl in Nantucket, whatever her name was, and Yvonne, just to challenge your father."

"But I never did anything with the girl in Nantucket."

"Yeah, well, I don't want to hear the details."

The waiter appeared, and they ordered some dinner. They sat in silence until the meals came.

"I loved her, Rach," he said hoarsely, finally breaking down. He didn't bother to wipe away the tears.

"I know, honey."

They finished the wine as they ate in silence. There was a bond between them to leave the rest unspoken, and that is how the evening ended.

That night he slept well, with just one dream—an odd sequence with Amos Coffin. *Saga* materialized out of the fog, Amos at the helm, flags flying in the rigging, and horns blowing. It seemed like a celebration. Nothing much happened. He was just there.

In the morning, Rachel called early. He was still drugged with sleep.

"Jacob, I wanted to thank you for dinner. I'm glad we did that." She paused while Jacob tried to wake up. "It was special."

"I don't think I ever took the trouble to understand you, Rachel."

"Water over the dam, honey." Neither one spoke. The line just hummed away.

Then he asked, "Is there someone else now, Rach?"

"Yes."

"A lover?"

"Yes, Jacob, a lover."

Jacob wondered whether the lover was with her now. "But do you really love her?" He knew it was a bad question, but he couldn't help himself.

"I can't answer that. I don't know how to answer. Let me put it this way—she means enough to me that I don't want to hurt her." There was a silence. "Hey, it doesn't mean I don't have a special place in my heart for you, Jacob."

"Is that the way bisexuality works?"

"I don't know, but it's the way I work."

Jacob changed the subject. "Listen, Rach, I appreciated your psychology lesson last night. And you're right about my father—I mean the old man. He was a bad dream, but I'm over him. He's dead and can't touch me anymore."

"That's not because he's dead. It's because you beat him. And I'm proud of you. Now go find a nice heterosexual girl. But maybe I should meet her before you go out on any limbs." She laughed.

"Really? You'd be interested?"

"Just kidding. You're on your own in that department."

He looked out his window at the long shadows of the new day. Rachel was a truly good friend.

"Thanks for taking care of me during the bad old years." Then he added, "And, Rach, it was a nice thing you did, finding out about Lynnette. It helped to know that. And I will call about the book. I promise."

"Well, you understand that I was being constructive, not nosy."

"Oh, I do. I do."

"Keep writing and telling the truth. You're good at it."

Jacob laughed. "You'll be looking over my shoulder?"

"You bet. Bye."

"Bye."

That was the last time they talked. Rachel probably moved away from the neighborhood or from the city with her lover. Maybe they went to Massachusetts and got married. He hoped so.

As he showered and dressed on that bright Sunday morning, his loneliness had dissolved, replaced by a feeling of profound responsibility. As a journalist with newly established credibility, he felt the need to say more about the plague of terror spreading across the world. It would be his way of giving meaning to the deaths of both Yvonne and Lynnette. In his own personal loss, he recognized something terribly wrong in the world. There was a binary chemistry in terrorism. It was always an act and a response. An eye for an eye. Saudis kill the radicals who want to oust them, and the radicals down a plane as revenge. Was this the way it would always be? He didn't have answers, but he was developing a point of view.

The quest for oil was corrupting the world and obscuring the more fundamental problems of the less fortunate. America had to use its power to lead in a new direction. The lies had to stop—so did the swagger. The talk of a "war on terror" had to stop, too. September 11 was a monstrous crime, not an act of war. Terror was a tactic, an act of desperation, a state of mind. It didn't start as a movement. It wasn't going to be defeated by declaring war. If there was a war to be fought, it was with ourselves—to do the right thing. The energies of the powerful needed to be refocused on the common good, not self-interest. If improving the common good were to become the goal, maybe … just maybe, the violence might end.

Jacob gazed out the window at the waking city, his city, still pink in the glow of the risen sun. It had brought him both deep tragedy and possibility—his tragedy, but the city saved. Today, the streets were quiet and the silent, unscathed walls of glass and steel were reassuring.

Epilogue

It was more than a year since Lynnette's novel had been published. Jacob followed its progress faithfully. He made a trip to Paris to interview her associates at the university and had written a foreword to the story. He even appeared at a few book events. Lynnette's *L'Histoire* made a very respectable debut. It was a compelling love story, bringing tears to his eyes each time he read it. His effort was a cathartic experience, helping to put his brief but tragic romance in perspective. He finally made peace with his loss. But he would never forget her.

The presidential election had come and gone with the Democrats returning to office. The occupation of Iraq was winding down, and negotiations in the Middle East had begun in earnest. The new U.S. president was finally bringing troops home, and Iraqis were trying to pull the warring factions together, at least for discussions of their own way forward. Both the Kurds and the Shias were insisting on full autonomy for their regions, while the Sunnis were stuck on a strong central government. At least they were talking instead of fighting. The huge U.S. Embassy in Baghdad was now awash with more diplomats than generals. Regrettably, it all could have happened sooner.

With the reduction of the U.S. military occupation of Iraq came salutary effects in other areas. The mood for negotiation was contagious—in Lebanon as well as in Israel. But there were troubling signs that the United States was going to hold on to a reduced military presence in Iraq for a long time to come. Of course, terror still lurked everywhere and continued to cast its shadow over world peace. But terror wasn't the only shadow. Competition for diminishing supplies of fossil fuels throughout the world would intensify, setting the stage for new conflict between nations.

Jacob was hard at work at his new job, furiously turning out articles for his magazine on subjects ranging from the underlying causes of terror to the endemic corruption in oil-producing nations. In fact, he had received a Pulitzer Prize for his three-part condemnation of the neoconservative notion that Jeffersonian democracy could be exported to Islamic nations. By any criterion, Jacob was a widely read and respected pundit.

Despite his success and improved financial position, he still lived in the same tiny apartment in lower Manhattan. It was only recently that he began to think of moving to more upscale digs. There was something about summertime that made him regard more enviously the glass and steel towers rising in the Upper East Side. He was just getting off the phone with his realtor when he noticed his second line blinking with a call. One of the luxuries Jacob had allowed himself was three telephone lines and an iPhone. Seamless communication was the cornerstone of journalism.

He glanced at the desk clock and wondered whether the incoming call was the one he was expecting from Tehran. He picked up the line with anticipation.

"Jacob? Is this Jacob, uh, Sellars?" It was a young-sounding feminine voice, with a familiar accent he couldn't quite identify.

"Yeah, this is Jacob."

"Oh, God, it *is* you. I can tell."

Taken by surprise, Jacob couldn't help smiling. He didn't have that many admirers. And it certainly was not Tehran calling. "Okay, who are you? I get the feeling I should know."

"It's Coffin. Remember me?"

There was only a moment of confusion. "Marilyn Coffin—of the whaling clan, the sailor girl."

She laughed. "Yeah, you do remember."

"Of course I do."

"Well, I can't open a newspaper without seeing you—I mean your name."

"I'm sure that's an exaggeration."

"Your column appears in the *Globe* twice a week—so there."

"It does?"

"Come on. Don't be cute. You're a famous guy. I had no idea … that night."

It was Jacob's turn to laugh. "I wasn't at all famous then."

"But you got to be—actually, notorious. And I think you know what I mean."

"Yes, I do. I'm so sorry that you got dragged into that. It was pretty nasty stuff they were pedaling. I wanted to call you, but if I had, there would only have been a brand-new story." She didn't respond, so he added, "I hope it didn't cause you too much unpleasantness."

"No, not at all. As a matter of fact I rather enjoyed the attention while it lasted." She paused a moment. "Listen, you know that money I got when Joshua died?"

Jacob wondered where this was leading. "Yeah, vaguely."

"Well, I bought a boat, a nice comfortable forty-footer—you know, a sailboat, a yawl, if you know what that is."

"I do."

"So, would you like to go sailing?"

"Gosh, I've never considered it … never have the time … but I do like sailing."

"Okay, consider it now. I'm in Connecticut, moored in Pequot Harbor without a crew. What do you think?"

"It's … it's only Thursday, I have … ah … a lot of …"

"Jacob, you're so successful I'm sure you call your own shots. And I'm a damsel in distress. I need a hand—will that do as an excuse?"

Jacob recovered his composure. "It sounds like a real nice invitation."

"So I can count on you?"

"I guess I could drive up tomorrow. Where are you exactly?"

"How about tonight instead? I don't feel secure alone."

"Uh, I don't know." He glanced at the clock instinctively. It was a little after 4:00 PM.

"It's only about a two-hour drive, and the directions are simple."

Jacob was mentally checking his Friday agenda. It all could wait. Nothing was urgent. Still, he had lingering doubts.

"I don't really have any, uh, gear."

"You're stalling. Don't you want to come? It's okay. You can tell me."

"No, it isn't that at all … it's just …"

"Look, there are two cabins. You'll have complete privacy, your own head. I'm not going to seduce you. I just want your company. Does that help?"

Jacob laughed nervously. "I wasn't worried about that."

"Yes, you were, too." There was a note of satisfaction in her tone. "Seriously, Jacob, I'd like to see you. I know a little about what's happened in your life. A famous guy like you just doesn't have many secrets. Come spend the weekend. You can take me out for dinner again, and we'll sail a little on the Sound. It'll be a change of pace for you. The winds are supposed to be light, ten to fifteen—no storms, perfect sailing weather for finding your sea legs."

His doubts were ebbing away.

"It's a date then. You said Pequot Harbor—like *Pequod*, as in Ahab's ship?"

"I guess."

How oddly ironic, Jacob thought. But the coincidence didn't bother him. "Just tell me how to get there."

The End

978-0-595-69072-5
0-595-69072-6

Printed in the United States
101056LV00004B/421-426/A